STRIPPING BARE

STEELE RIDGE SERIES

KELSEY BROWNING

STEELE RIDGE
www.SteeleRidgeSeries.com

Stripping BARE

A Steele Ridge Novel

Video game mogul Jonah Steele may be a billionaire, but as the youngest brother in a family of alphas, his struggle to prove his worth is all-consuming. Although he saved his hometown from ruin, he can't forgive himself for the biggest failure of his life.

As a teenager, **Tessa Martin survived one of the most devastating nights of her life.** Now, she's a corporate psychologist and stronger than ever. She also has her sights set on Jonah Steele, her former boss and the only man who can track down the hacker who compromised her confidential client files. But can she confess that Jonah's deepest secrets were exposed as well?

As the threat distorts into a real-life version of Jonah's legendary video game, his and Tessa's complicated emotional past—and the secrets buried there—could prove fatal. Will they strip away the past and reveal their feelings for one another, or allow it to blind them to a killer's twisted game of revenge?

Sign up for Kelsey's new release newsletter!

Published by Steele Ridge Publishing

To all the men and women who are vulnerable enough and strong enough to tell their own stories, however imperfect they may be.

AUTHOR'S NOTE

Dear Reader,

If you've read my Texas Nights series, you know I love to write lighthearted contemporary romance with plenty of snappy dialogue and sexy banter. Although you'll find some of both in this book, the Steele Ridge series has been my first foray into stories that lean more toward romantic suspense. Here, my villains aim to not only hurt but to kill.

So *Going Hard* and *Stripping Bare* both have a darker feel than you might be accustomed to with my contemporary romances.

Also, this particular book hinges on a devastating shared backstory between the hero and heroine. If you or someone close to you has been a victim of sexual assault, you may find parts of Tessa's story uncomfortable to read. Please know that I treated this topic as authentically as I was able, which means I didn't gloss over what I felt my characters would truly think and feel. At times, I questioned if I should be delving into this topic. But avoiding it would've been a disservice to the characters, the story, and my readers.

In addition to being one I needed to tell, I hope Tessa and Jonah's story will help both illuminate and heal some scars of sexual assault.

Respectfully,

Kelsey

1

Seattle, Washington
December 20
Three Years Ago

Even geeks needed downtime.

"Have a great holiday, y'all." Jonah gave a group of Steele Trap's coders a little salute as they filed out the door to take time off until after New Year's. The people at Steele Trap were dedicated to making the best video games out there, and they did it by working long-ass hours.

So every year at this time, he gave them bonuses, plied them with good booze and food, and then hustled them out the door for two weeks. Because that also gave him two weeks to hunker down and brood before getting the hell on with life.

Tonight, the strain of maintaining his happy face during the holiday party had worn on him, but he'd damn well kept it on.

With everyone gone for the night, he returned to his office, not bothering to turn on a light. After all, getting his drunk on didn't require more than the dim glow from the hallway lights. He could see well enough to reach into the credenza behind his desk and pull out a bottle.

Hello there, Mr. Lagavulin. Haven't seen you since this time last year.

He plunked the scotch and a glass on his chrome and Lucite desk. The interior designer who'd gussied up this place would probably blow an artery if he saw the tech stickers Jonah had slapped on the sleek piece of furniture. But every office, cube, and conference room on this floor was decorated in modern geek—Star Wars figurines, Legends of Zelda posters, and Rubik's cubes.

That was what made it home.

For the past eighteen months, he hadn't been comfortable in his own home, all because of a woman. But tonight wasn't about Tessa Martin.

Tonight was about drinking a birthday toast to his sister, just like he did every year on this date.

He kicked back in his office chair, feet up, and stared at the bottle of booze. This was part of the ritual, too. Looking at the damn thing until he couldn't resist opening it. Usually, that took about ten minutes. Tonight, he lasted seven minutes and twenty-three seconds.

He poured his first drink into the short glass and lifted it in a halfhearted salute. "This one's for you, Micki."

He and his twin sister hadn't celebrated their birthday together since they turned eighteen. They had always been so close. Until the party their senior year. Everything changed that night. Micki changed. He changed. The whole friggin' world changed.

Especially Tessa Martin's world.

Jonah had tried to repair it all, but his efforts had been too little, way too late. All the way around.

He was progressing nicely through the bottle, a warm haze taking up residence in his head, when he heard a noise from down the hall.

"It's the holidays!" he hollered, trying for a lightheartedness he didn't feel. "Get out of here. If you don't, I'll take back your holiday bonus!"

"Jonah?" A woman's sweet Southern voice floated back to him.

Of all people, it had to be her. Of course it did, because this was, after all, National Punish Jonah Steele Day. The one day of the year he allowed himself to shamelessly wallow in mistakes from the past.

He stared at the doorway, and she appeared there just as he'd known she would. She stole his breath in a way that liquor never could. Tessa Martin was a kidney punch, lung squeeze, and heartbreak all in one.

Dark ringlet hair controlled into some mysterious girl twist at the back of her head. Golden-brown skin, the stunning result of her biracial heritage. And a slender fragility that couldn't be eclipsed by the curves of her breasts and hips.

She stood in the doorway with one slim hand on the jamb and the other holding a digital recorder. Her style was classic and cool and so fucking sexy he tried not to look at her straight on. Whereas most of the women who worked at Steele Trap wore jeans and cargo pants, Tessa dressed in fitted business suits. Sometimes with pants, but nine times out of ten, with skirts that showed off her legs.

Tonight, her suit was a festive holiday red and hugged the curves he couldn't seem to ignore, even though he'd told himself a million times he should. That didn't keep him from wondering about what she wore beneath.

Was she elegant and classy all over?

"What're you still doing here?" She cast a doubtful glance at the bottle on his desk, and a dark corkscrew curl sprang loose from her neat updo.

"Spending some quality time with an old friend."

"You want to talk about whatever has you looking at that bottle like it might save your life?"

Uh-uh. Not even on a day when snow fell in hell.

But *he* was the one who'd asked her to come to Steele Trap as an organizational psych consultant. Because he still owed her. Owed her for something he could never make restitution for.

When he'd announced the company would now have her on retainer, his staff had given him the hairy eyeball. But after they got over their pissiness at having a head doctor around, they claimed she was good. A good listener, a calm sounding board, a positive influence. An all-around well-spoken, well-educated, well-adjusted psychologist.

She'd made something of herself when a lesser woman would've drawn inward for self-protection. Instead, Tessa had opened up and flourished. The day he'd walked into Steele Trap's breakroom to find her—shoes off and smile glowing—competing in a Ms. Pac-Man tournament with half the company's staff, he had known he was in trouble.

Had known he could fall for her.

She was sweet and smart and knock-a-man-on-his-ass sexy. And he wanted her with a fierceness he shouldn't feel. Should never act on.

"Thanks, but I'm good." He tried to smile at her like he'd smile at anyone else—casual and easy. Like with everything else when it came to this woman, he was a fucking failure. "Nothing to talk about."

She strolled into his office, her hips moving subtly from side to side under the fabric of her skirt, making him wonder what her skin there felt like. He'd seen her naked hips once years ago, and all he'd wanted to do then was cover her up. The full-blown memory of that godawful night tried to make an assault on his brain, but he refused to let it invade.

She raised her eyebrows pointedly and nodded at the scotch. "Then why don't you ask me if I'd like a drink?"

"Sorry, but this is a solo activity."

"Well, that's awfully selfish of you."

His protest didn't stop her. She simply pulled out one of his visitor chairs and made herself all comfy. Crossed one leg over the other, and he was mesmerized by the red high heel dangling from her foot.

"Tessa, you don't want to be around me tonight."

But rather than putting her off, his words seemed to darken her deep brown eyes with concern and curiosity. Yeah, his reluctance to talk had to be super-strength catnip for a psychologist.

Flailing for anything else to talk about besides himself and his crappy mood, he nodded at the recorder in her hand. "You know you can make voice notes on your phone, right?"

"This downloads straight to a secure database I use for all my client information." She slipped it into a pocket on her jacket, obviously settling in. "So about that drink..."

Well, it was a damn sight better to make this a social visit than some kind of head-shrinking session. As far as he knew, she was a white wine drinker, so his stash probably wouldn't be her gig anyway. "Scotch okay?"

"Anything but beer."

He located another glass and poured her a short shot, then filled his own to the rim. Just two friends, having an after-work drink. What the hell would friends talk about over a drink?

The holidays were always safe.

"Going back to North Carolina for Christmas?" he asked, injecting his words with casual good cheer.

With an absent hand, she reached for the glass and rotated it in a circle, gazing into the golden liquid. "Are you?"

"Not this year."

"Is that what's making you so unhappy tonight?" she asked, leaning forward. "That you're not making it back home for the holidays?"

Restless, he rose and sipped his drink as he paced around his desk. On his second pass, Tessa caught him by the wrist. "Talk to me. Please."

He rested his hip against his desk, but that meant he was close enough to Tessa to draw in her scent, cool and mysterious like a fall mountain morning. Trying to suppress the need she tripped off inside him, he blurted out, "It's my sister's birthday."

"Why would that make you so unhappy?"

"Because it's like she hasn't been my sister in years." Not really. Micki had withdrawn, day by day, as if she were fading away in front of everyone's eyes. And then, right after she and Jonah graduated from high school, she'd simply left. Later, they found out where she was—Vegas. And who she was working with—a fucking fixer with some not-so-savory connections. "And because she's my twin."

Tessa picked up her glass and took a quick sip before

pushing out of her chair. "Happy birthday," she said, her voice husky. "If I'd known, I would've—"

"Tessa, go home. Please." If she stayed much longer, he might spill more about his life. About how he felt. About what he wanted.

Her.

"Not while you're drinking."

He could play that game. His mouth quirked up and he tossed back the liquid in his glass. "All done."

"Then why don't I take you to dinner?"

He shook his head because what he was hungry for he wouldn't find on a menu at a downtown Seattle restaurant.

Tessa reached out—slowly—and touched his face. Just a whisper of her fingers against the three-day stubble on his jaw. But it rushed through him like the scotch, leaving a scorched trail in its wake.

Before he could stop himself, he turned his head and brushed his lips across her palm. Her indrawn breath made it clear he'd surprised her, but she didn't pull away.

In fact, she stepped closer and skimmed her thumb across his cheekbone. Her gaze was warm and soft, and her lips were parted. This was a woman who wanted to be kissed. By him.

God, he wanted that, too.

"Tessa—"

"Don't." Her touch shifted so that her fingers pressed against his lips, and he couldn't resist rubbing them against her soft skin. "I have a feeling I won't like what you're about to say. If you're worried this is inappropriate, you shouldn't. After all, you're the one person in this company who's refused to talk to me."

Yeah, he'd been dancing around that. Would keep dancing around it.

"I've been drinking."

"That's an excuse," she said mildly. "You're not drunk."

"I could be if you'd leave me alone."

"Nice try, McSurly. Something else is going on here. I can see your pulse beating in your throat. Am I making you uncomfortable? Or nervous?"

"Crazy," he said.

Her mouth tipped up in a smile that was a combination of sweetness and pure seduction. She moved into him so that the buttons on her jacket brushed the front of his T-shirt. Her scent wound around him, making him drunk in a way the single malt never could.

Without thinking it through, he spread his legs so she could step between them. He cradled her hips between his thighs, and her skirt rubbed against the fly of his jeans.

Her eyes filled with heat. "Then kiss me."

He set his glass on the desk with a definitive clink. Then his hands were in her hair and he was pulling her up to meet his mouth. God, if he thought she smelled like pure temptation, then her taste was the direct path to sin. A hint of cinnamon overlaid with the smokiness of the scotch.

She smelled cool and untouchable, but she was burning him with the heat of her kiss. She opened her mouth to him and angled to get closer until air couldn't squeeze its way between their bodies. Her tongue was slick and avid against his, invading his mouth like he'd dreamed of sliding into her body since the day she'd walked in here wearing her sexy suit and serious smile.

His brain did a wild loop in his head at the sensation of her mouth against his. At the reality of a kiss so long desired. So long denied.

Over the past eighteen months, he hadn't slept with a woman. Hadn't wanted to.

And it didn't take a PhD in psychology to figure out why. Tessa was the one woman his body craved, no matter how much his brain told him he shouldn't.

Without breaking their kiss, Tessa reached between them to work the buttons on her jacket. It slipped off her shoulders and swooshed to the ground. It killed him to release her mouth, but he needed to see.

One glimpse and he squeezed his eyes closed, his breathing ragged. "I'm glad I didn't know."

"Know what?"

"What you wear under there." She'd revealed a skimpy black camisole, all lace and silk with fragile straps that he could snap with a twist of his fingers. The urge to do so, just yank and rip, pounded through him. He wanted to bare her beautiful skin. Her tight, hard nipples.

He wanted to put his mouth on her. To put his teeth on her. Eat her the fuck up.

Dial it back. Dial it down. Dial it to fucking zero.

She ran a palm down the center of his chest, and his heart thudded so hard his sternum was vibrating. "Look at me," she said. "Be with me."

Then she slid her fingers under his shirt and touched the ridges of his stomach, making his abs contract with pleasure. His inner caveman immediately imagined what it would feel like to have her hand move lower. To have her unzip him and touch him with her soft hands. To have her wrap his cock in her fist and pump him from balls to tip.

"Are you breathing?" she asked.

"No," he said on a rush of air.

"That's dangerous."

"You're dangerous."

"Oh, I do like the sound of that." Her laugh was husky, and she pushed his shirt up his chest. Her tongue touched his right nipple just a flash before her teeth tugged, and the top of Jonah's head simply disengaged from his body. Rational thought was jettisoned.

With a jerky tug, he pulled his shirt over his head and tossed it on the conference table. The silky feel of her camisole against his chest rippled through him, setting off mini fires under his skin.

I want.

He cradled the back of her head and crushed his mouth to hers. But it wasn't enough.

He needed to put his hands on her.

Grabbing her by the waist, he swung her around and perched her on the edge of the desk. With frantic hands, he grappled with her camisole, trying like hell to push it up or pull it down. The result was a muffled ripping sound and the fragile fabric drooped around her waist.

He couldn't be trusted. Not with how damn badly he wanted her.

She's a piece of delicate china. You're a fucking bull.

He started to pull back, but she wrapped her legs around him and drew him closer. "It's fine," she breathed. "Old underwear."

He doubted that, but he was already too far gone to care. And when he had the soft weight of her breasts cradled in his hands, he forgot all about her clothes.

It was like holding heaven in his palms. Soft and warm. He wanted to savor the sensation.

But Tessa apparently had other ideas, because her fingers were at his waistband and she quickly unbuttoned his fly.

Fast. This was all happening so fast. Fast was bad.

Wild and uncontrollable.

Dangerous for Tessa.

He released his hold on her to catch her hands, but she shoved him away and worked his jeans off his hips, enough so she could shove down his boxer briefs.

The relief from having his erection freed sent another wave of lust over him, making his legs shake. And when she took him in hand, her grip warm and firm, he stumbled and braced his hands on the edge of the desk to stay upright.

She worked him, stroking up and down with the perfect pressure, while he buried his face against her neck. "That feels..."

"...amazing." she said, using her thumb to do something wicked and wonderful, making him even harder.

If she didn't let go, stop pumping him, he was going to come in her hand. He could feel it, the tightness in his belly, the tension on the inside of his thighs.

Something this good, this rare, should last. Intellectually he knew that, but his dick had other ideas.

He grabbed the hem of Tessa's skirt to yank it up. She wriggled against him and he somehow hooked her panties and slid them down. He blindly groped for his wallet and found the single condom inside. He carelessly tossed the wallet and ripped at the package.

"Let me—"

He just shook his head and roughly covered himself, not giving a damn how painfully pleasurable it was.

Now. Right the fuck now.

"Are you ready?" he ground out.

"So ready."

With impatient hands, he pushed at Tessa's knees, opening her legs wide. Then he yanked her to the edge of the desk and pressed inside her.

Oh, fuck.

The feel of her slick body, the tight heat, was almost

more than he could bear. It was like the world had coalesced into that perfect spot between her legs.

Dots of color flashed behind his eyes.

"Don't...don't stop." The kiss she smoothed across his collarbone pulled him under a wave of tenderness and possessiveness.

His breath was chuffing in and out of his lungs, but he could barely hear it for the blood rushing in his ears. With rough hands, he grabbed her hips and pulled her closer.

Then he leaned over her and drove in. Again and again and again.

Tessa made little noises in the back of her throat. Sounds that made his hips pump harder. Faster.

Until all that existed was the slide of skin on skin. Damp with lust and something else he wouldn't allow himself to name.

"Jonah," she breathed.

For some reason, hearing her say his name as if he was everything she'd ever wanted pushed the final button for him. He reached between their bodies to finger her clitoris in tight little circles. Her groan was low and lusty, and her muscles began to ripple around him.

That's when he completely lost his fucking mind. He pounded into her as the orgasm rushed over her. And when he felt her body begin to melt into his, he fucked her even harder.

The whole world narrowed down to his body touching Tessa's. She was everything good. Everything right. Everything—

His own orgasm slammed into him, coming from every nerve ending, every muscle, until his jaw clenched and his body stilled, buried deep inside Tessa's.

As he began to descend, all those nerves and muscles

began to shake. Almost a shiver, like he'd suddenly been hit with a case of untreatable flu.

Because what he'd just done was...was wrong.

His breathing hitched as hyperventilation snuck up on him. What had he just done? This was Tessa. Sweet, smart, serious Tessa.

Damaged Tessa.

He jerked away, pulling out of the haven of her body without thinking of the condom. He reached for it, but the damage was already done.

With horror, he stared down at her, palms braced against the desk, camisole covering one breast, the other exposed, her breathing making them rise and fall. Her skirt was bunched around her waist and her legs were spread wide, her inner thighs wet with...

In Jonah's mind, in his memory, all he could see was blood.

2

Asheville, North Carolina
One Year Ago

IT WAS NOVEMBER, AND JONAH WAS SWEATING HIS ASS OFF. But that was what standing on the porch of Tessa's parents' stone-and-timber home got him. A big ol' pool of flop sweat.

Because he hadn't seen her since the day he'd walked out of Steele Trap for the last time.

Trying to cool the hell off, he turned back his shirt cuffs, which revealed the tats on his forearms. An intricate triforce on one and a chrono trigger on the other, both done in black and jewel tones. Seeing as his own mom had cried a little when she'd seen them, it probably wasn't the best idea to leave them uncovered now.

Nice to meet you, Mr. and Mrs. Martin.

I'm Jonah Steele.

I'm the dickhead who once abandoned your daughter on this very porch.

Oh, and then years later, I screwed her on my office desk. And I now need her help to get my tattooed ass out of a sling.

Yeah, that wouldn't go over well.

He rolled down his sleeves and rang the bell.

"Hello?" The woman who answered the door stunned him. Although her skin was several shades lighter than Tessa's, she had the same dark eyes and welcoming smile. This was what Tessa would look like twenty or thirty years from now.

And Jonah would still want her twenty or thirty years from now.

"I'm...ah...you're..." Jesus, when had he developed a stutter? He stuck out his hand. "I'm Jonah, and I'm here to see Tessa. Is she around?"

He'd initially tried to call her in Seattle, but he'd been told she was away for Thanksgiving. So he'd taken the chance that she was here with her family.

"She's in the kitchen, helping me with a turkey casserole. Would you like to come in? I could get you a hot drink."

He wasn't sure he deserved to be invited inside their home, so he just said, "This will only take a minute if she's willing to come outside."

Mrs. Martin's smile wavered.

"We used to work together."

It must've all connected for her, because her pretty eyes widened. But she recovered quickly and said, "I'll get her."

Jonah turned to stare out at the scenery—trees losing the very last of their leaves, their piles heaped in yards and filling the ditches. The natural death of late fall, which normally depressed the hell out of him.

But this year was different. This was the year Micki had come home, and he'd be damned if she'd leave again.

But Tessa was the only one who could guarantee Micki could stay.

"Jonah? This is a surprise."

He whirled around to find her wearing an honest-to-goodness apron—with a white bib and ruffles along the skirt—over a black outfit. But in his mind, he pictured her naked, hip cocked in invitation and feather duster at the ready.

Dude, stay away from the sexy maid fantasies.

He definitely didn't have any right to those thoughts, not after what he'd done to her. After he'd deliberately kept his distance. After he'd sold his company to get the hell away from her.

"You look"—Kissable? Edible?—"good."

But she didn't smile at him the way her mother had. In fact, her eyes were guarded. "What are you doing here?"

"I need you."

The caution on her face switched to surprise faster than he could ping a server.

"I mean, I need your help. It's about my sister Micki, and it's serious."

"Okay..." She shoved her hands into her apron pockets, but he could easily see they were fisted.

He'd apologized, after that night in his office. But even he knew that he'd fucked things up even more. That was when he'd realized it was best for him to stay far away from Tessa. He couldn't seem to be around her without letting her down. Worse yet, hurting her.

And that was the dead last thing he wanted.

"Do you remember how I once told you I hadn't seen her for years?"

"Of course I do." Her tone made it clear she forgot nothing.

"Well, she's back in North Carolina, but there's a problem."

"I'm sorry, but I don't do individual counseling, if that's what she's looking for."

He considered that for a second. Micki probably *could* benefit from someone rooting around in that complicated brain of hers, but if he told her that, she'd tell him to go get his own damn head examined.

Not something he was fired up to do, especially if Tessa was the examiner.

"No, she needs you to talk with the State's Attorney and the Asheville DA." God, he was screwing this all up. No please. No thank you. Just wham ba—

Nope, not goin' there.

He paced along the length of the porch while Tessa watched him from her spot near the front door. "It's a long story. None of us knew it until recently, but Micki's craphat of a boss has been blackmailing her all this time."

"Why would he do something like that?"

Jonah squeezed his eyes closed for a few seconds. He didn't want to stir up bad memories for Tessa, but he needed her to understand. He opened his eyes and pointed to the stone porch steps. "Would you... Could we sit down for a minute?"

Her nod had a jerky quality about it, but she moved away from the door and settled on the top step. Blowing out a silent breath, he did the same, keeping a good two feet between them. But that wasn't enough to keep her cool scent from reaching him. He drew it in until his lungs couldn't take another molecule.

Sweetly scented torture.

"Tessa, this isn't easy. It's about that night. Harrison Shaw's party in Asheville."

"The night I was raped."

The word hit him like a cinderblock to the head. To the heart. It was raw and ugly, just like the shitheads who'd drugged her and... "How can you be so casual about it?" he demanded.

That seemed to spark something in her eyes, and they went hot. "I am not casual about it. But it happened. It's a part of my past. It's a part of who I am. I spent plenty of years stonewalling my way through sessions with therapists before I realized the person I was hurting most was myself. So, yes, I'm able to say it. To name it. To face it."

It wasn't something he wanted to face. Ever.

But Micki needed him. After all these years she was allowing her family—allowing *him,* even after the part he'd played in all this—to help her, and he had to secure this final piece for her to have the life she deserved. "There was video footage."

At that, Tessa froze and slowly turned her head toward him. "What?"

"God, no. Not that. Apparently the Shaws had some type of in-house camera security. Micki's boss, Phil Flynn, was the one who—"

"Is he slick—expensive clothes and gelled hair? Works out of Las Vegas?"

"How did you know?"

"Because he came here, after. Threatened my parents that he'd drag me through the mud if I went to the police. I was...fragile...for a while. They weren't even sure I'd hold up on the stand if we did file charges. Mom and Dad decided it was in my best interests to let it go."

Which was only one of the reasons Jonah had collected his own form of damages. Had demanded restitution for Tessa.

"I can see what you're thinking," she said. "That we shouldn't have let them get away with it. Believe me, I would never suggest it to a sexual assault victim. But at the time, my parents were doing the best they could."

Because they'd caved, Phil had been able to manipulate Micki for years, threatening to wrap a hangman's noose around Jonah's neck if she didn't work for him. Lie and deceive for him. "Haven't you thought about—"

"Have you heard how Harrison Shaw's life has turned out?"

Yeah, he knew a thing or two about that fucker and the four others who'd used Tessa. After that night, Jonah had made it his business to find out their names, their social security numbers, and everything else he could dig up on Charlie Cartwright, Matthew Levine, Andy Bledsoe, and Brandon Johnson. But in answer to Tessa's question, he just lifted a shoulder. "I haven't exactly added him to my LinkedIn network."

"He was a spoiled teenager, and as an adult, he's pretty much self-destructed. DUIs. Drug possession. For a while his dad kept him out of real trouble, but a few years ago he washed his hands, let Harrison finally take the rap for drug trafficking."

At least she didn't know about the incident—if "stealing" a hundred grand from his parents could be called an incident—that had started Shaw's downhill slide into most of that shit.

If she thought the guy had paid enough for his sins, she was sorely mistaken, but it wasn't a conversation Jonah and Tessa would have. So he took a breath and said, "Apparently, after that party, the Shaws gave Phil Flynn security footage from inside their house. I was caught on camera when I left you to get help. Between that and the DNA under your fingernails, Phil convinced Micki he could pin me with...with..."

"Jonah, say the word."

He swallowed, but it felt as though he had a medicine ball stuck in there. "He made her believe I could be charged with your rape and that conviction was a slam dunk."

Because in the state of North Carolina, there was no statute of limitations on rape.

"And you want me to—"

"I know I shouldn't ask, but if you'd be willing to tell the DA and State's Attorney that I didn't...didn't..." Hell, for the past two years, he'd felt as if he'd attacked her that night in his office. Unable to sit beside her for another second without touching her, without wrapping his arms around her and probably scaring the crap out of her in the process, he jumped up and pulled a business card from his jeans. "This is my attorney's card. You don't have to say yes or no right now, but if you could call him by the end of the day with an answer, I'd appreciate it. Then I promise never to bother you again."

Because with the turmoil and need inside him, that was the way it had to be. He couldn't see Tessa without wanting her. And he couldn't have her without hurting her.

And no man—him included—would ever hurt this woman again.

With a control he didn't feel, he placed the business card near her right hand on the step. Although his hand shook with the need to touch her, just a brush of his fingers over her shoulder, he drew back.

"Good-bye, Tessa."

He turned away and walked back to his car. This time, he would stay out of Tessa's life for good.

· · ·

IF SHE HAD A HUNDRED YEARS ON THIS EARTH, TESSA MIGHT never figure out Jonah Steele.

Brilliant, broody, and possibly broken.

Something told her she had played a part in his brokenness.

On his way to his car, he didn't look back once, just focused on that Tesla as if it were a transporter beaming him up. His shaggy brown hair gleamed in the sun and his jeans hugged his long legs. He was built like a swimmer—lean, but with the perfect amount of bulk to propel him through any obstacle in his path.

He was so good at bringing people together—to make games, to save his hometown, to create things bigger than just himself—but somehow, he seemed so alone.

Once again he was walking away from her, leaving only a hint of his leather and cedar scent behind. Just as he'd walked away the day he sold Steele Trap.

After the night she and Jonah had sex in his office, he'd been more distant than ever. His employees had picked up on that, some of them no longer attending sessions with her. When Jonah sold Steele Trap, the new owner wanted her to stay on for the transition, so she had.

But maybe now it was time to make a change in her life.

"Honey, why was Jonah Steele here?"

Tessa glanced back at her mother, who was watching Jonah's car zoom down the winding driveway. "How did you know who he was?"

"I recognized him from the cover of *Fast Company*."

He'd been on that magazine at the age of twenty-four, and Tessa had a copy of it stored in an archival box. She'd kept a clipping of every mention of him she'd ever come across. Business section articles, gaming magazine features, society pages.

Needless to say, her box was full.

And maybe that said it all. She had a box full of trivia about the man, but she didn't have the man himself.

"It doesn't look like his visit made you happy."

"He asked me to call his attorney."

"What?"

"Do you remember Phil Flynn?"

Her mom's pretty face went rigid, emphasizing the fine lines around her mouth and eyes. "He isn't a man I will ever forget."

"I had no idea, but apparently Jonah's sister has been working for him for years."

That seemed to take the starch out of her mom's spine because she dropped onto the step beside Tessa. "Why? I thought the Steeles were good people."

"He needs my help because he and his sister are being threatened by Flynn with video footage from the Shaw's house that night."

"Oh God, Tess..." Her mom's expression took on the horror Tessa had felt at Jonah's announcement, and she grasped her hand.

"From the hallway." Tessa squeezed her hand in reassurance. "But Flynn convinced Jonah's sister that he could take Jonah down for rape with the proof he had."

"That poor boy."

That made Tessa smile. "Not exactly poor, Mom."

"Monetary wealth doesn't have a thing to do with emotional wealth."

True. Which made her realize how bankrupt Jonah's eyes seemed any time he was near her, especially when the conversation edged toward the topic of her sexual assault. "I think it's painful for him to be around me. Either that or I repel him."

He wouldn't be the only man who couldn't handle her past.

Tessa stared at the box of Christmas lights her dad had hauled out of the attic earlier this morning, and they spun her back to the night of Steele Trap's holiday party.

After they had sex—hot, amazing, intense sex—on top of his desk, Jonah had pulled away from her and looked at her with the kind of horror that made her blood chill. His expression was a combination of disgust and shame, two emotions Tessa was no stranger to herself.

She'd worked so hard to put them in their proper place after she was raped. Seeing them so clearly displayed on Jonah's face ripped open a place in her carefully constructed emotional sanctuary.

So she slipped on her underwear and straightened her clothes.

But when Jonah tried to walk out, she grabbed him by the arm and pushed him into the nearest chair. "Talk," she ordered. "You owe me that."

How she hated to guilt him like that, but as many times as she'd dreamed of being in this man's arms, none of them had ended like this, with him looking at her as if she was someone he didn't know.

"I don't want to be like them," he said, his eyes glassy with pain. "They paid, but it wasn't enough."

"Like who?" she asked. Surely he couldn't mean... "Jonah, what just happened here was consensual. You understand that, right?"

"That doesn't make it okay." And he walked out.

Tessa blinked, bringing the box of lights and the present back into focus. "He needs me to talk with the authorities to clear him," she finally said to her mom.

"Is there any reason you wouldn't?"

Tessa leaned in and rested her head on her mom's shoulder. "Honestly, I'm afraid I'd do almost anything for that man."

3

North Carolina
One Year Later
Present Day

Someone had tried to make Tucci's, a downtown Charlotte restaurant, glimmer with holiday cheer. Fake mistletoe hung from doorways, colorful foil garlands swagged along the walls, and little Santas parachuted from the ceiling.

But for Jonah, it was suddenly too noisy, too hot, too crowded.

Any place where he and Tessa Martin were in the same room was too crowded. Made him feel as if his skin had been tossed in the dryer and shrunk like a wool sweater.

What was she doing here?

He hadn't seen her in person since the day he'd asked her to help Micki. To help him. After Tessa had called the DA and State's Attorney to clear his name, he'd told himself that an elaborate floral arrangement and a heartfelt thank-you note was enough.

Now it felt like nothing more than a dick move.

He took a sip of his beer and tried to keep his attention on the circle of people around him. He'd heard a few of his former developers would be in town and figured it was a perfect time to talk with them about a new project he wanted to launch.

"So when are you gonna tell us why you're plying us with food and booze when we're supposed to be at some boring conference dinner?"

Jonah flinched, realizing Jimmy Stafford, a Python whiz, had caught him staring at Tessa like a teenager jonesing for a prom date.

He forced himself to look away from her, but his brain was still mulling over her appearance. She was wearing snug black pants, heels that could fuel a thousand fantasies, and a silky red shirt. He caught himself rubbing his fingers together as if he could feel the texture of the fabric, so he shoved his hands into the pockets of his jeans and pretended he'd simply been glancing around.

At the bar, a dude with a martini in front of him was staring intently at someone. Jonah followed his line of sight directly back to Tessa. The guy's scrutiny made the hair on the back of Jonah's neck quiver. Then he looked down at his drink, and Jonah relaxed. Just a man looking at a beautiful woman.

He blinked, remembering Stafford had asked him a question, but instead of answering it, he asked, "What's Tessa doing here?"

Keith Benery, a self-taught young developer he'd hired at Steele Trap, was standing on the opposite side of the tall cocktail table. "Aw, shit. I didn't realize this was a private thing. Figured you were fine with anyone from Steele Trap coming, and she was going to be around, so—"

"Not a problem." It wasn't, because he wouldn't let it be.

Tonight was about making strides to shed his recent reputation as the bored Baby Billionaire. Baby Fucking Billionaire. His brothers had given him the nickname with a sort of twisted affection, but it still rubbed.

After he'd saved his hometown from the brink of bankruptcy, people had acted as if he was some kind of savior. A hero. But he wasn't.

Any idiot with a bank account could throw money around. And since he'd built his big cedar-and-glass house on the ridge, people had started to idolize him even more.

If only they knew they were wasting their time looking up to a man who didn't deserve their admiration.

"I wanted to feel you out about working on a side hustle," he said to the guys around him.

Keith hooked a thumb in his belt loop and knocked back half his IPA. It always struck Jonah as a little funny seeing the guy drink beer, because with his blond crew cut and freckles, he looked about thirteen.

"Another game like Steele Survivor?" Jimmy asked.

"Nah. Been there, done that." He could've made another game, since the timeline on his noncompete had expired. Steele Survivor was a game he'd first imagined when he was a kid. It was fun, and it had made him a rich man, but at the end of the day, it was just a game.

Now, he wanted to make something that mattered.

Before Jonah could explain his idea for a suite of personal safety apps, Keith turned and called out to the room, "Hey, guys, Steele's making games again!"

That brought the rest of the coders he'd invited his way,

drinks and snacks in hand. They crowded around him and peppered him with questions.

"Another survivor game?"

"What platform are you looking at? Console or iOS?"

Before he could correct Keith's assumption, a blond waitress hurried toward Jonah with a tray of appetizers. "Can I offer you something?"

By the husky tone in her voice, she wasn't trying to sell him on the deliciousness of those one-bite pork sliders.

"Thanks, but no..."

She smiled and leaned forward to give him a clear view of what appeared to be 400ccs of silicone. "Are you sure?"

He caught movement over the waitress's shoulder, and looked up to find Tessa walking toward the group. *Crap.* She probably thought he'd been ogling the woman's tits.

Why did she always seem to catch him at his worst?

He wasn't actually a butt-brained douchebag. At least not all the time.

Tessa touched the waitress on the elbow and nodded to the guys opposite Jonah in the conversation circle. "Those gentlemen were just asking for more sliders."

The waitress glanced at the other guys, dressed in shirts screen-printed with things like "Zelda is the girl" and "Video games don't make us violent. Lag does." Then she looked back at Jonah with disappointment clearly shining in her eyes.

Hell, it wasn't as if he had anything on them when it came to dressing like a grownup. His own shirt said "$\sqrt{-1}$ 2^3 $\sum$ π... It was delicious." But his credit card was the one that had been handed over for tonight's tab. And something about a Barclays Black Card seemed to get women's attention.

The waitress did a little eyelash flutter at him, then

headed toward the other guys, who greeted her and the sliders with a cheer and some juvenile backslaps.

Tessa moved closer, teasing Jonah with her scent. While the others momentarily gave the waitress and the food their full attention, Tessa sipped her wine and smiled over the rim of her glass. "It was nice of you to host this get-together. Are we celebrating something?"

"No, just catching up." He didn't want to tell her about his app ideas because they'd been inspired by her. By what had happened to her.

Something no one should have to endure.

If a person ever felt threatened, he or she should be able to quickly and covertly communicate with a small circle of people they trusted. People who could help them out of a dicey situation. The uses for an app like that could be wide-spread, but he wanted to roll it out to domestic violence and sexual assault victims first.

He shrugged and tried to avoid Tessa's scrutiny. Whenever she looked at him like that, as if she could clearly read all his thoughts, he didn't know whether to feel psychoanalyzed or turned on. "Heard a few people were in town, so..."

"Jonah, look at me."

"What? I am looking at you."

"No," she said, laying her soft hand on his scruffy cheek and almost stopping his heart, "you're staring at my left ear."

He couldn't help but let a small smile break through, because she was right. "You have nice ears."

Crazy thing was, his statement was true. Decorated with classic pearl earrings, Tessa's ears were dainty and perfectly curved. Sexy.

Sexy ears. This was what happened when he didn't have enough to keep him busy—he got juiced up looking at a woman's earlobes.

Her hand skimmed down his face, and she let it fall away. Even while surrounded by people, the loss made him feel alone. Hell, if it weren't for Tessa, he could be sitting alone in a jail cell.

"Thank you," he blurted out.

"For?"

"For clearing me," he said, turning more fully toward her to ensure others didn't hear.

"All I did was tell the truth."

"You made it possible for my sister to live the life she wants instead of the one she was forced into."

"And you? Are you living the life you want?"

"Please don't try to play shrink with me. I don't need you crawling around in my head." And fuck-all if that didn't make him think about her crawling into his bed.

Tessa simply took another sip of her wine and slowly placed her glass next to his, allowing her knuckles to brush his. "You're right. I'm not your therapist. I'm not your priest. I'm just a friend." With a sad smile, she reached up and smoothed his hair out of his eyes. "And a friend knows when another friend is feeling a little lost."

Hell, in one way or another, he'd been stumbling around in the woods since he was seventeen. Since the night he'd failed Tessa.

Something he'd been trying to make up for ever since.

He wanted to drop to his knees and ask her to forgive him. He also wanted to drop to his knees and—

"So, Steele, what's this new project of yours?"

Good. Saved from his own imagination.

Suddenly, a weird feeling crawled up the back of Jonah's neck, and he glanced toward the bar to find the same guy who'd been scoping out Tessa staring at him.

"I've kept all of you away from your conference for long

enough," Jonah told the developers. "Tell you what, I'll set up a video call next week with anyone who wants to hear more."

The man at the bar struck Jonah as familiar, but he couldn't place him. Maybe the dude was a Steele Survivor fan. That happened every so often. Someone recognized him from a picture on the Internet or some tech magazine.

But then the dude's attention shifted to Tessa once again and his expression changed. Hardened into speculative interest.

Uh-uh, buddy. No one looks at this woman like that.

Something on Jonah's face must've flashed like a neon light, because Tessa asked, "Are you okay?"

"Someone who looks familiar is at the bar. I should go over and..." *beat his ass.* But martini dude slid off his stool and into the crowd.

"I need to leave," he told Tessa. "Get your coat."

"What?"

"I want to walk you to your car."

"I valet parked. Besides, people are still here."

Damn, he hated to spook her, but he didn't like the way that guy had up and disappeared. "There was a guy at the bar who has been staring holes through that sexy red shirt you're wearing. And not in a good way. Now, I'd like to walk you to your car."

Her gaze flickered over to the bar and back.

He set his half-finished drink aside and quickly shook hands and bumped fists with his former employees. "Y'all stay as long as you want. Everything's on me."

He helped Tessa into her coat and grabbed his jacket from a nearby chair.

Outside, Tessa handed the valet her ticket, then turned to Jonah. "Something strange just happened in there. You asked people to come out and then you acted like you wanted to be anywhere else but here."

Blowing out a breath, he looked down the street where people were spilling out of bars and restaurants just like this one. Their laughter and smiles reminded him of his siblings. Happy, settled, freakin' content because they were doing something important and had someone to share it with.

Like Britt with the Steele-Shepherd Wildlife Research Center, and Reid with the law enforcement training center. Grif ran the city and had a great family. Evie was a modern-day Florence Nightingale, and Micki was teaching a cyber warfare class and developing education software.

He wanted that. A new purpose other than the status of former video game king.

That was why the app idea appealed to him so much. His initial thought had been to have some of his former employees help him, but maybe he should forget about involving them. Maybe he was trying to re-create something he had no business re-creating.

And the thought of talking with Tessa about his plans, as duct-taped and chicken-wired together as they were, made him feel strangely exposed. Besides, she might not appreciate that a hardship in her life was now giving him purpose.

The valet drove up in a silver BMW, a symbol of just how successful Tessa had become, and parked it at the curb in front of them. Compassion clear in her eyes, Tessa stepped closer to Jonah and placed her palm on his chest. "What's going on? For a few minutes in there, I thought you were going to turn and run."

He'd wanted to run from *her* and she'd seen it. He didn't need her to realize that how he felt about her made him vulnerable. So fucking defenseless.

So he went on the offensive, herding her toward her car. When her back was against the side, he lowered his face to her ear. "Stay out of my head. That wasn't your job when I hired you, and it isn't your job now."

"I'm just being a friend."

He couldn't afford for her to have any active role in his life. He'd left Seattle because a city of half a million people was still too small to hide that he wanted her with an intensity that wasn't in any way nice. Or easy. Or decent. "I don't want you to be my friend, I want..."

"You want what?" Her hand came to his waist and her lips moved, their glossy red sheen making a haze come over his vision.

"This." He put his arms on either side of her, caging her against the car, and covered her mouth with his. God, she tasted of expensive wine, hot woman, and somehow like cinnamon, just as she had the last time he'd kissed her.

For a few sweet seconds she responded, her lips nimble and mobile under his. But soon—too damn soon—she was pushing against his shoulder. "Stop. Jonah, stop!"

Her panic pulled him out of his moment of insanity, and he yanked his mouth away from hers and stood there staring down at her, both of them breathing heavily, their chests brushing with each harsh inhale and exhale.

They were standing on a sidewalk in view of tons of people, and he would've gladly done Tessa against this car.

He had to accept that he'd never be able to control himself around this woman. If anything spoke of the shadows inside him, it was this, his complete disregard for what was right when it came to her. She clouded what little good judgment he had and turned it into a swirling vortex of confused lust. "God, Tessa, I'm sorry. I didn't mean—"

"It's not you." She let her hands drop from his body and turned her face away.

How could it *not* be him? He'd caged her against the car and would've fucked her right here. No second thoughts.

"It's the beer."

"What?"

"I can't... I can't...beer..." She fumbled through her purse and held out a tin of breath mints.

He stepped back so quickly, his heel caught on the sidewalk seam and he had to do some fancy footwork to stay upright. He took the mints from her, popped a half dozen into his mouth, and crunched them violently between his teeth. Of course she couldn't stand the smell of beer on a man's breath. He should've realized that. "I didn't... This shouldn't have happened. It won't happen again."

"I wanted you to kiss me. It's just that certain things..."

Make you remember. "I understand."

"I don't think you do," she said softly. "Jonah, when are you going to stop denying that we want one another? Won't you at least give us a chance to see what this is? What it could be?"

He couldn't, and he was managing that by knowing she lived over twenty-six hundred miles away. "When do you fly back to Seattle?"

"I'm not. I've moved to Asheville to start my own corporate coaching company." Her lips curved in a small smile. "I'm back home to stay."

Looked like Santa had just taken a big ol' piss in Jonah's stocking.

4

In the hallway outside her newly purchased condo in an Asheville mid-rise, Tessa touched her lips, still tingling from Jonah's earlier all-consuming kiss and the scruff around his mouth. He'd kissed her as if he wanted to get inside her. Not just inside her body, but inside the deepest darkest parts of her.

From the second he'd walked into the downtown bar tonight, he'd been restless. It didn't take a trained mental health professional to figure that out. He'd smiled and chatted with the people gathered, but the easygoing expression had never touched his eyes.

Why did she seem to be the only one who ever saw that?

Other people constantly said things like "Jonah's so chill," "Doesn't get in much of a hurry about anything," and "Hard to rile."

Tessa unlocked her front door and placed her purse and keys on the foyer table—keys in the aqua art glass bowl and her bag in a gathering basket.

From his kennel, Badger was giving her a doggy grin and frantic tail wag.

"Hey there, King B," she crooned, hurrying over to release him. Tonight, she didn't care that she hadn't changed into her comfy clothes before he leaped into her arms. What was a little dog fur on a night like this, when she was feeling so uncertain? So shaken by her own decisions. "How's my good boy?"

From the way her piebald miniature dachshund was licking her chin, he was ecstatic.

Letting his wriggling body soothe hers, she blew out a breath and looked at her living room. Although her move was recent, she'd put a rush on her furniture delivery and everything was unpacked and in its proper place. Even the ten-foot artificial Douglas fir in the corner hung with white lights and matching ornaments.

Normally, having all her belongings organized made her feel calm and controlled.

Not tonight.

But her pup was helping. The feel of his smooth short fur under her hand. The warmth of his body against hers. The gift of his unconditional love.

She quickly kicked off her heels, purposefully allowing them to lie askew on the cool tile under her feet, and slipped on a pair of scuffs.

"Park time, buddy." She'd chosen this building because of the bark park in the central courtyard. When she reached for Badger's leash, his body went into overdrive, his tiny butt doing the bump with her chest.

In the hallway, she put him on the floor and he pranced down it as if he were ten feet tall, his head up and pointy chest bowed out.

If only Tessa could feel so confident all the time. She'd learned that little rituals—like putting her belongings in their appropriate place—helped to remind herself she was in control, that she had climbed her way out of something that might've wrecked a lesser woman.

But Jonah Steele could still wreck her inside if she let him.

Maybe she could call her mom and tell her about tonight. Then again, if she did that, her mother might give her the advice to move on, that she deserved a man who saw her for the woman she was now instead of the shattered girl she'd once been.

But Tessa wasn't willing to give up. Not until she'd really tried to connect with Jonah. When she'd first been brought on at Steele Trap, she'd been grateful, but had been intent on proving to Jonah that she'd made something of herself. That although she appreciated what he'd done for her, she no longer needed a protector.

She hadn't been prepared for what seeing him as a man would do to her emotions. The physical attraction had been electric and disconcerting. But she'd also found herself pulled in by the way he kidded around with the people who worked for him, the charitable donations he made without asking for acknowledgment, the spark in his eyes when he played video games in the employee lounge.

She wanted a chance to get close to *that* Jonah.

Outside in the doggie park, Badger did his business, then spent a few minutes trying to woo a Doberman. She ignored him, much to his disappointment.

"You might have more luck with that corgi from 603," Tessa told him.

The side-eye Badger gave her said, "I'll thank you to stay out of my love life."

Back in the condo, she scooped up her heels and headed for her bedroom, where she stored the shoes in their color-coordinated plastic box. She took off her pants and top, saw the amount of fur on them and tossed them into her dry cleaning pile. The camisole underneath she left on and pulled on a matching pair of silk lounge pants.

When she let her hair out of the twist, the kinky curls fell and brushed her back. Her chest loosened, allowing her to finally take a full breath. Jonah's kisses had the power to do that to her—steal all her air.

A glass of pinot grigio, a snuggle with Badger, and her cushy couch were exactly what she needed right now. But once she'd settled into the down cushions and pulled a cashmere throw around her and Badger, her nerves were still jumping just under the surface of her skin.

She placed her glass on the coffee table and reached for the TV remote. "How about a *Firefly* marathon?"

It wasn't Badger's favorite—he much preferred back episodes of *Meerkat Manor*—but tonight Tessa needed to escape into another world.

As if she could really be distracted from the way Jonah's mouth had felt on hers—strong and soft all at once—and the way his hands had felt on her body. Like he never wanted to let her go.

Maybe he wouldn't have if she hadn't pulled away. But the taste of beer on his lips had sent her hurtling back to a place she never wanted to return to. She'd worked hard to handle the smell in social settings, but still couldn't deal with it on a man's breath when his mouth was on hers.

So instead, she was spending the rest of her evening with Captain Malcolm Reynolds of the Firefly-class *Serenity*.

Her cell rang, making her heart jump. Maybe it was Jonah.

Stop acting like a twelve-year-old girl with a crush. You can call a man your own self if it's so important.

But when she checked the screen, it was a Seattle area code. She hit the talk button. "Hello?"

Badger, never one to be ignored, tried to insert his long snoot between her mouth and the phone. His nose touched her lips, and she pushed it down and tucked his head under her chin.

"Is this Tessa Martin?"

"To whom am I speaking?" She gave her corporate clients her private number for emergencies, but she wasn't stupid enough to give out information when she didn't know who was on the other end of the line.

"This is Carson Grimes. Remember me?"

He'd been a developer at Steele Trap, one of the first of Jonah's employees to see her after she was contracted to help the staff with things like stress management and work/life balance. She resettled Badger into the crook of her arm. "Of course. How are you?"

"Honestly, I'm not worth dick." His tone was harsh and his words were clipped.

Tessa tensed. He'd never once spoken to her this way while she'd been at Steele Trap. Now she was no longer on retainer, and Carson wasn't even an employee anymore. But she wouldn't turn him away. "Would you like to talk about it?"

"Not really," he said, "but you damn well need to do something about this."

"About what?"

"Get online and go to the Q13 website."

"Give me a sec to open up my laptop." Something was obviously very wrong here, so she scrambled up from the couch, which made Badger give an admonishing yap, and ran for the spare bedroom she'd set up as her home office. It took a few clicks to open her browser and navigate to the right site. "Okay. I'm here."

"Scroll down to the story about the Aurora Bridge."

That uneasy feeling inside her expanded. That bridge was a famous spot for jumpers in Seattle. She tried to swallow back her alarm, found the article, and quickly scanned it.

Oh, God. Her pulse quickened. "What happened?"

"Why don't you tell me?"

"Carson, I'm sorry, but you've caught me at a disadvantage. I don't know what you want from me. Obviously, I'm devastated to read this."

His laugh was raw and mean. "You don't know what I want? I want you to fucking stop e-mailing me."

E-mailing him? She'd barely had her laptop open recently. "What e-mail are you—"

"Davey was little more than a kid." He plowed over her question. "He couldn't take your bullshit. But I swear to God, you mess with me anymore, and you won't like the outcome. Davey killed himself. I don't know what your game is, but if one of us is going down, lady, it's gonna be you." The phone went silent on the other end.

"Carson? Are you there?"

Nothing.

Tessa's earlier agitation had been microscopic compared to what she was feeling right now, and Badger sensed it, because he hopped into her lap and put his front paws on the keyboard, making the article scroll back to the beginning. She pulled her chair closer to her monitor and reread the news slowly, looking for any clue as to why Davey Sinchilla, another Steele Trap employee she'd counseled and Carson's close friend, might've committed suicide.

But the write-up was all about the facts. David Stanley

Sinchilla. Age twenty-four and a native of Redmond, Washington.

"Oh, King B, this is horrible." Her heart felt as if it had been squeezed into a hard little ball. She'd met Davey's parents once. His dad was a high-school biology coach and his mom was a mail carrier. They'd been so proud of their son, working at a big, famous game company. Making excellent money. What parent wouldn't be thrilled to have their child find such purpose and stability?

Especially after he'd been such a wild kid as a teen. When he'd come to see Tessa, he'd given her his background, including all the drugs, rebellion, and a couple of rehab jailbreaks. When he was seventeen, his broken-hearted parents had been close to writing him off.

Finally, Davey had hit rock bottom after his so-called girlfriend had OD'd on a chemical cocktail of painkillers, sedatives, and muscle relaxers. He'd woken to find her dead beside him in the bed. That was when he'd gotten clean.

But it hadn't been without struggle over the years. He'd known the pressure of video game development would test him. Any time the pressure mounted, he'd schedule a coaching session with her. And between talking with her occasionally and keeping up with his NA meetings, he'd been coping well.

At least he had been the last time she talked with him. In fact, he'd been dating someone new, a woman he thought might be the love of his life.

As she scanned the scanty details in the article, Tessa's few sips of wine felt like Drano in her stomach. Davey's life had been reduced to less than five hundred words.

Tessa pushed away from her desk, and Badger jumped down to trot behind her. Absently, she picked up her glass, carried it to the kitchen, and poured the wine into the sink.

Then she washed the glass and placed it on the drying rack.

When she made another lap around the house and found herself opening the fridge and organizing the contents by food groups and color, she knew she needed to sit down and think. Some people sleepwalked when stressed. Tessa, on the other hand, woke to alphabetized canned goods in her cabinets.

She needed to understand what had happened with Davey. He'd had a regular therapist in addition to her. She made it clear to all her clients that her focus was on workplace coping skills, productivity, and performance.

Stress and overwhelm, she could handle. Addiction and suicide were on an entirely different level.

What had Carson said? Something about wanting her to stop e-mailing him. Which didn't make any sense because she hadn't seen or spoken to him for months.

She hurried back to her computer and again Badger hopped into her lap. She opened her e-mail and clicked on her sent items.

Scrolling through the outgoing e-mails, she mentally flicked through all the names. Her dad, the closing company for her new condo, the organizations she'd talked with about Martin & Associates corporate coaching.

This was stupid. She could just search, so she typed in Carson's name. A list of a dozen e-mails popped up, most of them to schedule sessions months in the past. But one was much more recent, just a few days ago.

That was the day the movers had delivered her furniture and household goods. All her time had been spent directing placement and unpacking boxes. She hadn't opened her computer all day, and she certainly hadn't sent an e-mail to Carson.

Something solid blocking her airway, Tessa clicked on the message.

Carson,

You trusted the wrong person. You should've been more careful who you told about that little stalking incident when you were in your early twenties. Because that information could sure be dangerous if it gets into the wrong hands.

But half a million could make it go away.

Let's stay in touch,

Tessa M.

With shaking hands, she stroked Badger's back. "King B, what is happening here?"

WHY SHE'D EVEN TRIED TO SLEEP, TESSA HAD NO IDEA. HER mind had whirled around like a lopsided ceiling fan all night. Turning, clanging against itself, making a godawful racket in there.

So at six she slid out of bed, pulled on a long sweater, and took Badger out to the doggie park. The chill outside made him frisky, and he bounded around the enclosure, his ears lifting parallel to the ground and giving him the appearance of a 747 during takeoff.

But he also knew breakfast was coming, so he didn't object when she put him on leash and headed inside. In fact, it was amazing how hard an eleven-pound dog could pull a full-size human.

While he was eating, she took her laptop out to the balcony overlooking Reuter Terrace. The sun was still trying to decide its plan for the day, creeping up like a skittish animal, only to be eclipsed by a horde of winter clouds.

I could use some Carolina sunshine today.

She flipped open her computer and stared at the e-mail

still on the screen. When she'd read it last night, it had been like a knife to the lungs, and she'd snapped the laptop closed immediately.

Denial. As a professional, she knew the label for her own actions. But all humans, no matter how self-aware, used defense mechanisms for a reason. Survival.

And fixating on that e-mail wouldn't get her one inch closer to figuring out what was going on with Carson and Davey, so she clicked it closed. The Seattle news channel websites didn't offer up much more information than they had the last time she looked. In fact, the newer articles barely mentioned Davey, and only in the context of the increase in suicides around the holidays, which was a myth.

It made Tessa want to pick up the phone and berate someone for their lack of fact-checking, but she reined in her displaced anger and refocused on the real issue.

Maybe something had happened with Davey and his new girlfriend. He'd been honest about how hard breakups were for him. Or maybe he'd quit attending meetings and started using again. His suicide could've been triggered by any number of things.

Suddenly, the lopsided fan in Tessa's mind straightened its trajectory and sped up to high. Trigger. The e-mail she'd supposedly sent Carson had triggered his call to her. If someone had been blackmailing Davey with her account, too, wouldn't that mean—

Her hands were shaking so badly that it took her three mouse clicks to switch over to her e-mails and access the sent folder again. She typed "Sinchilla" into the search box.

Of course, a string of scheduling e-mails popped up, but one was grouped alone, having been sent within the past few weeks. The subject line was "Things to think about."

That was ridiculous. She never sent messages with such

ambiguous subject lines. She used terms like "Upcoming appointment" and "Helpful resources" with her clients.

Her eyes narrowing as if it might make the words easier to read, she opened the sent e-mail addressed to Davey. Whoever had sent it wasn't worried about varying his or her approach much. Change out Carson's name with Davey's and insert a sly insinuation about his addiction and they were essentially the same text.

Whoever was doing this was efficient in their deceit. And if someone had sent two false e-mails from her account, what would've stopped him from sending more?

Her heart plummeted in her chest. She knew that feeling.

It was dread.

5

TESSA QUICKLY CHANGED HER E-MAIL PASSWORD, THEN FORCED herself to scroll through her outgoing messages. It didn't take her long to find another, similar to the first two with the exception of name and youthful transgression. Lauren Caldwell.

Surely Lauren would never believe Tessa was capable of sending something like this. After a few sessions together, Tessa had referred her over to a private practice therapist, explaining she felt Lauren would get better results with someone who specialized in addiction disorders. And since Lauren was no longer Tessa's client, they'd become friends.

Casual friends. Occasional weekend lunches and Pike Place Market shopping friends.

But friends nonetheless.

Lauren would understand an early morning call, so Tessa grabbed her cell and dialed.

"'Lo?" Lauren answered in a sleepy voice that said she'd either had a very late night or a very early morning. Tessa could picture her, blond hair cut in a messy shag and smudged eyeliner as black as the leather jacket she always wore.

"Lauren, it's Tessa Martin. I'm sorry to call so early, but it's urgent. I need to talk to you about an e-mail."

Some shuffling from the other end made it sound as if Lauren was sitting up in bed. When Tessa heard the flick of a lighter, her heart sank. Lauren had given up smoking over a year ago and had claimed nothing would make her go back to sucking down lungfuls of tar and death.

"Are you smoking again?"

Another long drag, then Lauren finally said, "What the hell do you care?" The sleepiness was long gone, replaced with a jagged bite.

"I care because I know how hard you fought to beat that addiction." Along with several others.

"So this is like a professional follow-up call. The psychologist making sure no more of her clients, my friends, take a header off the Aurora Bridge. At least not until she gets her money."

Guess that answered the question of whether or not Lauren would believe Tessa was capable of completely unethical and abhorrent behavior. "I did not send that e-mail."

From Lauren's side of the phone came another long inhale and an exhale with the force of a *fuck you*. "That's right. You don't care about anyone in Seattle, not since you left here to follow Jonah Steele."

Is that what people back there believed? That she'd run back to the North Carolina because of Jonah?

She should probably feel ashamed that Lauren's assumption held more than a little truth. Tessa had given herself three months to get Martin & Associates up and running. The same amount of time she'd set to convince Jonah that she was the woman for him. If she couldn't make him see they could be good together, then she'd promised herself she would finally move on. Write off any type of relationship with him.

But anything between her and Jonah was no one's business but their own. "I would never compromise client confidentiality—not for money or anything else."

"I'm not your client anymore."

"It doesn't matter. Privilege and privacy outlast the professional relationship." Why was she arguing about this? What really mattered here was that Lauren believed Tessa was threatening her. "I called because I need to find out what's going on. So far, I've found three e-mails that I didn't send, each of them demanding money."

"Carson told me you were on his heels, too."

"Has anyone else mentioned receiving an e-mail from me?"

"Besides Davey, you mean?" Lauren said, making it obvious she didn't believe a word of Tessa's denial.

"Yes."

"Not so far, but if someone hangs himself, I'll be sure to let you know."

And the line went dead.

Although Tessa was sick over Lauren's obvious anger and hurt, right now she couldn't do a thing to change her mind. Words alone weren't persuasive. She had to find out what was happening here and put a stop to it.

Badger must've sensed her mood because he trotted out to the balcony and scratched at her leg to be picked up. He burrowed under the hem of her cardigan and poked his head out far enough to watch for birds or squirrels. He felt it was his honor bound duty to protect her from anything feathered or furry.

Tessa stared at her computer. Now that she was starting to think clearly, she considered her client files. Maybe the company that kept confidential medical and mental health records had been hacked. Why hadn't she checked that earlier?

She opened the website and scanned the DataFort homepage. Nothing about a security breach, but some companies tried to keep mistakes like that out of the public eye. Since DataFort was in Florida, she dialed the customer service number.

Thirty minutes, four customer service reps, and a manager later, she'd heard the party line five times. Data-Fort denied all knowledge of their database and records being compromised. But that didn't mean it hadn't occurred. If she found out they were covering up that type of mistake, she would not only be changing record-keeping providers, but she'd be filing a complaint with the Department of Health and Human Services.

For now, the best she could do was change her account password to something complicated and cryptic. To memorize it, she repeated it aloud twice.

That done, it was time to figure out who was black-mailing people and hurting them with their own secrets. And if DataFort wasn't willing to give her information, then she'd have to go to someone who could out-hack anyone she knew.

Good morning, Jonah Steele.

THE MORNING CHILL FELT GOOD AGAINST JONAH'S BARE CHEST as he hurtled down the trail on his mountain bike. The trip up had been a sweaty bitch, but he loved summiting the ridge that overlooked the twenty thousand acres he'd bought to help save his hometown.

From up there, he could see the Steele Ridge Training Academy, built from the former sports complex, and Tupelo Hill, his mom's farmhouse. His oldest brother's cabin was tucked deeper into the forest and was shielded from view.

When Jonah cleared the last of the trees, his new house was sitting there like the glass-and-wood castle Reid accused it of being. Winter clouds reflected in the windows, and the cedars and hollies seemed to wrap the structure in their embrace. The house he'd designed and helped build, possibly to the annoyance of his general contractor, was pretty damn stunning. And it was the most constructive thing he'd done for himself since moving back here.

He'd been so hot to move out of his mom's place, have his own space. His privacy.

Yeah, what he'd needed it for, he wasn't completely sure, because he hadn't done much entertaining of the female variety lately.

Jonah took a slug from his water bottle, trying to wash away last night's taste of Tessa's mouth. But in comparison to the sweetness of her lips, the well water was bitter.

If that little scene outside the bar wasn't absolute proof he shouldn't be within a thousand miles of Tessa, he didn't know what was.

What the holy *fuck* was she thinking, moving back to Asheville?

Last night, he'd been too stunned, pissed off, and turned-on to ask her why she'd moved cross-country.

He scrubbed a hand over his face, feeling the stubble that he hadn't had the motivation to deal with this morning. Not after flopping like a hooked trout in his bed all night, thoughts of Tessa plaguing him.

Maybe that was better than sleeping, though, because too often she slipped her way into his dreams. Dreams that were sometimes full of sweet kisses and tender touches. Others that were full of sweaty sex and dirty talk. Those dreams that left him feeling disgusted with himself in the morning.

They'd started not long after she came on at Steele Trap, when he'd realized he was attracted to her, had feelings for her that had nothing to do with the past.

As he lifted his bottle to his mouth again, he caught a blur of movement on the gravel road that wound its way from the county road through the property.

A sporty silver Beemer. Apparently Tessa hadn't tortured him enough last night.

She got out of the car and walked toward his front door. She had a leather tote on her shoulder, and her dark curly hair was pulled up in what on another woman would be a haphazard ponytail, but on Tessa the hairstyle made Jonah think of carefree, breathless sex. Her deep pink blazer didn't come down far enough to disguise the way her gray pants cradled her thighs and ass.

And her ass was a Louvre-worthy work of art.

One side of his mouth quirked up at the thought. Somehow, he didn't think Tessa would appreciate him picturing her butt hanging on a museum wall. But it was exactly the kind of weirdo thought that kept him sane during the times when he felt anything but.

Stop ogling her ass and act like she doesn't affect you. Doesn't arouse the hell out of you.

But she did.

It didn't seem to matter how far apart he and Tessa were. He wanted her, which always made him feel like a complete piece of shit.

After the night they had sex in his office, he'd been so desperate to rid himself of the feeling that he'd seen a hypnotist. Maybe they worked for other people, but after the session Jonah still hadn't been able to control his thoughts of Tessa and the guilt that came with them. In fact, the only thing he'd come away from the session with was an unreasonable hunger for fried chicken.

He'd eaten buckets of the stuff for weeks afterward.

Now a part of him wanted to let her ring his doorbell, realize he wasn't inside the house, and drive away. But he wouldn't.

His heart thumping, feeling as if it was about to jump up his throat and cut off his air, he mounted his bike and peddled toward his house. He skidded to a stop a few feet from where Tessa was stroking his cedar doorjamb.

The sight of her slender fingers playing along the trim shot through him with the power of a fireball.

She's touching your house, dude, not your dick.

"Hey," he said.

Hand to her chest, she whirled around. "Oh my God, you scared me. Where did you come from?"

"Out there." He waved toward the trees. "Look, if this is about last night, I'm sorry that—"

"No, not about that," she said, her words barely audible as her gaze arrowed in on his bare chest, which gave him a raging case of man nip.

Self-consciously, he brushed at them with the shirt in his hand, pretending to wipe away sweat. His body couldn't handle her showing up places unannounced. Even the chill in the air couldn't cool him down right now. "Then what?"

"Can we...could we go inside and talk?"

"Sure." He leaned his bike against the house and reached past Tessa to open the front door. She slipped by him, her scent trailing after her and making him squeeze his eyes closed in pleasurable misery.

He kicked off his shoes on the porch and shrugged back into his shirt, the material clinging to his sweaty torso. He stepped inside behind Tessa to see her soaking in the great room. The ceiling soared three stories and one wall was constructed of massive glass panes. The view of prime North Carolina mountain landscape grabbed him by the heart and squeezed every time he gazed out at it.

Home.

The fireplace, an altar of river stones bisecting planks the color of wild honey, stretched the height of the walls. Rust-colored sofas were accented with some fluffy woolly pillows Evie had picked out.

"Your house is gorgeous."

"Thanks. Want something to drink?" he asked, then made for the kitchen without waiting for her answer. He needed to do something safe with his hands. Now.

She trailed him into the kitchen, another wide-open space with light-colored cabinets and open shelving above the countertops. "I don't drink much coff..." She trailed off as he bypassed the one-shot coffeemaker and reached for a kettle to heat water for her tea.

While the kettle did its thing atop his gas cooktop, he rummaged in a drawer and pulled out a pouch of loose leaf tea. He kept his hands moving—measuring out tea, finding the honey, grabbing a cup. Tessa settled on an acrylic and chrome bar stool and watched him.

When he finally placed the cup in front of her and poured her tea through a strainer, her beautiful mouth was open. Just slightly, but her surprise was clear. "You remembered."

Yeah. She'd kept some in Steele Trap's break room.

When he moved in here, he'd special-ordered some without a clue as to why he was stocking Tessa's favorite type when he wasn't a tea drinker himself. And he sure never offered it to anyone else.

Once, Reid had been looking for a bottle opener and had come across the tea. One sniff and he raised a smart-ass eyebrow at Jonah. "You drink this shit or bathe in it?"

With restless fingers, Tessa fiddled with the cup's handle, pushing it first right, then left, then back again. Finally, she said, "I need your help."

And that was the one thing Jonah had never been strong enough to deny this woman, regardless of what it cost him personally. But being this close to her, wanting to touch her but knowing he shouldn't, made him want to reach for something stronger than caffeine, like one of those fancy-ass imported beers Grif stocked in his fridge.

No. No beer around Tessa ever.

He stayed on his side of the counter, keeping an expanse of cold stone between Tessa and himself.

As if that would somehow block his feelings for this woman.

"What's up?" He propped a hip against the cabinet and sipped his now cold coffee, trying to project a casual don't-give-two-shits attitude.

"I got a call from Carson Grimes last night."

For the first time since he'd spotted Tessa in front of his house, Jonah began to relax for real. "That guy is a damn good developer. Few people can spot a bad line of code faster than he can."

Tessa's mouth gave a little quirk. "Those few people being you, right?"

"We all have our talents. Now what's with the call from Carson?"

She took a quick sip of her tea and frowned. "He thinks I'm blackmailing him."

Of all the things he'd expected Tessa to say, that came in about number four hundred thousand. "What?"

With distress in her dark eyes, Tessa met his gaze. Then she reached into a side pocket on her tote and pulled out a couple sheets of printer paper and handed them to him. The first was a news story from the *Seattle Times* detailing the death of a bridge jumper. Jonah quickly scanned the text and froze when he came to the person's name. David Sinchilla.

He looked up at Tessa to find her expression of worry had turned to desperation.

"What the fuck?" Almost in a trance of disbelief, he was flipping to the next page when his doorbell rang. He looked up to find Paula Smith, his mail carrier, flattening herself against one of his front windows. She gave another knock for good measure and waved at him.

Tessa pivoted on her stool to check out the disruption.

"I have to answer this," he told her. If he didn't, Paula would just stand there knocking and waving all day. She was like a mail-delivering Sheldon Cooper.

Jonah pulled open the door and tried to smile as if his stomach wasn't a churning mass of hellfire over Davey's death. "Hey, Paula. Whatcha got for me today?"

Far be it for the mail service in this small town to leave his envelopes and packages in the commercial-size mailbox he'd installed at the entrance of the property. But Paula took such pleasure in doling his mail out to him every day. Today she was wrapped up in some kind of navy blue scarf with bright green tassels. Above the knitted mass, her cheeks were a good-natured pink.

"Well, this looks like your light bill." She passed over a

white envelope as if she were counting back his change from a twenty-dollar bill. "Bet it's a doozy with all these windows." Another envelope. "And Lordy if this isn't another one of those black card offers. I think they're just gonna keep after you until you let them give you one." She winked at him, and he didn't have the heart to tell her he already had one.

The next envelope was a light yellow and had a row of hearts drawn across the top. "Now this one looks to be a birthday card, if I had to guess. Maybe from Aubrey?"

"Thanks for delivering these," he said, taking a step back inside the house.

"Oh, that's not all." She bent and scooped up a box he hadn't noticed resting at her feet. "This one didn't come with a return address. Maybe there's a card inside if it's a birthday gift."

He took the package and tucked it under his arm. "Appreciate it, but I know you're super busy with the holiday season and all. Don't feel like you have to drive all the way up here. You can just leave mail down at the road."

She patted him on the arm and, if he wasn't mistaken, felt him up a little. "Oh, it's no bother at all. You need to know that the Steele Ridge postal service is going strong and eager to serve our patrons."

He wanted to shake his head at her blatant hint, but he couldn't bring himself to disrespect a woman who was only a few years younger than his mom and, if rumors around town were accurate, was looking for her fourth husband. "Keep up the good work."

As she sauntered back to her Jeep, she gave him a flirtatious wave over her shoulder.

When he returned to where Tessa sat at the island—in

direct sight line of the front door—he was slightly dazed at the Paula whirlwind.

"Now that's personalized service," Tessa commented, humor clear in her tone.

"Small town." Jonah shrugged off his embarrassment at having her watch that little interchange and dumped his mail on the countertop to pick up the papers Tessa had brought with her.

"Have you been dating?" she asked.

The pages slipped from his hold and floated to the ground by his feet. "What?"

"She mentioned someone named Aubrey, but it's clear your mail person believes you're totally on the market."

"She's old enough to be my mother, and Aubrey is my niece." He leaned down and snatched the papers off the floor.

"Plenty of men date older women."

"I thought you were here because you needed my help, not because you want to hear about my personal life."

Tessa's eyes lit with interest. "If you want to talk about it, I'm all ears."

"No head-shrinking, Tessa."

"That's a derogatory term. You know that, right?" She tapped the side of her cup. "Besides, I don't think shrinking a head as big as yours is even possible."

"Wait until you meet my brothers."

"I'd love to."

Aw, shit. He hadn't meant it as an invitation.

"They all live here in Steele Ridge, right?"

It would serve Britt, Reid, and Grif right if he gave Tessa some family background and let her loose on them. "Lemme give you the rundown. Britt has a savior complex.

Grif has delusions of grandeur. And Reid has some kind of egomaniacal disorder."

"You don't say," Tessa said mildly. "And your sisters?"

"Well, Evie is the baby, so she's spoiled. And Micki..." Yeah, this was all fun and games until it got serious, so he just finished by saying, "...is too smart for her own good."

"And where does that leave you?"

Like hell he was going to take that bait. "It should be obvious. I'm the only normal one in the bunch."

Tessa's snort wasn't particularly ladylike, but he liked it. To his disappointment, she quickly tucked away her humor and her face became serious again. "About why I'm here..."

She was right. They needed to get back on topic. "Why would Carson accuse you of blackmailing him?"

Tessa pointed to the other piece of paper in Jonah's hand. "Read that one."

He scanned the short note signed with Tessa's name and looked up at her. "You didn't write this."

Her entire body relaxed and she leaned an elbow on the counter. "How do you know?"

"One, I don't think you'd be showing it to me if you had. Two, everything I've ever seen you sign is done with T. Martin. Sometimes T. Martin, Psy.D." He tossed the pages onto the counter. "What's going on here, Tessa?"

6

"I'm afraid someone hacked my files," she said, "so I checked with the data company where I store all my client notes."

"What did they say?"

"They completely denied a breach."

"Not smart." Most companies had learned it was far better to get in front of something like this. Because by the time the inevitable truth came out later, customers had lost all trust. His mom was still boycotting a national discount chain after her credit card number had been compromised and the company claimed they'd never been hacked. But Jonah had been inside their system and knew better. "Have you checked all your other accounts? If someone hacked one, they might've wiggled their way into everything."

"Identity theft?"

"Maybe. Or maybe someone's just doing it for kicks." He'd done his own share of hacking in the past, but never just for shits and giggles. It always served a purpose, and one specific purpose when it came to Tessa. "But you can't afford to ignore this. Did you report it to anyone?"

"Not yet, because I wasn't sure what I was dealing with. That's the reason I came to you." Her expression of relief turned wary. "Maybe you could call the company?"

Now he was the one to snort. "If they denied a security breach, it's doubtful they'll change their story. What's the company?"

"DataFort."

"Irony is running wild and free today, isn't it?" He reached for a laptop, one of six in his house. And that wasn't counting all the equipment in his command center down the hall from the kitchen. With a few rapid keystrokes, he pulled up the company's website just to get a feel for how the login process worked. Normal enough. "Do you keep your passwords stored on your computer?"

"No. I don't have to because I have a fairly good memory."

"You're way ahead of most people then." He clicked over and opened a program called Exposure, which scanned sites for vulnerabilities. After typing in the company's URL, he hit the "Achilles Heel" button. The search ran for several minutes, and he expected cracks to pop up right and left.

Nothing.

"Well?" Tessa asked.

He glanced up to find her leaning over the counter, the neck on her shirt gaping just enough to show her silky-looking purple bra.

Stop looking at her breasts.

The one time he'd had the pleasure of looking at and touching them had ended badly. Badly? It had been a shit show afterward, with him pushing away from her in self-disgust.

She, on the other hand, had calmly pulled on her half-torn camisole and made him talk to her. To this day, he wasn't totally sure what he'd said.

Now, out of sheer self-defense, he shifted his focus back to his keyboard. "They look pretty airtight in this scan."

But that was only one small trick in his bag.

The next piece of software he pulled up performed SQL injections and was humorously named *gulrót,* Icelandic for carrot, slang for penis. Penis. Penetration. Har-har. Who said geeks didn't have senses of humor?

"What are you doing now?"

"Trying to penetrate their database and grab usernames and passwords."

"Whoa, whoa, whoa." Tessa jumped off the stool and rounded the island in a flash. She grabbed one of his hands and pulled it away from the computer keys. Like that would stop him. He could type faster with one hand than most people could with two. "I just wanted you to find out if I *had* been hacked."

"Takes a hacker to catch a one."

"I changed my mind about this." When she saw that capturing his hand hadn't slowed him down, she inserted herself between him and the counter where his laptop was sitting. A space of about three inches, which meant her body gave his a full-contact sweep.

Every nerve in Jonah's belly and chest went on high alert. Hell, some of the ones in his back did, too. Tessa was a petite woman, with rounded hips, a definitive waist, and breasts that would make any man alive take a second look. And they were all pressed up against him.

He cleared his throat and tried to step back, but she caught him by the forearms, which had apparently become an erogenous zone.

"I was doing something here," he said, so damn glad his voice was even when he could barely think straight.

"Something illegal, which means you could go to jail for it. Haven't you had enough threat of that within the past few months?"

Yeah, things had been dicey there for a while after Micki had returned to North Carolina. He was still living with an assload of guilt over what she'd done for him. Ten years. She'd spent ten years of her life trying to protect him, trying to make sure her scum-wad of a boss wouldn't pull a bunch of backroom strings to have Jonah locked up. That son of a bitch was the one lounging around in orange pajamas these days because Tessa had been willing to keep Jonah's ass out of prison for a crime he hadn't committed.

A crime that had been committed against her.

She had been the victim, not him.

He had no right to feel an ounce of mental anguish, so he'd kept his mouth shut about how a crime against *her* had impacted him so damn much.

But her eyes were mesmerizing, so full of concern that he wanted to step into them. Just let the past and all his mistakes be swallowed up.

Unfortunately, life didn't work that way.

Becoming involved with Tessa would mean she'd inevitably find out what he'd done. And she'd hate him for it, especially when she realized he'd do it all over again.

So he sidestepped and tried not to eat up the feel of his body sliding across hers. "They would have to catch me to arrest me. Believe me, that ain't gonna happen." Cocky meant he was in control. Good. He was fine. On an even keel. But when he reached behind Tessa for his computer and saw the screen, he said, "Dammit."

She whirled around, one of her hips skimming his fly. "What?"

"My GET command pulled nothing."

"Is that good or bad?"

"Both. It means the company is smart and is walking their talk. But it's bad because it isn't simple for someone to grab your credentials."

"Which means they couldn't log in as me and access my case files. Then what happened? Any physical notes I make during a session are transcribed and then cross-shredded. I don't leave behind a paper trail. The information Carson shared with me about his past doesn't exist anywhere except that database."

Carson's past. Carson. Maybe this didn't have a thing to do with Tessa. "You can't be the only person in the world who knew the guy was once busted for stalking an old girl-friend. Hell, he told me about it. So who else? Old friends? Family?"

"But why the bogus note from me?"

"Maybe Carson told someone he was doing sessions with you and they saw an opportunity for blackmail that wouldn't be traced back to them."

Tessa ran a fingertip along her bottom lip in thoughtful silence. Jonah watched it slowly slide from side to side, her pearl-painted nail a contrast against her darker skin. Even the smallest detail about this woman made a hunger blaze in his belly. "I doubt it, because two more e-mails were sent from my account." She let out a shaky breath. "And one of them went to Davey Sinchilla."

"Fuck."

"Pretty much."

"I could try to talk my way inside the company, but

based on the nature of their data, it would take a long time, with my bet on exactly never."

"As much as I hate to say this, you're right. I need you to get in and look around any way you can. See if you can figure out who hacked in." She took a breath and reached for her teacup, but she didn't drink. Just stared down into the liquid. "Because this system was so secure, I not only kept my patient files inside, but I recorded an audio diary as well."

"And you're worried that was compromised, too."

She still wouldn't look at him. "Sometimes I documented important events. Sometimes I made observations about people who weren't officially my clients."

A bad feeling swarmed over Jonah, making his skin flash hot then cold. "What kind of observations and what people?"

"Family, strangers, friends, even lovers."

"What are you saying?"

When her head came up, an apology was swimming in her eyes. "I sort of recorded the conversation you and I had the night we had sex."

IF THE LOOK ON JONAH'S FACE HELD ANY MORE SHOCK, HE'D probably be comatose. And while Tessa watched, that initial expression of surprise slowly transformed. The muscles around his mouth, in his cheeks, near his eyes went from slack to stone.

Yeah, she'd been pretty certain this wouldn't go well. But if the sick, sloshy feeling in her stomach was any indication, it was even worse than she'd imagined.

"You...you did what?"

"Let me expl—"

"I am not your client, have never been your client, will never fucking *be* your client." With one swift movement, he slammed his laptop closed with a *swack*. He stood there gripping his computer, the tendons in his forearms making his gaming tats bulge. For the first time ever, they looked menacing instead of sexy.

Tessa swallowed back her ripple of unease. "I know that," she said in an even tone. "Recording a journal is a habit I started in graduate school. Harmless because I never forced my opinions—sometimes naive and untrained—on people. It was just a way for me to teach myself to observe and think."

"And diagnose people who didn't give you permission to muck around in their shit." With a careless hand, he gestured toward his computer as if it suddenly disgusted him. "And obviously not harmless if some hacker compromised your files."

"You're right. I'm sorry. If it makes you feel any better, some notes about my own past were stored there as well." Recording her thoughts were helpful when her memories—and the vulnerability that came with them—came roaring back. Like they had last year when Jonah had asked her to talk with the authorities and clear him.

"That was your own decision." The fire burning in his hazel eyes said this was a big deal to him. Very big. Maybe too big.

Jonah ran his hands up his cheeks, creating a subtle scraping sound against the stubble Tessa found so incredibly sexy. He pressed his palms against his temples and dragged his fingers up through his shaggy hair, making little tufts stick up on either side and giving him a Wolverine vibe.

Tessa wasn't able to suppress her shiver.

Uh-uh, sister. Not the place. Not the time.

She had a serious mess to clean up. "I'm sorry I'm asking you to do something like this, but if my files were compromised, I have an obligation to my clients."

"To your clients?" His lip twitched into a tiny snarl. "I sure as hell don't remember signing a consent form."

She reached for his arm, but he jerked away and stalked toward the refrigerator. The force he used to open the stainless steel door made all the condiments inside rattle against one another. He stood there, staring into the cavernous space, his hand curled so tightly around the door handle that his knuckle bones looked as they might suddenly burst through his skin.

Stop with the Hugh Jackman thoughts.

"I overstepped and I admit it." How would he respond if he knew the recorder had accidentally been rolling *while* they had sex? In layman's terms, he'd lose his shit. "I'm trying to make it right."

"No, you're asking *me* to make it right."

"What the hell do you want from me, Jonah?"

He swung around to stare at her, because of her acerbic tone or the curse word, she didn't know. And cared even less.

"You're right. I screwed up, and now things are a *fucking* mess. Are you going to help me or not?"

"I've never heard a four-letter word come out of your mouth. I didn't think you had it in you."

Oh, he had no earthly idea what was inside her. And it was a lot. Years ago, she'd been full of anger and self-pity, falling into complete victim mode after the rapes.

The nightmare Jonah had ultimately rescued her from. He'd carried her out of that house.

From what Tessa's mom told her later, she had been a

physical mess—clothes torn, nails jagged, skin bloody—when they found her lying on the front porch of their Asheville home.

And later, she'd been an emotional mess.

But she'd worked hard to get back on track. When she'd been awarded a full ride to University of Washington, she was elated. Finally, she was back in the driver's seat of her life. Professionally, at least.

Recovering personally had taken her awhile—both in time and therapy. Her therapist had guided her on a journey to regain agency over her own body.

Eventually, she'd been able to have consensual sex with a man. Unlike some sexual assault survivors, Tessa hadn't delved into a pool of promiscuity. Actually, she'd slept with only a few men. And she'd made her choices very deliberately.

So she had all kinds of hidden reserves Jonah knew nothing about. She stalked—her hips swinging and her head cocked in challenge—toward him.

The scent of evergreen and pleasantly sweaty man almost distracted her. Almost made her back down and try to smooth things over.

No, he needs to hear this.

Her pointer finger found a perfect spot in the center of his pectorals. Beneath her nail, his flesh and muscle gave until she could feel his breastbone. And she was shallow enough to be gratified when his nipples tightened under his shirt.

"You think you know me," she said softly. Deadly. "But you're wrong. Tell the truth—when you look at me, you still see a victim. A girl who had no choice, no ability to fight back."

His throat contracted as he swallowed. "I'm not saying—"

"Well, guess what? That girl is still a part of me, but she's the part that makes me strong."

"Tessa, I—"

"Did you know that I not only took self-defense in college, but that I taught classes in Seattle?" She could tell by his openmouthed expression that he hadn't. "That's right. I know how to drop a man with a hammer blow to the temple. I know all the vulnerable spots on the human body. I know how to take care of myself. But you see me as frozen in time. Regardless of my age, education, or work, you still picture me as I was that night."

"It's a pretty damn hard thing to forget, so don't expect me to ever do it."

Which meant coming to Jonah for help had been a mistake. She needed to finally admit the truth to herself. She saw Jonah as a man, but he saw her as a helpless girl.

So she removed her finger from the center of his chest and gave him a pat—noting that his heart was flinging itself against his ribs. If only things could have been different between them.

She rounded the kitchen island and picked up her bag. "Thanks for reminding me that I don't need you to play hero for me. I'll hire someone else to track down this hacker if I have to, because I *will* get to the bottom of this situation." And with that, she and her pride walked out his front door.

Stunned, he stood there staring at it. When his brain finally connected with his feet, he hurried to fling open the door, but Tessa was already driving away.

Dammit. What had just happened here?

Jonah's conscience nagged at him to follow Tessa, to make this right.

But his pride? Well, it didn't give a flying fuck what his conscience was whining about. She'd made *notes* about him.

If he were a lesser man, he'd sue her. Sue the pants right off...

The picture of cream-colored lace panties hugging her hips invaded his mind, filling every nook, every cranny.

Get your head on straight, Steele.

Years ago, he'd sworn to himself that he'd help Tessa in any way he could. And he'd done just that, behind the scenes. Yet now he'd let her walk out the door when she needed him.

Needed skills he'd used in her defense before. Skills he'd used to create havoc in Shaw's life and those of his buddies.

But where was Tessa's hero this time? She'd pissed him off, so he'd abandoned her.

Just like he had that night.

From inside his pocket, his phone vibrated, but he ignored it and stalked to his fridge to yank out a six-pack. The first can gave a satisfying *pshht* when he popped the tab. He lifted the beer to his mouth, but the smell of it suddenly turned his stomach. He upended the can over the sink and watched the pale yellow liquid gurgle down the drain.

Fuck it all.

One after the other, he opened the cans and dumped them out.

Tessa had treated him like he was just some head case off the street. Then again, she'd admitted that she had done the same for herself. Someone had pilfered through the most private details of her life.

Someone had violated her again.

When his phone buzzed again, he dug it out of his pocket and saw that it was a blocked number. It could be Dianne Baxter, the director of a women's and children's shelter in Asheville. He needed to get her a dedicated phone so he'd know when she was calling, but he took a chance and answered. "Steele here."

"Jonah, we have a problem."

He was relieved to find he'd guessed correctly. But he didn't like the tone of Dianne's voice. He'd never heard that combination of fear and anger from her. Adrenaline shot through his body. "What's going on?"

"We've got two kids missing, and the other children say a man took them from the play yard."

Son of a bitch. That area behind the shelter was privacy fenced, wired to a private security company, and secured with the latest, greatest electronic locks. "How?"

"He chopped through the fence with an axe. By the time the staff and security company were alerted, he was long gone."

This was Jonah's fault. He should've insisted on more protections for the outdoor area behind the shelter. If he'd already developed and rolled out the suite of apps he'd been mulling over for a couple of months, those kids might've been able to alert someone.

Waiting never pays.

"How's the mom?"

"Doris is frantic and blaming herself."

That was the last damn thing she needed to do.

Jonah willed the emotions thrumming through him to chill the fuck out. He had to keep a clear head in order to help anyone. "I can be there in less than an hour."

"I just wanted you to know. I'm not sure what you can—"

"When I hired you, I told you Sarah's Smile was yours to

run as you saw fit as long as I had say in the big picture. And keeping those women and kids safe is the biggest picture there is. I'll call you when I get there so you can meet me at the rec center and we can talk this through." He hit the end button and bolted up the stairs to get dressed.

Now all he had to do was convince Tessa to go with him.

Although Tessa wanted to gun her engine and speed all the way back to the city, she'd learned not to let those kinds of impulses overwhelm her. When things became too jumbled and messy, she couldn't breathe. Couldn't hold her thoughts together.

So instead of taking I-40, she found herself winding her way down from the property Jonah owned and into the quaint town of Steele Ridge. A cup of tea would be just the thing, especially since she'd barely touched the one at his house.

How had he known what type she preferred and why did he have it in his kitchen cabinets?

Don't read anything into it. Even the most experienced mental health professional would have a hell of a time figuring out why Jonah Steele does half the things he does.

She slowed and cruised down Main Street. The town wasn't a metropolis by any stretch and had a less funky vibe than Asheville, but there was something about it—a sense of warmth and connectedness—with the sparkling storefronts and the Smokies standing watch over it all.

People weren't bustling, but were taking their time wandering from the bakery to a handful of small shops. In front of the bakery sat a sandwich sign chalked with the day's special—reindeer cookies—and a quote: *Pain you must accept if love it is you seek.*

"Apparently Yoda is handing out relationship advice these days," she said to herself.

Tessa slowed to peer more closely at a shop named Triskelion Gallery. The window sign said "Reopening Soon Under New Management." Then there was La Belle Style rocking outfits just as hip as anything Tessa had ever seen in Seattle.

She pulled into a metered spot in front of Blues, Brews, & Books. Inside, she slid into a seat at a two-top and pulled her laptop from her tote. Since Jonah wasn't inclined to help her, she needed to reach out to people and do damage control.

She considered shutting down the e-mail account Carson and the others had received the blackmail threats from, but thought better of it. That was the only connection she had to the hacker right now.

So she ordered her tea, smiling up at the pretty blonde when she brought it and biscotti to the table. "Thank you. Would you happen to have Wi-Fi?"

"Not a place in town that doesn't these days." The blonde laughed and scribbled a combination of letters and numbers on a business card. $30+33621e.

Looked like some type of strange math problem, but Tessa typed it in and connected. She set up a new e-mail address and gave it a gobbledy-gook password that she whispered to herself to make it hold in her mind.

However, she wasn't willing to check her bank accounts for any strange activity over a shared Internet connection. That would have to wait until she was home. Instead, she pulled out a small notebook and sketched a mind map.

Fake e-mails

Carson

Davey

Lauren

Blackmail

Suicide

Secrets

Hacked files?

Tessa

Her own name seemed to radiate from the page. But the problem was, she didn't know exactly how the bubbles related to one another.

She'd walked out of Jonah's house as if she had a plan and knew how to execute it, but the truth was, her brain wouldn't stop churning. And that was something she tried to avoid at all costs.

One thing at a time.

Letting her mind settle, she gazed around the restaurant-slash-bar with an adorable Little Free Library in one corner. What she'd seen of Jonah's hometown so far, she liked.

The front door opened and in walked a gorgeous, curvy woman wearing a sweater duster with crazy flowers embroidered all over it. The colors were bright and bold—yellow, red, black, and teal.

Tessa glanced down at her own gabardine slacks and Brooks Brothers blazer. In her pursuit of professionalism, had she abandoned her sense of style? Had she built up a sort of silk and wool armor?

The woman strolled by on the way to the counter, and Tessa said, "That's a beautiful sweater."

"Thanks." The woman gave a warm smile. "It was made by a local textile artist."

"A very talented one."

"I'm Brynne Whitfield." She held out her hand and Tessa shook it. "My boutique, La Belle Style, is just down the street. No pressure, but I have another one in the store. Cream with an embroidered dragonfly on the back. It would look amazing with your skin."

A man the size of Montana stalked up, swooped the woman off her feet, and gave her an unapologetic kiss of possession. *Wow.* That was either insanely bold or wildly romantic. Tessa wasn't sure which.

When Montana Man sat the woman back on her feet, her face was flushed and she was beaming at him. Wildly romantic, then. "What was that for?" she asked him.

"Because I've heard a man should regularly sweep his wife off her feet, Mrs. Steele."

Steele?

He had to be one of Jonah's brothers.

Stopping here hadn't been a good idea. Tessa hadn't considered the possibility of running into other members of the Steele family. Shortsighted, considering the town was named for them.

She needed to leave now. She'd head back to Asheville and contact the police about her potentially compromised files. She gathered her things and shoved them into her bag. "Again, lovely sweater," she said to Brynne. "But I have to be on my way."

Brynne gave her husband the evil eye as if he'd just tanked a sale. Tessa didn't have the heart to tell her the duster wasn't her style anyway. "If you change your mind, here's my card." Brynne pressed a business card into Tessa's hand. "Please come by anytime."

Tessa had no intention of ever stopping in Steele Ridge again. Not after Jonah had made it more than clear he wasn't interested in her problems. Wasn't interested in her. Last thing she needed was to be hanging around like an eyelash-fluttering tweenager stalking the school's star athlete.

Still, she slid Brynne's card into her bag.

As she did, her phone played a snippet of a piano concerto and vibrated softly against the leather. Ah, the perfect excuse to make her escape. "Excuse me, I need to take this."

Brynne gave her a small wave, and Tessa hurried out the door. She quickly pulled out her phone and thumbed the accept button. "Hello?"

"Tessa." Jonah's voice meandered its way down her spine, leaving an unwelcome tingle in its wake. "I know you're pissed at me, but I need your help."

HE'D OFFERED TO SWING BY TESSA'S PLACE IN ASHEVILLE AND been surprised to hear her say she was still in Steele Ridge, right downtown. Hell, he was surprised she'd answered his call.

When he pulled his car into a spot just down from the Triple B, he was relieved to see that Tessa was, in fact, standing on the sidewalk. Her face was a placid mask of disinterest, but she was there.

He left the Tesla running and stepped out to wave at her. "Over here."

She pointed at her own car. "The meters are for a max of two hours and the lot is full. How long will this emergency take us?"

He had no idea, but from the sounds of the call he'd

received, the situation wasn't good. "Don't worry about the meter."

"Don't worry about it? If I leave my car here, I'll get a ticket."

His impulse was to snap at her. Because although his own family gave him plenty of shit, most of the rest of the world not only jumped when he told them to do something, but also asked if it should be a long or a triple jump. He didn't use that power often, but every once in a while, it came in handy. "Let me put it to you this way. My brother's girlfriend owns the place, my brother is the city manager, and my cousin Maggie is the sheriff. I think I've got you covered if you get a ticket."

Instead of walking in his direction, she patted one of the old-fashioned parking meters. "It says they'll also tow."

Fucking hell. He yanked his phone from his pocket and hit a couple of buttons. When his brother answered with "Grif Steele," Jonah said, "There's a silver BMW parked in one of the spaces near the Triple B. Can you please make sure it's not ticketed or towed?"

"Are you asking for gratuitous favors from a civil servant?"

"Civil, my ass. And *servant* isn't a word I'd ever associate with you. How about this? Tell Aubrey that if she'll feed the meter every two hours, I'll pay her twenty bucks on top of the cost."

"She'll be all over that. But what's the deal?"

"It's an emergency. I need to get to Asheville and Tessa Martin is going with me." He motioned for her to head his way, but she stubbornly stayed put. "She's worried her car will get hauled off while we're gone."

"Tessa?" Grif asked. "*The* Tessa?"

His family knew all about Tessa now, even though they'd never met her. "Yeah."

"Gimme the plate number." Jonah could hear papers shuffling from the other end of the line. "Go."

He stepped out into the middle of Main Street in order to see Tessa's license plate and recited the letters and numbers.

"Got it."

"Thanks, man."

"I live to serve."

At that, Jonah just snorted and cut the call. "It's all taken care of," he told Tessa.

"We could just go in my car," she said.

The impatience and fear that had been swirling around inside him since Dianne called boiled to the surface. The minutes were ticking away. "Are you doing some kind of defense or blocking thing on me? Is that what that is? Sorry, I don't have time. If you don't want to help me, fine, but I need to leave. Now."

"Maybe if you would tell me what this is about—"

"It's about some women and kids who're in a major crisis," he nearly shouted, turning the heads of Mr. and Mrs. Trambly, who were strolling down the sidewalk toward the Mad Batter Bakery.

That got Tessa moving. She finally abandoned her friend the parking meter and dashed toward his car.

He tried not to notice the way her breasts bobbed slightly under her jacket, but his eyeballs were like magnets when it came to her body. He swung himself back into the driver's seat. As soon as Tessa was inside and had the door closed, he reversed out of the parking spot and pushed the thirty-mile-an-hour speed limit through town to hit the interstate.

Once he was no longer worried about mowing down little kids and old ladies, he took the on-ramp and was doing eighty before he even hit the freeway proper. Then he added another ten to it once they were on the road.

"Look, Tessa, about earlier..." He glanced over to find her staring straight out the front window, one hand clutching the center console and the other dialing her phone.

She juggled it to her shoulder. "Hi, Katy. Could you add King B to your list today? I'm out and don't know when I'll be home. Thanks. I really appreciate it." She slipped her phone into her tote, readjusted her hold to the door handle, and eyed Jonah. "You're speeding."

"I drive this fast all the time," he said.

A puff of laughter escaped her. "I don't know whether that makes me feel better or worse. There are reasons for limits."

If Jonah had believed in all the limits people had tried to place on him in his lifetime, he wouldn't be where he was today. But then again, he could see why Tessa might want to keep a tight hold on her life's controls. "Who's King B and why is Katy putting him on her list?"

"Katy is a college student I hired off Rover.com because I knew with my schedule that I'd need backup care for Badger—aka King B."

"You have a dog."

"As do millions of other people," she said.

"Tessa Martin and something as messy as a dog don't go together in my world."

"Which just proves that you don't know as much about me as you think you do. Now, if you could give me a little more information about this emergency, I could be better prepared."

She was right. One thing at a time today. "It's called Sarah's Smile, and it's a women's and children's shelter."

"What?" By the way her mouth dropped open and her eyes widened, it wasn't at all what she'd expected to hear. "How in the world are you involved—"

"With a shelter?" Yeah, this was the part he didn't really want to disclose. If he did, then she'd probably dig around until she ferreted out all his plans. Although he didn't regret what he'd done on her behalf in the past, he was now trying to use his vast resources to help people rather than punish them. But these missing kids made Jonah want to find their dad and beat the shit out of him. "It's just something I help out with once in a while."

"Uh-uh." Tessa shook her head, a cautious movement. "That doesn't fly with me. Men are rarely allowed into shelters like that. After all, men are the ones the women and kids are trying to get away from."

Jonah had never hit a woman in his life, unless he counted a few recent paintballs that might've splattered his sisters. Or that time Micki had put him in chokehold when they were eight years old and he'd had to stomp on her foot to save himself. But Tessa's words made his stomach shrivel. "I don't go inside the shelter itself." At least not since it opened a few months ago. "But they let me work with the kids at the rec center across the street."

"Okay," she said slowly, as if she still didn't get the whole picture. Which she didn't, because he didn't want to give it to her, dammit. "So what's the emergency?"

The adrenaline that had flooded his body when Dianne called him released again, stiffening Jonah's muscles, and had him white-knuckling the steering wheel. "One of the spouses found out his family was staying at the shelter. Let's just say he came to claim what was his."

"Oh, God. What—" she cut off with a gasp as he took the off-ramp at twice the posted speed.

Jonah lifted his foot from the gas pedal and pulled air into his lungs. He wouldn't do the shelter any good this way. He needed to get his shit together and calm down. The last thing those kids needed to see was another out-of-control asshole. "We're almost there. They need some more counseling support because all the women and kids were thrown into chaos when it happened."

"You want me to do crisis counseling? That...that's not my area of expertise. There's a reason I chose corporate coaching."

He hadn't completely stopped to consider how Tessa might react to a situation like this. Had just seen what needed to be done and assumed. "If you can't do this, then—"

"I do have hundreds of clinical practicum hours from my doctoral work. It's not like I'm incapable."

"I never said that."

"Tell me more about the situation. I want to be prepared."

"He took the kids," he told her.

"Oh, dear Lord."

Yeah. But they were all going to need more than prayers. "They need all the help you can offer."

"I'll do my best."

That was all he could ask of her. "The director will brief you when we get there. I'll be over in the rec center with some of the older boys. She said they were acting all tough like they weren't affected, weren't scared, but they're posing." Something he knew plenty about. Acting A-Okay when you were actually bleeding inside.

A few zigs and zags through the streets in the West

Asheville neighborhood, and he pulled into the rec center's parking lot. "I never approach the shelter itself, so you'll need to cross there," he told Tessa as they got out of the car and he pointed to a skybridge arching over the street. That structure had been nonnegotiable because he wanted the kids to be safe in every possible way and the street between was just busy enough to make him nervous. "They're expecting you inside, but I'll text to let them know we're here."

But Tessa just stood there looking at him as if she could read his every thought, his every emotion, his every failing. So he ducked his head and let his thumbs fly across his phone to give Dianne a heads-up that he'd arrived and brought in reinforcements.

"We'll be here awhile," she said.

"Yes. As long as it takes." For as long as it took today, anyway. Some of these kids' scars would never go away. Just like Tessa's would be with her for the rest of her life. That was something Jonah could never steal, hack, or fix. And he hated that reality with a passion that had blackened something inside him.

"This conversation isn't over," Tessa said, straightening her jacket and putting on what he thought of as her I-can-fix-you face. "Afterward, I want to know what's going on here."

He scrubbed his knuckles over his scalp hard enough to make him permanently bald. "Yeah, you and me both."

8

Six hours after Tessa walked away from Jonah in the rec center parking lot, the last of the women waiting to talk left the "counseling office" the shelter director had set up in a utility closet. The scent of bleach and industrial strength cleaner had likely been blanketing Tessa the entire time, but now she noticed the sharp fragrance. It, combined with an empty stomach and the tension headache she'd been fighting off since Jonah called her, made nausea creep up on her.

She averted her gaze from the mop bucket in the corner because she would not allow herself to get sick here. It was unprofessional. Mental health professionals were trusted to remain calm and unruffled. Detached even.

But after hearing the terror the women felt when two children were snatched from the fenced backyard by their abusive father, there was no way she could be unaffected. She knew all too well how it felt to have your world destroyed by someone else's actions.

A knock came at the door, and Tessa breathed, willing her rocky stomach to cooperate. "Come in."

The shelter's director, a woman in her thirties with short red hair, poked her head inside. "Could you talk with one more person?"

Could she? She was so drained from today's emotional black hole that she was trembling. Or maybe her reaction stemmed from something even closer to home. "Well..."

At that, Dianne slid inside and quietly shut the door. "It's Doris."

The mother whose children had been abducted. It had taken the Asheville police over three hours to locate the kids and their dad, and during that time, Doris had been inconsolable. So overwrought that the shelter's regular counselor discussed having a doctor administer a sedative. But the mother had refused it, saying she needed to be on the lookout. After all, that was what had caused this in the first place —that she hadn't been watching her kids every second.

When the counselor had pushed the sedative idea, Tessa had stepped in to support the mother because she knew how terrifying it was not to be in control. "I...I thought she talked with the shelter's counselor earlier."

"She did, but she wants to talk with you."

Tessa uncapped the water bottle sitting beside her chair and took a quick swallow, hoping it would fill her rocky stomach. This wasn't her area. Yes, she'd been through trauma counseling herself, but there was a reason she'd chosen to focus on organizational psychology and corporate coaching. As with Davey and the others, she sometimes talked about people's deeper issues, but for the most part her work life was filled with team dynamics and helping people adjust to the workplace.

But she would not turn away a woman who was in pain. "Have her come on in."

When the woman shuffled inside, wearing the same ill-fitting jeans and oversized T-shirt she'd worn earlier, her face and eyes were puffy from tears. Her gaze flitted from Tessa to the mop bucket to the tall shelves of cleaning supplies and finally back to Tessa.

"Please be comfortable." Tessa gestured to the chair near her. "Well, as comfortable as you can be in a cleaning closet."

Doris rewarded her with a wan smile and slumped into the cafeteria-style chair. "You seem like a nice lady."

"Thank you. I'd like to help you any way I can."

"You tired, ain't you?"

Normally in control of her body language, Tessa jerked back as if she could dodge the woman's words. But she shouldn't pretend. Doris had likely heard enough lies, enough platitudes in her life. "Yes. I want to help people, but it takes a great deal of energy."

Was that the reason she'd steered herself toward the safety of corporate work?

Doris waved a hand toward Tessa's clothes. "A man buy you those?"

Tessa blinked. She wasn't sure where this conversation was going, but for now she was willing to let it play out. "I have my own work that allows me to support myself."

"So you ain't ever been under no man's thumb?"

"As a child, I lived with both my mom and dad, if that's what you mean."

"He ever hit you?"

The concept of Robert Martin ever laying a violent hand on her was so foreign she couldn't even comprehend it. Her father had sobbed when he'd seen her bruised and broken and torn. "Why don't we talk about what's happening with you?"

Doris's puffy eyes narrowed until her pupils were barely visible. "You didn't say yes or no."

"No, but—"

"What about yo' husband or boyfriend? He ever beat you up?"

Now they were entering boggy territory. Empathy was important here, but she never shared details of her past. "No, but I have been a victim of violence." She reached out and took Doris's work-roughened hand into her own. "Why do you want to know?"

"'Cause you look all nice and put together, like you got everything figgered out and all. I wanna know how you do that."

Oh Lord, sometimes with spit and safety pins. Other times with denial and duct tape. After the rapes, she'd never again wanted to be involved in any high-school activities. After a lot of talk and tears, her parents had agreed to allow her to get her GED instead of returning to school. When she'd insisted on applying to a university across the country, they'd protested at first. But she'd needed a clean slate, an environment where she could heal. Where she could breathe and regain her confidence.

In college, she'd continued to avoid rowdy parties. Even now, she fled the scene if she was in a social situation where men were drunk.

"Total control is an illusion," she told Doris. "No one has that, no matter how nice her shoes or clothes are."

"Ain't what I want to hear. If a real nice lady like you don't run her own life, how'm I ever gonna do it?"

Gently Tessa turned Doris's hand palm up and touched the callouses below her fingers. "How did you get these?"

With lowered eyebrows, Doris glared at her own hand. "I

done worked my whole life. Everything from fast food to janitorial. Ain't too proud to work."

"You should be proud of each one of these," Tessa said. "Tell me, did you develop them all in one day?"

"What you mean?"

"I mean did you mop and develop these callouses in a single day?"

"Naw. It took me all summer the year I turned nine. They been like this ever since."

It broke Tessa's heart to hear that this woman had been scraping and getting by since she was a child. "Building a life—a good and healthy life—is much the same way. It doesn't happen overnight. And we have to be willing to work hard for it."

Maybe she'd forgotten that when it came to Jonah. She felt as if she'd been working hard to get close to him for years now, but for some reason he wasn't ready, even though he'd proven that he was physically attracted to her. How much time would he need? And how long was she willing to wait?

"I go to the job every damn day. But Barney show up here anyway and grab my kids. That ain't good. Ain't healthy. My Kyra done cried herself to sleep tonight. I had to rock her in my arms and promise her he won't be back, won't hurt her no more. I had to flat-out lie. And then she up and tells me she misses him. I can't win for losin'."

"What scares you the most about what happened today?"

"Everything, but mostly what if he'd taken my kids and nobody found them again? What if he taught Kyra that it was okay for her daddy and her boyfriend and her husband to knock the shit outta her?"

"You've worked very hard to get your children out of a

dangerous and unhealthy situation, and I would imagine today felt as if all your hard work was for nothing."

"Made me wonder what was the use." Doris squeezed Tessa's fingers. "Do you think it was a lie to tell my daughter she could be safe? Do you think it's a lie to tell her not all men get mad and hit like her daddy?"

The assault on Tessa hadn't been about anger. Those boys hadn't bloodied and bruised her because they were mad. Tessa believed, based on her years of therapy, they'd done it because she'd rejected Harrison Shaw earlier that evening. And because he'd been attracted to her in the first place.

Although her memories of the physical events had been almost obliterated by the drug he'd given her, she remembered the moment when he called her a half-blood bitch.

It had taken her a long time to believe any male outside her family was safe and trustworthy. She still didn't trust easily, and she did everything she could to avoid risky situations—elevators with only one other passenger, dark parking lots, parties where people were drinking too much.

"I think all children need to be taught to protect themselves and advocate for themselves," she told Doris. "But you also have the power to help her connect with men who don't abuse. Maybe someone in your family or church."

Jonah's image drifted through Tessa's head. Messy hair, searing gaze, restless hands.

He was just a man.

In her recovery, she'd had to accept and embrace that although she'd been attacked by boys, another boy had been responsible for freeing her from that room.

Had she overcompensated and idolized Jonah for rescuing her?

Maybe.

But he'd been a critical touchpoint for her in therapy. In healing.

Yet, he distanced himself. From her. From others as well. He was a complicated man who held himself to high standards. Standards he might never believe he was meeting.

"Don't know that I trust no man right now."

"I understand why you might think that way." Feeling like a kindred spirit with Doris, she stood and pulled the woman into a very nonprofessional hug. "Maybe you could talk with Dianne and she could suggest someone. I know men aren't allowed in the shelter, but at the rec center—"

"You talkin' about that rich white boy what built this place?"

The equilibrium Tessa had been fighting so hard to regain all day fled, whooshed out of her like a breath that had been punched from her lungs. He'd built this shelter? Why hadn't he mentioned that earlier? No, she hadn't idolized him too much. He was a hero, whether or not he accepted it. "I...I wasn't thinking of anyone in particular."

"Kids 'round here all like him," she said. "I'm sure them fancy computers he bought don't hurt none."

This was all beginning to make more sense. What had spurred Jonah to become involved with a shelter like this? And why had he been so resistant to talking about it?

An even more disconcerting question was why she suddenly felt as if her own work was lacking. Was it because she'd avoided people in this kind of pain?

"But Dianne, she think a whole lotta him, too," Doris said. "So there must be somethin' good about him."

Tessa was beginning to understand that Jonah didn't realize just how good he really was.

· · ·

To hell with having a team help with the suite of safety apps. Jonah would do it all himself as soon as possible. He'd just have to work on it and Tessa's hacker problem at the same time.

If he'd already created the app, the cops would've been able to find Doris's kids much faster.

He was waiting by the car, the sharp December breeze raking his hair and cutting across his face, when Tessa came across the walkway. He strode across the parking lot toward her.

She was moving slowly, cautiously, as if she was in physical pain. As if the stress of today had beaten her up. No, he would never again let anything in this world beat her up. He'd been a complete asshole earlier today, shoving off her concerns about her files. She'd hurt him, and all he'd wanted to do was push her away.

Yet she'd come running when he asked for a favor. Okay, maybe she hadn't run, but she'd come. Even without all the details. Tonight, he owed her an explanation and an apology.

"I should never have asked you to do this." With more control than he felt, he smoothed a hand over Tessa's cheek. Fatigue shadowed her beautiful eyes.

For a split second, she leaned into his touch. Then she drew in a breath, took a step away, and lifted her lips in the sorriest excuse for a smile he'd ever seen. "I'm fine."

With everything inside him, he wanted to lean down and kiss away her weariness. Breathe some of her burden into his own lungs. But after the way he'd reacted this morning, he didn't have the right. So he lightly took her elbow and led her to the car.

She slid inside with a sigh.

Jonah skimmed her shoulder and let his hand linger

until she finally looked up at him. "Thank you," he said quietly.

She gave a quick nod and looked away.

This wasn't what he'd expected. Based on their earlier conversation, he'd imagined she would come out with guns blazing and demand he tell her why he'd dragged her to a shelter she had no involvement with to help women she didn't know.

He got in the car and said, "Are you hungry?"

Her hand immediately went to her stomach as if protecting it from the idea of food. "Yes and no."

"We can get something here in town—"

"No restaurants." She rested her head on the seat and closed her eyes.

"Then I'm taking you back to Steele Ridge."

"Just drop me at my condo. I can Uber out there tomorrow to get my car."

Wasn't gonna happen, but he kept his trap shut, pulled out of the parking lot, and headed toward downtown.

A few minutes later, Tessa opened her eyes and frowned. "How do you know where you're going? I never told you my address."

He tapped the steering wheel with his thumbs. "Master hacker here, remember?"

"That's an invasion of privacy."

He sure wasn't going to tell her that he knew a whole damn lot about Tessa Imani Martin. Or he thought he had until getting blindsided by her last night. First thing he'd done when he returned home from Charlotte was dig around for her new address.

Stalk much, Steele?

How had he missed the tidbits about her having a dog and becoming a self-defense instructor? He was slipping.

He pulled the car in front of her condo building and cut the engine.

"This is a no-parking zone. You *will* get towed if you leave your car here," she said. "Besides, I didn't invite you in."

He held out his hand. "If you'll give me your key and tell me what you need, I'll be back in five minutes. I doubt they'll tow with you sitting here."

"What? No. I'm going inside, pouring myself a glass of wine, and sinking into a hot bubble bath."

Uh-uh. He would not think about Tessa sliding into the water, white bubbles enveloping her gorgeous skin. "Your car is in Steele Ridge. Tell me what you need and I'll pack an overnight bag for you."

"Even if I were going back to Steele Ridge to pick up my car, I wouldn't stay the night."

"Fine. If you won't hand over your key," he said, sliding out of the driver's seat, "I'll get a master from the building manager."

When Tessa hurried into the building behind him, he was chatting up the building manager. She strode toward Jonah as the manager handed over a key to him. She glared at them both with more force than a .68-caliber paintball blasting out of Reid's new fully automatic guns. "Why did you give this man a key to my condo?"

"He...he said you were right outside and—"

"Never hand over my key to a stranger," she told him before turning on Jonah. "And what do you think you're doing?"

"Getting your things."

"Go home, Jonah."

"I thought you wanted to talk about why I asked you to help me today." At this point, he was willing to give her part of the shelter story if it would make up for how he'd reacted to her request this morning.

She bit her lip, which meant he was tempting her. "Fine, give the key back to the manager, and you can walk me to my condo, but I'm not going back to Steele Ridge with you."

Jonah returned the key to the manager. He walked beside Tessa down the hall and glanced over to find her watching him with a combo confusion-and-death stare. He'd take her confused. He'd take her pissed off.

Hell, he'd take any way he could get her.

She unlocked the door to number 102, and he followed her inside. That was when everything went to shit.

9

"OH MY GOD," TESSA BREATHED, SHOCK RICOCHETING through her.

"What?" Jonah moved quickly, hooking his arm in front of her and sweeping her behind him in one smooth move. "Shit!"

That was one word to describe her formerly ecru living room wall. On it, someone had spray-painted the words PLAY OR DIE. The strokes were so heavy that the paint had run in fat drips like the title of a cheesy horror movie.

The nausea that had threatened Tessa earlier made a reappearance. To tamp it down and calm her breathing, she leaned her forehead against Jonah's back. His muscles were rigid beneath his jacket. The leather was cool, bringing momentary relief, so she pressed her cheek against it.

But the comfort didn't last long because Jonah shoved her back out into the hallway and tried to shut the door on her.

Panic swarmed over her. "Wait. I have to get Badger." He hadn't made a sound when they'd entered the door. What if someone had—

"I'll get your damn dog. Stay here until I come back." Without another word, he quickly closed the door in her face.

She blinked. Had he just tossed her out of her own home? Who did he think he was to walk in and take over? She tried the doorknob only to discover it was locked from the inside.

She was fumbling with her keys when the door opened again and Jonah stood there holding a lethargic Badger.

"He's sick. Someone hurt him. I will kill whoever—"

"Based on the smell of the cheese in his kennel, he was drugged, but he's already coming around."

Sure enough, Badger's brown eyes opened and he wiggled his way out of Jonah's hold and jumped. Used to his antics, Tessa grabbed him mid-flight.

Jonah said, "Whoever was here is long gone, but why don't you wait out—"

"No. I get why you pushed me into the hall, but it's my house and I want to see if there's any other damage."

"The front door was locked, but that obviously doesn't mean shit, seeing as the building manager just handed over your key to me."

"You said I was right outside. He wouldn't have given it to just anyone."

Jonah grunted with obvious skepticism. "Anyone else have a key to your condo?"

"Besides me, just my parents." Yeah, and the spray-painted message on her wall, although done with red and green, didn't exactly look like the type of holiday greeting her parents would send her.

Badger seemed to shake his daze enough to realize there was another human in his midst because he did a gymnastic move that allowed him to brace his paws on Tessa's shoulder and stare at Jonah. He gave one bark as if to say, "Stay back until I decide if I approve of you."

"Who would've done something like this?" she asked. "I haven't been back in Asheville long enough to upset anyone. Maybe it was kids."

"Maybe." But Jonah's tone was doubtful as he stroked Badger from head to hindquarters. That was all it took for her dog to decide he wasn't the enemy. He scrabbled in her hold trying to fling himself toward Jonah.

Thinking about anyone, especially a pack of teenage boys, invading her space sent a chill through her and she hugged Badger to her chest. Okay. She would be okay. She'd faced much worse in the past. Yes, someone had come into her home, had defiled it. But it was just paint. It could be fixed easily.

Still, physical damage could have lasting emotional effects even when all the signs of it were gone. She might be able to paint over that wall, but she'd still be able to imagine the words under the new coat for a long time to come.

Jonah must've seen how torn she was, because he wrapped his arms around her and Badger. How could one man exude so much fierceness and gentleness at the same time? It didn't escape her that he was blocking her from seeing the message again through the open doorway. Standing between her and ugly words.

"You're not staying here tonight," he said evenly. "Close your eyes."

"What?"

"Close your eyes so you don't have to see that shit anymore."

"I'm not a child."

"Then do it for me."

"Fine." She closed her eyes and he took her hand, sending warmth winding its way up her arm.

He urged her forward and a few steps later, a door closed behind her and he said, "You can open them now."

Sure enough, he'd led her to the correct bedroom. She placed Badger on her bed and he ran around it as if he'd won the lottery.

"You have a purse dog?" Jonah stared doubtfully at her dog, who was now burrowing under a ruffled pillow sham. He was trying to distract her from what they'd found in her living room, and she wished it were that easy.

"No, he's a hunter."

"He can't weigh more than ten pounds. What's he gonna hunt?"

By this time, Badger had dug his way through all her throw pillows and they were flying left and right. This day had been the complete opposite of enjoyable, but Badger made Tessa smile. "He's tenacious."

"And he's coming to my house with you."

Tessa grabbed Jonah's shirt and pulled him down to her for a kiss. Just lips against lips, but it helped ground her.

"What was that for?"

He wouldn't want to hear how sweet he could be sometimes, so she just said, "My dog."

"You gave me a kiss from your dog?"

"He's demonstrative that way," she said, her voice shaky from the feel of Jonah's lips on hers. "I'll need Badger's kennel. His food is in the pantry and he has a bag in the entry closet."

"Why don't we get you packed up first and then..." Jonah turned away to yank at one of her dresser drawers and stopped with his left hand hovering over her lingerie collection. She liked nice underwear, so it was quite a stash.

Get more than you bargained for, buddy?

"I'll pack my own underwear," she told him. "You're in charge of Badger's bag."

"Huh?"

For goodness' sake, Badger could pack for himself faster than this. But it was nice to know Jonah wasn't unaffected. While he stood there entranced by her undies, she went to the closet.

It didn't take long to get what she needed. Although she planned to return in the morning, she never traveled without at least two sets of clothes, so she selected a few items and zipped them into her tweed hanging bag.

She poked her head out the closet door. Jonah hadn't moved positions, but now he held at least half a dozen bra and panty sets. His fingers flexed and released around the bundles of silk, satin, and lace.

Seeing him standing there looking down at her underwear made something hot spark low in Tessa's belly.

Uh-uh, sister. This isn't the time or place for sparks. You're mad at him, remember?

But he was being so sweet to Badger. To her.

"I need to grab a few items from the bathroom. Think you could get Badger's things now?"

"Kennel, food, and bag."

When she went to her en suite bathroom, she braced her hands on the countertop and breathed. Her nerves felt as if someone had tightened them with tuning knobs and was plucking at them. *Twang, twang, twang.*

Her body was simply processing the adrenaline from finding someone had broken in to her home. This wasn't about Jonah and how he affected her.

Right. Her insides were one big tangle of competing

emotions—shock at what they'd found, gratitude she hadn't been alone.

Make room for the feelings. Observe, but don't let them overwhelm.

Unfortunately, she was finding it hard to follow her own advice.

No time for a mini-breakdown, so get moving.

She scooped up a handful of personal items and dropped them into a small train case she stored in her linen closet. When she returned to her bedroom, Badger's overnight supplies were sitting on the bed and Jonah was working his phone with his thumbs, so fast they blurred in front of her.

The man seriously had bionic thumbs

"What are you doing?" she asked him.

"Texting with my cousin the sheriff. Maggie's going to give the Asheville police a call to have them come out to take a look at this and talk with the building manager."

A heavy feeling invaded her chest. That meant they would have to stay here for hours. And for some reason, that bubble bath in her own tub didn't feel so appealing right now. "You said you thought kids were just—"

"I said maybe. But it doesn't feel right." He looked up from his speed texting, and his eyes were bright and sharp. Pissed off. "We're not going to downplay this. Not after the hacking deal."

"You think the two incidents are related?" Her client files and the message on her wall didn't seem to have anything in common.

"I'm not much of a believer in coincidences." He glanced back down at his phone and gave a grunt of satisfaction. "Grab your dog and his stuff. I'll get your bag. We're outta here."

"What about the police?"

"They can get access from the building manager after they question him up and down about who else he might've given a key. If the police need to talk with us, they can wait until tomorrow."

"Before you called earlier, I'd planned to contact the Asheville police about my files being hacked. I need to talk with them."

"I'll find this hacker my own damn self. I can do it faster than they can. Once we have something to go on, we can fill them in." He took the train case from her, then draped the garment bag over the same arm so he could take her hand.

"What about all the things you said earlier today? You had every right to be angry with me. What I did was unprofessional at best and unforgivable at worst. Jonah, I'm sorry."

"That doesn't matter now," he said gruffly.

"How can you say that?"

He swiped a hand over his face, emphasizing just how tired he looked. "Look, it's not like you printed massive copies of your assessment of my mental state and handed them out like pizza coupons. It's done. Neither of us can do anything about the fact that someone dug around in your files. But I can help you find the person who did it."

"So now, after someone defaced my wall, you're willing to help me?"

"Look, I was an asshole this morning. But if you want to ream me for it, can it wait until we get out of here?"

"I don't want to *ream* you. I want to say thank you."

"Don't look at me like that."

"Like what?"

"Like I'm some kind of hero."

Outside, Jonah stowed her bags in the backseat and took

Badger's kennel and bag from her. He placed them in the floorboard behind the driver's seat. "So you can see him."

That one detail. One thoughtful act almost broke her cool. "Thanks." She opened her own door and slid inside before he could see she was struggling to contain her emotions.

Once he had the car in drive and had pulled out, Jonah reached for her hand. "You okay?"

Tessa swallowed, trying to clear the choked-up feeling. "Thanks for doing all this. I'm sure you didn't count on houseguests, especially a dog."

"Hell, Badger's smaller than some of my remote controls. Not like he'll take up much space." Jonah's grin was strained around the edges, but it was genuine. "Besides, Tessa, there's nothing I wouldn't do to keep you safe."

JONAH RUBBED HIS EYES. AFTER HOURS OF STARING AT HIS bank of computer screens, he'd hit one dead end after another, trying to trace the scum-wad who'd gone digging around in Tessa's files. Maybe a cup of coffee would kick-start him again.

He'd make a cup and then spend an hour on the app development project. Maybe changing gears would spark an idea about this damn hacker.

He hauled his ass out of the chair his siblings liked to call his throne.

In the hallway connecting his tech cave and garage to the rest of the house, he caught sight of movement outside the windows. Someone was on his property.

He quickly backtracked and retrieved the handgun he kept stashed in a drawer. He clicked the magazine into place and shoved his feet into a pair of boots.

Using the external door off the hallway, he slipped outside into the darkness. His sense of hearing seemed heightened in the early-morning mountain chill. An owl hooted and from around the side of the garage, he heard what sounded like wood scraping against wood. Was someone trying to jimmy one of the windows into his house?

Aw, fuck no. Not gonna happen.

Jonah crept around the side of the house. Sure enough, a bulky figure was hunched down near the door that opened from the great room onto his back deck.

So help him, if this was the same guy who'd painted all over Tessa's living room wall, he'd put a bullet in each of his kneecaps. Then they'd sit down and have a friendly little chat while the shithead bled.

Jonah dashed up the stairs, grabbed the intruder around the neck, and jammed the gun against his cheek. "What the fuck are you doing?"

The intruder's empty hands rose above his head. "Jonah," he rasped, "It's me, your dad."

Sounded a lot like him and the height was right, but the guy was bulked up in a coat and had a hood pulled over his head. "Who was the 1989 NASCAR Rookie of the Year?" Jonah asked him.

He and his dad were far from best buds, but everyone knew Eddy Steele loved him some car racing.

"Dick Trickle. He was forty-eight at the time."

Jonah withdrew the gun and dropped his arm from around his dad's throat.

His dad turned, hands still in the surrender position, but he was clearly wearing a grin. "You been taking lessons from Reid?"

"I know exactly how to defend what's mine," Jonah

said. "And I can shoot a real gun just as well as an imaginary one. You might want to remember that the next time you're skulking around my house in the middle of the night."

His dad had never much understood him, the son more interested in the make-believe worlds of video games than tracking, killing, and skinning a deer. Sometimes he'd caught his dad looking at him, studying him as if trying to figure out where Jonah had come from. If he'd ever be a real man like his older brothers.

"Why are you here, anyway?"

"Just dropping off some stuff I had laying around." His dad jerked his chin to indicate something behind him.

At least a cord of firewood, perfectly stacked. "You brought me wood?"

Stupid question seeing as the evidence was right in front of him.

His dad's shoulders moved under his coat, and he glanced toward Jonah's outdoor fireplace. "You know I ain't much for Christmas gifts and the like, but I figured all you kids could use some with the weather turning colder."

Mixed feelings clashed inside Jonah. Part of him wanted to give his dad a big hug, but another part of him wanted to reject the gift. Eddy Steele showed up when and where he wanted. He hadn't been there for his family day in and day out.

Not like Jonah's mom had. She'd worked her ass off to afford birthday and Christmas presents for her kids. She'd always been the stable one, the one who made sure they were fed and educated. This man just popped in like an uninvited guest.

Dropping off wood in the middle of the night was the perfect example of his MO.

"So you decided to drop it off before sane people are awake?"

"You ain't exactly in your pajamas," his dad shot back. "Besides, didn't see a reason to make a big hullabaloo about it."

More like he didn't want to have to talk to his own kids. But maybe bringing wood was his own hermit way of showing he cared.

"This your first stop?"

"Yeah, figured I'd do a couple loads a night. Tonight, it's you and Britt. Tomorrow, I'll catch Evie and Micki."

"You might want to give the others a heads-up. Otherwise someone will put a bullet in you."

"I see your point." He squeezed Jonah's shoulder and gave a rusty chuckle, both of which brought a warmth to Jonah's chest he didn't really want to feel. "Happy holidays, son."

And with that, he strode off the deck and into the woods.

"Happy friggin' holidays, Dad."

10

THE MOTORIZED WHIRRING SOUND OF THE WINDOW SHADES rising woke Tessa as sunlight angled across the bed. The mattress in Jonah's guest room must've been made of stardust and gold. She would've sworn she wouldn't get a minute of sleep last night, but she'd dropped off almost immediately.

Surprisingly, Badger was still snoozing in his kennel this morning, so Tessa slid out of bed. She stretched, working out some of the leftover tension from last night. A few knee kicks and elbow strikes warmed her muscles and encouraged the blood to flow throughout her body. She had a feeling she would need all her strength today.

The view from outside called to her, and she wandered to one of the windows. The sun was just peeking over the ridge, sending its warming rays through the bare branches of the maples and oaks that covered Jonah's mountain. She'd grown up in Carolina, so seeing the sun and the mountains shouldn't take her breath away, but it did. Even in the heart of winter when everything was brittle and brown and dying.

But life was still out there, some of it dormant until the right amount of sunshine and warmth came along.

People were much the same. When life became too harsh, they protected themselves. But the strong ones, the hardiest ones—like Doris and her children—would bloom again.

Sometimes the flowers would return a little more ragged than before. But they came back, year after year.

Blossoming again was so much easier with the right soil and sunlight and care.

What would it feel like to be the sunlight for those tender and broken buds? If yesterday was any indication, it would be exhausting.

But for the first time she considered that it might also be exhilarating.

Something to think about later, after she dealt with the immediate problems in her own life.

A high-pitched doggie yawn came from Badger's direction, and Tessa crouched down to open his kennel. He went through his hilarious yoga stretches—a true downward dog and some kind of back foot dragging cobra pose.

She shrugged into a short robe, grabbed her laptop, then clipped on Badger's leash. His toenails made a pleasant tip-tapping as they headed downstairs. On the first floor, the sun had found its way over the ridge and was splashing its golden aura over the wooden floors. But otherwise, the large open-concept living-dining-kitchen area was empty.

The security system was off so after taking Badger outside for a quick pit stop, Tessa went to the kitchen and fixed his food bowl. Remembering where Jonah stored the tea, she slid open the drawer. Inside she found not only Pu-erh cacao citrus, but also another half dozen of her favorite blends.

What reason would he have had to stock her favorite teas? The man was maddening.

And apparently she was fascinated by his madness.

Once she had a cup of tea, she sat at the kitchen island to take care of some business. This week, she was supposed to present consulting proposals to three companies—two in Asheville and one in Charlotte. And even though her mind was still ticking over how she felt after helping at the shelter yesterday, she had to protect her professional reputation.

Thankfully, her contacts in the companies' HR departments were understanding that she'd run into some moving snags and were willing to reschedule her meetings until next week. The weight that took off her shoulders was immense. But it meant she had only a few days to get control of the e-mail blackmail situation.

Maybe Lauren had calmed down enough to talk with her. She dialed and the call connected. But it disconnected immediately, as if Lauren had screened an unwanted solicitation call.

Okay, she'd head in a different direction, then. Next up, she logged into her banking app to check her accounts. Still no unusual deposits, which might've been a good way to track the hacker. Surely if money was deposited, he would want to take it out. Or maybe he'd set up another account altogether. And she had no way to trace that, not unless they figured out who the hacker was.

Last night, Jonah had promised to help her hunt down the person. "So let's go find him somewhere in this huge house, King B."

As if he owned the place, Badger trotted toward a hallway leading to the one-story portion of the house. The hallway itself was lined with windows on the east side, making it a virtual sunroom. He gave her a doggie smile and stretched out in a sunbeam. Give him three minutes and he'd be snoring blissfully.

Tessa let him sun himself and moved on in her search for Jonah. The first door she came to opened into a mudroom the size of Rhode Island. It connected to a four-car garage, and a flip of the light switch revealed that Jonah hadn't denied himself a few nice toys—his Tesla, several other vehicles, half a dozen mountain bikes, and two ATVs.

Back inside, she found a game room guys of any age would kill for. A pool table, air hockey, foosball, and more classic video games than she could count. Pacman, Galaga, Donkey Kong.

Was Jonah Steele a man or a perpetual fourteen-year-old boy? Based on the things he made her feel, she'd have to come down on the side of full-grown man.

She eased open the second door off the hallway to find another large space, but this one looked like NASA Mission Control. Massive curved screens on the walls, long tables with blinking equipment, and racks filled with other bits of metal and wire. The low-level humming from the electronics was strangely calming.

But the man sitting in the middle of it all, surrounded by a wraparound workstation and cradled in some kind of high-tech recliner, did not make Tessa feel the least bit calm.

In fact, he made her restless and needy.

Jonah wore headphones that had to be noise-canceling, because he never glanced her way. His face was a study of concentration as his fingers flew around the keyboard suspended in front of him with the *click, click, click* of a tap dancer on fast forward.

His facial scruff was a little scruffier than normal and his brown hair stood out in little tufts here and there. The only strands under control were those mashed down by the headphones. His mouth was a solid line, and shadows lingered under his eyes. The fact that he still wore yesterday's clothes was the final bit of evidence she needed to conclude that he hadn't slept.

"Hey," she said quietly.

His focus didn't waver. He was still glaring at the monitors surrounding him.

So Tessa strolled into the room and stood between him and his view of the massive screens. She figured if it worked when she was trying to get her dad's attention during football season, it would be effective here, too.

Jonah's warp-speed typing came to an abrupt halt, and he jerked at his headphones, letting them drop around his neck. "What're you doing up? You should get some sleep."

"I got plenty, thanks."

"You couldn't have slept more than..." He glanced around the windowless room as if it could give him some indication of the time of day. Tessa lightly tapped on a screen that showed the current time in the upper right-hand corner.

"Seven fifty-four."

"In the what?"

She couldn't help but smile. When she'd been at Steele Trap, she'd noticed that he often kept unusual hours, working long into the night and coming in at three in the afternoon. "In the morning."

"Monday?"

"Yes. Why? Have you skipped days before?"

"Yeah, I think once it was forty-two hours." He rubbed both palms over his face, making a raspy sound that gave her a girlie ping between the legs. She pressed her thighs together, but the feeling was like an itch that shouldn't be scratched in a public place.

And thinking about an itch like that only made you want to scratch it that much more.

Problem was, she needed Jonah for that.

His words from last night came back to her. *There's nothing I wouldn't do to keep you safe.* But wanting to keep her safe and wanting *her* were two different things.

"You sat in a chair working on your computer for almost two days straight? How is that even humanly possible?"

"I have an exceptional ability to focus."

"Still, it can't be healthy."

Suddenly, Jonah swung out of his chair. "Excuse me for a sec." Then he loped toward a door near the back of the room. Several minutes later, Tessa heard the muted flush of a toilet and the sink water running.

When he emerged again, he was rubbing his stomach. It let out a sound that would've scared small children.

"You haven't eaten either?"

"I don't like crumbs on my keyboard."

"C'mon." She motioned for him to follow her. In the sunny hallway, Badger ran over to Jonah and scratched at his leg to be picked up.

Apparently, her dog had no loyalty to the kibble provider.

Without breaking stride, Jonah scooped up Badger as they headed back down the hallway to the kitchen. "I never would've taken you for a dog person."

"Why not?"

"They're...messy. And you're so...neat." He scratched Badger's chest, and her dog somehow wiggled his way onto his back so Jonah was cradling him like a baby. His brown eyes were begging Jonah for a belly rub.

Pet me. Stroke me. Love me.

Geez. She and her dog both had the same man-crush. "He came to me from a dachshund rescue group, but I'm pretty sure Badger's the one who rescued me. Sure, he sheds and poops, but when he snuggles, there's nothing else like it in the world." It was like having her own mini canine therapist. She couldn't count the number of nights she wouldn't have made it through without him. "He's a great listener, too." With a commanding finger, she pointed Jonah to a stool. "Sit and I'll fix you something to eat."

A smile touching his lips, he obeyed and let Badger hop to the ground. "My mama would like you. She's a general, too. Little bitty thing, but she can bring her kids to their knees. In Reid's case, that's like chopping down an oak."

If he was the brother she'd seen in town, she'd describe him more as a redwood.

And Jonah's mother sounded like a woman Tessa would very much like to know. Jonah had never shared much about his family during the time they'd both been at Steele Trap, but she knew they were all successful in their own right.

With efficient movements, she moved around the kitchen—fixing coffee, checking the fridge and pantry, and pulling out everything she needed to make breakfast.

Within fifteen minutes, she was sliding a plate piled with a ham and cheese omelet, home fries, and fresh fruit in front of Jonah. He stared at it as if he'd never before been introduced to the concept of breakfast.

"What?"

"Where did you learn to cook like that? Hell, how did you learn how to chop like that? You looked like one of those ninja chefs."

"It's not any different from how fast you can work a

keyboard. My mom taught me how to prep fast and clean as I go." As a child, Tessa had rolled her eyes. But after the rapes, the chopping, dicing, and slicing had become a kind of therapy for her. She could control the size of the onion, bell pepper, and carrots. She could control the thickness of a slice of ham.

She couldn't control what had happened to her.

She fixed herself a bowl of fruit and sat on the stool next to Jonah. But she wasn't hungry for food. She wanted answers. "Tell me about Sarah's Smile."

"There's not much to tell."

"You built it and that rec center, didn't you?"

He cut and chewed. Cut and chewed. "Tessa, we really need to talk about last night. About why someone is targeting you."

"We will." And they would, but he was avoiding answering her question. Why would he want to hide his involvement in the shelter? "After yesterday, you owe me some answers about the shelter."

"What's there to know?" He stabbed at a potato. "Those kind of places need money, and I have money, so I give it to them. Simple."

"Why a women's shelter?"

His attention didn't waver from his plate. "Because they and their children are..."

"Easily victimized?" she said quietly, the rightness of her guess settling inside her. "Are you involved with others?"

"Does it matter?"

Oh, it mattered. So much. He was standing up for and doing for those who couldn't always stand and do for themselves.

But she didn't want to be lumped in with those he thought couldn't do for themselves. Yes, she needed his help now, but she didn't like the idea that he might believe she needed his protection.

Mulling it over, Tessa absently dipped her fork into her bowl and caught Jonah staring down intently. Following his trajectory, she found that her robe had parted and was revealing a long expanse of her thigh. Her skin rippled with awareness and tiny goose bumps popped up.

She crossed her legs, which hiked her robe up to the tie belt and inched her short nightgown farther up her legs. If she revealed any more real estate, she'd be flashing him her panties.

Jonah swallowed hard and stabbed at his food without hitting a bite of it. He wanted her, but he didn't *want* to want her.

Their entire problem was that too much haze and too many half-truths had always stood between them. And she'd never pushed him for more because she'd been afraid of his rejection. But she wanted a relationship with him, and if she continued to wait, it could take him millennia to come around.

Over the years, she'd been very, very careful about who she warmed up to. But no man had ever made her hot like Jonah Steele did. So she was taking off the gloves. And hopefully all her other clothes, too.

She rolled her shoulders so that her robe slipped down one arm, revealing the thin strap of her gown and the champagne-colored lace that barely covered her left breast and dipped into a deep vee. Behind the fabric, her nipple hardened to a tight point.

Jonah rubbed his hands over his cheeks, and again, the sound set off an ache between her thighs. What would he do if she told him she wanted to feel the rasp of his facial hair across her skin? Along the insides of her thighs? Against her—

Jonah grabbed the neckline of her robe and yanked it up to her shoulder, covering her exposed breast. "It's cold," he said gruffly and dug back into his food.

What was she going to have to do—strip naked and jump up on his breakfast bar? This feeling building inside her was a combination of impatience and frustration and anxiety. Dangerous, because it made her feel reckless and impulsive.

The fruit in her bowl no longer appealing, she used her fork to pursue a strawberry with a slice of mandarin orange. Somewhere along the way, other fruits became involved in the high-speed chase and a plump grape and a blueberry flew over the barrier, bounced off the counter, and made a break for the floor.

"I got it," Jonah said, but she beat him to it and slid off her stool.

Fruit in hand, she was straightening from her crouch when Jonah swiveled on his stool and she came face to face with the zipper on his jeans.

The distended zipper on his jeans.

He either really liked her cooking or he'd gotten hard from looking at her thigh and breast.

She couldn't help herself. She stayed there in a strange crouch staring at Jonah's crotch until he drawled, "Wanna give me that fruit? A few more seconds and you're gonna have a smoothie."

His words shocked her out of her fascination with his erection, and she felt pulp and juice squishing through her fingers. "I need sex, Jonah."

Silence.

"With you."

More silence.

Extended silence. And he'd suddenly become fascinated with the one piece of ham left on his plate.

Damned man. To keep from either kissing or choking him, she reached for a napkin to clean the fruit from her fingers. Shaking with anger and need and a sliver of embarrassment, she marched around the bar, swiped the mess into the trash, and cranked on the faucet to wash her hands.

When she turned, Jonah was standing there, so close she could feel his breath on her skin. His hands rose and fell. "I don't know what to do with you, Tessa."

She could give him a list, starting with a long, hard kiss and possibly ending with him lifting her to the countertop and screwing her blind. Why couldn't he see what was between them? What *could* be between them?

"Why do you always turn away from me?" she asked, waving a vague hand near his hip. "Because unless your reaction really was to the omelet and not me, then I don't know what I'm doing wrong."

"You're not doing anything wrong."

"Based on our history, I've been making the assumption that you *are* attracted to me. Did I miss a turn somewhere? Am I just imagining it?"

"No."

"Then why do you avoid touching me? The times you have, you've been ashamed and beaten yourself up afterward, haven't you?"

"Can we drop this? We need to focus on your break-in and the hacking incident."

"Is helping me something you feel like you have to do? Because if you can't look at me without that strange combination of guilt and need, I'm not sure this is smart. You're obviously uncomfortable with any role you play in my life—

lifesaver, reluctant friend, even more reluctant lover. And I am tired of wanting a man who won't allow himself to want me back."

He squeezed his eyes closed. "I keep my hands off you because..."

"Because when you look at me, you see her, the helpless Tessa, don't you?"

Jonah's phone rang, and he grappled for it like a drowning man might reach for a life preserver. "Hello... yeah, this is a fine time. C'mon over."

When he hung up, Tessa touched his arm, a light stroke of fingertips. "Jonah, talk to me."

"We can't do this right now." He removed her hand from his arm and pressed it against her side. "Not when someone is threatening you."

"Then we're done here. Take me into town to pick up my car."

"Not happening," he said. "Maggie is on her way so we can talk about that son of a bitch who painted on your wall."

11

TESSA SNAPPED HER FINGERS FOR BADGER AND MADE FOR THE stairs.

Jonah only indulged himself by watching her ass swing from side to side for three steps before going after her and catching her by the elbow. She, her bouncing breasts, and her stellar ass were going to kill him.

D-E-A-D. Dead.

She swung around and the anger flashing in her eyes only made him hotter. "What?"

Near the windows, her pocket-sized dog was giving him the stink-eye as if thinking: *Man up, dude, or I'll fuck you over.*

"Stay," he said. "Please."

If she walked out right now, she'd be facing whatever this threat was alone. And the thought of that made his body and brain rebel. Safe. He wanted her safe and happy.

This morning, she was neither.

"I know we have some..." he rolled his hand as if that might make the words flow more easily, "...unresolved history."

Her snort made it clear she thought he was Captain Obvious.

"If I promise you that we will talk about what's between us, can we table it for now?"

"It's been tabled for years already."

"I know. You're right." He intertwined their fingers, admired the contrast of their skin. Maybe it was time for him to try to untangle his mixed feelings about Tessa. Could he do that and survive? "But that's damn hard to do while I'm worried about your safety. We—I—need to figure out who was in your files, because that'll tell us who broke into your place."

"Is that what you were doing all night last night, trying to track down my hacker?" Tessa asked him.

"Yes, and I came up empty-handed." And it was making him fucking crazy. Just like Tessa was. He couldn't hide the truth much longer—that he wanted her so ferociously that it scared the shit out of him.

A knock on the door announced Maggie's arrival.

Tessa said, "You're right. We need to focus on this for now."

He pulled open the door. "Come on in," he said to Maggie and led her to the kitchen. "You want some coffee?"

Her eyebrows went up at his offer of hospitality. "Sure."

Badger trotted over to her and reared up on his hind legs to sniff at her uniform. "Hey there, little guy." She reached down to pet him and shot Jonah a questioning look. "When did you get a dog?"

"Maggie, meet Badger. He's Tessa's bodyguard."

Maggie turned her attention on Tessa and held out her hand to shake. "Hi, Tessa. I'm Maggie Kingston."

"I'm impressed that Haywood County elected such a young sheriff." Tessa's smile was genuine, but her eyes were shadowed, leading Jonah to believe her mind was still on their earlier conversation. Why couldn't she see what was inside him? See the need that bordered on obsession and understand how dangerous that was for her?

"And a female to boot," Maggie said. "We're not as backward out here as a lot of people think."

Jonah made a one-shot cup of coffee for his cousin and slid it in front of her. "So what's the news from Asheville?" His patience and hospitality only went so far. He wanted answers.

"Just talked with my contact in the Asheville PD this morning. They went door-to-door on Tessa's floor of the building and talked with the staff. But..."

Maggie's hesitation told Jonah he wasn't going to like what she had to say a damn bit.

"...in a pricy place like that, the neighbors make it a point to stay out of other people's business. None of them saw or heard anything."

"What about the idiot building manager? Did he give someone else a key?"

"He swore he didn't. Said the only reason he handed one over to you was because Tessa was with you."

"And the other staff?"

"One of the maintenance guys remembered seeing a dude in a navy hoodie. But hell, it's December. That didn't strike him as suspicious. He figured it was a resident going out for a jog."

"What about security footage?" he demanded.

"They asked for it, but apparently the state-of-the-art system the building owner promised residents has yet to to be installed."

"But there are cameras in the hallways," Tessa said.

"Yeah," Maggie said, "but they're not connected to anything."

"Unfortunately, hardware doesn't do dick without the proper software behind it." Disgust rolled through Jonah. He would be having a friendly chat with that building owner soon.

"What about tracking down the dude in the hoodie?"

Maggie's gaze flickered away and slowly back to him. "Asheville PD wasn't willing to put that kind of manpower into it. After all, nothing was missing from Tessa's condo. And three words of graffiti didn't warrant a full-out investigation."

"What the fuck, Mags? That was a threat."

"Has anyone tried to directly hurt Tessa?"

"Hey, you two," Tessa said, waving a hand in front of Jonah's face. "I'm standing right here. And no, no one has tried to harm me. But I received an odd call from a Steele Trap employee."

"Someone local?"

"He worked at Steele Trap in Seattle. I'm not sure where he is now."

"Did he threaten you?" Maggie asked.

"Not exactly."

"What the hell does *not exactly* mean?" Jonah demanded. "That's a yes or no question. When you first told me about Carson, you didn't mention that he'd scared you in any way."

"He was obviously unhappy with me, but that's because he thinks I'm blackmailing him. Which I'm not. But someone hacked into my confidential client files." Tessa cut him a quick look. In response, Maggie's gaze narrowed. Tessa hurried to say, "And the company denied a breach."

"So you're telling me you plan to just accept that at face

value?" Now Maggie's attention was on Jonah. She knew exactly what he and Micki were capable of when it came to digging through data. She turned to Tessa. "Tell me about the call."

"Fuck." Jonah paced and brooded while Tessa gave Maggie the lowdown on Carson's call. He didn't like these new details. Maybe he needed to look more closely at Carson. "What can you do about this?" he asked his cousin.

Maggie lifted a shoulder. "Honestly? Not a lot. None of this has occurred in my jurisdiction. I'll stay in touch with Asheville PD, but unless something else happens, I doubt they'll put any more time into it."

Maggie finished her coffee, rinsed out her cup, and put it in the sink. Then she gave Jonah a slug in the shoulder. "Sorry I couldn't do more. Let me know if you need anything, and please stay on the right side of the law."

Once she left, Jonah returned to his pacing. This time, he added some muttering. "If they won't find this fucker, then I will."

He rolled Tessa's mention of Carson Grimes around in his head. Originally, he'd just considered him an innocent bystander, but what if there was more to it?

Jonah checked the time on his phone. Not quite nine, which meant it wasn't even six on the west coast. If he called Steele Trap's HR director at this hour, she would get on the next plane to North Carolina and castrate him.

Wait a sec, Carson had called Tessa. "Where's your phone?"

"Upstairs."

"I need it. You should have Carson's call-back number on there."

"You don't really think—"

"I don't know what to think."

It didn't take Tessa long to go upstairs and come back with her phone. She tapped in her password and handed the phone to Jonah. Unfortunately, Grimes didn't pick up, so Jonah left a message, trying not to sound like he planned to strangle the guy. "Grimes, this is Jonah Steele. I have something I need to talk with you about, so call me back."

His brain clicking through options, he picked up the box that had been delivered yesterday. Turned it over in his hands as if it were a Magic Eight Ball that could tell him the chances of success.

Something inside rattled.

"If you keep tossing that around, you'll break whatever's inside," Tessa commented. "I don't know how you can stand to have an unopened box sitting around. That would make me crazy."

"Have at it." He slid the box in front of her, then rummaged around in the kitchen drawer for scissors. He passed them over and Tessa attacked the tape on the box.

She withdrew a wad of packing paper and two smartphones in protective cases with Steele Trap's logo on them. "What in the world?" She dug into the box again and pulled out controller gauntlets and what looked like military night goggles with an attached headset and mic. "What is all this?"

"Looks like a VR—virtual reality—setup." Jonah grabbed the phone and turned it on. A text immediately popped up.

Luv ur work. Chk out mods to SS. CUS, $1RB@L1N

CUS. See you soon. What the hell?

"Huh," he said. "Some dude calling himself Sir Balin had the balls to port Steele Survivor over to an app and send me his game mods."

"Don't most people try to stay under the company's radar when they do something like that?"

"Well, I'm not a part of Steele Trap anymore, so maybe he thought I wouldn't care." He tapped the phone against the countertop. Something about this whole thing made the back of his neck itch.

He'd been so damn sure he could track down the source of her compromised files by the time Tessa woke this morning. Whoever had been snaking their way through the Data-Fort system was a pretty decent hacker.

But he was better.

He just needed a plan of attack.

And there was no one smarter to bounce ideas off of than his sister. He pulled out his phone.

It rang three and a half times before Micki answered. "'Lo?"

"I need your brain."

Her chuckle was more than amused—it was evil. "I always told Mom you'd gotten the raw end of the twin deal. And finally you've realized which of us got all the smarts. Only took you thirty years."

"Mick, I'm serious."

"Me too, little brother."

Whatever. He wouldn't rise to her bait this morning. "I'm trying to track down a hacker, but I haven't been able to trace the SOB. Spent all damn night last night chasing him from one IP address to another. Every time I thought I was getting close, his path darted in another direction."

Jonah heard murmuring from the other end of the line and what sounded like the slide of sheets. Something he didn't want to hear, since she and Gage were apparently doing the very thing Tessa wanted to do with him.

Something he damn well wanted to do with her, but knew could be a huge mistake.

"I need your help," he told Micki.

"Why don't you do something to clear your mind? Sounds like you're knocking your head against a wall."

What he really wanted to do to clear his mind was to take Tessa to bed, but that wouldn't do a thing to find this hacker. "Someone sent me a modded copy of Steele Survivor."

"Ballsy," Micki said. "But it could be your answer. Play it. Sink in, and something on this hacker might pop for you. Later."

And *click,* she hung up.

"Did your sister have any suggestions?" Tessa asked.

"She suggested I play a video game to try to unstick my brain."

"Because what else would you do?"

"Sometimes it's like a form a self-hypnosis," he explained. "I've had some of my best ideas, my most innovative concepts, come to me while playing."

"Kind of like taking a shower or driving." She nodded thoughtfully. "Hey, if it works, it works. Can I play, too?"

"I'm going to play the modded version of Steele Survivor."

"Okay."

"It's a first-person shooter game." Even if the weapons weren't machine guns and hand grenades, they were used to inflict a certain amount of damage on the other players.

"Jonah, I contracted for Steele Trap. Of course I know about the game."

Resigned, he led her back to his dim tech cave. Badger trotted along and settled into Jonah's favorite gaming chair.

He clicked the smartphones into the VR goggles and

outfitted Tessa with a pair, along with a headset and controller gauntlets. She looked as if the hardware on her head would tip her over, but she rocked the gauntlets like a pair of Wonder Woman bracelets.

When she thrust her arms this way and that, making little *pow* and *whoosh* sounds, he wanted to hug her.

"Be careful not to lose your balance or bump into anything," he warned her. "You can just move in place."

The game's opening sequence played as normal, with a cut scene of four guys joyriding in the back of an old pickup that closely resembled the POS truck Britt still drove. They wound their way down a mountain road, then cruised Main Street under the baleful eye of a stereotypical potbellied Southern sheriff. As closely as Jonah had modeled the dude on Sheriff Caldwell—who'd lorded over Haywood County before Maggie—he should've been sued.

But when the old sheriff had seen the game, he'd strutted around for days telling people he was famous and that it was only a matter of time before Hollywood came calling. Far as Jonah knew, he was still waiting at some retirement community in Georgia.

At the far edge of town, the truck stopped and all the characters piled out. They were joined by a few more guys loosely based on Jonah's high-school friends. But there was no mistaking the four main characters as Jonah and his brothers.

"They look like you," Tessa commented.

"Since I'm the youngest brother, they would say I look like them."

"Did they have any idea you were immortalizing them?"

"Britt had a shit-fit when he found out." Jonah chuckled. "But by that time, I had people beta testing demos. Reid and Grif didn't have a problem with any of it."

"Why are all the characters guys? Where are the girls?"

Yeah, Micki and Evie had asked that a million times. "It just wasn't made that way. I was ten years old when I first came up with the idea. It was a game for guys."

"You're honestly too young to be that sexist."

"It's not sexism, dammit. But even on-screen, I have a thing against hurting women."

"Seriously? It's a game."

"Holy shit." His attention was snagged by what was happening in front of him. The lineup of eight male characters was expanding as more people strolled onto the playing field. Tessa had certainly gotten her wish, because the new characters sure looked a helluva lot like Jonah's sisters and mom. His heart was thumping painfully. But that was nothing compared to the way it seized when another character joined them. She was wearing a red business suit and high heels—ridiculous for playing a shoot-'em-up survival game.

The person who'd modded his game had rounded up all the people Jonah cared most about in this world.

Including Tessa.

WELL, HOW ABOUT THAT. SOMEONE OBVIOUSLY THOUGHT enough of the women in Jonah's life to add them to his male-dominated game. "Who did you say sent this to you? Because I like him, whoever he is."

When Tessa peeked out from under her goggles, Jonah's face was immobile except for a tiny twitch in his jaw.

"What's wrong?"

"He fucked up my game."

She didn't agree. Anything could be improved with a

little girl power. "Maybe he or *she* thought your character diversity was a little shortsighted."

"I don't like it."

Tessa might be a psychologist, but that didn't mean she'd ever completely understand the male ego. It was elusive and mysterious—like the Loch Ness Monster or Sasquatch. She used her gauntlet controller to select herself as the character she'd use to play the game. "Why am I wearing work clothes?"

"How the hell should I know? You weren't even in my version."

She had a feeling he was also trying to keep her out of this version of his life. But she wasn't going to let that happen. "Next time, I want cargo pants and sneakers."

"I'll submit a change ticket to whoever modded this," he said, his tone as dry as burnt toast.

"Who's the woman with long dark hair and blue eyes?"

"My baby sister Evie. Micki's the one in the skull T-shirt."

In the game, Jonah's twin was dressed in skinny jeans and black boots with silver buckles running down the sides. Her dark hair was styled in a jagged cut that, combined with her delicate bone structure, made her look like a badass fairy. "She looks fierce."

Jonah laughed. "Tell her that and she'll love you for life."

He skipped over his sisters and chose his own avatar.

Now that they both had their players, the intro scene faded and Tessa faced a crazy-realistic 3-D scene with a small inset in the lower left corner. "Why do I have two views?"

"The big one is yours."

"And the other is..."

He didn't answer, but she could hear him moving beside

her and the small inset view changed. Ah, that was what his character was seeing. Nice.

She turned her head and the full effect of the 3-D hit her. "Whoa. This is kinda wild." By holding out her arms, she was able to convince her brain she was on solid ground.

With even, controlled breaths, she studied the scene in front of her. By the looks of the background, she and Jonah were at different starting locations. Before she could blink, his character was rushing along trails surrounded by native mountain trees and rhododendron. He shimmied up a sweet gum, the leaves rustling realistically. When he dropped back to the ground a few moments later—graceful as a cat—he held a wooden sword in his hand.

"Where did that come from?" And why didn't she have one?

"You gotta find your own weapons."

"Where?"

"Everywhere."

That wasn't incredibly helpful, especially when her on-screen character had yet to take a step.

With some effort, she was able to walk toward a massive oak. Unfortunately, she didn't "climb" it as easily as Jonah had. Instead, she ran into the trunk again and again. *Ow!* If this were real life, her forehead would be full of bark chunks. "How do I get up there?"

All she got from Jonah was a distracted grunt. Not helpful. But it sure fueled her competitive spirit. So she moved her arms and legs until she found a combo that allowed her to jump and move her arms at the same time. With renewed determination, she made modest progress up a tree. But when she tried to inch her way out on a branch to grab for what looked like some type of water gun, it cracked and she fell through the air.

On-screen, she landed on her back with an audible thump. Although she used every move she could think of, her character didn't budge. "Why can't I get up?" she demanded.

"Had the air knocked out of you," Jonah said. "Creates a ten-second freeze on movement." Meanwhile, he was vaulting over dead trees and finding stuff like gold coins and stashes of acorns in abandoned hunting cabins and deer blinds.

"I want treasure, too," she said when VT—Virtual Tessa —was finally able to sit up, then get to her feet. "Is that the point of the game? The person with the most stuff wins?"

"Nope, it's kinda like capture the flag. You round up everyone on the opposing team and disarm them."

"And I assume we're enemies?"

She momentarily lifted her goggles and glanced over at him. *Whew!* If she'd had a free hand, she would've fanned herself at the sexy flash of his smile. The force of it tingled its way through her system, and she dropped her arms. The gauntlets knocked against her thighs and her character vaulted off the ground and into a nearby bush. She emerged with a gun, and a thrill of accomplishment raced through the real Tessa. After a few false starts, she figured out how to run and weave, although she was still clumsy.

Her attention snagged on something at the edge of her screen, a glimmer of movement behind a cluster of azalea bushes. Before she could determine exactly what she'd seen, the foliage swayed and settled. "Are you chasing me?"

"Whether I want to or not," Jonah muttered.

"What's this weapon I'm carrying?"

"Dammit, Tessa, we're playing."

"Yes."

"You won't quit talking."

Oh, that's right. Apparently men weren't able to walk and talk at the same time. Too bad she couldn't use her feminine charms on-screen to distract him. Or...maybe she could.

In real life, she untied the sash of her robe, but Virtual Tessa's clothes remained on her body. Sexy distractions were out. Shoot, if seduction wouldn't work, then she'd have to play it his way. "I need to know how to use whatever this weapon is."

"Aim and pull the trigger."

Fine. She'd figure it out by herself. For several minutes, she directed her character to hunker down behind some rocks near a stream. She fiddled with her finger and hand movements until she figured out a combo that would allow her to not only shoot the strange gun, but also jab it like a bayonet and swing it like a club.

Oh, yeah. She was going to take him down.

Then she studied the terrain on Jonah's inset view. Somehow he'd found his way to the towering tree she'd fallen out of, which meant he was gaining on her. If she didn't figure out the game soon, he'd find her and capture her.

The thought of being chased and captured by him in real life sent a delicious tremor through her body. It would be intense, challenging, and downright thrilling.

But that was reality. Steele Survivor was a game she planned to best him at.

She waded her way across the stream, almost feeling the chill of the current against her skin. On the other side, she found an incline where she could watch the area around her. Watch and wait.

Jonah was so intent on his pursuit that he apparently didn't realize she was on to him. Now that she knew how to maneuver, she shimmied up a small tree to get a better view. To assess her opponent.

Jonah's character—dressed in the incredibly realistic torn jeans and graphic T-shirt—jogged up to the rocks Tessa had sheltered behind. He crouched down and ran his fingers across the indentions made by her heels.

"Why can't my character take off her clothes in the game?"

The inset of Jonah's screen wobbled as if he'd missed a step. "Wha...what?"

"It seems like I should be able to kick off those stupid heels if I want to. Clothes should be optional."

"If I'd been fifteen when I came up with the idea for this game, there would've been female characters and they probably would've all been naked." He studied the terrain for a few seconds and waded into the water, headed directly for her hiding spot. "Gotcha," he mumbled.

Damn him.

There was no way she could get down from the tree without him spotting her now. At least not in the normal manner. But her small perch had benefits as long as she could be patient.

It didn't take long until Jonah was circling the area, checking behind bushes and edging his way around trees. He studied the branches, but Tessa had miraculously camouflaged herself in the leaves. He crept in the opposite direction while she waited. And calculated.

She drew in a breath, let go of the tree, and jumped. With a real-life victory cry, Virtual Tessa shot at Jonah with her weird gun and crashed into his back, forcing him down onto his belly.

His character gave an *oomph* as though he'd really felt the impact of her weight. Then he somehow dislodged her and flipped over, sending her gun flying and skittering away.

Shoot. She'd been so close to getting the drop on him.

"This is when it changes to hand-to-hand," he told her. "Kicks, punches, hair-pulling. Anything goes."

Well, hand-to-hand sounded good, but she doubted if it included any sexy times. Since she no longer had a gun, she expected his character to cast aside the weapon in his hand.

But before her character could scramble to her knees to engage with him, on-screen Jonah pulled back his sword. Then the massive blade arced around and time—on-screen and IRL—slowed to quarter speed.

"What the fuck?" Jonah said in a rough voice.

"What's happen—" Before Tessa could finish her question, the sword sliced cleanly through her character's neck. Her severed head thudded to the forest floor and rocked to a stop, face up. Eyes still open and filled with surprise.

12
—————

JONAH YANKED OFF HIS GOGGLES WITH NUMB HANDS AND THEY clattered to the floor. Yet he could still see Tessa's headless avatar inside them.

Killing had never been programmed into Steele Survivor. That was what had made the game so different, had created an appeal for both kids and parents.

"Uh...was that part of the game?" Tessa asked tentatively.

"No." He hustled to her and slid the goggles from her eyes. "I would never hurt you." Not even in a fucking game.

"I know that." When Tessa touched his throat, her fingers were warm against his skin. But nothing could soothe away the chill sinking into Jonah's bones. "I don't understand what happened just now."

Unable to help himself, he gripped her waist and sank into a gaming chair, drawing her down into his lap, more for his reassurance than hers. He pulled her close and she wrapped an arm around his neck, which surrounded him with her rich scent. He pressed his face into the curve of her shoulder and tried to breathe away the lung-freezing feeling of seeing her headless body on that screen. "Someone else made those mods to the game."

"I know that wasn't really you."

Her soft skin tempted him, and he trailed his lips along her collarbone just to assure himself that she was here in his arms. That she was safe. That she was whole. He couldn't live with himself if Tessa was ever physically harmed again. "In some very wrong ways."

Tessa's breasts grazed his chest, making it obvious in her braless state that her nipples were tight underneath her robe. Without thinking it through, Jonah replaced his lips with his teeth, bit down lightly on her shoulder as if he could control her like an animal might his mate. Her breath hissed in, but her body became pliant against his. "Jonah..."

He wanted her like this. Wanted her to give up the control she'd obviously worked so hard to develop, because he wanted her to come apart for him and only him.

But he was scared shitless that the real him and his real needs would terrify her.

He carefully skimmed his hands up her shoulders and neck to frame her face in his palms. Then he took her mouth. She tasted of exotic tea and didn't hesitate to meet his kiss, immediately opening her mouth and searching for his tongue with hers. Sexy little sounds came from the back of her throat.

The silk of her nightclothes brushed against his arms, electrifying his skin and sending lustful impulses through him. His body knew exactly what his next step should be with Tessa.

If only his brain would shut the fuck up. He reached for his mental remote control and clicked the hell outta the off button.

As if she sensed something had changed, Tessa moved into the kiss, taking it deeper and more desperate.

Cool fabric pooled on his lap. Her robe. That meant she was wearing only a slip of a nightgown and whatever she had on under it. Jonah slid a finger under the thin strap, testing its silky strength. It would take nothing to rip it away.

No. No ripping, tearing, or yanking.

He brushed at the strap and followed its path to her upper arm, tracing little patterns against her skin as he sank further into her kiss. But Tessa groaned and disengaged her lips, her breath coming in sexy little puffs against his jaw. "Don't...don't play with me," she said, her voice quivering, shooting through his system like a fast-acting drug.

He caught her earlobe between his teeth and whispered, "This has never ever been a game."

"Then touch me." She shimmied, sending her gown to her elbows. His hand tightened reflexively on her arm, but she grabbed it and repositioned it over her breast.

Soft, round, warm.

Perfect.

He could spend a lifetime smoothing his fingertips over the swells of her breasts, slowly tracing circles inward, until he made it to her nipple.

The thought of tweaking that peak, of scraping it with his teeth, sent a shudder through his body and hardened his dick. He wanted to press her breasts together, bury his mouth there, and consume her.

His thoughts were interrupted by Tessa's gasp, and he realized he'd taken her nipple between his fingers and was working it ruthlessly.

Fuck. This was the reason he forced himself to resist her. He couldn't be trusted to control himself around her. He wanted her so badly that it bordered on violence.

He released her breast and grabbed her waist to urge her off his lap.

"If you push me away this time," Tessa said, her voice low with a combination of arousal and resolve, "I won't come back. You say you're not playing a game, but it feels that way to me. You can't pull me close and then shove me away."

"Look at my hands." He held up the one that had been mauling her breast.

"What about it?"

"It's shaking."

"From adrenaline and norepinephrine, most likely."

"Don't you get it, Tessa? I can't be trusted around you. I lost control once. I won't do it again."

"That's what this is all about, isn't it?"

He rubbed his palm over his head as if he could scrub away his desperate need for her. Hell, if that were possible, he would've exfoliated his brain years ago.

"You're scared of hurting me." She yanked his hand away and slapped it against her breast. "Grab it."

His fingers twitched, but he resisted tightening his grip on her soft skin.

Tessa should never have to endure pain to receive pleasure.

With a huff, she jumped off his lap. Her gown fell to her hips, leaving her breasts bare. She grabbed his other hand and covered her breast. Her nipples were burning holes in his palms and his mind was melting from the heat. He could lean forward—just a few inches—and suck her into his mouth. Use his teeth on her until she was hot and wet and begging.

"My God," she said. "I've seen better moves from men choosing tomatoes in the grocery store."

A wave of shame—red and ugly—rushed over Jonah, suffocating him. Who he was, the things he wanted... She deserved better.

"I'm sorry," she said. "I shouldn't have said that. I know better than anyone that everything about sex should be a choice."

"I care about you, but..."

She leaned toward him, pressed a kiss to the side of his mouth. "I know you do, but you're holding back. Why?"

He'd just killed her on-screen. Didn't she remember that? Jonah tried to close his mind against her video game character's fate. "What do you want from me?"

"I want you to treat me like a normal woman. Last time I checked, I wasn't made of glass. You can't break me."

Oh, but he could, and when he did, it would break him.

Maybe he could restrain himself.

Slow and easy.

She'd made it clear he wouldn't get another chance. He slid a hand down to her hip, and urged her closer. Taking his time, he drew her breast into his mouth and flicked her nipple with his tongue.

Slow.

This time her groan was full of satisfaction, and she shoved her hands into his hair to press his face closer. He sucked gently, savoring the flavor and texture that was uniquely Tessa. When he released her, she tried to wriggle closer.

Easy.

He could do this. Was doing it.

Jonah took her other nipple in his mouth and lightly fingered the recently abandoned one, keeping it hard and tight. With one hand, Tessa released her death grip on his hair and snaked it down between their bodies to slip it inside her panties.

Shock and body-shaking lust drove through him. "What're you doing?"

"What does it look like?"

"You...you do that often?"

"Are you asking if I masturbate?" Her chuckle was somehow both amused and aggravated. "Of course I do."

The little blood that had still been flowing in the non-penis parts of Jonah's body took the exit ramp to Dickville at ninety miles an hour. "I want to watch you."

"Now?"

It was his turn to laugh. Anytime. Now, later, whenever. That would be the best way to learn what she liked, how far he could push her. To be with her, he needed to replace all the old images he'd been carrying around for a decade, and he had a feeling that watching Tessa make herself come would be better than a thousand hours on the therapy couch. "How about I help you out today?"

He'd barely gotten the words out, and Tessa's hands went into overdrive, shoving her panties down her hips and thighs. Standing naked before him, she was all amazing curves and delicious skin.

He wanted to visit all the places on her body.

Visit? To hell with that. He wanted to become a permanent resident in Tessa's friggin' garden of Eden. He would stay there day and night sampling all her forbidden fruit.

When he slipped his hand between her legs, she adjusted to give him room. If he'd thought her breasts had burned him, the feel of her slick and needy against his palm was a completely different level of fire.

He wanted inside her. Wanted to drive into her until they were skin to skin, heart to heart.

Maybe being with Tessa would make him whole again, give him back the piece of himself he'd been unable to reassemble all these years.

She tilted her hips, and his fingertips grazed along her clit. "Please," she whispered, undoing him. "Now."

Anchoring his thumb against her clit, he eased two fingers into her body. Where the tremor started—with Tessa or him—he had no idea.

It didn't matter because this was so fucking right.

With a delicate sweep of his thumb and a smooth glide of his fingers, he concentrated on Tessa's pleasure. At first, her hips did a slow thrust, a languid movement.

But it didn't take long until she was jerking against him, all rhythm forgotten as she strained toward orgasm. "I...I need..."

"What?"

She tugged on his wrist, pulling his hand flush against her body and burying his fingers inside her with one sure stroke.

God, yes. She was so hot, burning for him. He pumped his fingers into her and circled her clitoris with his thumb.

A cry tore from her and she arched her back and rose to her toes to ride it out. Her pulses ended in a shudder that seemed to take all the bones from her body. With a sigh, she slumped down, sprawling into his lap.

Jonah's heart was thumping, an out-of-control rhythm against his chest. He wanted to do that again. Wanted to press her spread-eagled on the floor, get between her legs, and make her come until she didn't know her own fucking name.

Remember. Slow. And. Easy.

In an attempt to practice his slow and easy, Jonah

wrapped her in his arms and rested his chin on her shoulder.

That was when he glanced at the floor and saw the red words scrolling inside his VR goggles. That sick fuck of a modder had left a message inside Steele Survivor.

PLAY OR DIE.

TESSA FELT THE IMMEDIATE CHANGE IN JONAH. ONE SECOND, he was radiating male pride and the next, his entire body snapped to a rigid wall of muscle and bone.

"Whatever you're beating yourself up for," she said, "stop it."

She'd been so hopeful that once he touched her again, he would forget about her past.

"That motherfucker," Jonah breathed near her ear as he released his hold on her.

The loss of his touch made her want to cry. Just slide to the floor, curl up, and weep out all her frustrations over how she felt about this man. As euphoric as she'd been after Jonah had driven her up and over, tumbled her into the most delicious orgasm she could remember, now she felt hollow. Her body and mind were aching vacuums. And her heart?

She was tired of trying to hold it together for Jonah, of wishing that he would take what she so desperately wanted to offer.

Using his shoulder as leverage, she scooted off his lap. Now her nakedness made her feel vulnerable instead of powerful, so she scrambled to pick up her nightgown and slip it over her head. Her underwear had disappeared to somewhere unknown, and she smoothed her hands over her butt, trying to assure herself she was covered.

Jonah scooped up his VR goggles, came to his feet, and absently shoved his hand down the front of his jeans, adjusting what appeared to still be a partial erection. At least he hadn't been unaffected. He'd wanted her, whether or not he'd wanted to.

"Look," she said, "I'm just going to get Badger, gather our things, and get out of—"

"You're not going anywhere." His steely tone invited no argument.

"I can't do this with you. I thought I could, but your hot-and-cold act is too much for me to handle."

That seemed to grab his attention, and he glanced down at her. "Dammit, Tessa. You'll be lucky if I let you out of this house, and you're sure as hell not going anywhere alone."

Who did he think he was? And how had *her* orgasm flipped a circuit in *his* brain? "You push me away and then you want to tell me what to do?"

Unbelievable.

"Put this on," he demanded, shoving the goggles into her hand.

"What?"

"Look in the fucking goggles." He held them up to her face.

The visual had gone black except for three words. The same words that had been painted on her condo's wall. Before she could process exactly what that meant, the letters faded like blood soaking into the ground. Then a new character—dressed in jeans, white T-shirt, and blue coat—strolled onto the screen, hands stuffed into his pockets. "Grab the other pair," she told Jonah. "Hurry."

Above the neck, the on-screen guy slowly morphed from one character to the next. Short, choppy hair. Micki. Then a man with shaggy golden blond hair—one of Jonah's brothers—who transformed into a head with Tessa's own wild corkscrew curls. Her curls faded into Jonah's messy brown hair and facial scruff.

If that weren't eerie enough, the on-screen Jonah began to speak. "In every game, there are the strong and the weak. Winners and losers. Killers and victims. I know your secrets because I'm inside you. The only way to find me is to chase yourself. And in the end, there can only be one survivor."

The Jonah-esque character turned and walked away, into a faint background image. It was a street with shops lining each side, and there in the middle of it all was the sign for La Belle Style, Brynne's boutique.

The scene once again faded away, replaced with two words this time. GAME ON.

"What...what is this?" Her voice shook and her arm fell to her side, the goggles resting heavily against her thigh. Her subconscious was clanging—*danger, danger, danger*.

Whoever had tinkered with Jonah's game was the same person who was blackmailing Carson and the others.

Jonah lunged for the box that had come in the mail and rooted through it, tossing packing paper right and left. "Empty, dammit. And no return address." He tossed it aside and reached for her. The kiss he pressed to the top of her head slowly reunited the fragments of her heart. He turned her in his arms and pulled her close. "Someone is fucking with us."

Tessa rested her cheek against Jonah's chest, listening to the reassuring thump of his heart. "We should call someone."

Jonah gently pressed his thumbs under her jaw and tilted up her face. His hazel eyes seemed to burn with a fire —not a quick flame-and-out blaze, but one that smoldered and hid depths that could sear skin and soul. "You realize this is the same person who was in your condo, right?"

"Yes, and it means the hacking and the game mods are somehow related."

"Whoever this is has an agenda that includes both of us."

"Then why aren't we calling the police right now? You said we'd inform the authorities in Asheville if we discovered anything."

"Did you notice anything about that cut scene?" he asked her.

"You mean the guy at the end? He was walking down Main Street in Steele Ridge."

"Where Asheville PD has no jurisdiction."

"But Maggie does. She needs to know about this."

"I'll let her in on it."

But something in the way he drew out the words warned Tessa they didn't share the same idea of informing the authorities. "Then why aren't you dialing now?"

"Because this modder is flipping me the big fat finger."

"And he knows you won't be able to say no to that kind of bait." The chill of fear solidified in her chest. This was bigger than Jonah or her alone, yet he was taking this very personally. "What do you think he meant about knowing secrets?"

"He obviously got his hands on info from your files. Doesn't get much more secret than that. Now he's bringing whatever this is to my turf. To my goddamn home."

And one thing she knew from being at Steele Trap, Jonah was intensely loyal. To the people who worked for him, to his family, to the people he cared about. The way he'd helped his hometown proved that a hundred times over. "Do you really think Carson could do something like this? It doesn't seem like him."

"There's only one way to find out."

"You can't go after him. That's what he wants."

"And that's exactly what he's going to get. He couldn't have made it any clearer that he's willing to go through the people in my life if that's what it takes to get to me. I've gotta stop this guy. Now."

"Jonah, you make video games. You're not a cop."

"I may not be law enforcement, but being a gamer is way more valuable right now."

"You think this person is actually in Steele Ridge?"

"I know he is," Jonah said, his voice as hard as his last name. "And if he wants to play, then I sure as hell plan to win."

13

"No," she said immediately, a bad feeling invading her bones. Pulling out of Jonah's embrace, she scanned the room for her phone, only to remember she left it in the bedroom. "I'll call your cousin myself."

But Jonah caught her by the wrist to keep her in place. "He's out there right now. For all I know, he could be hurting someone. Shit..." He shoved his hand into his pocket and groped around. "I need to call my family."

In his haste, he fumbled the phone and Tessa caught it before it hit the floor. He snatched it from her, pushed a button, and jammed the phone against his ear. His face relaxed a few seconds later. "Mom, are you okay?"

Indistinct words came from the other end of the line.

"What about the girls? Have you talked with Micki and Evie today?" His breath released in a rush. "Okay, good. That's good. What about Britt, Grif, and Reid?"

Tessa wanted to wrench the phone from his hands and hear for herself that his family was fine, but she restrained herself. She didn't even know the Steeles and yet she'd somehow brought danger straight to their door.

"Yes, they are good sons to call you every day. I'll try to do better, Mom," Jonah said. "No, nothing's wrong. I'll talk to you later." He slipped the phone back into his pocket and closed his eyes.

"Why didn't you tell her?" Tessa demanded.

"Tell her what?"

"That some maniac is out there and wants to hurt you."

"I don't think this is about me, Tessa."

"How can you say that?"

"Because he targeted you first."

She wasn't buying it. Not for a nickel. Not for a dime. Not for a million dollars. "Were you watching that jump scene?"

"Cut scene," he corrected.

"Whatever," she said. "But he was talking directly to you."

"How do you figure that?"

It made Tessa stomach rocky, remembering the way her head had separated from her body and how her eyes had stared in death—glassy and empty. "Because I was dead, Jonah."

"Fuck." His tone was low and rough, but he pulled her in and wrapped her tight in his arms. It didn't completely soothe all the crazy emotions swirling through her, but his touch set off something inside her. Something primitively feminine. Something needy and frightened.

Something that made her want to seek out his protection.

And although she appreciated that Jonah had once helped her out of a horrible situation, she wouldn't let any man make her feel weak. But Jonah would go after this person, whether or not Tessa approved. She'd been around him enough at Steele Trap to know when he pledged action, he wasn't merely tossing the idea around. He was already committed.

"If you're going after him, I'm coming with you."

"Not happening."

"You can't do it alone." She waved a hand toward the VR goggles. "Tell me you can navigate in that thing out in the real world."

The way his jaw flexed said he hadn't thought about that, which meant he was really off his game. Jonah could run angles and options faster than anyone Tessa had ever met. His impulsiveness now scared her, but if he was determined to go on the hunt, then she refused to be left behind. "I guess you plan to call one of your brothers or Micki for help with this," she said with the perfect lilt of innocence.

He rested his cheek against the top of her head. "Fuck. It. All."

Yeah, she had his number.

"I'm already in this," she said softly. "I have been since the minute Carson Grimes called me."

What did this person have against both her and Jonah?

It was obvious they'd missed something. Some reason this person wanted to lash out at them. What did they have in common? Steele Trap and the night of her attack, primarily.

"From his little speech at the end," Jonah said, "it looks like he wants me downtown."

"When I was there yesterday, it wasn't packed, but enough people were on the street that you'll need me to help you navigate and run interference."

"You won't get out of the car."

"How do you expect me to help you when I can't see you or talk to you?"

He gave her a quick squeeze, then stalked over to a floor-to-ceiling cabinet. When he opened the door, it became apparent that he owned every technical gadget, charging cord, and device known to man. He rummaged through, cussing under his breath until he found what he apparently wanted.

"We'll connect you to my headset for sound. Then I'll wire you with a different mic so you can communicate with me." He turned back to Tessa and gave her a once-over that was more clinical than sexual. "Which means you have to put on some clothes."

He was right. This was more important than their unfinished business with one another. Within ten minutes, Tessa had changed into a pair of pants and a collared silk shirt and was back downstairs.

Jonah took one look at her and said, "Unbutton."

What she wouldn't give to hear him say that in a needy tone instead of one that was all too businesslike. But when she slipped the small mother-of-pearl buttons from their holes, she noticed that Jonah was staring hard at the bundle of wires in his hands.

He wanted her. She knew that now. She just needed to figure out how to get him to admit it and act on it. Act on it *all the way.*

"This battery pack can hook to your waistband." He hesitated, his hands hovering near her waist.

She grabbed the fabric and pulled it away from her body. When he clipped the gizmo onto her pants, his knuckles skimmed her stomach, making goose bumps break out on her skin and causing her nipples to tighten. Impossible to miss since her blouse was hanging open, exposing her bra.

"Then this wire goes up and you can clip it to your..." He motioned in the vague vicinity of her chest.

Uh-uh. He would not get off this easy. She moved her shoulders, which allowed her shirt to slip down her arms. "Why don't you do it? Make sure it's secured correctly. Or if you're not willing to put your hands on me again, then I'll go out and find this person myself."

"The hell you will." He grabbed her by the waistband and jerked her toward him. And oh, was it wrong that his action sent a little thrill through her body that landed directly between her thighs?

She wanted to make Jonah Steele lose the restraint he always seemed to have around her.

His hands were steady and sure as he threaded the black wire under the middle of her bra. The plastic was cool against her skin, but nothing could tame the heat Jonah's nearness kindled in her. He fastened the clip to her bra cup, skimming her nipple in the process.

But the second and third time he brushed his knuckles across the fabric? Those were no accident.

They were going to finish what they'd started earlier if she had to tie him to a bed. And oh, wasn't that a picture for the memory books? His long, lean body stretched out for her to look at, touch, and taste at her leisure.

"What..." She had to clear the frogginess from her throat. "What about video?"

"I have a Bluetooth transmitter that'll relay a camera feed to the display on my dashboard."

"I'd rather track him with you."

"I'd rather you weren't there at all."

Car display it was. Tessa buttoned up her shirt and reached for her purse while Jonah stuffed gear into a backpack.

It only took them a few minutes to drive from Jonah's house into town. But rather than park on Main as Tessa had yesterday, Jonah veered off to a side street and pulled in near a Barron's Park sign.

He rummaged through the backpack until he came up with the goggles, headset, and gauntlets. Once he'd fiddled around with some settings, he slipped the phone into the front of the goggles, then clipped on something else. "External camera," he explained, tapping above the car's display screen. "It'll feed straight into here. You'll need to keep the car in auxiliary mode so it'll stay on."

"Anything in particular I should do?"

"These goggles switch from full VR mode to AR mode."

"AR?"

"Augmented reality. Gives you a view of reality overlaid with computer-generated stuff like sound, video, or data coming from a GPS. Think Pokémon Go. Based on that, I'm hoping they'll show me any obstacles in my way, in one form or another. But if you see me about to walk into a tree, you could let me know."

"Anything else? What are you going to do if you're actually able to track down this guy?"

"Beat the shit out of his sorry ass."

Sometimes she forgot that Jonah was, at heart, a Western Carolina good ol' boy. Persistent, possessive, and protective.

Is that what I really want in a man?

In Seattle she'd seen the mellow, urban-dwelling video game mogul. This Jonah was someone else. And she'd be lying if she didn't admit the North Carolina Jonah was keeping her hormones revved up.

She liked him edgy and rough.

He slipped the goggles onto the top of his head and reached into the backpack once again. What he came out with socked the breath from Tessa's chest. With clinical detachment, he looked over the handgun, released the magazine to check the bullets, then clicked it back into place.

"What is that?"

One side of his mouth lifted, the most amusement she'd seen from him since her avatar had died a bloody death in the game earlier. "A Glock 19. You didn't think I planned to go out there unarmed, did you?"

"But there are no *real* guns in Steele Survivor. Isn't that what he wants you to play?"

"No real machetes in the game either," he said. "That didn't stop this fuckwad from modding them in."

"You think he's going to be armed out there?"

"I'm sure of it."

Tessa tried to keep her breathing steady. If Jonah ran into real trouble, all she had to do was dial 911.

"Don't," he said.

"Don't what?"

"Do whatever you're thinking about. The fewer people involved in this bullshit scheme, the less potential for them to get hurt."

"What about you?"

He leaned in, his eyes a mesmerizing tiger yellow now. "I created this game. I know this town. I'll be fine."

Then he kissed her. A slow plunder of her mouth that took her under and rolled her. Seduced her into the dangerous sea of Jonah Steele. He touched all of her—lips, teeth, tongue—until she felt as if he'd marked her as his. When he finally shifted away, she was breathing as if she'd climbed ten flights of stairs.

"You... I... We..." Her heart was giving her ribcage a workout. "We're finishing this."

"Yes, we are." Then he got out of the car and pointed downward, indicating she should hit the automatic locks.

Before they'd clicked into place, he was off and running. Tessa jammed the buds into her ears and the sound of Jonah's breath steadied her. "Be careful," she told him through her mic.

"I'll be back soon."

She didn't try to extend the conversation because she wanted him one hundred percent focused on what was in front of him. Jonah was scanning the landscape. From her vantage point, it was wild because she was seeing what he was seeing as he loped down Main Street.

Blues, Brews, & Books. Brynne's beautiful boutique. The bakery with the sandwich sign out front. Today it said: *Mesa rescuing yousa or yousa rescuing mesa. Thisa good. Thisa very good.*

First Yoda and now Jar Jar Binks. Was someone there a Star Wars fan?

"You never know about Jeanine. She's the lady who writes those each day," Jonah said.

"Sorry, I didn't mean to ask that aloud. So you can see Main Street?"

"Yeah, but it's a wreck. Paint peeling, windows broken, sidewalks buckling." At that, he jumped over a perfectly sound piece of sidewalk.

"Do you see him?"

"For the most part, the people look like NPCs. Non-playable characters."

Just then, a woman stepped in front of Jonah and held out a hand as if to stop him.

"Slow down," Tessa warned him. "She's real."

Jonah came to a skidding stop and Tessa heard the

woman say, "Jonah Steele, what're you doin' running down the street lookin' like a scuba diver?"

"Just trying out some equipment and getting a little exercise, Mrs. Cuddleford."

"I'd think you'd have plenty of room to run around out there on that ridge of yours. In fact, I heard Reid's put in a bunch of stuff to train up policemen and the like."

Jonah's head tilted down, giving Tessa a view of his hands clenching and unfurling.

Mrs. Cuddleford poked Jonah's chest. "You may have saved Canyon Ridge, but everybody had to buy all new return address labels and send out change of address cards. Do you have any idea how much those things cost these days?"

"No, ma'am," he said on a sigh.

"Over ten whole dollars."

Tessa's view shifted when he looked down and pulled out his wallet. Retrieving a twenty, he said to Mrs. Cuddleford, "Would this help with the address labels?"

"I suppose so." She sniffed, but quickly plucked the money from his finger. "Get on with yourself, then. But don't be stirring up any trouble."

"No, ma'am."

Tessa couldn't help but laugh because Mrs. Cuddleford hadn't realized that Jonah's response could be taken as either "No, ma'am, I won't stir up trouble" or "No, ma'am, I won't *not* stir up trouble."

It was as if the woman still saw Jonah as a little boy. Had he been mischievous or studious? Outgoing or shy? Popular or one of the crowd?

"Jesus Christ on a saltine cracker," he muttered.

Once he was on the move again, Tessa asked him, "Is everyone here like that?"

"Up in your business, you mean?"

"If that's what you want to call it." In one way, it was sweet the way people all knew each other and looked out for one another.

"Let's just say that it won't matter how long my brothers and I live here as adults. Some people will always see us as the Steele boys."

"I want to meet them."

Jonah's stride hitched, but he regained his footing and put on more speed. "Why?"

"Because I know you love your family." And because she wanted true insight into Jonah. The entire person. Carolina boy. Brother. Son.

Town scoundrel. Town savior.

"Dammit," he said as the buildings and people on Main began to thin out.

"Nothing?"

"No one dressed in blue with a white beanie." He looked left, then right. "Main Street would've been too easy."

"Fewer people on the side streets." Tessa pointed out.

"True." By this time, Jonah was doing a fast jog and his breathing was deep and rhythmic, lulling Tessa. So far, the camera wasn't showing anyone. Maybe the person who'd modified the game was just yanking Jonah's chain.

"I'm starting to circle around to the car. If I don't find him before I get back, I'll check the area past the park."

A shiver rippled up Tessa's arms. Someone was playing a twisted game of hide-and-seek. "Just be careful."

"Son of a bitch," Jonah breathed.

"What? What do you see?"

"He's here. In the fucking park. Are your doors locked?"

Tessa double-checked. "Yes. Where is he?" The camera

was showing only a pavilion, part of a parking lot, and a kid's slide.

"Just sitting on a bench waiting, like he doesn't have a problem in the world. Well, I'll show him a problem. I'm fixin' to take down this bastard." When he was angry or stressed, Jonah's Southern drawl intensified.

But his honey smooth voice didn't calm Tessa's jumpy stomach. After she'd been assaulted, she'd developed the ability to recognize risky situations. And right now that sense was going haywire, yelling that he was running straight into a trap. Something was wrong, very wrong here. "Stop. Jonah, don't go after him."

"Too late."

Jonah angled off toward a park bench, and suddenly Tessa caught sight of the person sitting there. Wrapped in a blue coat and wearing a white knitted hat, the park visitor was tossing out what looked like cracker crumbs to a small flock of squabbling blue jays.

Although Tessa could only see what the camera was showing, something about the person didn't seem right. "Are you sure that's—"

Her warning was cut off when Jonah executed a flying dive over the bench, hitting the person behind the right shoulder. From the force of the momentum, a jumbled ball of arms and legs crashed the gravel path in front of the bench, and the birds took off in a flurry of squawks and feathers.

Tessa's view went topsy-turvy, flipping over and over, then bouncing to a stop. The camera had come loose from Jonah's goggles.

Everything seemed to slow as if Tessa were watching the scene through sorghum syrup. She blinked, trying to clear her vision so she could understand was she was really seeing. Small feet wearing white thick-soled tennis shoes. Birdlike, mottled hands. Wisps of gray hair peeking out from the stocking cap.

Jonah reared up and straddled the person, pulling back his arm for a punch.

"Jonah, stop!"

"You SOB, I'm gonna—"

"Don't hit her!"

"What?"

"Take off your goggles."

"Tessa, this guy—"

"Do it. *Now.*"

He shoved them to the top of his head and looked down. "Oh, God. What the fuck did I do?"

That told Tessa all she needed to know. That wasn't the person they'd been trying to find. She pressed the door lock and fumbled with the handle. It took three tries before she was able to shove open the door and jump out. She dashed toward the bench as Jonah scrambled off the prone form.

She skidded to a stop and looked down. Jonah's head was bowed and the woman he'd attacked lay unmoving on her back. Her eyelids fluttered and she blinked, flooding Tessa with relief.

"Are you okay?"

The woman's mouth moved, but nothing came out.

Tessa yanked out her phone and dialed 911. She gave them location details and all she knew, which wasn't much. Once she was sure they were sending help, she knelt down next to the woman and took her frail blue-veined hand.

One glance at Jonah told her that he wasn't doing much better. His eyes held a faraway glaze and his throat was working as if he couldn't swallow properly.

"Ma'am, can you tell me your name?" she asked.

A tiny head shake was the only answer.

"Don't let her move," Jonah ordered. "She could have a spinal cord injury. I probably snapped her in half."

When he looked up, a fist of emotion rammed into Tessa's chest. Tears filled his eyes and he didn't even try to blink them away.

Tessa stroked the older woman's white hair. "Do you know her? Who is she?"

"Eva Vanderwinkle. One of the nicest ladies in Steele Ridge. Does stuff like make blankets for foster babies and read to sick people at the hospital. Hell, she didn't even bit... gripe about having to change her address when I bailed out the town."

"Mrs. Vanderwinkle," Tessa said softly. "Help is on the way. Jonah didn't mean to hurt you. He thought you were someone else."

The woman's mouth lifted a tiny bit. "Those Steele boys," she whispered. "Always stirring up trouble."

14

IT TOOK THE AMBULANCE LESS THAN FOUR MINUTES TO ARRIVE at the park, and Jonah had never been so fucking glad that he lived in a small town.

He'd body-slammed an old lady. Shame made him want to turn his head away to keep from looking at her tiny body splayed out there on the path, but that would be a chicken-shit move. So he hunkered down near Mrs. Vanderwinkle, but didn't touch her. Didn't let his ham hands near her.

Of course, the emergency personnel put a C-collar on her and were extra careful when they transitioned her to the gurney and lifted her into the ambulance. It was a small comfort to Jonah that one of the emergency responders was Maggie's brother, Cash.

Before Cash could swing into the cab of the ambulance, Jonah grabbed his arm. "Is she gonna be okay?"

"I can't tell you much now, but it's a good sign that she never lost consciousness. We're taking her to St. Elizabeth's if you want to check on her later."

Cash climbed in, and the ambulance took off with lights whirling and siren whooping.

Jonah sank onto the bench where he'd attacked poor Mrs. Vanderwinkle. This was just proof that he couldn't control the aggressive impulses inside him.

She'd be fine if he'd stopped to really look at who he was taking down. If he'd called out instead.

But no, he'd let loose and hurt a sweet lady.

"It was an accident." Tessa sat beside him and placed a comforting hand on his shoulder.

He didn't want to be soothed. Didn't want to be forgiven for such a dumbshit move.

A cop cruiser pulled up and Maggie got out. Her face one huge scowl, she strode up to Jonah and Tessa and planted her hands on her hips, emphasizing the utility belt around her waist. Too bad she couldn't just pull out her service gun and put him out of his misery. "What the hell happened here?"

"It was a mistake..." Tessa started to explain, but Jonah shrugged out from her under hand and stood.

"I jumped Mrs. Vanderwinkle."

"Is this what you do when you get bored up there on the ridge—come down and wreak havoc on innocent citizens?" Maggie nudged the VR goggles, still lying on the ground, with the toe of her boot. "What're these?"

"It's a long story."

"Handy, since I have all the time in the world to hear it," she said. "You want to do this here out in the cold or come back to the office where you can have a cup of shitty-ass coffee?"

Turning to Tessa, he said, "You can take my car back to the house and Maggie will drop me off later."

"Not happening," Tessa said, her mouth pinched stubbornly.

"She's right." Maggie scooped up the goggles. "I'll need to talk to her, too."

"Keys still in the car?" he asked Tessa.

"I didn't take the time to pull them out."

"Then I'll ride with Maggie and you can follow."

Something flashed in Tessa's dark eyes, something that looked like hurt. But Jonah couldn't comfort her right now. Hell, he didn't deserve to comfort her or to be comforted by her.

It was late afternoon and evening was creeping over the mountains to shadow Steele Ridge by the time Jonah and Tessa finally walked out of the sheriff's office.

Maggie had ripped him a new asshole. Said Jonah should've come to her the minute he suspected this guy was on her turf.

But in the end, the only crime committed today was by Jonah. Bodily assault.

Mrs. Vanderwinkle had kindly decided not to press charges, and he needed to make amends. He would track down this bastard, one way or the other.

"I'll drop you by the house," he said to Tessa, hearing and hating the clipped tone of his own voice.

Still, she reached for his hand and he let her lace her fingers with his. "What happened wasn't your fault."

"Tell Mrs. Vanderwinkle that."

"You're going to see her, aren't you? I could go with—"

"No, I need to do this alone."

"I understand."

She couldn't. Not really. No one in Jonah's life had ever completely understood him, not even Micki. The youngest of four brothers, he'd just wanted to be a protector like them.

Yet the first time he'd had the chance to truly help someone, he'd done a completely half-assed job. A real hero would've stayed with Tessa, protected her from that last son-of-a-bitch who used her. A real hero wouldn't have left her —alone and bleeding—on her front porch because he was too damn afraid of getting into trouble.

He was still doing a half-assed job at protecting people he cared about. When they drove up to his house, he pulled the door key off his ring and held it out to her.

"Maybe...maybe I should just go back to Asheville."

Anger tried to boil up in Jonah again, but he wouldn't let it. Tessa didn't deserve that. "No." He pressed the key into her palm. "This guy is still out there somewhere. You're safer here than you'd be in your condo."

Indecision flickered in her eyes, stirring up all Jonah's feelings of lack of control. So he took her hand and looked at her, really met her gaze the way he'd been avoiding since he'd ripped off the goggles to find he'd almost killed Mrs. Vanderwinkle. "Do this for me, please. I don't know what's going on here, not completely. But this guy is playing a dangerous game, and it's obvious he's not above using the weak to get what he wants."

"I'm not weak."

Hell. "I didn't mean that."

"I can't just sit around and play the damsel in distress. This all started with me, and I won't cower away while you're trying to find whoever is responsible."

Jonah dug the heels of his palms into his eye sockets. Damn, it felt as if he hadn't showered or shaved in a decade. "I think he's using you to get to me."

"Even if that's the case, he compromised my files, spray-painted my home, and made threats that may have caused Davey to kill himself. I can't let that go. I've been thinking about who could be behind this."

He had, too.

"We know it's someone with a certain amount of technical skill. Would Carson really be able to do something like this?"

Part of him wanted to believe Carson was their guy, but that martini dude at Tucci's the other night had stuck in Jonah's mind. Who the hell was he and why had he been staring at Tessa?

"I'll call Steele Trap's HR director and see if I can get a line on him."

"*We.* It has to be *we,* Jonah, or I walk."

"If you'll stay here while I'm gone, I promise I won't cut you out. But I need to go apologize to Mrs. Vanderwinkle on my own." He shoved out of the car and went around to open her door.

"I want to talk this entire situation through when you get home," she said, stepping out.

Home. As if she considered his house her home, too. If only.

If only he could stop blocking every attempt she made to get close to him.

He took her hand, walked her to the front door, and unlocked it. He handed her the loose key, then framed her face in his palms.

She was so precious to him. All he wanted was to protect her from ever being hurt again.

"Don't wait up, but I promise we'll talk this out." He pressed his lips to hers, breathing in her scent, letting it wash over him, surround him. If he could just draw her into his lungs, into his body, he could be a better man.

Although he hated to, he ended the kiss, and her lips clung to his. "I'll set the house security system from my phone. If you need to go outside, you can hit pause, then reactivate it with this code." He gave her a random jumble of numbers and letters, expecting to have to repeat them several times.

But Tessa closed her eyes, silently recited the sequence, and said, "Got it."

On his way to St. Elizabeth's hospital, Jonah called the restaurant in Charlotte. He was able to get one of the bartenders on the phone. "Hey, I was at your place Saturday night and I thought I saw one of my old college buddies there, but he left before I could catch up with him. Could you check your receipts and give me the name of a guy who was drinking martinis? Three olives."

"Dude, I'm not sure—"

"Do it, and I'll call your manager and add more gratuity to the bar bill for that night."

A sigh came from the other end of the line. "I'll need a little time to check the system."

Jonah gave the bartender his callback number.

When he arrived at the hospital, he strode up to the information desk and flashed a strained smile. "I'm looking for Eva Vanderwinkle's room."

"Room 212."

On the second floor, a nurse stopped him as he tried to enter the room. "Are you family?"

With no reluctance at all, he lifted a bouquet of flowers and said, "Her grandson."

"You can stay ten minutes. They recently brought her up from recovery."

Crap. That meant she'd needed surgery. "Thanks."

He strolled toward the other end of the hallway and rounded the corner. Thank God for walls because he leaned against the nearest one and tried to catch his breath. He could've killed Mrs. Vanderwinkle.

When he got himself together and found the correct room, he walked in to find Mrs. Vanderwinkle alone and hooked up to all kinds of beeping and flashing machines.

The sight made his insides go cold. Where was her family?

He placed the flowers, so damned inadequate as an apology, on a nearby rolling table and went to the bedside to take her hand.

Her thin eyelids fluttered open, and she pinned him with sharp blue eyes. "Jonah Steele."

"Yes, ma'am. How're you feeling?"

She waved toward a pitcher sitting next to the flowers he'd brought and rasped out, "How do you think I'm feeling? Like a Yugo that's been flattened by a semi."

With unsteady hands, he hurried to fill a plastic cup with water and shoved a straw in it.

"Lift the bed a little."

He found the button and increased the incline enough so she wouldn't choke on a sip of water. He held the cup and straw, and she took two halfhearted sips before lying back on the pillows.

After a few bolstering breaths, she said, "Who was that pretty girl you were with?"

"A friend." Seriously? He'd put her in the hospital and she wanted to know about Tessa? "The nurse said you had surgery, but I wasn't able to get any other information."

"Just a pin in my hip."

Just a pin? That meant recovery time and physical therapy. He pulled out his phone and sent himself a reminder text to hire her a private physical therapist. "Do you have someone to stay with you here at the hospital?"

"My daughter's on her way down from Alexandria. Don't you worry. I'm eighty-three years old. I didn't get to my age by being a dainty little flower. I'm a tough old broad."

He took her hand again, conscious of the birdlike bones beneath his fingers.

"Don't let my size fool you. My Henry used to say I was the hardiest heifer in the pasture." Her smile reached her tired eyes. "Poor man didn't exactly have a way with the compliments, but he meant well. Point being that we women are made of sterner stuff than you might think."

What would Tessa say if he told her she was the hardiest heifer in the pasture? Based on all she'd said to him lately, he had a feeling she'd take it as a compliment. Maybe Mrs. Vanderwinkle was right. He was still seeing Tessa as delicate instead of strong. "Please know that I never meant to hurt you. I thought you were someone else."

"Jonah, you're a good boy," she said. "You saved this town, so why in the world would you go around attacking the senior citizens here? That doesn't make a bit of sense. Besides, your mother raised you better. But I would like to know who you mistook me for."

The words Jonah wanted to use to describe the asshole who was using innocent women to mess with him weren't fit for polite company. So he forced a smile and told Mrs. Vanderwinkle, "No one you need to worry about."

Because Jonah was damn well going to make him pay.

JONAH'S HOUSE WAS WARM AND WELCOMING DESPITE ITS massive size, but when Tessa went to the guest room to change clothes and let Badger out of his kennel, she suddenly felt alone and vulnerable. Since she'd returned from Seattle, she hadn't yet rekindled any of her childhood friendships. Tonight would be a perfect night to curl up on the couch with a girlfriend to share a bottle of wine and talk about their troubles.

Brynne Whitfield Steele flashed into Tessa's mind. Tessa took out the business card Brynne had given her, which listed the boutique's Facebook page.

She opened the Facebook app on her phone and brought up La Belle Style. From there, she clicked on Brynne's profile. Her dark hair and gorgeous face were immediately recognizable in her profile pic.

Tessa's finger hovered over the *friend* button. To press or not to press? Was it just weird and pathetic for her to stalk Brynne, friend her, and then message her asking her to come over for girl time, when they didn't know one another?

Before she could talk herself out of it, she poked at the phone. Lots of people friended folks they didn't know very well, and business owners tended to accept all the requests they received. She took a bolstering breath and messaged Brynne through the boutique's page.

Hello. I'm Tessa Martin. We met briefly at the Triple B.

Brynne: *Hey there! Did you change your mind about checking out that sweater? Wait a minute. Tessa Martin. You're* THE *Tessa.*

Apparently word had gotten around after what had happened today. And they all knew she'd been critical to clearing Jonah last year, which meant they were all privy to her history.

There went her idea. She didn't need Brynne to look at her with pity.

Tessa had started this PM, but now she had no idea what to type back. In the end, it didn't matter because three dots appeared on the screen.

Brynne: *Maggie called Reid earlier to tell him about what happened in the park today. He's been hitting up Jonah's phone for hours, but no answer. He and the other guys went up to Jonah's place earlier, but the lights were off and the Tesla wasn't in the garage.*

Tessa: *He's out right now.*

Brynne: *Are you at his house?*

Tessa debated. If she said yes, would Jonah's entire family descend? She had a feeling Jonah wouldn't be very happy to return and find them all sitting in his living room. Not after the day he'd had.

Everyone else seemed to think Jonah was such an easy-going guy, but Tessa knew the truth. He was much deeper than his smart-ass smirk and his sarcastic T-shirts. He had an intensity and an edge of darkness that no one else seemed to see.

Tessa: *Yes, but Jonah's gone to see Mrs. Vanderwinkle. Do you think you could keep everyone away, just for tonight?*

Brynne: *Do you know the Steele brothers?*

Not really. Only what Jonah had told her, which wasn't much. But if they were anything like him, they were forces of nature. Reid, in particular, seemed like a cyclone.

Besides, she and Jonah needed to talk this through. If his brothers showed up, she might get shut out of the search for the hacker. And she'd be damned if she'd let that happen.

Tessa: *Will the others follow Reid's lead?*

Brynne: *It's possible.*

Not a sure thing, but it would have to do.

Tessa: *Can you convince Reid to leave it alone until tomorrow? Jonah hasn't had much rest and I have a feeling the whole thing could blow up.*

Brynne: *What whole thing?*

Tessa: *Jonah can explain it all in the morning.*

Lord, he would kill her for making that promise to his family, but what was she supposed to do? He'd be even angrier if she let them come here tonight and she told them everything. Angry? He'd go apeshit.

Brynne: *I'll use every wile I have, but you're gonna owe me.*

Was Brynne one of those women who played the give-to-get game?

Tessa: *What will I owe?*

Brynne: *You have to come see the sweater I think is perfect for you.*

The breath Tessa had been holding released. That she could do.

Tessa: *Deal.*

Brynne: *Be prepared. Night. :-)*

With a flick of her thumb, Tessa dismissed the Facebook app. Well, that certainly hadn't gone even close to the way she'd expected. And it was still just Badger and her alone in this huge house.

Tessa changed into a pair of jersey pajamas before pausing the security system and taking Badger outside. While he did an exploration of Jonah's front yard, she stood on the porch with her arms wrapped around herself. Full dark had fallen and it seemed to press in on her as if it were alive.

You are safe. You are strong. You can take care of yourself.

She squinted, trying to spot Badger among the rhododendron and mountain laurel. Patting her thigh, she called, "C'mon, King B. Let's go inside and get your dinner."

Normally the word *dinner* was enough to bring him racing back to her, but not tonight. A big clump of bushy ferns moved off to Tessa's right. *Gotcha.*

"Out of there, Badger."

A series of sharp high barks came from the edge of the yard. That was Badger's I-will-mess-you-up bark, and the sounds of it made Tessa's stomach contract.

Probably just a rabbit.

Still, she picked up a landscaping rock and tiptoed toward where Badger's barks were coming from. When she found her pup, he was standing at attention—tail rigid and the fur on his back in a mohawk of alarm—staring into the wooded area leading away from the house.

She grabbed him under the belly, settled him against her shoulder, and bolted for the front door. Badger's growl vibrated against her chest until they got inside and she locked the door and reset the security system.

Her heart was thumping in an uneven rhythm as she poured Badger's food in his bowl. He didn't give it a second glance, which never happened. Instead of going nose-deep into his kibble, he trotted back and forth in front of the great room windows.

This was western North Carolina, critter wonderland. Besides, Badger had scared off whatever had been out there.

Nothing to worry about.

15

TESSA FOUND A WET BAR TUCKED INTO ONE WALL OF JONAH'S living room and poured herself a generous serving of Far Niente cabernet. "King B, let's take your dinner upstairs."

It made no logical sense, but she would feel safer on the second floor.

For a second, she debated texting Jonah to see when he'd be back. No. She was just spooked. Maybe if she settled down with a movie, the story and the wine would center her.

In her room, Badger circled her feet until she picked him up. "I'm restless, too, buddy."

She flipped through the movies on her phone, choosing *The Empire Strikes Back*. Han and Leia's first kiss never failed to make her heart sigh, and the asteroid scene always made her blood pump faster.

Han Solo: *Never tell me the odds.*

That was probably also a good adage when it came to getting close to Jonah Steele. Because if Tessa had known how hard it would be to crack his shell, she might've talked herself out of pursuing him.

She glanced at the cushy reading chair in the corner. Comfortable as it appeared, it wasn't calling to her tonight. So she strolled down the hall until she came to a door she thought led into Jonah's bedroom. Some creative juggling allowed her to turn the doorknob and flip on the light.

Wow.

Two entire walls were floor-to-ceiling windows. The other two walls were paneled with horizontal heart pine boards. A king-size platform bed was tucked against one of the wood walls and above it hung a stylized depiction of a blond woman in a blue skinsuit. On her arm was some type of cannon, making it clear she was no one's damsel in distress.

Okay, so Jonah *wasn't* a sexist when it came to video game characters.

Tessa just needed to make sure he saw that she could be just as kick-ass as Ms. Blue Skinsuit. Maybe she didn't have weapons strapped to her arms, but she was far from defenseless.

She'd made damn sure of that.

The bed was covered in a down duvet and a woven throw, and on either side, pendant lights were centered over side tables. The corner area between the walls of windows was set up like a sitting room, with a leather love seat, a couple of mid-century chairs, and an ottoman serving as a coffee table. The ottoman was littered with haphazard stacks of graphic novels, manga, and gaming magazines.

She saw Jonah echoed everywhere. Smart design. Natural textures. Creative art. And sleek lines that deceptively camouflaged complexity.

Unable to help herself, she went to explore the master bathroom.

If the bedroom was *wow,* this room was *wooooow.* The

floor was covered with intricately patterned green and gray tile that led to a shower big enough for a cocktail party, but the fixture that captured Tessa's attention was the bathtub. If something that sumptuous could be called a tub.

With two levels, one built above the other, the continually running water cascaded. During her years of active recovery, her therapist had recommended that Tessa reconnect with her body. To reclaim it for herself. That process had started with warm, relaxing baths. Then she'd moved on to looking at her body through the water, reacquainting herself with what someone else had tried to take from her.

Water had helped her reclaim her confidence. Helped her regain comfort with her body.

The thought of being in that tub with Jonah, both of them slick and naked, made awareness sluice through her. Her nipples hardened and her thighs clenched. She wanted to back him against one of the sides, straddle him, and ride him until they were both out of their minds.

She could all but feel his big hands on her hips, lifting her, then pulling her down to fill her. Chest to chest, her arms around his neck, her lips on his.

The truth was she wanted to fuck that man's brains out. Wanted to screw him until he was too endorphined-out to resist her, to fight her anymore. She wanted him to see her as the woman she was now.

Wanted him to truly accept how amazing they could be together, both physically and emotionally. She and Jonah were meant to be together. She knew that as well as she knew her own name.

She returned to the sitting area in the bedroom, drank her wine, and watched half of the movie. But for once, it wasn't holding her interest. The day had finally worn her out. She wasn't willing to let Jonah slip past her when he came home.

She could've stretched out on the love seat, but the bed called to her. Of course Badger trotted over with her and scratched at the side of the mattress. "How about a pillow tonight? I'm not sure Jonah wants Badger fur in his bed."

Badger dropped back to all fours and gave her a disgruntled look over his shoulder. But when she placed a king-size pillow on the floor and patted it, he curled up on it with a huff.

She fiddled with the switch for the bedside light and discovered she could dim it rather than black out the room, which would make her rest easier. For the most part, she'd left the past where it belonged, but she liked to be able to see her surroundings.

Sliding between the smooth sheets, she caught Jonah's scent—cedar and leather—on the pillow. Yum. She wanted to bury her face in it. To satisfy her sensory urges, she settled onto her stomach and rubbed her cheek against the cool fabric. Within minutes her eyes were drooping.

I'll just rest them for a little while.

When Tessa woke, the room was black except for a fingernail moon glowing from outside the massive windows. Her fingers clutched at the sheets under her, but she refused to panic. Maybe the bedroom lights were on a timer. The switch was about six inches above the bedside table. All she had to do was reach out and—

A big hand landed on her right butt cheek and she squealed. With a desperate shove, she hit the switch and low light glowed. She fish-flopped to her back, which only moved the hand from her backside to her frontside.

Her thundering heartbeat throttled back slightly. She knew that hand, because it was attached to the dark-haired, scruffy-faced man currently breathing rhythmically in deep sleep. Why hadn't he woken her when he came in? Why hadn't Badger alerted her?

Thanks a lot, King B.

The duvet had been pushed down, revealing the broad bare expanse of Jonah's back. A tender impulse made Tessa want to press a kiss to each bump along his spine.

How could she get out of this awkward position without waking him? By his deep breathing, it was obvious the day had worn him out as much as it had her. Probably more, since he hadn't slept the night before.

To shift his hand away, she circled his right wrist just below his tattoo. The three connected triangles each held a jewel-toned gem. Every time she saw them, his tattoos set off heat low in her body. They were even sexier from this vantage point. Would they stretch over his forearm when he slid his fingers inside her? Would they flex and bunch when he withdrew and thrust in again?

She wanted to see that so badly. But not like this. Not while he was unaware.

Her touch must've set off some reflex. Because Jonah's fingers curled possessively between her legs, pressing the fabric of her pajamas against her and sending a jolt through her body. Her hips instinctively lifted.

Jonah's eyes opened. No sleepy haze. No foggy confusion. Just asleep one second, and awake the next. "What are you doing?" His voice was a sexy, sleep-roughened rumble.

"Um...ah...I was trying to..."

He glanced down and seemed to realize the location of his wayward hand. To her surprise, he didn't pull it away. Instead, one side of his mouth lifted in a bad-boy half smile.

And oh, that did her in. Set her on fire. Made her wet. Made her want.

He had to be able to feel her response.

And if he didn't do something about it, she would go to her room, dig out her vibrator, and stomp back here and...and...

"Something fierce just went through your mind," he said. "What was it?"

"That if you don't follow through on your hand's promise, I'm going to trade you in for a sex toy."

At that, he blinked.

"I was just trying to move your hand. I didn't want you to wake up and think I somehow tried to take advantage of you."

"Seeing as it's my hand on you, that doesn't really compute. Were you waiting on me in my bed?"

Oh, put that way, it did look more than a little calculated. "I had a glass of wine and watched part of a movie. I was sleepy, but didn't want to go back to my room because I knew you wouldn't wake me to talk."

"You were right."

"So this wasn't some big seduction plan."

"Then let's go back to sleep."

"I've had sex," she blurted out.

"I know because—"

"I've had sex with men besides you. Before whatever we did in Seattle and after."

"Oh." The word was more of an annoyed grunt than an expression of relief.

"Remember when you asked me about touching myself?"

"I'll remember until I'm a hundred."

"That was part of my recovery, learning that I had say-so over my body. That I could enjoy being touched again. That I was capable of sexual satisfaction. Now, I make my own choices about sex."

"That...that's good."

"And I choose you. But you have to choose me back. Why do you keep pushing me away?"

"I'm afraid I want you too much."

"How is that even possible?"

"I damn well don't deserve you!" He sat up and shoved his fingers into his hair. "Think about what happened when we were together in Seattle."

"Besides the five-star orgasm, you mean?"

"I ripped your clothes."

Yes, she still had that camisole tucked inside her bedroom drawer after all this time. Pulled it out on occasion to refresh her memory of what it felt like to be loved by Jonah Steele. "Thin straps and men don't always get along."

"You don't understand."

Oh, but she thought she might. "You're worried about something."

"I don't want to hurt you. In any way."

"And you think a seam popping somehow damaged me?"

"Tess, what you looked like sitting on my desk, top ripped, skirt shoved up to your..."

A flash of insight so bright that it almost blinded her bolted through her. He'd had some kind of flashback that night. That was why he'd pushed her away.

"You didn't hurt me. You won't hurt me. You can't."

"Maybe you haven't noticed that I'm twice your size."

Oh, she'd noticed. She'd also noticed he was half hard. Had been since he'd woken up with his hand between her legs.

"This isn't a good time," he said.

"When will it be a good time? Truth is, whether we do

this tonight or next month, I will still be a rape victim. People live and love with baggage all the time. If you really want to be with me, we have to get past it. Together."

With a flip of his wrist, he captured her hand and pressed it against the front of his shorts. "That's what you do to me." Each word was dripping in self-disgust. "And it makes me want to tear at your clothes, get between your legs, and..."

"Not made of glass, remember?" She squeezed his erection through the fabric of his sleep shorts, felt him expand in her hand. "You don't scare me."

His eyes closed and his jaw tightened as though he was fighting off pain, but he wrapped his hand around hers until they were both fisting his cock. "What's that feel like to you?"

"About the right number of inches for satisfaction."

The sound that came from Jonah's throat couldn't be mistaken for anything but what it was—an animalistic growl. And it rippled through Tessa's body, raising pricks of pleasure along her nerve endings.

16

"JONAH, YOU CAN'T HURT ME BECAUSE I WILL ALWAYS TELL YOU if something makes me uncomfortable," Tessa said. "And I trust you to listen."

I trust you. Her words reverberated through him.

Tessa pulled him down to the bed, rolled over, and aligned her body on his so they were pelvis to pelvis, chest to chest, face to face.

When she slid her lips across his, he was sunk. He'd been fighting his hunger for this woman for years, but he was all out of fight tonight. Honestly had no idea of what he was fighting anymore.

She was right. Who was he to judge and decide what was best for her?

He drew his hands up to cradle her head, sinking his fingers into her wild bedhead curls. With his mouth, he coaxed her lips open so he could taste her fully. Before they were done, he would know her entire flavor.

He wanted so many things when it came to this woman, it would take a lifetime to explore them all.

Lifetime. The word spiraled around in his head.

What would it be like to spend a lifetime with Tessa?

He didn't know, but tonight he would try to be what she needed.

Reluctantly, he drew away from her to reach for the bedside light switch.

Tessa opened dazed eyes. "What are you doing?"

"Turning off the light."

"I like to have the light on."

An uneasy feeling drew tight in Jonah's gut. In the dark, he could do this. But when he could see her, all of her, he just didn't know. Maybe they should just—

"I know that look on your face."

"What look?"

"It's the one that says you're on the verge of changing your mind."

"I prefer the dark."

"It's because of me, isn't it?"

He wasn't about to say yes. It *wasn't* because of her. It was because he hadn't allowed himself to forget a single thing about that night. Because he still had nightmares about it sometimes. But he couldn't replace those images with happier ones, healthier ones, if he never let go of the old ones. Let go of his fear about hurting her. He held out his hand to her. "How about a compromise?"

Now, she was the one to look uncertain as she stared at his outstretched hand. "I feel like we've been playing a strange game of sexual musical chairs. I'm ready for the music to stop for good."

His stomach still jumping, he said, "I promise."

When she took his hand, everything settled inside him. Into certainty. Into peace. Into smooth desire.

"Come with me." He led her from the bed into his over-the-top bathroom. Even his designer had lifted an eyebrow at the overkill in this room, but now Jonah was glad he'd fought for every detail. Nothing less would do justice to what was about to happen between Tessa and him.

He tapped a controller on the wall, and the waterfall stopped recirculating and began filling the tub. With another adjustment on the controller, a muted glow came from under the water.

Tessa leaned over to drag her fingers through the water. With her hair tumbling down her back, her beautiful skin and rumpled PJs, she was like the promise of a sunrise. And he could see her as if it were the first time. A new first time.

Smiling sheepishly, she looked back at him over her shoulder. "I snooped in here while you were gone."

"So you went through all the cabinets, made sure I had the proper number of towels and toilet paper rolls?"

Her laugh was soft. "No, I mean I came in here and gawked. I'm sorry I invaded your privacy."

He walked toward her and nothing else but Tessa existed for him in that moment. "You were sleeping in my bed when I came home. Do you really think I care if you opened every door in my house?"

"I overstepped all the way around."

"No, you were exactly where I wanted you."

He reached for the waistband on his shorts to shuck them, but before he could push them down, Tessa was on her knees running her fingers along the scar on the left side of abdomen. "What is this?"

Although the nerves under the slice of skin were shot, his dick twitched at her touch. Just the sight of her in front of him was enough to fill his head with pictures. Dirty, delicious pictures.

Her taking him in her mouth, taking him all in. The feel of her hair as he held her head and... He forced himself to focus on her question instead of the proximity of her mouth to his cock. "Stab wound."

Her head reared back and she stared up at him, her mouth open in surprise. "What?"

"Micki's boss wasn't too happy with having her family get in his way."

"You could've died."

"Nah." He chuckled. "He missed all the important stuff."

"Where else?" Now she was the one to grab for his waistband. "Where else were you hurt?"

Tessa was damn quick when properly motivated. One second, he had clothes on. The next, his shorts were on the floor and his dick was showing her its best snappy salute. But she ignored it, grabbing him by the hips and forcing him to turn.

Her sigh was one of relief, but the feel of her breath on his butt didn't bring him a bit of relief. She caressed his ass and scratched her fingernails over his skin.

He stepped out of his shorts, almost losing his balance in the process.

Tessa slid a hand between his legs to cup his balls, tight against his body. She pressed a kiss to his backside. "Jonah, I want to—"

"No." He knew exactly what she was about to say, and if she sucked his dick into her mouth right now, it would be over. He would snap, and she wouldn't trust him anymore.

Because tonight was about trust as much as it was about making love.

He grabbed her hands and drew her to her feet.

"Then at least let me look and touch." She shimmied out of her own pajama bottoms and kicked them away. Then she nudged him so they were facing the expansive mirror on one wall. She peeked around him, her curves—unfortunately still covered—plastered to his naked back.

When her hands began a slow drag over his skin, Jonah's body quivered with the perfection of her touch. They smoothed over his pectorals, stimulating his already hard nipples. Down they went, skimming his abs and the line of hair below his navel. She traced the length of his scar and gripped his hipbones.

Ignoring his rampant hard-on, she caressed his thighs, explored his knees, and spent way the hell too much time checking out his calves and ankles.

On her way back up, the soft fabric of her pajama shirt brushed against his already electrified skin. And when she finally circled his cock with both hands and pumped, he couldn't control the thrust of his hips.

"I like the way you look, Jonah Steele," she said softly. "I love the way you feel."

Something hard lodged in his chest—the pressure of doing all the right things, making all the right moves with Tessa. She was too important for anything less.

"This is your show tonight," he said. "You're totally in charge."

"Then why don't we check out that crazy tub of yours?"

He forced himself to move away and adjust the water controller back to the waterfall setting.

"I didn't just look around when I was in here earlier," she told him.

Hell, he wouldn't care if she'd dismantled the whole place as long as she stayed. His home—his life—felt right with her in it.

"I took one look at that tub, and I fantasized."

He wanted to give her every fantasy she could dream up. "About?"

"About you." She sauntered in his direction, slipping buttons loose on her pajama top with each step. Then she let it fall to the floor. Her naked breasts never failed to steal his breath. She looked like a woman was supposed to, with curves a man could sink into. Could lose himself in.

Could find himself in.

Tessa reached for her panties, but he grabbed her hands and pushed them away. "Mine."

He eased the fabric down her legs and the scent of her—hot and ready—waved over him. God, he was so needy, so hungry for her, that he could lay her out on this cold floor, push her legs wide, and drive in—

No driving. You're a passenger on this trip.

No matter what he wanted, her needs were more important. And a woman like Tessa would never want to be possessed the way he wanted to have her. So he pressed a quick kiss to her stomach and took her by the hand to lead her to the tub. He steadied her while she climbed two steps up and back down. With the lights glowing from below the water, an aura seemed to surround her. She glowed with beauty and vitality and feminine strength.

He went back to the vanity and riffled through a drawer for a condom. Covered, he climbed into the tub and lifted Tessa to sit on the side.

"Your body is...I don't even have words for it," he told her. "A damn miracle. I want to know exactly how you like to be touched."

She caught him around the waist with her legs and tried to draw him in. "Then come here and—"

"No. I need you to show me. I need you to touch yourself so I understand. So I can give you what you need." She'd been touched in such cruel and inhumane ways. He couldn't change the past, but he could make the future all about her.

She must've heard the rawness, the sheer truth of his words. "Where do you want me to touch myself?"

"Anywhere. Everywhere."

Her hand went to her breast and squeezed. Then she trailed her fingers down the outside. "My skin is sensitive here."

Jonah mirrored her movements on her other breast, and she shuddered. Her nipples were tight and dark, tempting him to reach out and touch, but he was playing by her rules.

Tessa's head lolled back as she circled her breast with two fingertips. When she reached the underside, she moaned and her calves moved restlessly under the water.

Jonah's muscles were taut with the need to push, go further and faster. But not until she did.

She moved her fingers to her nipple. There, her touch wasn't gentle. She twisted and tugged, and her knees parted.

"Stop," he demanded. "That has to hurt."

Her laugh was breathless. "Do you really want a lesson on sexual arousal and the accompanying increase in pain thresholds right now?"

Was that really a thing? He filed the relationship of pain to pleasure away for further research later. His hand was far from steady when he followed her lead and gently rolled her nipple between his fingers.

"Harder," she demanded.

"I don't want to—"

"I promise, I'll tell you if it doesn't feel good."

Fuck.

He applied a little more pressure, and her legs opened wide, revealing the glistening tender skin between them.

In. He wanted in.

When she moved her hand between her legs, Jonah's body went into a vacuum state. No freaking air anywhere.

He wanted to watch her pleasure herself for hours. She rubbed her clitoris, making it stand out stiff and proud. His heartbeat was pounding through his body so hard, he could barely hear the harsh sounds of his own breathing. "God, Tess, I want—"

"Mmm? What do you want?"

About her. About her. About her. It will always *be about her.*

"Whatever you want."

Her fingers still moving nimbly between her legs, she shook her head. "That wasn't what you were going to say."

The words and desires and needs whirled inside him, building and building. What was he supposed to say, that he wanted to put his mouth on her and tongue her until she screamed? That he wanted to turn her over and drive into her from behind? That he wanted to shove her up against a wall and fuck her until neither of them could stand upright?

A sly smile crossed her beautiful face. "Well, if you won't tell me, then I'll have to do something about this myself." She pushed off the tub's edge and waded toward the waterfall. Eyes narrowed, she put her hand under the stream of water and glanced around. She crooked a finger at him. "Looks like I need you after all."

"You have me." For anything that brought her pleasure.

"Stand right here and put your hands under my back." With that, she reclined in a float position and hooked her legs over the edge of the tub. Which positioned her clitoris directly under the water flow.

Oh, fuck. Made perfect sense now.

She moaned her approval at having the water pound down on her. And all he could do was stand here holding her and watch a faucet do all the work. Within seconds,

Tessa's hips were working, doing whatever necessary for the water to flow over the right spot.

When she came, it was on a long, lusty groan that emerged from somewhere deep inside her. After, she went limp in his hold, but Jonah was feeling anything but satisfied and mellow. In fact, the condom he'd put on felt as if it was about to cut off circulation to his dick.

He tugged her back toward the side of the tub. She was as malleable as a rag doll when he settled on a built-in seat and pulled her into his lap so they were chest to breasts.

"That's the way—uh-huh, uh-huh—I like it," she sang softly, making him laugh. She melted against him, wrapping her arms around his shoulders, spreading her knees to straddle him and pressing her mouth to his.

Her kiss kicked what little control he had to the curb. She was using her tongue aggressively, making it clear she wanted him to follow her lead.

Jaw tight, he grasped her hips and lifted her until his cock was snug against the entrance to her body. "Are you sure?"

She released his mouth and looked—really looked—into his eyes. "I want you, Jonah. I want you inside me."

His hips surged up and he pushed into her silky heat. Ah, Jesus. It was better than he remembered. She was tight and so fucking hot. Still, he made himself keep control, using short, shallow thrusts.

Her smile was lazy and relaxed. Not exactly the reaction he was looking for. "Tessa!"

"Hmm?"

The last thing he wanted to do was ask if it was good for her. Obviously, he wasn't rocking her world the way a stupid waterfall could. "I want you to feel good."

"I do."

"I want you to lose your mind, it feels so good."

"You sure?"

Nah, he was just fucking around. "Yes, dammit!"

To his supreme disappointment, she pushed up from his lap, separating their bodies. She held out her hand to him. "You need to understand that I'm not fragile. Come here."

She led him to the plush rug in front of the full-length mirror. Okay, fine, they could do this again. But she shocked the shit out of him when she dropped down on all fours, and lowered her head. A submissive position no man could misinterpret.

When he didn't follow, she glanced up at him. "I'm choosing, Jonah. And I choose you."

A chunk of cement he'd been carrying around in his chest loosened. She trusted him. Really trusted him. And that was a gift he would kill himself before he squandered.

He knelt behind her, ran a hand down her back as if he were touching a religious object. She turned her head to meet his gaze in the mirror, and in that moment, with hot honest need and desire in her eyes, he was lost.

She arched her back and opened for him. And this time, when Jonah slid inside her, her expression wasn't relaxed. It was full of stunned pleasure.

Her heat surrounded his cock, tightened his belly, and spread up his chest. The feeling traveled to his head and scorched his brain.

With each stroke, he pushed a little harder, went a little deeper. Until Tessa was on her elbows, her cheek against the rug. Their eye contact never broke until her arms splayed out to her sides and her body began to ripple around his.

He drew back, almost out of her body, then thrust forward and held. The orgasm ripped through him, squeezing his balls and stealing his breath, while she continued to come around him.

With the force of it all, Jonah's body went into pleasure shock. But when Tessa smiled at him, that was when his world exploded and reassembled.

17

BECAUSE HE HADN'T ENGAGED THE ELECTRONIC BLACKOUT shades over his windows last night, the inevitable North Carolina sunshine splashed across Jonah's bed. But rather than aggravation at being awakened too early, a feeling of contentment filled him.

That sense of satisfaction had everything to do with the woman snuggled against his side. Being with Tessa—*really* being with her last night—was better than anything he could've imagined. She'd understood his needs, his wants, and hadn't turned away.

Hadn't been threatened. Or disgusted. Or frightened.

He smoothed his hand over her hair and spiraled a curl around his finger. Although he needed to get up and get to work on tracking down the hacker, he couldn't resist leaning in for a kiss. She came awake slowly, her muscles engaging, and she slipped an arm around his waist so they could turn fully into one another.

Maybe, if they kept making love the way they had last night, he could be himself with her. Let her see inside him in a way he'd never believed he could. Had never believed she would want.

He worked his thigh between hers and found that her body—though still pliant with sleep—was totally on board with his touch. He was reaching for her breast, his anticipation rising, when his bedroom door slammed against the wall.

"What the fuck, Baby Billionaire? Why are you still in bed?"

He was going to kill them. Slowly. And painfully.

He'd start with Reid. Then he'd let Grif and Britt flip for next in line.

Then he would change the code on his security system and never give it to them again.

Jonah angled his body to shield Tessa and yanked the sheet up to cover the breasts he was just about to get up close and personal with. He looked over his shoulder to find his three brothers crowded inside the room. Reid's hands were making mallet-sized fists, Britt's were on his hips, and Grif's were brushing at lint on his pressed dress shirt. As if lint would have the balls to taint his clothes.

"Get out," he snapped.

"Nuh-uh," Reid shot back. "You cut us out once. What the hell were you thinking by not letting us know you put Mrs. Vanderwinkle in traction?

"She's not in traction, you assbrain." Like a pin in her hip was any better. Jonah was still sick over it.

"We're not gonna turn around and leave, pretending something isn't going on with you."

Grif gave Jonah a half smile. "I sure as hell can't carry him out of here. He weighs as much as a silverback."

That was an exaggeration, a slight one.

Jonah glanced back at Tessa, who was lying there, eyes

and mouth open wide. Not surprising since they were both buck-ass naked.

"For once," Britt said in his calm eldest brother voice, "Reid is right. Our name is on this town, too, and we need you to tell us why you put a senior citizen in the hospital."

"If you shitheads will give me five minutes, I'll—"

"Screw that." Before Jonah could react, Reid stomped over and yanked the comforter off the bed. Then he froze and squeezed his eyes shut. "Oh, hell." Without looking, Reid shoved the big wad of fabric toward Jonah. "I'm sorry. We didn't realize she was...you were..."

Grif's laughter was loud and clear. "Wait until Brynne hears about this snafu. She's gonna send you to etiquette classes. Maybe make you do a cotillion."

Even serious Britt cracked a small smile at that. "Why don't we head back downstairs and wait for Jonah in the kitchen?"

Reid did an about-face, and they filed out.

Tessa's hands flew from where they'd been clutching the covers to her face. "Do you think he saw anything?"

God, he was at a loss here. Would knowing that his brother had probably gotten a good eyeful of her beautiful body freak her out? Would she see it as some kind of violation?

"He closed his eyes immediately."

"Because he got a gander at my ass."

Wisely, Jonah didn't mention it was unlikely, based on the fact that she was lying on her back. It was more likely that Reid caught a glimpse of her stellar tits. "He didn't mean to, and he's sorry. It's okay. None of them would ever do anything to hurt you. Reid's just a big oaf sometimes."

She pushed at his shoulder and struggled to sit up. "I'm

not scared of them, but I didn't want to be naked the first time I officially met them."

"It does make handshaking slightly more complicated, doesn't it?" He was trying like hell not to laugh, now that he knew she wasn't traumatized.

"It puts me at a disadvantage," she huffed, and her breasts bounced near his face.

"This isn't some kind of judgment. They're my family." The idiot part of the family, but still.

"It's a little easier to make a good impression when my hair is fixed and I'm fully dressed."

Unable to resist the temptation any longer, he leaned forward and kissed her right nipple. "You make a hell of an impression just like this."

When he drew her into his mouth and scraped his teeth across her delicate skin, she gasped and arched her back. With her skin gleaming in the sunlight, she was the most beautiful woman Jonah had ever seen. Like a goddess that women prayed to emulate and men prayed to serve.

He certainly wouldn't mind settling between her legs and serving her all day long with his mouth. "Tessa, I want to—"

"Uh-uh." She pushed him away from her breast, nipple gleaming and pointing. It needed his attention. Immediately.

"Maybe the three stooges will go away."

Tessa's supremely kissable lips twisted wryly. "You really think so?"

"Fuck," he sighed. "Not really."

"Then maybe you should go down and fill them in while I put myself together." Tessa patted her wild hair. "I just need a few minutes to get in the shower and tame this."

He picked up her hand and pressed a kiss to it. "Tessa, I

want you to remember something. Put together or not, you are perfect."

With every minute he spent with her, he was beginning to believe she was perfect for him.

TESSA DIDN'T DAWDLE IN THE BATHROOM, DID A QUICK SPLASH and dry, then twisted her hair up into something she hoped looked respectable. She pulled on a pair of wool pants, a white shirt, a cashmere blazer, and loafers. But when she and Badger hurried down the staircase to the main level, she knew something was wrong. Four men together were never this quiet. Maybe they were in Jonah's tech cave.

She gave them the benefit of the doubt until she opened the door and found the room soundless except for the hum of the arsenal of computer equipment. Damn him. She'd made it perfectly clear that she wouldn't play powerless princess to his rescuing prince.

She checked the garage for his Tesla. Still there. Then she looked for a car out front. Nothing.

Which meant Jonah and his brothers were gone.

On the security panel near the front door, he'd left a hastily scrawled Post-It. *Brothers demanding answers. Back soon. Sit tight. J-*

Sit tight? He was out of his mind. Without debating the wisdom of what she was about to do, she ran back upstairs to grab her phone. As she had last night, she PMed Brynne.

Tessa: *Would you happen to know where the Steele men are?*

Brynne: *Last I heard, they were headed up to Jonah's. Haven't you seen them?*

Did *she* see *them*? Not exactly. But how could she tell Brynne that her husband had *seen* her head to toe?

Tessa: *They stopped by. I hopped in the shower and when I came out, they were gone.*

Brynne: *Reid was pissy last night. I had to watch him pace and cuss for half an hour.*

Tessa: *I'm really sorry about that.*

Brynne: *LOL. It happens at least once a week. That's just Reid. But when the guys get mad at one another, they tend to settle it with guns.*

Tessa's throat twisted.

Tessa: *What?*

Brynne: *Yeah, they've got a bunch of old toys they apparently started out playing with, but now they've moved on to big-boy paintball guns.*

The tight feeling in Tessa's throat eased a little.

Tessa: *Do you know where I could find them?*

Brynne: *Tell you what, drive to Miss Joan's house and we'll go find them together.*

Tessa: *Which is where?*

Brynne: *White farmhouse down the road. You passed it on the way to Jonah's.*

Normally, she wouldn't have minded what had to be a mile walk, but she hadn't thought to bring tennis shoes on what was supposed to be a quick overnight stay.

Tessa: *I don't have a car. Mine's still in town.*

Brynne: *Take one of Jonah's. He won't miss it. Keys are in the freezer. See you in ten.*

It went against Tessa's grain to take someone's possession without asking, but what choice did she have? She certainly wasn't going to wait around for Jonah to mosey back home.

She fed Badger, let him out to potty, and then kenneled him. Much to his annoyance. He gave her a doggy huff and turned so his little butt was pressed against the metal door, a sure sign he was pissed at her.

Back in the kitchen, she shoved aside a package of steaks in the freezer and spotted a plastic baggie that held keys. Honest to goodness old-fashioned keys rather than modern key fobs.

In Jonah's garage, she studied his toys with a closer eye. They sure ran the gamut. A shiny blue truck with wooden sideboards that seemed like something a hip organic farmer would drive. A silver Mercedes with the gull-wing doors. A little white Fiat convertible that looked as if it still needed some TLC. The Tesla. And an orange car sporting a spoiler taller than the roof panel. It had the back-end of a road-runner and the sleek, sloping front-end of a shark.

Oh, yeah. She wanted that one.

She dug through the bag of keys and pulled out one for a Plymouth. A small pang of guilt shimmied through her when she slid into the black leather driver's seat. But when she pushed the button on the visor to raise the garage door and cranked the car, that pang was drowned out by the sound of the engine rumbling.

She shivered at the vibrations shimmying through the metal and into her seat, reawakening all the nerve endings Jonah had turned on last night. What would he say if she suggested a make-out session in his car?

It would be fun to do something so carefree and youthful. Normal. Something she'd never done as a teenager.

The road from Jonah's house to his mom's was too curvy for Tessa to push the car. It reminded her of making love with Jonah—a lot of restrained power in a sleek package. But all it took was the right touch to turn potential into reality.

Last night, he'd been cautious, resistant at first. But

when she'd finally convinced him to stop being careful...
Whew. That had been brain-bending. She had light burn
marks on her knees. Marks she wouldn't show Jonah for
fear he'd see them and feel guilty.

He was so sure he would hurt her that he wasn't willing
to reveal himself and his true desires. His true wants.

His true needs.

And if he wasn't willing to share those things with her,
their relationship would come to a standstill. Because she
wasn't willing to settle for anything besides the truth.

And Tessa's truth was that she wanted Jonah like he'd
been last night. But even more out of control. Completely
out of control.

And probably not what she should be thinking about
when she was about to meet his mom for the first time. She
pulled into the drive in front of the white farmhouse.
Cheerful Adirondack chairs were scattered along the deep
porch. Holiday greenery was looped around the porch rails,
and two potted evergreens flanked a front door decorated
with a wreath made of magnolia leaves and red ribbon.

She'd barely knocked when the door was pulled open to
reveal a small woman with short silver-shot hair and a
welcoming smile that emphasized the laugh lines around
her eyes. "You must be Tessa."

How had she known?

"I know all kinds of things about my kids they don't
know I know." She waved Tessa into the farmhouse and led
her toward the kitchen. "Then I have insurance when I
need it."

"It's nice to meet you, Mrs. Steele."

"Call me Miss Joan. Everyone else does."

"I'm sorry to just barge in, but I'm looking for Jonah
and—"

"Brynne called to tell me to expect you. Give her a few minutes and she should be here. Would you like a cup of pecan coffee and some breakfast while you wait?"

"I wouldn't want to be any trouble." What she wanted was to find Jonah and line up their next move against the hacker, but Tessa's stomach folded into a hunger cramp at the mention of food. And thanks to the delicious, nutty scent coming from the welcoming kitchen, she'd break her I-don't-drink-much-coffee rule.

"You can't be more trouble than one of my own kids," Miss Joan said, her voice full of love and pride. "Stubborn and strong-minded, the lot of them."

"They're lucky to have you." Talking with her and smelling the scent of a real home made Tessa long to see her own parents. She'd lived on the other coast for so many years that it didn't faze them if she only called once every couple of weeks. But since someone had breached her files and started playing head games with Jonah and her a few days ago, she hadn't spoken with her mom and dad at all.

Miss Joan pulled out a chair at the expansive wood and metal farm table and bustled over to the counter. "Sit and I'll fix it for you."

Having Jonah's mother treat her like a family friend unnerved Tessa. "You don't know me from Adam."

She turned back to meet Tessa's gaze. "Sweetheart"—both her eyes and tone held sympathy—"I probably know more about you than you wish I did, what with all that trouble Micki was in last year."

"If I'd known sooner about her boss's threats, I would've—"

"Of course you would have." With a wave, Miss Joan turned back to the coffeepot. "I know who your people are, what kind of girl you are."

It seemed Tessa was at quite a disadvantage here. Would Jonah's family ever stop catching her with her pants down... *Don't think about that.*

A mug of delicious-smelling coffee, cream, and sugar seemed to materialize in front of Tessa. She stirred in a little cream and had taken her first sip when Miss Joan said, "Reid told me you were something else."

Coffee backed up mid-swallow and tried to make a detour up Tessa's nose. She coughed, covering her mouth and nose with a napkin. When she had herself more or less under control, she croaked out, "Reid?"

With a grimace, Miss Joan propped a hand on one hip. "Sorry, but we're a nosy family. He looked into you quite a bit last year."

Thank. The. Lord. Jonah's older brother hadn't spilled the beans to his mom that he'd caught her naked in Jonah's bed this morning.

"Gave me the background on your family and what you've made of your life since...since..."

"The rapes."

This time, Miss Joan was the one to swallow, and her eyes filled. "Tessa, I know you may not feel totally comfortable with this, but would you let me give you a hug?"

Although she *was* unbalanced by the request, Tessa stood and Miss Joan hurried over to wrap her in her arms. It wasn't a quick squeeze. She gave Tessa a loving mom's I-can-hold-you-together hug, one that made you feel as if the chipped and jagged pieces were being glued back together. Tessa knew them well because her mom had given them so many times, especially in the first few years after the rapes.

Tessa returned the hug and they were still standing there, rocking right and left, when Brynne walked in. "I see you two are already fast friends," she said with a sweet smile. Today, she was dressed in black skinny pants tucked into brown wedge boots and a sweater that sparkled gold, silver, and bronze in the kitchen light.

Miss Joan finally released Tessa, but gave her a soft pat on the cheek. "Sweetheart, you will do. You will do very well."

Tessa wasn't completely sure what she meant, but Miss Joan's oblique approval warmed her inside.

"Are the guys already at it?" Brynne asked Miss Joan.

"Oh, mercy yes. They stormed in here like a bunch of hooligans, grabbed go-cups of coffee, and loaded up the back of Reid's truck with paintball paraphernalia from the barn."

"So they play war games on a regular basis?" Tessa asked. That wasn't particularly convenient this morning, when she and Jonah needed to talk through everything that had happened the past few days.

Brynne and Miss Joan exchanged a look that was half affection and half exasperation. "Apparently," Brynne said, "you can take the man out of the mountains, but you can't take the mountain out of the man."

"They tend to go off and shoot at each other when one of them has a problem to work out," Miss Joan added. "Women are civilized. We have a cup of coffee and talk. Men need to burn off some of that intense emotion before they're able to have a sensible conversation about anything."

Didn't anyone besides Tessa realize Jonah beat himself up for his own intense feelings and desires?

She turned at the sound of a door opening and closing, and a few seconds later, a woman walked in who could only be one person. Jonah's twin. Micki was tall and lean like Jonah and her eyes were that same shrewd hazel that missed nothing around her. The Micki avatar the hacker had added to Jonah's game was right on the money.

"I heard there's a paintball game," Micki said.

"They're already out in the woods."

"Those jackasses went without me," Micki fumed. Then, with a sheepish look, she said to her mom, "Sorry about the language."

"If I worked myself up into a tizzy every time one of you said a bad word, I'd be spun up like the Tasmanian Devil all the time."

That's when Micki seemed to realize Tessa was standing there. "Oh, hey. You're—"

"—Tessa. It's nice to finally meet you." And it was a true first meeting, since Tessa didn't remember much about the last and only time they'd seen one another.

She held out her hand, but Micki completely bypassed it and grabbed her in a fierce hug. Wow, apparently the Steeles were huggers. And for such a thin woman, Micki sure was strong. Her tone was just as fierce when she said, "Thank you. I wanted to call you myself, but Jonah told me it might stir up things better left alone. But I want you to know not a day goes by that I'm not grateful for what you did for us last year."

"And I'm just as grateful for both of you."

"Enough said, then." Micki blew out a breath and released her. She looked Tessa up and down, then nodded —a slow, thoughtful motion. "You know how to shoot a rifle?"

Ah...what? Tessa blinked. "It's been awhile, but—"

"Good, because not only does Brynne here dress for the runway instead of the battlefield, but she's also a pacifist. However, she *is* good for carrying ammo." Micki sauntered over to the coffeepot and poured some into a thermal cup. "Ladies, let's adjourn to the barn."

Before Micki could make for the back door, Miss Joan pressed a kiss to her cheek. "Don't hurt them too badly, okay?"

Micki's grin was pure wicked intent. "They'll all come back alive. That's all I can promise you."

Miss Joan heaved a dramatic sigh, but it was clear by the sparkle in her eyes that she enjoyed her grown kids' shenanigans. What an intriguing family they were. If Tessa had known that when she was doing her graduate work, she might've used them for a case study. The dynamics were multifaceted and downright fascinating.

And whether or not she realized it, by inviting her to play paintball with them, Micki had thrown out a challenge Tessa couldn't resist. Time to unleash a little kick-ass girl power. She would track down Jonah and shoot a paintball right between his eyes so they could get back to their search.

She glanced down at her loafers. "Don't guess you'd happen to have an extra pair of sneakers, would you?"

Miss Joan kicked off the Chuck Taylors she was wearing. "Size six work okay?"

"They'll be a little tight, but—"

"Mom," Micki said, "don't expect them to come back clean."

Miss Joan's response was a careless wave. "Tessa, how about you bring them back for a victory lap?"

"I'll see what I can do."

Before Micki could drag them outside, her mother fixed go-cups for Brynne and Tessa, putting the perfect amount of cream in Tessa's.

Sharp, sharp lady.

Tessa, Brynne, and Micki trooped out to the barn, and Brynne never missed a step in her tall boots.

Micki hooked a thumb toward her. "She's a marvel, isn't she?"

"Brynne or Miss Joan?"

The laughter that came from Micki was low and genuinely amused. "Both, but for different reasons. I've never known a woman who could get as much done in a four-inch pair of heels as our Brynne can. And Mom, well, she's the best. No other way to describe her."

After Micki had been estranged from her family for so many years, it appeared she was now happy and whole.

Then why was Jonah still fighting to do the same?

Inside the barn, Micki rummaged through a rack of paint-splattered coveralls. She pulled out a pair and held them next to Tessa, looking her up and down again. "The guys, Evie, and I all have our own custom gear, but we keep a few extra on hand for guests. This one'll be a little long on you and with your bodacious rack, it might be a little tight across the chest."

Tessa eyed the heavyweight khaki canvas. She was going to strain that thing in the bust and butt. "Do I just put this on over my clothes?"

"They're thick," Micki said, "but sometimes the paint still bleeds through." She fingered the sleeve of Tessa's jacket. "This doesn't look like something you want ruined."

Lovely. She was about to get almost naked in front of Jonah's sister and sister-in-law. No better way to get to know the family. She toed off her favorite pair of Stuart Weitzmans and dropped Miss Joan's sneakers to the ground.

Micki stripped down efficiently, revealing a sports bra and a pair of boy shorts emblazoned with the Captain

America logo on the rear. She shrugged into her coveralls and zipped them up.

Much as she might want to, Tessa refused to turn her back to change. She slipped off her blazer and slacks to hang them over a hook on the wall, then unbuttoned her shirt.

Micki's whistle echoed in the cavernous barn. "Holy shit, that is some underwear."

For once, Tessa wished she wore cotton bras and panties.

With an avaricious gaze, Brynne sidled close to Tessa and held out her hand as if planning to check the tags. "Are those La Perla?"

"No, they're made by a small company in Atlanta. I...ah... they're probably overkill, but..."

"But they make you feel like a bazillion bucks," Brynne said. "Don't feel guilty for spoiling yourself. Those are decadent."

"Good going, Martin," Micki said. "You've just given Brynne a panty-gasm."

"I won't rest until I track down the manufacturer and convince them to let La Belle Style sell their merchandise."

Tessa tried to step into her coveralls but her foot became caught. She would've face-planted if Micki hadn't grabbed her arm.

"Bet our boy Jonah is a big fan of their wares, too." Micki wore a half smile as if waiting for Tessa to confirm or deny.

Nope. Not today.

"I'm not trying to be a nosy witch," Micki said. "But I love my brother."

"Things are complicated right now."

"Life is complicated. Ask any one of the Steele siblings. None of us have gotten our happy ever after without a decent amount of struggle."

Except for Jonah. And Tessa would love to give him that.

She shoved her arms into the coveralls and shrugged them over her shoulders. She pulled the zipper only to find Micki had been right on. Getting the thing to fasten over her boobs was a struggle. When she finally zipped it to her throat, she looked down to find her chest smashed like a pancake.

Brynne chuckled at Tessa's plight. "Think of it this way. You don't have to worry about support while you're running around in the woods."

"Enough girly tits and panties bonding crap." Micki thrust a helmet and gun into Tessa's hands. "Let's go kick some ass."

———

18

WHEN JONAH WOULDN'T OPEN UP AND IMMEDIATELY SPILL HIS guts about the clusterfuck with Mrs. Vanderwinkle, his brothers decided they needed to take this thing to the woods. *If we can't talk it out of you, then we'll shoot it out of you.*

But he knew what would come after paintball. His brothers would nag the shit outta him until he spilled everything about what had happened the past few days.

Yippee.

Sometimes it really sucked being the youngest brother.

Good thing he knew he could win this paintball game fast. After checking the traps he'd come out and set up a couple weeks ago, he climbed his cold ass up into an old deer blind.

And waited.

He really didn't have time for this. He should climb down, hoof it back to his house, and try to nail that modder-hacker-bastard. He still hadn't heard back from the bartender at Tucci's, and it was making him twitchy. But on the way to his mom's house, he'd gotten in touch with Steele Trap's HR director and learned that Carson Grimes had recently taken a job at a Charlotte biotech. He intended to pay Grimes a visit pronto.

The forest around him was alive with the sounds of bird calls and scuffling in the underbrush, which either meant none of his brothers were in the area or they were being so stealthy that even the animals didn't realize they were around.

Out of his peripheral vision, he caught a shimmer of movement. *Gotcha.*

Grif came strolling out from behind a tree as if he were meandering down Rodeo Drive. His coveralls were pristine and his helmet gleamed as if he'd waxed the damn thing. What guy looked that put together to play paintball? Made Jonah want to nail him in the ass just for that.

"I know you're up there," Grif called, his voice muffled by his protective helmet. "Go ahead and shoot."

Fine. The sooner he took them all out, the sooner he could get back to the business at hand.

Jonah's finger twitched on the trigger.

"You know you want to."

He did. Right now, he wanted to take aim and leave a big red splotch right in the center of Grif's visor.

"Hurry up, or I might decide to shoot you instead," Grif taunted. "Britt and Reid are over in the ravine. If you take me down, you can get over there and sneak up on them from behind."

When it came to playing games, most people believed they had to work within the rules. But Jonah knew there were always more ways to get what he wanted, was always a back door. He reached into the pocket of his coveralls and fingered the secret weapon he'd stashed there when they'd been suiting up in the barn earlier.

If Grif would just take half a dozen more steps to the west, Jonah could...

Hands on his hips, Grif strolled over and looked up at the blind Jonah was ducked down in. Damn, his brother was the perfect target. But rather than blast him with a paintball, Jonah pulled the trap he'd rigged for just this occasion.

One second, Grif was standing on so-called solid ground, the next he disappeared into a holding pit Jonah had dug when they were excavating for his house.

One down.

"You cheating son of a bitch," Grif called from the hole. "This is paintball."

Jonah climbed down from the blind and peered into the well-padded ten-feet-deep temporary prison. It wasn't meant to harm, just hold someone for a little while. "Nuh-uh. This is Steele Survivor."

"Reid and Britt are gonna annihilate your ass."

"We'll see about that." Grinning so hard it strained his cheeks, Jonah loped off toward the ravine. After days of uncertainty and frustration over this hacker, it felt damn good to be at the top of his game.

Jonah found Reid and Britt exactly where Grif said they'd be. Apparently, they'd decided to partner up until they took out Grif and Jonah. *That's about to go sideways, you lunkheads.*

Good thing Jonah had been secretly preparing for a day like today. He tossed a pine cone off to the right of where his brothers were hunkered down behind a cedar tree. As expected, their heads swiveled in that direction.

C'mon. This one's for Britt.

Sure enough, Reid gave the hand signal for Britt to check it out. Although Britt was the unofficial head of the

Steele family, when it came to battle plans, they all deferred to Reid.

Just three more steps and—

Whomp! From a nearby tree, the modified mace Jonah had crafted swung and broadsided Britt, the pine sap-covered volleyball connecting with his helmet and sticking. Jonah would probably owe his brother new gear for that, but seeing Britt scan the woods feverishly for the enemy was so worth it.

Two down and one to go.

As if he had all the time in the world, Jonah patiently waited for Reid to realize his comrade in arms was no longer in the game. Sure enough, Reid went to investigate and stomped around Britt when he found him standing there, volleyball glued to his head.

Reid didn't release Britt because that would be breaking the rules of engagement. But his face took on a determined stubbornness that in Jonah's younger days would've meant a wedgie or a toilet dunking was in his future.

Not today, big brother.

Jonah had deliberately laid a very subtle trail on his way to the ravine. Of course, Reid picked it up quickly and a smug smile crossed his face. At one point, he squatted down to check the leaves in his path. He swung his head left, then right, and just as Jonah had anticipated, he chose the path less traveled.

He'd taken all of ten steps when Jonah's trap engaged. A camouflaged rope tightened around Reid's ankle, pulled his feet out from under him, and yanked him three feet off the ground. Hanging there upside down, Reid used every cuss word in the book and some even Jonah had never put together. He was especially impressed with *ass-chatting fucknut.*

Whatever that meant.

With the way Reid was thrashing and cussing, it was a good thing Jonah had decided on a one-inch diameter bungee shock cord rather than some old rope from the barn. Feeling pretty damn proud of himself, Jonah climbed down from the tree the net was hanging from and sauntered up to his older brother.

"Don't walk up here looking like you own the world," Reid said. "Grif is still out there. He may dress like a city boy, but he shoots the way he was raised."

"He's currently cooling his heels in a pit."

"Sheeeeeit," Reid drawled.

"And since I'm the Steele Survivor, the three of you have to do anything I tell you to for the next twenty-four hours."

"What the hell? That's never been part of the game."

"Winner makes the rules." Damn, it felt good to get the better of his brothers. As a kid, Steele Survivor had been Jonah's way of melding real life with his video game ideas to get the best of both worlds. Taking the beautiful North Carolina mountains and making boys' play accessible to kids all over the world.

"And you have no intention of telling us why you body-tackled Mrs. Vanderwinkle, do you?"

"My problem, and I'll solve it."

"That's not the way it works. We're a family. We handle things together."

"I—" Before Jonah could finish his rebuttal, something whacked him in the center of the back with the force of a...a paintball. "That doesn't—"

"Don't say it doesn't count," Micki said. "Tessa got you fair and square."

Tessa?

He swung around to find Micki and Tessa grinning at

him from the trees. Brynne was behind them carrying an armload of ammo. In a helmet, sneakers, and coveralls clinging to her curves, Tessa looked as if she should either be a mechanic in Grand Theft Auto or a driver in Ridge Racer.

His dick took one look and woke the hell up.

Great. Now he'd never again be able to play two of his all-time faves without getting a stiffy.

"And didn't I just hear you say that the Steele Survivor gets to make the rules for a day?" Tessa asked sweetly, so sweetly it made his teeth ache.

"You and Micki are still both live players."

Without so much as an eyelid twitch, Tessa shot his sister in the foot.

Tessa was still glowing from her victory after she and Jonah changed out of their paintball coveralls and were back in street clothes. He held the farmhouse's front door and followed her outside. "I need to make a quick trip to Charlotte."

"You just told your family you would explain what's going on."

His mouth was turned down, making her cuddle him. But this wasn't the time to be sympathetic. He needed to let his family in. "I will. Later."

Uh-uh. Something about this was hinky. "Keeping people in the dark never comes to good."

"This isn't their deal, and I don't want them in anyone's crosshairs."

Crosshairs. Charlotte. "Why the sudden need to go to Charlotte?" she demanded.

She made her way down the steps and realized halfway

to the car that he wasn't behind her. He was standing on the porch staring at his shark car, the one she'd taken from his garage. "You drove Clementine?"

Oh, yeah. That was a perfect name for this delicious car. Sweet with a distinctive bite. "Yes."

"She's a four-speed."

"I know what to do with a gear shift."

At that, he cut her a speculative look, which served to remind her exactly what she'd done with *his* gear shift last night. If she had her way, she'd be test-driving him again soon.

"She's a 1970 Plymouth Hemi Superbird," he said.

No wonder it had made her think of a roadrunner. "I like her. A lot."

"The interior is all restored original."

Tessa rolled her eyes skyward. "I didn't take a box cutter to the seats."

"Don't joke about that. It actually happened to Grif once."

Trying not to get defensive because Jonah was looking at her as if she'd threatened his firstborn, she waved at the car. "You left me. I came downstairs and you were gone. What else did you expect me to do?"

"Sorry." He winced. "Since I moved out of Mom's house, I'm not used to checking in with anyone. And my brothers can be very *persuasive.*"

"Next time, do more than leave a note." She unlocked the driver's door and glared at him across the top of the car. "Get in. I'm driving you to Charlotte. Can you ask one of your brothers to check on Badger?"

"Dammit, Tessa."

"After last night, I thought you'd stopped shutting me

out. You can't do one thing with your body and another with your mind."

His face took on a stubborn cast.

Uh-uh, buddy.

She would use whatever weapon she had to. "Last night, I was so tired and then I was so *busy* that I forgot to mention something."

"What?"

"When I took Badger outside, something was rustling around at the edge of the yard." Now his expression turned dangerous, so she hurried on. "It was probably nothing, but now I'm a little nervous about staying alone."

"If something else like that happens, you tell me immediately. I mean it."

Success! "So why are we going to Charlotte?"

"To talk to Carson Grimes."

He'd planned to do it behind her back. He would've if she hadn't pushed the issue.

Once Jonah was inside, Tessa cranked the car. She was tempted to gun it just to spite him, but she and Clementine had bonded earlier, so she wasn't eager to take her frustration out on her new friend.

Wow, she'd made a lot of new friends today, hadn't she? Miss Joan and Brynne and Micki.

And she'd won a game of Steele Survivor. She was kind of a badass.

She injected that into her voice when she told Jonah, "Don't do it again. Don't ever leave me behind to protect me."

By the time he and Tessa made it to the Charlotte biotech company where Carson Grimes worked, Jonah was so on edge it took all his acting skill to smile at the receptionist and casually lean a hip against her desk. "We're looking for a new employee of yours. Name's Carson Grimes."

The receptionist's brow furrowed for a few seconds, then her face brightened. "Oh, you mean the one from Seattle."

"That's him."

She picked up her phone receiver, her finger hovering over the buttons. "May I give him your names?"

Jonah upped his smile a notch even though it pained him. "We'd really like it to be a surprise. We're old friends and we wanted to welcome him to town."

"Gotcha." She hit a couple of buttons and smiled flirtatiously at Jonah while she waited. "Is this Carson? Great. You have some people here to see you. You can meet them in the reception area."

When she replaced the receiver, her expression turned apologetic. "Sorry, but I can't let you in the office since you don't have an appointment."

"No problem," Tessa chimed in, her voice cheerful. "We completely understand corporate espionage when it comes to R and D." But her smile at Jonah was edged with shark teeth. Yeah, she still hadn't forgiven him for trying to ditch her.

Rather than standing in eyesight of the hallway he assumed Carson would emerge from, Jonah waved Tessa toward the exterior door, "We're going to step outside for some fresh air," he told the receptionist. "Carson can meet us out front."

Outside, Tessa asked, "Why not talk to him in the lobby?"

"Because I didn't want him to bolt." He urged her to the opposite side of a neatly trimmed holly bush.

A few minutes later, the front door whooshed open. With the speed he normally used on a keyboard, Jonah rounded the shrub.

Carson's eyes popped wide. "What the hell—"

"I'm asking the questions today." Although Jonah wanted to grab the guy, he tried to breathe through the tension wadded in his stomach.

Slow and easy. You don't know that he's behind all this.

"Jonah?" Tessa's tone was soft, as if she instinctively knew his control was fraying by the second.

Carson's skinny chest was rising and falling rapidly, and his eyes were darting left and right. "What...what are you two doing here?"

"I ran a multibillion-dollar gaming company. You don't think I got there by being stupid, do you? You weren't hard to track down. Now you're going to tell me why you're threatening Tessa or I will reach down your throat and turn your organs inside out."

Great. That was sure to convince Tessa that you won't lose your shit on someone else.

"You two need to leave me alone." Although the temperature was hovering in the low forties, the dude was sweating as if he were trapped in a sauna, and his gaze was ping-ponging between Jonah and Tessa. "If you don't, I'll go to the police."

"Oh, that'll be handy. You can march your ass in there and explain how you hacked Tessa's files and painted threats on her walls."

"I...I don't know what you're talking about." His Adam's apple convulsed, and he nodded toward Tessa. "She's the one threatening me. Telling me to give her money or she'll blab to people about our counseling sessions. She did the same thing to Davey and he ended up dead. There's something wrong with her."

"You could've written that blackmail e-mail, trying to throw suspicion off yourself."

"Dude, I just started a new job. I don't have time to play games like that even if I wanted to."

"I think he's telling the truth," Tessa said softly.

"What about me?" Jonah demanded. "What do you have against me?"

"Other than the fact that I think you were stupid to sell your company? Not a damn thing. I liked working for Steele Trap."

"Then why did you quit and move all the way to Charlotte? Why did you follow me to North Carolina?"

Carson's laugh was strangled, but it was real. "Dude, I didn't move here because of you. I came because I met a girl. She works for a real estate company here, and I knew we'd never make it work long distance. I want to get married, have kids and shit. She could be the one."

She could be the one.

Jonah glanced at Tessa, standing there so fierce. She'd proven again and again that she had a soul of forged steel. She was tough and resilient.

She could be the one.

It reverberated through Jonah's mind. Tessa was his one. He loved her. He knew it to the end of his soul, and now that he was willing to admit it to himself, he felt like he was fighting shadows to keep her safe.

Could he have made a mistake about Carson? "When's the last time you were in Asheville?"

"Uh...half after never?" Carson said. "I've only been here for a couple of weeks. Haven't exactly had time to play tourist." His focus shifted to Tessa. "You really aren't using the stuff you know to try to squeeze money out of people?"

"Believe me when I say I would never do that," she said. "Someone hacked my files and is using the information to hurt all of us."

"Then you'd better figure out who's behind this, because I'm not your guy."

19

When Tessa climbed into the driver's seat again, Jonah didn't balk. Didn't say a word. In fact, he said not a word for 130 miles. When they were closing in on Steele Ridge, he finally spoke. "Your car should be at my place by now."

"How? My keys are in your house."

"I've got a talented family. Between the lot of them, they could've broken it down for parts, then put it back together again during our jaunt to Charlotte."

When they drove up, her car was sitting in front of his house. Once they were inside, Jonah held out his hand for Clementine's keys, but Tessa skirted around him. "I want her."

"Huh?"

"I want to buy Clementine."

"You drive a BMW."

"Yes, but now I want a 1970 Plymouth Hemi Superbird."

"She's my car."

Good grief. Men really were possessive, weren't they?

"Remember what you said? Winner of Steele Survivor gets to make the rules for twenty-four hours." In fact, that was the reason he'd grudgingly agreed to let his family in on what was going on. Because she'd insisted on it. "Well, I'm making a rule that you have to sell that car to me."

"She's not at all your style."

Tessa's lips curved and she moved in on Jonah. By the wary look in his eyes, it was clear her smile was just as predatory as she'd intended. "What style is that? She's flashy and I'm not? She's fast and I'm not? She's powerful and I'm not?"

"No, I—"

She poked him in the chest. "You think you know me. You think you have me all figured out. Put Tessa in her good-girl, head-shrinker box in the corner. You have no idea what I'm capable of, Jonah Steele. And the next time I have you naked, you're going to find out just how flashy, fast, and powerful I am."

A throat cleared behind Tessa.

They were here. His family.

Wanting to drop her hot face against Jonah's chest, Tessa closed her eyes for a second to regain her equilibrium. Then she opened them and whispered to Jonah, "Please tell me it's Reid again."

At least then, she could contain her embarrassment. After all, he'd already gotten an eyeful of her goodies.

"I like this girl, baby brother." Okay, not so bad. Just Micki, who'd seen her in her underwear.

"Finally, someone who can match wits with him." If the flooring under her feet had suddenly turned to quicksand and sucked her under, Tessa would've died a happy woman. Because that last comment had come from Miss Joan.

And the totally smart-ass humor in Jonah's eyes made Tessa want to...to...

"Breathe," he whispered before pressing a gentle kiss to her forehead. "Welcome to the Steele family."

At his touch and his words, Tessa's heart jumped. After a mere morning in their company, she was pretty sure she would love to be a part of this big, rowdy, crazy family.

She was still frozen, contemplating that turn of thoughts, when Jonah clapped his hands once. "If you want to know the whole story, let's go into my cave." He pointed, and Tessa turned to see his finger was directed at Reid. "And don't touch anything unless I say you can."

Not to be left out, Badger barked from his kennel, and Tessa carried him into Jonah's tech cave. Inside, Jonah took over like the CEO he'd once been. He gave the group the low-down on what had happened with Tessa's files, the game mods, and their dead-end field trip to see Carson Grimes.

"Who is this guy and what the hell does he want?" Reid asked.

"I'm running some theories around in my head," Jonah said. "But—"

"He hasn't been able to backtrack to him through the file-holding company's network yet." A sly smile on her face, Micki stretched out her hands as if she were about to go into the boxing ring. "But now I'm here."

"It was more convoluted than you might think," he grumbled.

"That's just because you didn't have the right woman working on the job." She settled into one of the chairs and pulled a keyboard toward her.

Jonah did the same, and before Tessa's eyes, they seemed to disappear into their own world. Miss Joan patted Tessa's arm. "Don't be concerned. Those two have been like that since the day they were born, somehow able to communicate, work in tandem, and block out everything around them."

Reid snorted. "They used that superpower more than once to run roughshod over the grading system in school."

Miss Joan's mouth puckered up. "I don't want to hear about it."

"Gives you plausible deniability," Tessa murmured.

"Exactly."

Britt shoved his hands into the front pocket of his jeans. "Watching those two do their Wonder Twins act always makes me feel like some kinda weird voyeur. Maybe we should let them—"

"Fuck me." The soft but heartfelt words came from Jonah. He slid a quick glance toward his mother. "Sorry, Mom."

"What's up?" Micki asked.

"Dickh...ah...dude sent me another modded game file via OnionShare."

"Ooooh, let's play."

"Not sure I trust a file sent through the dark web."

"Don't tell me you don't have an air-gapped machine you can use to install it on the phones."

Now they were talking their own language.

Micki waved an arm at everyone standing around the room. "Peanut gallery needs to move along so Jonah and I can concentrate."

The rest of the family began to shuffle out of the room, but Tessa hesitated. She liked Jonah's sister—a great deal—but a sudden jealousy came over her. Being pushed out of something that had begun with her didn't sit well.

"Not Tessa." Jonah caught her by the wrist. "This is her gig, too."

That eased the spot of envy in Tessa's chest.

He fiddled with the goggles, doing whatever had to be done to run the game, while Tessa looked into them over his shoulder. The starting credits scrolled inside the goggles as they had before, but instead of launching the game itself, the character in the blue coat walked on-screen. His arms were crossed and he took a wide stance. Both defensive and aggressive.

Like last time, his face continued to morph—cycling through each person in the Steele clan and ending with Tessa's head on the stocky male body, nothing like Carson Grimes's lanky frame.

S/he smiled and it was the most gruesome thing Tessa had ever seen on her own face. "Today starts a new game in a new world."

Jonah grabbed a gauntlet, desperately stabbing at the buttons like a new player who had no idea which controlled the game functions.

Meanwhile, the on-screen character said,

"As destructive as life,

As healing as death,

An arrow of strife.

Just as prone to bless.

It is all that is good,

Yet with an evil trend.

As it was at the beginning of all things,

It can also be the end."

Then, as he had before, he turned and walked down a computer-generated representation of Steele Ridge's Main Street. The scene slowly faded to black.

"Whoa," Micki said. "That's creepy."

"Did you expect a fuzzy bunny?" Jonah let his head droop and rest against the back of his chair. "What the hell was that little ditty? Something about the beginning and the end."

"Play it again," Micki said.

When Jonah tried to restart the sequence, he had no luck. "Dammit."

Tessa had been repeating the refrain in her head, and she recited it aloud, letting the words glide through and expand in her consciousness.

"Impressive," Micki said. "How did you do that?"

"It's a form of eidetic memory."

"Like photographic?"

"Sort of, except it's auditory."

Micki chuckled and slapped Jonah on the arm. "You are so screwed. That means she'll remember every idiotic thing you ever say."

"It's a riddle," Tessa said as she listened to the words echoing inside her head. "Fire. It's a riddle about fire."

"He said a new game in a new world," Micki mused.

"A world of fire." Saying it aloud sent a shudder through Tessa. "And he was in Steele Ridge again, right?"

"Yeah."

"What about the fire station? Could he be directing us there?"

"Little brother," Micki said. "This one's a keeper."

It looked as if she'd received the Micki Steele seal of approval. And with the look of admiration and affection Jonah turned on her, Tessa almost believed he thought she was a keeper, too.

JONAH STARTED FOR THE DOOR, BUT TESSA OUT-JUKED HIM. "Don't even think about it. I'm going with you. Steele Survivor twenty-four-hour rule, remember?"

He could've danced around that some way, but now that she knew where his spare keys were, he had no doubt she'd simply follow him.

He'd have to wait to call the restaurant in Charlotte again to find out if the bartender had drummed up the martini guy's name for him.

Micki stayed at his house to monitor anything else that might come through from the Mega Douche Modder. When he and Tessa left, Badger was happily sprawled across Micki's lap like a sausage-sized blanket.

They headed to Steele Ridge's single fire station with Tessa once again at Clementine's wheel. He had a sinking feeling he'd never drive the car again.

"Do you think he wants you to play again?" she asked.

He was pretty damn sure the guy had a hard-on for jerking him around. "I brought all the equipment, just in case."

When they pulled into the fire station parking lot, a trio of guys had the big engine pulled out of the bay and were polishing it to a gleaming shine. Jonah and Tessa got out of the car, and one of the firefighters turned to greet them.

"Look who the cat dragged in," Cash said. "Hope you're not planning to run around town knocking down more women."

"What're you doing here today?" Cash had been on duty yesterday and normally the firefighters worked twenty-four-hour shifts.

"Pulled a double. Traded with Callahan because his wife went into labor. First kid." Cash folded the chamois cloth he'd been using. "Did you come for the package?"

"What package?"

"The one we found outside the station doors this morning. It has your name on it."

The hair on the back of Jonah's neck quivered. "Why the hell didn't someone call me?"

"I planned to drop it by your place after my shift."

Jonah clenched his jaw to keep from lashing out at his cousin. Cash couldn't have known how important this might be. "Did you see who left it here?"

"Nah." Cash scratched his ear. "We took a call about two this morning. Got back here around four. Didn't see the box then. Wasn't until the lieutenant came out to grab the paper at six-thirty that we found it. What the hell, man? Didn't your fancy house come with a mailbox?"

"Where is it?"

Cash looked pointedly at Tessa, then shot a sharp glare at Jonah. "Things were too busy for chitchat yesterday, but maybe you could introduce me to your friend here."

"Cash, this is Tessa. Tessa, this is my nosy cousin, Cash."

"It's a small town. Everyone is nosy here." Cash laughed and waved for them to follow him into the bay and through a door into the interior of the station.

"So nice to meet another member of Jonah's family," Tessa said. "How big is the Steele crew, anyway?"

"If you count both my mom's and dad's sides, we have a cousin or two," Jonah said.

"Or twenty." Still chuckling, Cash led them to the kitchen where a small box sat on the countertop.

Jonah approached the box carefully and lifted it. Probably weighed less than a pound. Too light for a bomb? Reid would know for sure. "I'm gonna take this outside to the open grassy area behind the building."

Cash's easygoing expression tightened. "Why? What's in it?"

"I'm not sure. Last time, it was VR goggles and some other stuff."

"You had me worried there for a second."

"Mind if I borrow a turnout suit and headgear?"

"Now I'm worried again."

"It's probably nothing," Jonah said.

"You're thinking bomb, aren't you? We could call in a squad from Asheville."

Something told Jonah they didn't have time for that. Besides, whoever was toying with him and Tessa was enjoying the game too much to end it this way.

"Stay with Cash," he told her.

"I don't think so."

Shit. He shot Cash a look, one that men all over the world knew. It was the take-care-of-my-woman nod. "Then at least stay inside the bay."

"You said you're going behind the building."

"There's an exterior door with a window at the back of the bay," Cash told her. "You can watch him through that."

From Tessa's drawn eyebrows and downturned mouth, it was obvious she wasn't happy about that solution. So Jonah carefully set the box aside and pulled her into his arms. Instinct shouted for him to get her the hell out of here. He loved that she was so strong, so resilient. But her strength warred with his need to protect her. "Please do this for me. If something happened to you, I would lose my mind."

She reached up and skimmed her fingers down his cheek to linger at his lips. Last night, that same touch would've felt sexual. Today, it felt like something more. Something both comforting and dangerous. "Then how do you think I feel?"

If it was a fraction of what was inside him, they'd need more than a few minutes to discuss it. "We're not finished with everything we started last night, and I'll be damned if I'll let this jackass interfere with that," he whispered against her hair. Then he pressed a hard kiss to her lips and reluctantly released her to lift his chin at his cousin. "Let's get me suited up."

Ten minutes later, Jonah stared down into the box. He held up the contents so Cash and Tessa could see from inside that it was okay to come out.

Tessa busted through the door and came at him in a full-out run. "What is it?"

"From the male input jack and these silver electrodes, it seems like some kind of sensor shirt that can be plugged into the VR goggles."

"That something you came up with?" Cash asked.

"No." Because honestly, the thing looked rudimentary. But at least the modder had been busy building something interesting, which was more than Jonah could say about himself. "Haptic suits aren't new, but no one's perfected them yet. It takes a shitload of money to develop new tech like this. And investors don't usually like companies to do R and D when it won't pay for itself."

Cash whistled. "So are you telling me someone one-upped the techie king?"

Not necessarily, but it did rub him wrong. Anyone could code a little old mobile app like Jonah's. Maybe he should set his sights on something bigger...

No, it's not about complexity. Or accolades. It's about safety. Don't forget that.

Tessa reached inside the box and opened a slip of paper.

"What's it say?"

She slid a guarded look toward Cash. Whatever was on that piece of paper, she didn't want his cousin to hear.

"Hey, Cash, can you give us a minute here?"

"There's something fishy about this whole thing," Cash

grumbled. "Don't do something else I'm gonna have to clean up."

After he stalked back into the building, Tessa took a deep breath and dropped down to sit on the grass. "I think they're instructions."

Jonah scanned the paper over Tessa's shoulder. It was another freaking riddle, this one not as obscure as the one they'd received via the modded game.

> I am always hungry.
> I must always be fed.
> The finger I lick
> Will soon turn red.

Below the riddle was a list.
La Belle Style?
Blues, Brews, & Books?
Tupelo Hill?
The wood-and-glass castle?

> Only one will fall.
> Only two will play.
> If others join, all will pay.
> The clock starts now.
> Play or Die.

"Does that mean what I think it does?" Tessa's voice held a tremor as she pulled out a cheap timer that had been obscured by the padding around the sensors.

Only two will play.
If others join, all will pay.

"It sounds like if we let anyone else know what's going

on, all the places will burn." He grabbed the timer from Tessa. Thirty minutes.

The clock starts now. That motherfucker was watching them. Jonah jumped to his feet and turned in a circle, trying to get a bead on the person who obviously had eyeballs on them.

Jonah reached down, yanked Tessa up by the elbow, and shoved the car keys into her hand. "We have to go now."

As they ran toward the car, Jonah was already plugging the sensor web into the goggles. *God, please let this shit work.* He yanked his T-shirt over his head, dropped it to the asphalt, and slid into the passenger seat. "We need to hit the closest locations first. Drive to Triple B," he ordered.

He'd start there and work his way through them all. His fingers itched to call his brothers, but now that he knew this SOB was aware of his moves, he couldn't afford to. He wiggled and wrestled his way into the sensors, almost tearing the wiring as he forced his arms through the armholes. Once he'd patted down the sensors, making sure each touched his skin, he pulled on the goggles and gauntlets.

"Please tell me you won't jump anyone else," Tessa said, her voice full of worry.

"I promise to use my words this time instead of assuming what I'm seeing is real." The buildings on Main Street remained in real life order, although they took on the same abandoned quality as before. He pointed at Triple B, the bar and restaurant owned by Britt's girlfriend, Randi. "Park by the front door."

The car hadn't stopped rolling when he shoved open the door and jumped out.

The sensors against his skin were vibrating and turning warmer as he strong-armed his way through Triple B's door and found it full with the pre-happy hour crowd. *Fuck.* He didn't have time to explain to Randi what was going on. Each second that ticked away could mean the difference between people living or becoming victims of this fucked-up game.

Cupping his hands around his mouth, he hollered, "Get up and get the hell outta here. Now. This is not a warning. Not a joke."

"I just got my damned cheeseburger," some zombie with a John Deere cap on groused. "I ain't goin' nowhere."

"I'll pay for your fucking burger. I'll pay for every burger you eat for the rest of your life. Just get your ass outta here."

People were rushing out the front door when a blond-haired zombie marched up to Jonah. Had to be Randi. "What are you doing? Why are you forcing all my customers out the door?"

"Randi," he said, grabbing her hands and tossing the dishtowel she was holding to the ground. "I can't explain. Just trust me. I need you to get yourself and all your employees out of the building immediately."

"Does Britt know about this?"

He would soon enough. "How many others are here?"

"Three. Kris, Grady, and a new waitress I just hired."

He tugged Randi toward the door to the office and storage area. It opened and a petite zombie with black and purple hair emerged.

Randi told her, "Kris, get out of the building."

"Wha—"

"Just do it."

Jonah and Randi made a sweep in the back and followed her two other employees into the parking lot behind the building.

"Now, will you explain..." Randi started, but Jonah was

already running around the building toward where Tessa was waiting.

He didn't bother to close the car door this time, and the cold air swept over his sweating torso. "U-turn toward..."

But she was already on it, tires squealing as she did a tight about-face and gunned it.

At La Belle Style, it took slightly less time, since the boutique wasn't packed. Only a salesgirl, Brynne, and two customers. Jonah would've been in and out if Brynne hadn't insisted on grabbing the till and an armload of merchandise.

When he dived into the car this time, Tessa hit the gas and said, "Breathe. You'll hyperventilate. Maybe we should go ahead and text your mom. Have her get out of the house."

With the sensors rapidly generating more heat, he hadn't realized his breathing was becoming more and more shallow. "We don't have any idea how he's tracking us. I can't risk it based on that damn riddle."

The drive out to Tupelo Hill from town had never taken so long.

"We're going to beat him," Tessa reassured him. "You're doing great."

But the clock on the dashboard kept ticking away as she took the country roads and weaved around a tractor and a couple of pickups on the two-lane blacktop. They turned into the family property and Tessa blew right past one of the security patrols Reid had hired when people had threatened the Steeles in the past.

Dust and gravel flew, probably scratching the hell out of the car's paint job as Tessa fishtailed to a stop in front of Tupelo Hill.

In his haste, Jonah stumbled up the porch steps and burst inside the house. "Mom! Hey, where are you?"

No answer.

"Is anyone the fuck here?" Where had all his useless siblings gone after he'd filled them in about this psycho? Why had he sent them away?

He tugged at the sensors because they were starting to sizzle against his skin like butter on a hot skillet.

The sound of bare feet came slapping down the hallway from his mother's bedroom. "Jonah Stewart Steele, you can use that kind of language in your own home, but—"

"Anyone else here?" He lunged and scooped her up in his arms, barely registering that her hair was wrapped up in a towel and she was wearing a short bathrobe.

She gave a squeaking squawk. "No, just me. If this is some new part of your latest paintball game with your brothers, I swear, I will take away all your guns."

He had no idea how far away he might need to get her, so at the car, he swung her to her feet, yanked open the door, and shoved her into the backseat.

When he jumped in, his mom was saying to Tessa, "I don't know what this is all about, but I don't appreciate being manhandled by my own son."

Tessa didn't acknowledge his mother, didn't look toward the backseat. She just put her foot on the gas and ate up the winding road toward his house as if she'd been studying under Danica Patrick her whole life.

20

EVEN THOUGH SHE'D ADVISED JONAH TO KEEP HIS BREATHING under control, the air was backing up in Tessa's lungs. She reached over to touch his thigh. "She's going to be fine."

And she was saying a silent prayer each second that Badger had decided Micki was good company and stayed in Jonah's cave with her. But as they raced over the last rise toward his house, Tessa could see she might've spoken too soon. Although the countdown timer indicated they still had five minutes, smoke was curling up from the massive wood-and-glass structure.

"Oh, Lord have mercy," Miss Joan breathed from the backseat. "Jonah, what's going on? Is Micki still in your house? If she had on headphones, she might not have heard the smoke alarm go off."

"I've got this, Mom."

But Tessa could tell from the way he swallowed, as if he had a grapefruit stuck in his throat, that he wasn't as confident as he claimed. She put on a little more speed, cringed at the rocks pinging against the car, and navigated the heart-jolting curves up the steep ascent faster than was probably smart.

But smart didn't matter right now.

Again, Jonah barreled out before the car stopped rolling and ran toward the wing of the house that held the garage and his tech cave. Smoke seeped out from under the garage doors, and never missing a step, Jonah changed his trajectory toward another part of the house.

"For goodness' sake," Miss Joan exclaimed. "We need to call 911!"

"We can't," Tessa told her. "Not yet."

"Why not?"

"Because he might burn down everything."

"Who? Who are you talking about?"

"We don't know who he is." While Jonah was inside and out of sight, the seconds ticked off as if they were centuries.

"Give me your phone," his mom demanded.

"Miss Joan, I mean it. You can't call the fire department. Not until he has Micki out of there."

"But if she's not still in the house, then he's risking himself for nothing."

Tessa pulled her phone from her purse and handed it over.

From the way Miss Joan kept it smashed against her ear with a strained expression on her face, Micki wasn't answering. Finally, she dialed again. "Gage, have you seen Micki in the past hour or so? Oh. Oh, no. I'll call you back."

Her eyes were terrified as she held out Tessa's phone in a limp palm. "Maybe we should go help—"

"No." The last thing Jonah would want was for more people to be in jeopardy. Tessa was mentally reciting every prayer she could remember from Sunday school as a child, especially the ones that requested deliverance from evil. "He'll get her."

Four interminable minutes later, Jonah came running around the side of the house, carrying his sister in a fireman's hold over his back. His hair was dripping with sweat and his face was smeared with soot.

Miss Joan pushed the seat forward, and Jonah stuffed Micki inside the car. She was holding a very disgruntled-looking Badger.

Tessa's terror that Micki might not be breathing was alleviated by the creative four-letter words Jonah's sister was aiming his way. "I was getting out, you idiot. You didn't have to carry me like I'm some helpless girl."

Badger bounded from Micki's arms into Tessa's lap. He burrowed down, pressing his little body as close to her as he could get.

Jonah flopped back into the front seat, his chest expanding and deflating with his labored breaths. "Drive... drive back down the ridge."

"What about calling 911?"

"Once we're far enough away. That bastard obviously doesn't play by his own rules. Who the hell knows what other surprises he might have stashed inside my house."

Tessa shivered, remembering Jonah and Cash's earlier conversation about bombs.

As they wound their way back toward the farmhouse, Jonah yanked at the sensors on his torso.

Micki leaned over the front seat, "Whoa, what're those?" Her voice was hoarse from the smoke, but her curiosity verified that she wasn't hurt too badly.

"Don't stop at Mom's," Jonah directed Tessa, rubbing at the fiery red spots where the sensors had been attached.

"Get off the property. Once we're on the main road, we'll call."

"You're blistered."

"Based on the fact that these things didn't do more than warm up until we got close to my house, I should've known those other locations were just decoys."

"They looked like they burned the shit outta you." Micki poked at a spot on Jonah's shoulder. "That's cool."

"Mikayla Steele!" Miss Joan exclaimed.

"I don't mean cool that he looks like he's contracted some kind of exotic disease. I meant cool technology. Do they hurt?" she asked Jonah.

"Like a bitch."

Once Tessa drove the car off the Steele property, she swung it around by doing a less-than-elegant U-turn on the grassy shoulder so they had a view of the ridge where smoke was still rising from Jonah's beautiful home. She reached for his hand and squeezed before releasing it so he could call for emergency services.

Quickly, he gave all the pertinent details, ones Tessa wasn't sure she could've been half as calm about. His home —his uniquely beautiful home—was on fire. "They're on their way," he said.

"I was involved in backtracking through that network, and I didn't smell the smoke as fast as I should've," Micki said. "Actually, I didn't smell it until Badger started barking like a maniac. He jumped off my lap and ran to the cave's door. Did three frantic laps before I figured out what he was trying to tell me. God, Jonah, I'm so sorry about your house."

He patted her hand. "It's just a house."

"Your dream house."

"Which can be rebuilt. You, on the other hand, are one of a freaking kind."

If his mom and sister hadn't been in the car, Tessa would've grabbed for Jonah and given him a soul kiss. He might not believe it, but he was a hero in all the ways that counted.

"The builder put in a few extras," he said. "I was able to close off the metal door between the kitchen and the hallway that connects it to the tech cave, game room, and garage. Hopefully, the rest of the house should be okay except for a little smoke damage here and there."

"But your cars."

He reached for Tessa's hand, a crooked grin on his streaked face. "At least we saved Clementine."

Oh, to hell with their audience. Tessa threw her arms around Jonah's neck and practically climbed into his lap. Badger gave an indignant yip and jumped in the back toward Micki. Later, Tessa would make it up to him and reward his heroism with his favorite sweet potato and peanut butter treats. "I was so scared."

"Sweet Tess," he said, pulling her close and wrapping his arms securely around her. "I may have failed you once, but never again."

THAT EVENING, ONCE HIS MOM'S HOUSE HAD BEEN CLEARED BY the fire marshal, Jonah's family was gathered there. After the fire and the threats on other Steele properties, everyone's state could only be described as what his mom would call a tizzy.

With his siblings, their significant others, and Grif's daughter, the living room was crowded with people all talking over one another. If Reid stomp-paced across the rug one more time, Jonah would knock him to the ground and sit on his ass.

It had taken hours for the emergency personnel crews to carefully pick through Randi's place, Brynne's boutique, and the farmhouse for any type of incendiary device. Come to find out, the modder had planned to target Jonah's house all along because the others had been completely clean.

It hadn't been declared arson yet, especially since a couple of gas cans had been stored in Jonah's garage, but he knew this was no accident. He'd been lucky that only the one-story wing was destroyed and that he'd gotten Micki the hell out of there. If something had happened to her...

Gage was obviously harboring the same gut-shredding feeling, since he'd had Micki wrapped in his arms pretty much nonstop since meeting them at the hospital earlier.

Jonah had to find this dickwad and bring him down. For Micki. For his family. For Tessa.

Her expression tired and shell-shocked, she sat in a chair in the corner, petting Badger one stroke after another. He went to her and hunkered down to still her hand on Badger's back. The tremor he felt came from her, not the dog.

He needed to get her out of here soon, because he couldn't stand to see that blankness on her face.

If his family's racket hadn't been enough to make Jonah's head ache, the smoke that had irritated his sinuses would be. Although he knew it would make the brain pain worse, he put his fingers in his mouth and produced a whistle that cut through the chatter and speculation.

"We aren't going to solve this thing tonight." *They* weren't, at least. But he'd slipped away earlier and talked with the Charlotte bartender and his nerves were still vibrating from what he'd discovered. Martini dude was none other than one Charles Cartwright. At first glance, a boring banker. But Jonah knew the truth. He was a bastard and a rapist.

But did he have the tech skills to pull off such an elaborate setup?

Jonah couldn't let Tessa find out his suspicions. She wouldn't understand why the guy was targeting her and Jonah, and he sure as fuck didn't want to explain. Because if Cartwright was after her, Jonah had done this. He'd brought all this shit to her front door.

He urged her up from the chair. She looked as if she was about to nod off, even with all the noise. "Tessa and I are going back to my place. I need to think. The first person who calls or texts and interrupts my deep thoughts will pay a steep price."

Reid was the first to react, stalking toward Jonah. But Britt put an arm out to clothesline him. "I got this." He turned to Jonah. "Going back there isn't smart."

"It's been cleared. And Reid's upped security all over the place."

"The problem with that, as always, is guarding every inch of twenty thousand acres is impossible. This guy probably hiked in from land adjoining ours. Somehow, I don't think those owners would be happy to let Reid's security guys invade their privacy. Randi's land only borders so much of our property line."

Grif gave an agreeing nod. "He's right. Which is why I brought these." From his pants pocket, he pulled a keyring with two keys on it. "These'll give you access to the Murchison building. The apartment is still set up."

When Grif had first come back to Steele Ridge, he'd lived above his City Manager's office for a while.

"And that'll put you both closer to the sheriff's department and the fire station," his mom said.

"What about you?" he asked her. "If I'm in town, I don't want you out here."

"I already have a bag packed to stay with Grif and Carlie Beth. Aubrey and I are planning a cookie-baking marathon."

"I don't like it." Jonah glared around the room at the people he loved most in the world. "This fu...idiot is running us out of our homes."

Reid clapped him on the shoulder. "Just for the time being. We'll get him."

Which only reminded Jonah that his roomful of equipment was toast. What hadn't actually burned, the heat had compromised. Finding the cash to replace it wouldn't be a problem, but some of it had been custom built. He didn't have time to replace and rebuild, not if he wanted to drop this guy quick.

Honestly, he wouldn't have imagined Cartwright had this deep well of creativity. After Jonah had tanked the guy's odds of getting into law school, he'd gone on to become a mid-level grunt at a bank, a loan officer or something. Not exactly a visionary.

Could he have hired someone to come up with a revenge plan?

From her spot in Gage's lap, Micki said, "I know what you're thinking. My setup isn't as expensive as yours was, but it's good. If Grif doesn't object, we can move it over to the Murchison building. That'll give us room to work."

Jonah slid his hand across his eyes. He wanted them all completely out of the picture. "I called a travel agent earlier. I can have all of you on a cruise out of Miami tomorrow afternoon. Hotel in Charlotte is already booked and the flight goes out first thing in the morning. You can load up now."

His mom recoiled as if he'd slapped her. "You cannot be serious."

He pulled Tessa's hand up to hold it against his still painful chest. "Including you."

Her eyebrows went up. "So you want us to take off and leave you here to find this person on your own."

"He's already made it clear that he's willing to inflict collateral damage."

"I sure hope you didn't put down a deposit," she said, her voice sharp. "Because you'll lose every dollar of it." She smiled in Grif's direction and held out her hand for the keys he'd offered. "Thank you for the place to stay."

"I dropped off some clothes and toiletries while y'all were still at the hospital," Brynne said.

"We'll plan to check in with y'all in the morning," Reid said.

Fuck. He wasn't six years old anymore, yet his older brothers were taking charge like they always had.

Think with your head instead of your ego.

Micki broke away from Gage's embrace and did something that had happened way too little in the past ten years. She put her arms around Jonah's waist and laid her head on his chest.

When he wrapped his arms around her, a weight lightened inside him. He and Micki would always share something visceral, something special that came from floating around in a womb together. "Please let us help."

"Micki, I don't need—"

"Don't," she sighed. "We were apart for long enough. I may have excluded you from my life for years, but now that

I'm back, please don't do the same to me. You're in trouble, and this time I want to help you and Tessa face it head-on."

Tessa looked at him, her eyes telegraphing that she was waiting to see what he'd decide—to cover up the fact that he needed the people in his life or to show them he wasn't an island.

He knew Tessa wouldn't leave Steele Ridge, wouldn't let him handle this situation alone. Which meant he needed his loving, meddlesome family to help protect her.

"Fine," he said to Micki.

She smiled and pulled Tessa into their hug. "Go get some rest, you two. I'll be knocking on your door first thing tomorrow morning."

He squeezed her shoulder. "Bring your best stuff. I can't work with inferior equipment."

The tired smile on Tessa's face told him he'd said the right thing.

21

JONAH'S DAD, RARELY SEEN IN TOWN, WAS WAITING OUTSIDE the Murchison building when Jonah and Tessa arrived. The last thing Jonah had the patience for right now was introductions and explanations, but if Tessa's curious expression was any indication, he wouldn't be able to avoid it.

At least his dad's mountain man appearance was relatively tame tonight. His hair was smoothed back and secured at his neck, and his beard looked as if it had been recently trimmed.

"You all right?" he asked Jonah gruffly.

"How'd you know to find me here?"

"I was listening to the police scanner earlier. Called Maggie and she said Reid let her know your whereabouts so her people could keep an eye on things."

Jonah grunted. The beauty and the hell of living in a small town again. People cared. They cared so much that sometimes it was hard to keep things hidden. "We should probably get off the street." Because who the hell knew where that son of a bitch was tonight?

Once inside, he said to Tessa, "Tessa Martin, this is my dad, Eddy Steele. Dad, this is Tessa, a...friend of mine."

Her smile was genuine and completely nonjudgmental when she reached out to shake his dad's hand. "So nice to meet you, Mr. Steele."

"Same here." He made eye contact with Tessa, then his attention shifted back to Jonah. "Son, can I have a word?"

There was no way he'd let Tessa go upstairs alone, and she must've seen his hesitation because she said, "I'll step over here while you two talk."

When she sat down on the staircase leading to the second floor, Jonah's dad said, "That was some nasty business today. You sure everyone is okay?"

His patience running low, Jonah said, "You could check on them all yourself, you know."

"Don't think I don't keep eyes on things, boy."

"Britt taught us that real men protect and take care of the people in their lives."

His dad's flinch was visible. He obviously understood everything Jonah was saying with that one statement. That Eddy Steele wasn't a real man because he left his family. Britt had been the true father figure to Jonah and the others. "You got that high IQ. You think you know everything, but you don't."

"Then why the hell don't you explain why you withdrew from your family?" Jonah shook his head. Why was he opening this old can of worms tonight? He had plenty weighing on his mind already without adding in his dad's lifestyle choices.

"Because a man shouldn't shit where he eats."

Rage boiled up in Jonah's chest. For the most part, he'd simply written off his dad, not nearly as hurt or angry as his older brothers were, but now, he wanted to deck the old man. "What the fuck is that supposed to mean?"

His dad patted the left side of his chest. "When a man feels too much here"—he tapped his temple—"and can't control his darkness here, he needs to be man enough to get the hell out of situations where he might hurt the very people he claims to love." He shot a quick glance toward Tessa. "Looks like you'd do well to remember that."

IN AN ATTEMPT TO CENTER HERSELF, TESSA SMOOTHED FRESH sheets on their borrowed bed while Jonah took a shower in the second-floor apartment overlooking Main Street. Once she'd tucked in corners that would've made an army commander happy, she unpacked the La Belle Style bags that Brynne had dropped off earlier.

In one, she found items that couldn't be a part of the boutique's inventory. Men's jeans, a leather belt, tennis shoes, soft sleep shorts, underwear, and half a dozen T-shirts. Brynne obviously understood Jonah's sense of fashion.

Tessa shook out one of the shirts to check out the screen printing on the front. It was some type of math graph and said, "Holy Shift! Look at the asymptote on that mother function." Tessa wouldn't have believed anything could make her smile tonight, but Brynne deserved an award for this one.

Tessa put away Jonah's new clothes, then dug into the bag she assumed was for her. The first item brought hot tears to her eyes. It was the gorgeous dragonfly sweater Brynne had described to her. On it, she'd placed a note.

Please accept this as a gift from me. Tessa, honey, it was made for you. Wear it and think about how richly colorful your life could be here in Steele Ridge.

This family certainly didn't play fair, did they?

Tessa wasn't completely sure how Jonah felt about her, but his family seemed like they were her fans.

She was smiling and holding the sweater to her chest when Jonah limped out of the bathroom across the hallway. He wore a thick gray towel around his waist, which left his burn-marked chest bare. When they arrived at the apartment, Tessa had wanted to toss that damn sensor shirt into a dumpster, but Jonah insisted on bringing it inside.

If she had her way, she'd use a pair of wire cutters on it and snip it into tiny pieces.

"What's that?" He nodded toward the sweater in her hand.

"Oh, just something Brynne left."

Strolling closer, he brought a clean tropical scent with him. He took the sweater from Tessa's hands and looked it over.

"It's not really my style. I'll probably—"

"Keep it."

"What?"

"You should keep it," he said. "It's beautiful." Somehow, one of his hands found its way around to the back of her neck and stroked the sensitive skin there, sending a shiver of awareness through Tessa. "Just like you."

For some reason, that made Tessa's cheeks heat. Something about Jonah's rough and intimate tone threw her off balance. She'd been trying to capture this man's attention, his affection for so long. Now she wasn't sure what to do with it.

"With all the craziness today," he said, "I don't think I ever said thank you."

"For what?"

"Not sure I can count them all. Dealing with my crazy family, staying calm when things went off the rails, maneuvering like a freaking race car driver."

"I was just—"

Her protest was cut off by his mouth covering hers. The stress and fear of the day finally hit Tessa like a brick to the heart, and her legs shook.

This—Jonah's demanding lips on hers—felt different.

Deep.

Desperate.

Dominant.

Today's events had scratched away a little of his veneer. Exactly what she'd wanted, but was she ready for this? Ready for the real Jonah?

A trembling started in her midsection and radiated its way out to every part of her body. Apparently, the sensation was truly physical because Jonah rubbed his hands up and down her arms, but Tessa's involuntary reaction only intensified.

He must've realized she was about to break apart in his arms because he eased away and said, "Hey, hey. What's wrong?"

She wanted to drop her head and rest it against his chest, to reassure herself that he was alive and real, but his burns looked so painful. "He could've killed you. I think that's what he wants. What do you call it...killing you is his end..."

"End game."

"How can you say that so calmly?"

"Because I know I'm going to stop the son of a bitch."

I. Not *we.* She needed him to understand she had to fight her own fights. Yet his concern for her was tempting her to lean on him more than was healthy. More than was safe.

She needed a minute to get herself under control, because they had to talk and think about this situation clearly. "I could use a shower."

"Tessa..."

"Yes, it's temporary avoidance," she said. "Classic defense mechanism. I just need a few minutes." If she could wash away the dried layer of fearful sweat on her body, she might be able to regain her equilibrium.

"I left you a towel on the sink."

She pressed a soft kiss to his bristly jaw, scooped up Badger, and fled. When she stripped out of her clothes, she realized just how dirty she felt. Not only from rushing around trying to outsmart a madman, but also from her complete lack of control in this situation. Her world didn't work that way. Things had their places.

And right now, everything was decidedly out of order. Why had she believed that she could bring Jonah into her life without it going topsy-turvy?

In retrospect, it was silly and nearsighted. After all, he'd been tilting her world for years.

"C'mon, King B. You're a mess."

Her pup flattened his ears back at the prospect of getting under the spray.

"There's a cookie in it for you."

Those were the magic words. He let her place him inside the tub and he backed into a corner.

The shower water felt like heaven on Tessa's skin, easing the gut-wrenching fear that she hadn't been able to allow herself to feel while she and Jonah had been racing around town. She slid down the tile to sit, letting everything rain over her. When Badger let out a low whine, she picked him up and held him close. "I was so scared. Were you scared?"

He licked her ear and she rested her forehead against his slick fur.

"So many people in danger and they didn't have a clue. And when Jonah ran inside the house, I thought he might not come back out. If I'd lost you and him, I would've..."

She didn't know what she would've done, because her mind wouldn't allow her to fully form a picture of a world without Jonah in it. It was a vacuum she couldn't imagine filling.

And afterward in the car, when he said *I may have failed you once, but never again,* her heart had cracked into tiny pieces.

How could he possibly believe that he'd failed her? If not for him, she might not be alive. She certainly wouldn't be the woman she was today. Because of him, she'd been able to recover.

To believe she had the strength to build the kind of life she wanted.

It wasn't until a knock came at the bathroom door, and Jonah called out, "Tessa, let me in. I can't stand hearing you like that," that she realized she was making a deep sobbing sound that resembled a wounded animal left on the side of the road to die.

The knob rattled hard. "Talk to me or I'm busting down this door."

"I'm okay. Just give me a minute," she called back, her tight throat making the words come out creaky. "Go to bed and I'll be there soon."

"Tess..." Something thudded against the door as if he'd dropped his head against the wood. "Let me help you."

"I've got it under control. I'm serious, just leave me be a little longer."

"If you're not out in five minutes, I'm coming back."

Good. He'd jolted her out of a self-indulgent boo-hoo fest. Yes, feelings needed an outlet, but her little breakdown was something else. Something that made her feel raw and incredibly vulnerable. She turned off the water and dried herself and Badger. When she turned to study herself in the mirror, the foggy surface couldn't hide her swollen, pink-rimmed eyes.

Good thing Jonah liked the dark.

But when she walked across the hall to the bedroom, the overhead light was still on. Jonah was sprawled on top of the covers, his chest bare and the towel unwound but covering the essentials.

He nodded toward the corner. "Brynne found a kennel for Badger, and I put a kitchen towel in there. Thought he might sleep better if..."

If he could burrow.

Tessa's chest felt as if it had been cracked wide open. This man was so much more complex than he looked from the outside. He was insightful and thoughtful and so damn caring, but he rarely let it show, preferring to mask it all behind a dismissive shrug. Why?

"Kennel, King B," she said, and although Badger gave one longing look at the people bed, he trotted inside the new kennel and scratched at the dishcloth until he'd formed it into a suitable nest.

After giving him the promised treat, Tessa rummaged through the bag of clothes to find a soft cotton chemise and matching yellow panties. She casually dropped the towel to slip on the gown and step into the undies as if she did this in front of Jonah every night. With steadier hands than she'd had earlier, she reached for her hair to pull it out of her face.

"Leave it down," Jonah demanded, his gaze locked on her.

She shivered at his tone, but released her hair and let it fall down her back. She padded over to the wall switch, but before she could flip off the lights, Jonah spoke again. "I want them on. I want to see *you*."

But did he want her to see him?

A lick of awareness went through her, but the red splotches on his body reminded her that he was in pain. He hadn't followed the instructions he'd been given at the hospital. "You need ointment and bandages."

He groaned like a little boy told it was time to come in for supper. "It isn't that bad."

"I'm not compromising on this."

"Fine." He sat up on the edge of the bed, barely keeping the towel in place. "But I can't reach the burns on my back."

"You take care of your chest, and I'll get your back." She realized her mistake when she climbed on the bed behind him to find his butt revealed in all its muscled perfection. It was like a piece of delicious ripe fruit. She could just lean down and bite...

"Tessa!"

She blinked and looked up to find Jonah holding the tube of ointment the clinic had prescribed.

"Need this?" he asked, his tone full of amusement. "Or did you find something else you'd rather do?"

Why she was embarrassed to have been caught contemplating the texture and taste of his ass was beyond her.

It took a vast amount of concentration to apply the ointment to the multiple burns on his back with steady fingers. The feel of his skin, his muscles, his spine sank into her like sand soaked up water. She carefully placed a Band-Aid horizontally over each wound.

When Jonah twisted his torso to check her progress, Tessa laughed. He'd slapped on his bandages willy-nilly, and he looked as if he'd contracted some kind of latex measles.

He took all the packaging and tossed it on the nightstand, then sprawled out on his side as if they did this every night. As if they hadn't just become lovers.

If that's what they actually were.

Because *lovers* implied that they loved one another. She'd been a little in love with him for years, but over these past few days, she'd begun to fall in love with the real man.

Jonah tugged one of her curls and absently wrapped it around his finger. "You said you were scared he would hurt me. Can you imagine how I felt?"

"Most men don't want to admit when they're afraid for their safety," she said.

"Not that. I meant how fucking afraid I was that you would get hurt."

"It's become pretty obvious that I was never the target in the first place. He has some beef with you. He just used me to get the ball rolling."

He tugged harder, and Tessa turned to face him. "Which means he's obviously not above using people I care about to further his agenda."

"Do you think he knew Micki was inside your house?"

"I don't know. But he has eyes on all of us somehow. How else could he have delivered that package and set the fire? Or have known if we called the cops? I don't like that. Don't like the idea that someone is watching you."

"If you're about to make another pitch for everyone else taking a tropical vacation while you find this person, just shut it. Can you imagine your family playing shuffleboard on the Lido deck while you're here fighting for your life?"

"No, guess not." A chuckle rumbled up from Jonah's chest, warming Tessa.

"They love you. You know that, don't you?"

"What about you?" He kept his attention on the lock of hair he was playing with as if it were a mesmerizing piece of art.

Was he asking what she thought he was asking? Her heart was beating up her ribcage, but something kept her from blurting out how she felt, still too afraid he would push her away. "I'm not much of a shuffleboard player, either."

At that, his mouth turned down in what, on a three-year-old, would've been a pout. Tessa couldn't resist. She leaned into him and put her lips on that pout, taking care not to brush Jonah's blistered chest.

His fingers tightened in her hair, just the pleasurable side of desperation. "I want you, Tessa," he said against her lips. "I need you."

He hadn't said he loved her, but for now, she would take what he was offering.

22

Tessa's skin smelled of the body wash from the apartment's shower. Tropical—coconut and mango. It made Jonah want to eat her up with a ferocity that shook him.

Truth was, his feelings for her had always shaken him. At first pity, and then shame. He'd tried to make restitution and stay detached, but that hadn't been possible.

Now, she was in his life under the worst circumstances, and he had fallen in love with her.

Tessa deserved tender care and slow lovemaking. But every time Jonah was around her, every time she touched him, he felt as if the universal clock had been twisted back to the Pleistocene era. His gut told him to grab her and run so that some other knuckle-dragger couldn't scoop her up first.

She lifted her sweet lips from his. "What are you thinking about?"

The question every man in the world dreaded. But after all she'd done for him, Tessa had a right to know what his fucked-up mind was chewing on. "That I don't think I'm good for you."

An adorable little line appeared between her eyebrows. "You don't get to decide that."

"You'd decide that for yourself if I told you everything that goes through my mind when I think about you. Tess, I'm not who you think I am. The laid-back me is just a freakin' paint job. But when I'm around you, it starts to chip away."

And that scared the shit out of him because she deserved more. Someone better. Safer.

"That's an excuse you use to push people away. To push me away. And you are not a man who was made to be alone."

She would drop his ass if she knew just how dishonest he'd been with her. "How do you know I'm not meant to be alone?"

Because that was what his dad had been saying, right? If you're not good for your family, for the people you love, then you should just leave them the hell alone.

Tessa's smile, when it came, was like a beacon. Something Jonah would crawl through fire and broken glass for. "Because God saw to it that you had a big, nosy family. And whether you know it or not, you try to gather people together. You want to make people's lives better."

How could she say that, much less believe it?

"You don't agree?" She tapped a finger against her lips as if trying to dig up ways to convince him. "Besides how much you love your family, there's the fact that you built a company of people you cared about. Cared enough to treat them like people instead of coding machines. You bailed your hometown out of bankruptcy. You built a women's and children's shelter—a gathering place for people in need."

He glanced away, but she touched his shoulder and

asked, "Why did you bring some Steele Trap folks back together the other night? You never said."

"I had an idea for a new app." Something that could mitigate situations like what happened to Doris's kids. And like Tessa's.

"And you wanted to involve people you care about."

"It was stupid. I could do the whole thing myself."

"Of course you could," she agreed. "But that's not the point. The point is I think you miss being part of a team."

Was she right?

Since he'd returned to North Carolina, he'd been happiest when he was in the middle of a project involving other people, most often his brothers and sisters.

"Maybe." But that wasn't something for him to figure out tonight. Tonight, the person he needed to connect with was Tessa. He reached out and trailed his fingers down her arm.

"Jonah, your chest..."

Fuck his chest. He'd strip off pieces of his skin if it meant he could be with her—be inside her—now. "It's fine."

Her fingertips brushed one of the bandages, light as a breeze, and the resulting sliver of pain electrified him, made him shudder.

"See," she said. "That hurt you."

"I can honestly say that nothing has ever felt as good as you do."

Her gaze fell from his face, telling Jonah all he needed to know about her belief in his words. How could he show her, convince her, he felt more for her than he had any other woman? That he might, just might, be worth her time? Her love.

His dad's warning floated through his head again. But Jonah knew that real emotional pain was caused when one person abandoned another. When he was unwilling to be vulnerable enough to tell the truth.

"That thing you said about pain and pleasure? How they sometimes work together? I...I think I'm wired that way."

She glanced down at the towel that was barely covering the substantial hard-on he'd developed as she bandaged his blistered skin. "So you like pain with your pleasure?"

"I don't want to scare you. I would never hurt you."

Her palm was soft and warm against his cheek. "I know that. Tell me what you mean. Bondage? Discipline? Rough sex?"

God, when she said it like that, it made him want to walk the fuck away from her and never come back. Jonah rolled off the bed and to his feet, and his towel dropped to the wood floor. He reached for it, but Tessa caught his hand. "Talk to me."

"I'm not into whips and shit. I don't mean that."

"Okay. But even if you were, that wouldn't make you a bad person."

"I...just like to run the show."

"And that worries you."

"When it comes to you, yes."

"Have you ever forced yourself on a woman?"

"Fuck no."

"Then as long as whatever you do, whatever you want, is consensual, you have no reason to feel bad about it."

"But what I *want* and what you *need* aren't the same thing."

"You don't know that. And the only way we'll figure it out is to try it. Turn out the light and come back to bed."

He glanced at the switch, instinct and habit making him want to flick off the overhead light. "I want it on."

He realized that he meant it. He had a real chance to

change the images of Tessa—blacked out and bleeding—in his head. Exorcise them from his soul. He ran a hand down her thigh, urging her to turn sideways on the bed. "Scoot to the edge."

"Are you sure about the light—"

"I am. Do it, Tessa."

Her eyes flared with arousal, and she scooted around until her hips were at the mattress edge.

His breathing already uneven, Jonah sank to his knees and slowly ran his hands along her legs, giving special attention to the fragile bones in her ankles and touching each of her red-painted toes. "Damn, your feet are sexy."

She laughed. "I think you have a fever."

"Seriously. I didn't realize feet could be a turn-on." He traced a pattern on the sensitive skin of her instep and watched the way her thighs tensed and released. Oh, yeah. There were distinct advantages to being able to see every move Tessa made. It would take him years to find all her secret spots, all her hot buttons.

For long minutes, he skimmed his fingers up her calves and explored the topography of her knees. A light touch behind one almost made her jackknife off the bed.

"Ticklish?" he asked.

Her breath was coming fast and shallow. "I...I don't know how much of this I can stand."

"Don't like it?" By the scent that was coming off her skin —hot and spicy—she liked what he was doing just fine. "Spread your legs."

She did so immediately, revealing a delicious landscape of smooth golden-brown skin. With the movement, her nightie rode up, revealing a skinny strip of lace between her legs, the center dark and damp.

The need to rip away the fabric covering her hummed

through his blood. He wanted to put his mouth right there, suck and tongue-fuck her until she screamed. Then he would do it all over again with his fingers. And again with his cock.

But he forced himself to concentrate on her inner thighs, stroking and kissing until her hips were arcing off the bed.

His own arousal was at the edge, his dick pulsing with the blood surging into it.

"Take off your gown. I want to see your breasts."

Slowly, Tessa pushed herself up and crossed her arms to draw the soft fabric over and off her body. Her breasts—fucking amazing under any circumstances—were spectacular. Swollen with pointed dark nipples.

The sight made him want to push her back, climb on top, and just...fuck her. Trying to will away the intensity of his need, Jonah closed his eyes and breathed.

"Are you hurting?" she asked.

"Like you wouldn't believe."

"I knew we shouldn't have—"

"I'm talking about this." He reached between his legs to circle his cock with his fist. The pressure of his own touch almost had him shooting off.

Tessa laughed softly. "Do men ever think of anything besides their penises?"

He snorted. "Cars, the remote control, football, and women."

"And with that last one, we're back to penises."

"You have to admit they're pretty handy inventions."

"They would be if you'd ever do something with yours."

That forced a bark of laughter from him. "Are you sure?"

"I will tell you if I don't like something, so stop worrying and touch me."

He splayed a hand in the center of her chest, savoring

the lush feel of her breasts against his fingers, and pushed her back down to the mattress. He grasped her hips and dragged her forward.

Without warning, he put his mouth on her, biting lightly through her panties. Her body convulsed and she let out a strangled moan.

"More?" he murmured against her inner thigh.

"Much, much more." Her body went lax, was his to command. The sheer trust she was giving him wrapped around Jonah's heart and squeezed.

"You might want to hold on, then." Because he wouldn't let up until she couldn't take any more. And he'd already discovered she was tougher, stronger than he'd ever imagined.

He hooked a finger through the lace covering her and ran his knuckle along her silky skin, giving extra attention to her clitoris. Soon her hips were lifting and she was making needy, greedy sounds. Jonah's stomach jumped with excitement and visceral need. Hands shaking, he yanked her panties down her legs and let them fall to the floor.

Sweet, sweet, sweet. The sight of her, bared to him, made Jonah want to drop to his knees and thank God. Since he was already kneeling, he did send up a little manly chin lift to the one responsible for the perfection of Tessa's body.

She was a gift. Maybe a gift meant just for him.

He edged her knees wider so he could fit his shoulders between her legs. His first lick was long and slow, a delicious taste of ice cream after years of summer.

"Fuuuck," she moaned, and Jonah pressed his face against her to suppress his laughter. She patted his head, a little harder than strictly necessary. "Jonah..."

So he gave her every bit of his skill and attention, licking and sucking and love-biting. The noises and words she was rambling made his balls draw up and his nipples harden. He brought her to the point of sobbing, then circled his lips around her clitoris and plunged two fingers inside her.

She was coming before he could seat his fingers to the palm. Hard, unrelenting clenches of her muscles. Her orgasm rolled on and on, bringing Jonah a mind-blowing pleasure and pride. They were so damn good together.

This time, when she touched his head, it was to pet his hair. "Wow," she slurred.

His laugh came from deep inside.

"You should get an award."

Jonah didn't even want to think about the shape of the trophy he might be given for his oral sex technique. "The only thing I want is you."

Her eyes heavy and satisfied, she lifted herself on her elbows. Her hair was a wild halo. "Pretty sure you just had me."

"What was that promise about showing me how flashy, powerful, and fast you are?"

She reached out as if to pat his chest, but stopped before she touched his skin. "That was before this."

There were positions that would make his burns a nonissue, one of them with Tessa on her knees and him behind like last time. His cock liked the idea of that just fine, but it didn't fit with what was happening inside him. He wanted to watch her eyes, see her pretty face, when he made her come hard.

He scrambled to gather up the bed pillows. He'd owe Grif an entire linen replacement after tonight, but who the hell cared.

"Lift up," he ordered.

She did a clumsy roll to one side and he shoved three pillows under her back and ass.

"That okay?"

"Ah...yes."

It was perfect, actually, lifting her almost to his hip level. Jonah leaned over her body, supporting himself with his arms, and kissed her. The feel of her mouth against his, the sweep of her tongue was as exciting and intimate as the taste of her on his lips.

Her hands hovered at his sides.

"Touch me," he said.

But instead of winding her arms around him as he expected, she fisted his dick, lying hard and tight against his belly. Jonah gritted his teeth against the eye-crossing bliss of her hand sliding up and down him.

But he needed more. Needed to be a part of her. Needed to *have* her.

That's when reality struck him, almost gutting him with his idiocy.

"Fuck, fuck, fuck," he chanted.

"Yes, please," Tessa said.

"Condom," he gritted out.

"Check the bag on the dresser."

"Huh?"

"Brynne is going to be your new favorite sister-in-law."

Jonah pushed himself up and stumbled over to the bag. He shoved his hand all the way to the bottom and came up with a row of foil packages. Yeah, Brynne would get a big ol' thank-you from him.

When he returned to the bed, Tessa's smile told him she knew exactly how thankful he was. He ripped into the package and rolled on protection.

"By the way," Tessa said softly. "I'm on the pill and I'm clean. Since... Well, I get tested regularly."

The indirect reference to her attack knotted up Jonah's

stomach. *Don't fuck this up,* he told himself. *She's moved on. It's time for you to do the same damn thing.*

"Me too. Clean, I mean. Not the pill."

"Then how about this?" Her smile and gaze never wavered as she reached down and rolled the rubber off his dick. Jonah's brain knocked against the top of his skull, making him woozy and stupid. He was about to slide inside a woman without a barrier for the first time in his life.

Her smile wavered. "I'm sorry. Maybe I was too forward—"

"No. It's just...I need a sec to get my mind around it. I've never—"

"Neither have I."

A beginning. A fresh start. Isn't that what he'd wished for for years? He couldn't turn back time, but he and Tessa could experience this as a first, together.

He bent over her, supporting himself with one arm, while he positioned himself between her legs. He went light-headed at the feel of her—hot and wet—against him.

Tessa raised her knees and reached between them. Together, they led him inside her body in a slow, smooth slide. Once they were fully joined, Tessa let her hand fall away. Jonah lifted it above her head and twined their fingers together. Did the same with the other.

Tessa's dark eyes were wide open, and Jonah had a feeling if he looked closely enough, he could see into her heart and her soul.

"Be with me," she whispered. "The whole me."

Her words wrenched something inside his chest. They were multilayered, asking him to open himself fully to her and to accept that she wasn't broken.

"Yes."

Her fingers tightened around his, and she lifted her hips

to draw him deeper. When he moved, it was like a spiritual experience. Slightly unreal, yet blinding in its satisfaction. Its sheer rightness.

Their bodies touched at only two points, but Jonah couldn't have felt closer to Tessa if he'd been able to climb inside her skin with her.

"Feels so good," Tessa said, her eyes taking on a dazed expression. "Like...like..."

"Being complete." He changed the angle of his thrust to rub against her G Spot.

Her legs wound around his hips and clasped him tight, limiting his range of motion. God, if only he could lie chest-to-chest with her. He could get his hands under her ass and love her with long strokes. Instead, he pressed kisses to her wrists, each in turn, and disengaged their hands.

"Don't..."

"I'm not going anywhere." Not ever again. He'd run enough. Avoided her for far longer than he should have. He gripped the backs of her thighs and, much as it pained him, unwound her legs from around his hips. That gave him the leverage he needed to slide in and out of her at an angle that had her moaning and shaking within seconds. "Like that?"

"I'm...oh, I can't..." She clutched at the sheets, wadding handfuls as she tried to get closer to his touch, to the thrust of his cock.

Another small adjustment and Jonah was rubbing her clit on every stroke. "Let go. You're safe with me."

The way she was writhing under him, he knew she was close. Probably would've been climbing his body if she could. He'd be a liar if he said that didn't feed his ego.

He wanted this to be the best she'd ever had. He wanted to be the last man she ever wanted.

"Please," she said, her thighs struggling against his tight hold. She was fighting him. She didn't want this.

Uncertainty rose up in him and he almost released her. But a tiny rational part of him understood she was fighting to get closer to him, not fighting to get away from him.

He drove into her harder, his ass clenching with the effort to hold off his own orgasm.

Her muscles bore down on him as she started coming, and Tessa reared up and nipped his shoulder. And holy fuck, the feel of her sharp little teeth sent a current of pure electricity through his body and out his dick.

Unable to control his instincts, he flat-out fucked her. Without thought, without concern, definitely without remorse. And when his own orgasm rose and spilled over, he came close to blacking out. At the last second, he caught himself before he collapsed and crushed Tessa beneath him.

"Jonah?" she asked, her voice seeming to come from miles away. "Are you okay?"

Somehow, he managed to roll them to their sides, barely registering that his own sweat was seeping under the bandages and stinging the wounds on his torso. "Tessa, God...I think I love you."

23

JONAH'S FAMILY OBVIOUSLY HAD SOME STRANGE AFFINITY FOR early morning visits, because when Tessa woke, someone was knocking at the bedroom door. The Steeles also had a problem with house key sharing.

It felt as if she and Jonah had plunged into a sleep coma only seconds before. He was sprawled on his back, one arm hanging off the bedside and one covering her pelvic area. That man had sleep groping habits.

Last night, he'd said he thought he loved her. Did he truly love *her* or was he simply relieved that she felt there was nothing wrong with a man who liked to take control in the bedroom?

The way he'd handled her body hadn't scared her. It had thrilled her.

But this morning they obviously didn't have time to discuss the hot sex or the emotions brought on by it. She nudged his shoulder. "Jonah. Jonah, wake up."

"No breakfast, Mom. Not hungry," he mumbled.

She rolled her lips in to keep from laughing. "If you don't get up, your brothers are going to see me naked again."

His eyes opened—*pop*—and he stared at her with complete lucidity. "What time is it?"

Tessa checked her phone on the nightstand. "Eight."

"This time, I *will* kill every last one of them."

"Even your mom?"

His mouth turned down. "No. Because she makes kick-ass biscuits. And because, well, she's my mama."

Tessa's heart turned a slow, sweet loop de loop. Her own mother had always told her to watch how a son treated his mom because that would tell her what kind of man he was. And what she saw in front of her was a loyal, protective, caring man who had a hard time accepting help. A hard time accepting himself for exactly who he was.

A hard time believing he and Tessa could belong together.

So she would just have to keep proving it to him day after day until he believed it. Starting when his family wasn't standing directly outside the door, probably picturing what she and Jonah were up to.

She scrambled to get out of the bed, but Jonah caught her hand and drew her back for a soft kiss.

"What was that for?" she asked.

"Are you okay?"

She knew he meant physically, but she hesitated because her emotional state wasn't on an even keel right now after hearing him talk about love.

"I'm sorry if—"

"You have nothing to be sorry for. You worry about me feeling safe, but you need to understand you're safe with me, too. I loved being with you—the real you—last night. I never want you to be anything less than honest with me."

He blinked and a shade seemed to come down over his eyes. Then he about-faced with a wicked grin and a pat to her ass. "You might want to put clothes on before going into the living room."

"You think?"

His deep laugh warmed her, inflated her heart, and pulsed through her body. Tessa realized it was a feeling of everything being right. In alignment.

She quickly slipped into a pair of surprisingly comfy jean leggings, a shirt, and the beautiful sweater from Brynne. When she and Jonah walked out of the bedroom, most of his family was gathered in the apartment's sparse living room. Tessa hadn't noticed it last night, but against one wall sat a psychedelic green, pink, and yellow couch with sagging cushions. With his knees spread, Reid took up two-thirds of it, while Grif glared in that direction. Whether his displeasure was directed at his brother or the couch, Tessa wasn't sure.

Badger arrowed directly for Micki, and she hefted him like a football. "I'll take him out."

From a basket, Miss Joan was unpacking enough biscuits, ham, and jam to feed half the population of Steele Ridge. She glanced up, looked between Tessa and her son, and gave a tidy nod. "I figured everyone could use some fuel."

Reid reached for a biscuit and she slapped at his hand. "Tessa and Jonah first."

"I think you love him more than the rest of us," Reid playfully groused.

"Of course I do," his mother said with a glint in her eye. "Are you just now figuring that out?"

Reid shot a look at Grif. "That's a good reason for Aubrey to stay an only child. She won't have to vie for top spot in your family."

Grif glanced down. Then his focus moved to the tall

windows overlooking Main Street. In the next few seconds, his attention seemed to light on everything but one of his family members.

Miss Joan's mouth opened and she pressed her palms to her cheeks. "Oh, Griffin, a baby? Are you serious?" She rushed over to Grif and manacled her tiny arms around his waist. "Tell me it's true."

His sigh had a resigned air to it. "We weren't planning to announce it for another couple of weeks. Carlie Beth's gonna kill me."

But Miss Joan was too busy doing some kind of joyful River Dance around him to acknowledge his words. His brothers crowded around him, shaking his hand and slapping his back.

"You're working hard to oust Jonah as the favored son, aren't you?" Reid asked him. "Between Aubrey and this new baby, you're trying to get a corner on the grandkid market before any of the rest of us."

Grif's grin was wide and cocky. "I can't help it if my sperm are stronger than yours."

Behind his mom's back, Reid gave his brother the middle finger.

Their brotherly ribbing warmed Tessa. Reassured her that although Jonah could be closed off, he had plenty of people around him who would always draw him out again.

"I'm so excited that I almost can't think." Miss Joan waved her hands in front of her face. "But as much as I want to talk about a new grandbaby, we have to refocus on Jonah and Tessa this morning. Micki made some progress last night."

With Tessa's dog in her lap, Micki was slumped in an easy chair that didn't look much better than the couch. She appeared a little strung out, her normally sharp eyes slightly dull and her spiky hair flat on one side. Jonah obviously recognized the signs of an all-nighter, too, because he said, "I planned to attack the problem this morning."

Micki reached for his hand and he dropped down to sit on the arm of her chair. "I figured we could work it in shifts. I went back into DataFort's records," she told him, her voice raspy.

"And?"

"I was able to get a thread on our hacker this time. Looked like he'd been poking around again."

Jonah's attention lasered in on his sister. "You traced him?"

"Well, yes...and no. He was smart enough to bounce his tracks through multiple servers—Hong Kong, Mumbai, New York, and several others. I lost the trail in Rio. And unfortunately, I also tripped some trigger that locked up Tessa's account."

"No big." Jonah waved away Micki's words. "It'll take you less than fifteen minutes to fix that."

Tessa closed her eyes. None of this was legal. Then again, they weren't exactly battling someone who played by any kind of rules or moral code.

"But I started thinking about the hardware he sent you." Micki said. "We assumed he modded it himself."

Tessa saw where Micki was going and jumped in. "But if he's been so busy setting up the ground rules and scenarios for the game, would he have time to build all the hardware from the ground up?"

Micki's smile was tired but admiring. "Finally, someone besides me who can give you a run for your money in the brains department."

When Jonah turned his attention toward Tessa, his expression was conflicted, as if he couldn't decide whether to draw her into this conversation or push her out. Finally, he said, "There are a helluva a lot of hardware manufacturers in the US alone. And if he bought his components overseas, it could take us years to track them down."

Micki pulled something from a canvas tote bag sitting on the floor. "Hope you don't mind, but I detached one of the sensors when you took the vest off in the car yesterday. Don't worry, I closed the wiring circuit." She held the pieces of the lone sensor in her palm. "These are made by the same company as the vibrating motors Steele Trap uses for its controllers."

"How did you figure that out?"

"I had a hunch and called the head hardware engineer at about two in the morning Seattle time. He wasn't too talkative at first, but I promised him you'd send him season tickets to the Mariners' games."

Jonah nodded thoughtfully. "And?"

"And all this mess didn't start until Tessa left Seattle, too, right?" Micki asked. "That has to mean something."

EVERYONE BUT MICKI, TESSA, AND JONAH FILTERED OUT OF the apartment when he reminded them that they wouldn't be any help with the technical aspects of tracking down this bastard.

"The hacker-modder has to be someone I counseled," Tessa said.

Jonah disagreed, but if going down that Steele Ridge employee path again would keep Tessa and his sister busy while he dug deeper into Harrison Shaw's buddies, he was all for it. "You're right. Maybe we missed something."

"I need to go back through every file." Tessa looked at Micki. "Can you get me access?"

"Sure thing."

"While y'all work that angle, I'll take a look at the hardware." Because it still wasn't making a damn bit of sense to him why one of Shaw's compadres would've set up this elaborate scenario. There were infinitely easier avenues for payback.

He sat down on the floor with the hardware in order to make a good show for Micki and Tessa and to keep his mind busy. Otherwise, he'd overthink the fact that Tessa hadn't said "I love you" back last night.

Yes, he'd blurted it out during the heat of an intimate moment, but he meant it.

He grappled with the tiny guts of the sensor, using an eyeglass screwdriver and precision tweezer, and Badger trundled over to sniff at the hardware. Obviously unimpressed, he sneezed on one, then decided Jonah's thigh was the perfect place to stretch out and take a siesta.

While Micki once again violated firewalls to get Tessa into the client records she'd been shut out of, Jonah stroked Badger's back and studied the sensors for any clue they might give him. When he'd asked Maggie about dusting the equipment for prints, she'd bagged the timer. But she'd shaken her head at the sensors, telling him that by sweating all over them like a linebacker during two-a-days, he'd no doubt washed away any evidence.

The welts from the sensors were starting to itch, and he had to keep his hands busy to keep from scratching the hell out of them.

Right now, he had nothing solid to connect Cartwright to all of this except a different kind of itchy feeling. What if he was all wrong in thinking this had anything to do with Harrison Shaw and his buddies? Had he made a mistake in assuming Tessa had simply been a way to get to him?

He needed to track down Cartwright. Alone.

Shutting Tessa out again was a dick move, but after the fire he didn't want her near any of those men.

Which meant he needed time and space to get to Cartwright.

"Are y'all in the files yet?" he asked.

"Of course. Everyone from Keith Benery to Sharon Vrana." Micki was obviously dragging ass if her jaw-cracking yawn was any indication, but she said, "I'm just setting it up so we can download the files and have the computer read them back to Tessa."

Jonah casually scratched Badger's head and tried to mask the tension squeezing his body. "Hey, I need to run over and check in with Cash and Maggie on a couple of things."

"Did you learn anything new?" Tessa studied him as if she could get inside his mind and dig out whatever she wanted. With a grapefruit spoon.

"No." Which wasn't strictly a lie. "That's why I want to walk through some thoughts with those two. They might have a flash of insight that's escaped me." It took all of Jonah's strength to meet Tessa's gaze and maintain an air of innocence. "Why don't you two take all this out to Mom's house and finish up your research there?"

Micki's eyes went squinty. "Why would we do that when we already have everything set up here?"

"Because Grif said she insisted on going home this morning, and I don't like the idea of her being alone at Tupelo Hill with what happened yesterday. There's plenty of room to spread out and space for you to take a nap."

"I'm fine." The fact that she said the words around another massive yawn pegged her as a liar.

"The sooner y'all pack it up and head out, the sooner I can pick Maggie's and Cash's brains."

Although Micki was obviously dragging, she and Tessa scooped up the laptops and their notes. Within five minutes, they were packed up and ready to roll.

Jonah passed a still snoozing Badger to Tessa and gave her a kiss. "I'll be out to pick you up a little later."

"If you find out something important, call us immediately."

"If I come across anything you need to know, I will." He hated deceiving her this way, but he wasn't willing to jeopardize her safety. This guy had already proven he didn't give a shit about sacrificing the people Jonah loved.

24

When Tessa and Micki arrived at Tupelo Hill, Miss Joan threatened to permanently take away Micki's laptop if she didn't give it a rest and go lie down. Micki frowned and stomped up the stairs to the second floor with Badger on her heels.

"Do people realize you rule with the iron-fist-in-a-velvet-glove strategy?" Tessa asked Miss Joan.

With quick competent movements, she was transferring four different types of holiday cookies into gift boxes. "Early on, I only gave my kids two choices, both of which were acceptable to me."

"Like juice or milk?"

"You get the idea."

"That's downright brilliant." And a strategy she'd be slipping into her back pocket for any future children she and Jonah... No, it was too soon to start conjuring up hopeful images of bright and broody little boys who looked like Jonah.

"That's the only way I could handle six of them without being trampled on."

"I understand you raised them primarily by yourself." Wheedling out that little detail had taken Tessa months of *accidentally* running into Jonah in the Steele Trap break room.

"You're asking about Eddy, aren't you?"

"I met him last night. He stopped by the Murchison building."

"Really?" She paused in her cookie box packing. "Do you know why?"

"Jonah didn't"—or wouldn't—"say. They had a private conversation that he didn't share with me."

"I was brought up believing that the good Lord doesn't give anyone more than she can bear. But when my Eddy started disappearing for longer periods of time, I sometimes thought God had finally blown his perfect record." She chuckled. "Especially on cold days when all the kids were cooped up inside. Britt tried his best to be an impartial referee for his younger siblings. But it's not a role he ever should've had to take on." She slid a platter of cookies onto the table and went back to the counter to fetch two big mugs filled to the brim with hot chocolate and fat marshmallows. "Micki'll pout when she gets up and realizes we had cookies without her."

With the mound of them—sugar with red sprinkles, almond biscotti, shortbread, and gingerbread people—on the plate, Micki didn't have to worry about leftovers. But Tessa might have to start worrying about her waistband if she spent more time with Jonah's mother.

That would be a reasonable price to pay if she could get to know this wonderful woman better.

Miss Joan eyed the laptop. "I know you're chomping at the bit to get back to your research, so feel free to snack and work."

"How did you know?"

"Two of my children are technology prodigies, although how that happened, I will never know. For years, I've watched the way they fidget when they can't wait to get their hands on some kind of machine because they just *have* to know something."

Oh. She had been tapping her fingernails against the side of her mug, hadn't she?

"So don't mind me. I'm going to grab a pad of paper and start thinking about all the ways I want to spoil my new grandbaby."

Tessa needed to go back though all her Steele Trap sessions, but found herself opening the recording she'd made the night she'd strong-armed Jonah into talking with her after they had sex. She should've deleted it when Micki regained access to her files.

No, she should've deleted it long ago.

What she hadn't realized until later was that when her jacket had fallen to the floor the night they made love in his office, her recorder had clicked on. Had captured every word, every sigh, every moan of pleasure between them.

She fast-forwarded past the illicitly recorded sex and listened to the conversation—if it could be called that—they'd had after.

"I don't want to be like them," she heard him say. "They paid, but it wasn't enough." The few times she hadn't been able to resist listening to the file in the past, she'd always focused on Jonah's first statement. But now, the words *they paid* seemed louder than all the others.

Who hadn't paid?

He couldn't have been talking about Shaw and the others because they hadn't paid. Unless...

Had Jonah decided to somehow make them pay?

Stirring that pot now might destroy this tenuous bond between her and Jonah, but she had to know.

She angled her computer away from Miss Joan and hunched closer. Her fingers were shaking, but they hit the correct keys, typing out Harrison Shaw.

Still, she hesitated before she hit Enter.

Nothing. No mention of him since he went to prison for drug trafficking.

Breathing a little easier now, she typed in another name.

Matthew Levine. Over two hundred names came up on LinkedIn alone. That would be like searching the Mojave for a grain of sand.

She didn't even know the names of a couple of her attackers, but one guy's last name had been Cartwright. The other guys had called him Cartwheel, but his real name was Charles.

When she typed in his name, a few Charles Cartwrights in North Carolina popped up with LinkedIn profiles. One was an insurance salesman in Wilmington. Another worked at a bank in Charlotte. And yet another was a high-school coach in Greenville.

But LinkedIn profiles weren't going to give her the kind of information she was looking for. People used the platform to brag about their professional accomplishments, not reveal the mistakes in their lives.

Tessa wasn't completely sure what she *was* looking for, but she'd know it if she found it. On the third page of her Google search, she spotted it. The *Daily Tar Hill,* the UNC newspaper, listed an old article about Charlie Cartwright. He was a senior accused of cheating on the LSAT by hacking into the Law School Admission Council's network and stealing test answers. Apparently, the student had denied it, but the accusation had ended his plans for a law career.

They paid, but it wasn't enough.

Oh, sweet merciful God.

She jumped up from the table so quickly that her chair almost toppled over, and Miss Joan looked up in surprise. "I...uh...sorry, but I need the restroom."

Miss Joan pointed her down the hall, and Tessa grabbed her phone and hurried toward privacy.

She dialed Jonah's number, but it went to voice mail. Should she leave a message or not?

Finally, she just said, "Jonah, I have some information that might be relevant. Call me immediately."

She dabbed at her face with cool water, trying to keep the sick feeling of betrayal from overtaking her. Once she had most of her composure back, she returned to the kitchen.

If Jonah had done what she now suspected, she might have just stumbled on the truth about who was behind the hacking and game-playing.

Still, she scrolled through the list of Steele Trap employees who'd scheduled more than one session with her.

Benery, Caldwell, Grimes, Vrana, and a few dozen others.

Wait a minute. Keith Benery was from somewhere in the South. Not only was he one of the few people in the company besides Jonah and her to have a drawl, but she remembered once having a lively conversation about where to find the best Carolina barbecue.

So she clicked onto Keith's file and refreshed her memory on why he'd spent several sessions with her, primarily to talk about the death of his younger brother. As she remembered, he was very closed-mouthed about how his brother had died, only saying it was an accident. In fact, he'd never even told her his brother's name.

His brother's death had obviously hit Keith hard, because he'd been in her office regularly until...

She clicked through the files, checking dates. His last scheduled appointment had been on December 18, a few months before Jonah sold Steele Trap. Maybe he'd finally worked through his grief and hadn't felt he needed any more support. Or maybe it was something much darker.

Pausing the recording, she clicked over to her web browser and typed in *Benery obituary* and *North Carolina*. The site for the *Smoky Mountain Times* in Bryson City listed an obit for Steven Benery.

But it reported no cause of death.

CHARLOTTE BANK AND TRUST WAS BUSTLING WHEN JONAH walked in. On his way into the city, he'd called to confirm that Cartwright was at work today. It would be his last day if Jonah had anything to do with it.

He strolled up to a desk occupied by a perky blond twenty-something. "Hey, there. I wanted to talk with someone about a home loan."

"Absolutely, Mister..."

"Smith," he said. "A friend of mine recommended Charles Cartwright."

Her smile dialed back a few notches. "Of course." Hm. Someone else wasn't crazy about ol' Charlie, either. But she made a quick interoffice call and hung up. "You're in luck. He happens to be free right now. Just down that hallway. Second door on the left."

"Appreciate it."

Like many bank offices, Cartwright's was surrounded by windows from the waist up. Jonah walked inside and closed the door behind him.

Without looking up, Cartwright waved a distracted hand toward a visitor's chair. "Have a seat, and I'll be with you in—"

"Now, *Cartwheel*," Jonah said pleasantly, clenching his hands to keep from jumping over the fucker's desk and killing him in front of everyone in this bank.

Like an animal that had caught a predator's scent, Charlie lifted his head slowly.

"Recognize me?" Jonah asked, casually picking up a paperweight.

"I...ah..."

"Don't bother lying, because I saw you at Tucci's the other night. You were staring at Tessa Martin. Surely you remember her."

Cartwright went to reach for something under his desk, but Jonah was faster, slamming the paperweight across the guy's knuckles.

"Keep the other hand on the desk, too."

"Who the fuck are you?"

"You know exactly who the fuck I am."

"I don't want any trouble from you, Steele."

"Then why did you bring it to my front door?"

"I don't know what you're talking about," Cartwright said. Jonah was pleased to see sweat circles forming under the arms of Cartwright's snappy white button-up shirt.

"Who did you follow into Tucci's—Tessa or me?"

"I went in there to have a fucking martini before I went home to my fucking wife."

"Does she know you're a rapist?"

The color in Cartwright's face leached out. "You're insane. I never—"

"Harrison Shaw's house. December before you graduated high school." Jonah glanced around the nondescript office. "Bet this wasn't the future you expected to have. The first Cartwright in four generations who didn't get into law school and eventually pursue a career in politics. Mommy and Daddy must be so disappointed."

"How the hell did you know I..." His words trailed off as his mouth opened wider. "You set me up. I thought you made video games."

Jonah's laugh was low and decidedly unfriendly. "Dude, fucking up your life took me less than ten minutes."

"I'm calling the pol—" Cartwright reached for his phone, but Jonah slammed him with the paperweight again.

"You could call the cops," Jonah told him. "But you couldn't prove anything to save your life. And the statute of limitations for some things is *way* shorter than the one for rape. Now, were you following Tessa?"

"I had no idea she would be in that restaurant."

"So you were watching me."

He actually looked as if he didn't know what Jonah was talking about. "Why would I have done that if I didn't know you were the one who blew my shot at law school?" *Ding, ding, ding.* Understanding dawned in Cartwright's eyes. "You did it to all of us, didn't you?"

Jonah dug the weight into Cartwright's hand and enjoyed the sound of bones grinding against one another.

"Son of a bitch," Cartwright breathed. "You fucked us all."

What Jonah couldn't bring himself to say was that how he'd fucked them over was nothing compared to the way they'd hurt

Tessa. But Cartwright was pretty damn convincing. Had he really not known that Jonah had manipulated his life behind the scenes? "Then what about the others—Levine, Johnson, and Bledsoe? Maybe one of them decided to come after me."

"Believe me, if anyone had figured out you were the one behind all our bad luck, he would've let the others know. You screwed up our lives, probably cost us millions of dollars."

"Boo-fucking-hoo. You're lucky I didn't use a more *permanent* solution." With a smile, he lifted the paperweight and rammed it down across three of Cartwright's knuckles. The guy made a sick gurgling sound. "I want you to think about this real hard. See if you remember anything. I'm taking one of your business cards, so you can expect my call in an hour. Between now and then, get on the phone with your buddies and ask them who's been coming for Tessa and me. If I find out any of you lied, your lives won't be worth living."

And with that, he tossed the paperweight into Cartwright's lap and walked out.

Fuck. He thought he had it all figured out, but if Cartwright was telling the truth, it meant Jonah had jack-shit, and this modder was still playing the game.

25

Tessa's insides were in a jumble over what she'd discovered about Charlie Cartwright, but she had to set that aside for now. Had to set aside that Jonah had been anything but honest. The most important thing she could do now was to find Keith Benery.

"Do you think Micki would mind if I borrowed her car?" Tessa asked Miss Joan, keeping her tone as casual as possible.

Apparently not casual enough, because Jonah's mom looked up from her grandbaby-spoiling list and frowned. "Why?" Her attention locked onto Tessa's computer. "What did you just find out?"

Even as an adult, she found it hard to lie to a parental figure, and Tessa wasn't much of a fibber to start with. She sighed. "Apparently, one of the men who raised a red flag for me when I was going back through my client files grew up not far from here. His parents still live here, so I thought—"

"That you'd just run off and check out the situation yourself?"

"After I text Jonah and ask him to meet me." She almost choked on the lie.

Miss Joan patted at the part in her hair. "I swear, this is the reason I have to use Miss Clairol on a regular basis. Kids grow up, but that doesn't mean they ever grow any darn sense." She pointed at Tessa's phone. "Go on, then. Send him a text."

Tessa typed up the text and pretended to hit send. *Keith Benery. His parents live in Bryson City. 1612 Connamere. Meet there ASAP.*

"Done," she said, pushing back her chair to stand. "Do you know where Micki put her keys?"

"Nope," Miss Joan said cheerfully, "but I know exactly where mine are."

"But—"

"Sweetheart, you didn't think I would let you go alone, did you?"

That was how Tessa found herself riding shotgun in Miss Joan's sturdy little Subaru with the radio tuned in to an oldies-but-goodies station. Buddy Holly crooned out "That'll Be the Day" as they headed west on Highway 74.

Before long, though, Jonah's mom turned down the volume. "You love him, don't you?"

Tessa had a feeling she wasn't talking about one of the 1950s heartthrobs on the radio. And honestly, after what she'd uncovered today, her feelings for Jonah were swinging from one extreme to the other. Her body felt achy and slow from the toll of discovering what he'd done behind her back. How he'd kept it from her the past few days when he knew how important the truth was to her. "And you don't pull any punches, do you?" she asked his mom.

"I should've expected someone in your profession to answer a question with a question. He would die if he ever heard me say this, but Jonah's always been sensitive. Big heart with a huge capacity for being hurt. That's one of the reasons he alienates himself from other people, even his family sometimes."

Tessa held her thoughts for several minutes before asking, "How was he, after?"

His mom drew in a long breath. "Withdrawn, moody. But we all chalked that up to Micki taking off right after they graduated. You think he was impacted by what happened to you."

"Yes, and I...I think he might've tried to get back at my attackers."

"What do you mean? How would he have done something like that?"

"I don't know exactly. He just told me once that he didn't feel as if they paid enough. I don't think he liked the fact that my parents and I never went to the police."

She shouldn't have mentioned it. Jonah's mother loved him and would always come to his defense. It was what parents did. *Change directions, Tessa.*

Miss Joan grabbed for Tessa's hand, hung on tight. "One time when Evie was in middle school, some kids were teasing her at recess. Jonah caught wind of it somehow, and the bullies found themselves signed up for thirty hours of community service, cleaning up a piece of public property where folks had dumped a bunch of trash. If I remember correctly, there were piles of dirty diapers and rotten food out there. Jonah went out there every day to watch them. He tries to hide it, but he has a very protective streak when it comes to those he loves."

"Which means he's willing to do just about anything for them, right?" The only thing keeping Tessa from screaming right now was the fact that Jonah's punishing her rapists meant he'd had feelings for her for years. Maybe not the feelings she wanted, but the violence she'd faced all those years ago had jumpstarted something inside him.

They were drawing close to the Benerys' home, so Tessa shelved her thoughts. They pulled up in front of a neat brick rancher that looked as if it had been built in the 1960s. The lawn was dormant, but a trio of evergreens added some seasonal cheer.

Miss Joan unhooked her seatbelt. "I'm coming with you."

"No."

"Sweetheart, I wasn't asking for permission. I wouldn't let you drive out here alone, and I'm certainly not going to let you walk up to the front door alone."

A quick debate waged in Tessa's brain and conscience. If anything happened to his mother, Jonah would never forgive Tessa. Then again, Keith's parents weren't the potential threat. He was. "If you see a man, blond and in his twenties, I want you to come back and lock yourself inside the car."

"Mm-hm." Miss Joan's noncommittal answer told Tessa all she needed to know about who the Steele siblings had inherited their stubborn qualities from.

"I need to ask a few questions. The plan is to get in and out in less than ten minutes."

"I'm just here for moral support."

The small front porch was decorated with a waist-high Santa perched on a pair of snow skis. A trio of elves hung on for dear life behind him, while a dozen mini reindeer served as the manpower in front. The wide grin on Santa's face said he was a fan of extreme snow sports.

Tessa rang the doorbell.

The woman who answered was probably in her late

fifties, nicely dressed in black pants and a paisley tunic top. "May I help you?"

"Mrs. Benery?"

"Yes."

"I'm Tessa Martin." She held out her hand, and Keith's mother took it. "I work at Steele Trap Entertainment with your son." A small fib since she was no longer there. "I'm actually here looking for him."

"If Steele Trap is trying to convince him to stay on, I can tell you that you're wasting your time. He's made up his mind to move back home."

"Are you saying he's quit his job?"

"He's given his notice, yes."

When she'd chatted with him for a few minutes at Tucci's, he'd said nothing about leaving. In fact, he'd acted as if he was happy at Steele Trap and eager to help Jonah with another project. "Mrs. Benery, when's the last time you saw Keith?"

Her mouth twisted as she looked up in thought. "Probably three days ago. Said he was planning to do some camping up around Lake Junaluska."

That certainly confirmed Tessa's suspicions that Keith had been close by, because the lake was just northeast of Steele Ridge. "Any specific campground?"

"He didn't say."

"Mrs. Benery, I need to ask you a question that could be painful, but please know I wouldn't ask if it weren't so important."

As expected, the woman's face closed up in preparation. "Okay."

"I came across an obituary for your younger son, Steven. Can you tell me what happened to him?"

Keith's mother closed her eyes, breathed, then opened

them again. "Both my boys were always heavy into video games, but Steven also liked to play outside. He would beg Keith to come out with him. That wasn't Keith's thing, but the times when he gave in, Steven was so excited."

Tessa sustained eye contact and gave a nod to encourage Mrs. Benery to finish the story, even though she had a horrible intuition about where this was headed.

"One day when Steven was about thirteen, they were out playing and Keith came running back to the house. He said Steven was hurt. My husband and I hurried to the wooded area at the end of the cul de sac. We found him on the ground. He wasn't breathing."

"I'm so sorry." Sympathy overwhelmed Tessa, and judging by the tears in Miss Joan's eyes, she had been affected, as any mother would.

"We found out later that a pellet from Keith's air rifle had lodged in Steven's brain. No entry wound, so they believed it went up his nose. Keith never touched that pellet gun again."

26

Once Tessa gave Mrs. Benery her most sincere sympathies over the loss of her son, she and Jonah's mother slowly walked toward the car.

"I can't even imagine what she must've gone through," Miss Joan said. "A child isn't supposed to pass on before his parents. That kind of pain has to be huge."

The pain of being responsible for your sibling's death would be devastating as well. "I think Keith is the one who's behind everything that's happened over the past few days. I think he's the one who tried to burn down Jonah's house."

"I don't understand. Do you think he's still harboring some kind of guilt for what happened to his brother?"

"It's entirely possible." Tessa had been mentally flipping through her sessions with Keith. He'd been angry and upset about his brother's death, but he'd never expressed that he himself was to blame. But something was wavering at the edge of her psychologist's intuition. She just couldn't seem to grasp the trailing thread and pull it, so as much as she hated to lean on Jonah, especially after what she'd discovered, she needed his insight. She reached into her purse for her phone. "Maybe Jonah will understand why Keith decided to target us."

"Highly doubtful," a male voice said from behind her.

Tessa whirled around to find Keith Benery standing at the edge of his parents' property. With his boyish face and freckles, he looked like an innocent teenager, but the handgun he was holding confirmed he was an angry adult. "Keith, we just had a nice visit with your mother. I'd love to sit down and talk with you about what happened to your brother. Why don't we—"

"Give me your phones. Both of you." Keith's unwavering stare made it clear he expected them to cave to his demand. Tessa pretended to fumble hers and prayed she'd hit the button that would send the draft text to Jonah.

Both she and Miss Joan handed over their phones, and Keith stuffed them in a duffel over his shoulder.

"Get in the car." He jerked his head toward the Subaru.

"You're right. It's cold out here. We'd be more comfortable there. But we told your mother we'd be right back." She shot a meaningful look toward Jonah's mom. "If you'll just let Joan go back and make our excuses—"

"I know who she is," he said. "She's Jonah Steele's mother, and she's not going anywhere. Now get in the car. Front seats, both of you."

"If you don't want to talk here, I bet there's a coffee shop nearby," Tessa said, trying to will away the sinking feeling that with every word, Keith was the one taking over as dictator of this situation. "I'll drive."

If she was in the driver's seat, Miss Joan would have a better chance for escape.

Once they were inside the car, Keith settled into the back with the gun trained on Jonah's mother.

"Wh...Where are we going?"

"Steele Ridge." He sneered the last two words. "Mr. Big Dick's ego is so huge he had to have a town named after him."

Tessa glanced in the rearview mirror. Keith's eyes were narrowed, but his focus never wavered from Miss Joan. Tessa said, "It sounds like you're upset with Jonah for some reason. Maybe you'd like to talk about that."

"I don't want any of your psycho-mumbo-jumbo. Didn't work before. Sure isn't gonna work now."

Yeah, she obviously sucked at it if this was the outcome from her one and only grief counseling client. But all she needed now was to keep him talking. "Counseling is most effective when you're completely open and honest. You told me about your brother, but I'd like to hear—"

"Shut up, bitch."

Miss Joan kept her hand out of sight as she reached over and squeezed Tessa's. A warning or a reassurance, she wasn't sure.

Every few seconds Tessa risked a look back at Keith. He wasn't frothing at the mouth or talking to himself. He was obviously very much in command, and that terrified her more than any breakdown. Keith knew exactly what he was doing and was stone cold about it.

When they were a few miles outside Steele Ridge, Tessa said, "We're almost there. Can you tell me where we're going?"

"Take the third right off Main Street. And don't try anything as we're driving through town. You make any move to communicate with people outside the car, and Mama Steele's head will be a splatter against the windshield."

Tessa had tried to remain calm, but his threat made terror rock her belly. "She has nothing to do with this, Keith.

Obviously, you're upset with Jonah and possibly me. Why don't I drop her off and then we can—"

"If you stop the car before I tell you to, she'll be dead."

Once they made the turn he'd indicated, he gave Tessa directions that navigated them onto Hidden Hills Drive. The street was in a residential neighborhood filled with modest but sturdy ranchers and split-levels built on multi-acre lots.

Miss Joan's grip on Tessa's hand tightened. "What?" Tessa mouthed.

Her response was a barely perceptible head shake.

"Park there." Keith pointed to a large wooded lot between houses. "We're going to get out and take a little field trip. If either of you tries to call for help, I will kill the other. Understand?"

"Young man," Miss Joan said in a disappointed mother tone, "you're making a choice that won't turn out well for you."

He grabbed Tessa by the hair, hard enough that tears welled in her eyes, and yanked her back awkwardly so she was wedged between the two front seats. That pain was nothing compared to him jamming his gun into the space beneath her skull. "Lady, if you want to lecture me, I will get rid of her right now. Then you'll have to explain to your son how you got his girlfriend killed."

Girlfriend...

The first time she and Jonah had seen one another in almost a year was at Tucci's the other night. Why would Keith think they were...?

She closed her eyes. The recording. Keith had listened to all her recorded files, including the one of her and Jonah. What if she could convince him that she and Jonah weren't involved? Would that make a difference? "I know what you're doing, Keith," she said in a calm voice. "You want to punish Jonah for something." Something she still didn't understand. Normally, she didn't advocate lying to a client, but this wasn't exactly a normal appointment. "But if you're angry with me because you think Jonah and I are involved, that's just not the case."

The gun dug deeper. "Oh, really? Then explain why you let him screw you in public then. Little Miss Professional fucked the boss right there in his office. I thought you were different, that you were on my side, but no. What Jonah Steele wants, Jonah Steele gets. Guess he wanted your hot little pussy."

Tessa couldn't hold in her gasp or control the heat that rushed to her face. What mortified her more—Jonah's mom hearing this or that Keith had listened to something so private—she couldn't say.

So that was why Keith had never been back to see her. Her mind clicking, she said, "That...that was a one-time thing."

He snorted. "Which is why you're sleeping in his bed now. You suck as a therapist and you suck as a liar. Then again, those are the same thing, aren't they? You told me the pain of Steven's death would be bearable one day. That was bullshit."

He was right. She'd been in over her head thinking she could guide him through his grief. Why had she even toyed with the idea of helping people through traumas? Keith was proof that she had no business doing anything more than team building and making referrals to real counselors. "I was—"

"Kinda like your fuck buddy has been feeding you BS for years." Keith rolled right over her words. "After I figured out you were hot for him, I did a little digging on our boy Jonah. Hacked the hacker. Bet he didn't tell you what all he's been up to over the years. How he was the one who funded that big college scholarship for you."

"Wha...What are you talking about?"

"Did you really think you were good enough to get a full ride to college? Nah, our boy Steele robbed Shaw to pay Martin. A hundred grand or so."

"That doesn't make any sense." Her brain started a continual loop, trying to work it out. Was Keith saying Jonah stole from Harrison Shaw to pay for her education?

Oh, God. Somehow, Jonah *had* found a way to punish them, and all these years, he'd allowed her to think she was a strong, self-made woman.

"You'll have to ask him for the lowdown. If you're alive long enough. Now get the fuck outta the car," he demanded, shoving her back toward her seat.

The gun was Tessa's steady companion as they got out. Keith didn't even look down when he grabbed his bag from the backseat. "Into those trees." He shoved Tessa toward the wooded lot.

They trooped through the woods, dead branches and leaves crunching under their feet. Tessa tried to remember how far they'd gone, counting each step and looking up to catch the direction of the waning winter sun.

A few minutes later, Keith pulled Tessa up by the back of her beautiful sweater. He tossed the bag he'd been carrying toward Miss Joan. "Unzip that and take out the sensor vests."

"Keith, can you at least share what you're trying to—"

Whack. Tessa's knees wobbled at the feel of the gun slamming into the top of her spine. "Take off your sweater."

Tessa couldn't do this again. If Keith tried to rape her, she'd fight with everything inside her, until one of them was dead. But she didn't want Miss Joan to die in the process. She glanced at her and mouthed, "Run."

Another head shake from her. Damn them, the Steele family really needed to take a course in Stubbornness Management.

"You too," he said roughly to Jonah's mom. "Both of you. Now!"

Tessa didn't like the way his demeanor had changed. He was becoming more aggressive by the minute. "Keith, you promised we would talk about Steven—"

With one yank of his arm, he swung her around and ground the gun into her forehead. "What the fuck do I have to do to get you to shut the fuck up? No more talking about Steven."

"But isn't this game all about him?" She had to try to get through to him. "If you'll just tell me—"

He backed her against a tree and pushed the gun against the center of her head so hard, Tessa felt the metal cut through her skin. "It's time to shut up and play. If you don't want to play, then I'll take you out now and Steele can kill his mother."

Kill his mother? What did that mean? But before Tessa could figure it out, Keith grabbed one of the sensor vests from Miss Joan and shoved it into Tessa's hands. That action had mercifully moved the gun inches away. "Take off your shirt and put this on."

Willing her hands to remain steady, Tessa let her gorgeous sweater drop to the ground, then unbuttoned her shirt and shrugged out of it. She would do whatever it took to keep his attention off Jonah's mother. From her peripheral vision, Tessa saw that Keith was staring at her breasts. From fear and the cold, her nipples had peaked. "You don't have the right to look at me and you sure as hell don't have the right to touch me. You may have us at gunpoint, but you don't own my body. Touch me there, and you'll have to murder me to keep me from killing you."

She'd thought she could do anything it took for Miss Joan, but not that. No man would ever control her that way.

No man would take away her choice.

Keith cleared his throat, and his gaze darted away from her breasts. "Then hurry up and put on the sensors."

Pulling the tangle of wires over her head was awkward.

"Make sure they're attached," he said. "If I find even one is loose, the game is over."

That's right. Play or die.

When she stepped toward Miss Joan, Keith jammed his gun into Tessa's ear.

"If you want the damn things attached," she ground out through the pain, "then we'll need to secure the sensors on each other's backs."

His nod was grudging. He shifted the gun toward Jonah's mom. "Do Tessa first."

Her fingers were chilled against Tessa's skin, and she whispered, "I'm sorry." After checking each of them, she told Keith, "All done."

They traded places, and while she was working behind Jonah's mom, Tessa angled her body to block Keith's view of her movements. She attached each of the sensors as he'd instructed, but she yanked on the wires leading into the battery pack resting against Miss Joan's lower back.

"It's cold," Tessa said. "Can we please put our shirts on over the sensors?" That would also hide what she'd done to Miss Joan's wires.

Keith grunted his assent and gestured toward the bag on the ground. "Get the rest of it out of there."

Tessa squatted down and pulled out two sets of goggles

and gauntlet controllers like the ones that had been sent to Jonah. "I assume you want us to put them on?"

"Hurry up."

Helping Miss Joan with her shirt and equipment gave Tessa an excuse to get close to her again. She slipped the goggles on her head, which made her look like an old-fashioned pilot. "If we have to play, you'll want to pull those down over your eyes," she said where Keith could hear her. But as she loosely secured the controller gauntlets, she lowered her voice to a half whisper. "Once it starts, get away."

"But Jonah will—"

"Jonah probably has no idea where we are. This time, I'll take care of myself."

27

On the road back from Charlotte, Jonah thought about what the hell he'd missed. Harrison was in prison, Cartwright had been genuinely clueless, and Carson Grimes wasn't their guy.

That left the other two fuckwads...unless Tessa had been on to something by looking back at Steele Trap employees.

Maybe the hardware had actually been the important clue all along. Steele Trap had been one of the few companies that had developed software and designed specialized controllers.

He dialed the company's main number and asked for the manager over the hardware development area.

"Hello?"

"Gary, it's Jonah Steele here."

"Hey. I...uh...talked with your sister earlier. Really early."

"Yeah, Micki has no concept of boundaries. Look, I've picked through every part of the hardware she mentioned to you. It all looked like stuff that could've come from Steele

Trap stock. Have you noticed any inventory missing in the past few weeks or so?"

"You know we don't usually do any kind of count except twice a year. When inventory was done in early November, all the numbers lined up."

"Is the normal shrinkage percentage still the same?" They'd never had a huge sticky finger problem at Steele Trap, partially because electronic components weren't exactly hot resale items.

"I should probably talk to the new owner before handing out more information. Your sister didn't give me the details on why you need all this. Are you looking to develop games again?"

How many times did he have to answer no to that question for people to start believing him? "No problem. I understand. If I need anything else, I'll call the CEO directly. But hey, we missed you here at the meet-up in Charlotte."

"Yeah, we've got some critical ship dates around here coming up soon."

"Then I'm surprised anyone was on this coast."

Gary grunted. "Some people just aren't as committed now that you're gone. In fact, a couple of guys recently up and quit."

Jonah's instincts went on high alert, but he didn't want to spook Gary into clamming up again. "That sucks."

"Two of our best," he grumped. "Carson Grimes and Keith Benery."

"Really hate to hear that," Jonah commiserated. "They were always good guys." Except one of them wasn't anything close to good, he thought as he disconnected.

Before he could call Tessa, his phone rang. "Where the hell are you?" Micki snapped.

"On my way back to Steele Ridge, and I need to talk to Tessa. Now."

"Well, that's a problem, seeing as I woke up from the nap Mom forced me to take only to find her and Tessa gone."

"What do you mean gone?"

"Like not in the house and the car isn't here gone."

No, surely Tessa wouldn't just head out on her own. She knew how damn dangerous this situation was right now. Who would protect her if... *Stop that shit. You will find her.* "Did you look for a note?" he asked Micki, putting more pressure on his accelerator.

Maybe Tessa hadn't stumbled on the same thing he had. Maybe she and his mom had just taken a quick trip into town.

"I'm not a moron," Micki said on a huff. "And when I called Mom's phone, it went to voice mail."

His phone beeped with an incoming text, which was always a pain when he was already on a call. "Lemme call you back." But when he pulled the phone away from his ear, the notification had already disappeared. And hurtling down the freeway at ninety wasn't a good time to flip through his phone. He pressed the home button and said, "Read text."

Siri's voice came through the car speakers. "Two new messages from Tessa Martin. Message one. *Keith Benery. His parents live in Bryson City. 1612 Connamere. Meet there ASAP.* End of message. Would you like to reply?"

Jonah's heart went into overdrive. Oh, fuck. He had made the mistake of a lifetime, had been so sure he knew where the threat was coming from. He'd been trying to protect Tessa by keeping the truth from her, but by pushing her out, he'd done the exact opposite.

He fumbled his phone and it fell under his feet.

But Siri didn't seem to notice, just droned on. "Second message. *Get your gear. It's time to play or die.* End of message. Would you like to reply?"

"Yes," he yelled.

Shit, he was going to kill himself this way. He took the next off ramp and pulled to the side of the interstate frontage road. When he finally laid hands on his phone, he called Micki back.

"What the hell? You hung up on me." His sister's voice was increasing in volume with each word. "What is going on?"

"Phone took a tumble, but I pulled off. I got two texts from Tessa's number. The first said she was going to Keith Benery's parents' house in Bryson City."

"Why in God's name would she do that?"

"The second text wasn't from her."

"But I thought you said—"

"It was from Keith Benery. He worked at Steele Trap. He's the one. The hacker."

"How do you know?"

"Because his message was Play or Die."

"Oh, God." Micki's breathing suddenly changed, and Jonah knew what hyperventilation sounded like since he was on the edge of it himself.

"What?"

In a strangled voice, Micki said, "A text just came from Mom's number, and it says 'Tell your brother to suit up unless he wants to know what it feels like to kill a member of his own family. Location to come.'"

Jonah pulled back onto the road, swerved around a minivan, and raced through a hard yellow light to get back on the highway. "Can you meet me at the Murchison building? I have the sensor shirt with me, but I need the other hardware he sent."

"What's the plan?"

"To beat this fucker at his own game."

When he double-parked in front of the Murchison Building, Jonah didn't give a shit that he was blocking a Ram long bed, a VW Bug, and a ragged-out Honda. He was out of Clementine, inside, and up the stairs without conscious memory of taking the steps.

The apartment door was wide open, and he rushed in to find his sister and his dad, of all people, bent over one of the controller gauntlets with tiny screwdrivers. "What're y'all doing?"

Micki glanced up, and her eyes, a reflection of his own, were full of worry. "I don't like anything about this, so I inserted a tracking device."

Jonah checked his phone. "He's supposed to contact me with a location any time now."

"But how do you know he won't change the plan mid-game? We need to know where to find you."

"You mean where to find Mom and Tessa."

The beep of his phone sent a painful jolt though Jonah and he tightened his sweaty hold on it.

564 Hidden Hills Drive. The house he'd been raised in.

"Something about this seems so personal," Micki said.

"You think? The guy's only been trying to kill people around me. That wasn't personal enough for you?" And right now, he didn't have the luxury of time to scratch his head over why Keith Benery would be pissed enough to come after his family and him. Because whether she believed it or not, Tessa was his family. Part of the small group of people he would do anything for.

He wanted a lifetime with her if she wanted him back.

For the first time in years, he believed that was possible for him. For them together.

His dad placed a steady hand on his back. Jonah wanted to shrug away from it, but he held on to his composure. The old man was here to help and that had to count for something.

"I know we can't talk you out of meeting him, so Micki and I will be in charge of rounding up Maggie and her team."

Jonah's brain was on overload, working all the angles of how he might take down Benery. The guy wanted to play? Then Jonah would go old-school. "Tell Maggie to have Reid and Britt set up the old tiger trap behind the house. They'll know what I mean. They have to use caution. He has two hostages."

"Your cousin knows her business and so do your brothers," his dad said. "And you need to have some faith in your friend and your mom. Women are a lot stronger than we give them credit for most of the time."

"That doesn't mean I plan to let them fend for themselves."

His dad's grip tightened, and his eyes hardened. "Sometimes that's the best way to keep them safe. Hiding the truth hurts the ones you love most. It always comes back to bite you on the ass."

"Thanks." For what, he wasn't a hundred percent sure, but his dad was making an effort. But Jonah didn't have time for family therapy hour right now. He snatched up the gauntlet controllers and fumbled to secure them.

"Let me do it." Micki latched the plastic sleeves and held on when he would've pulled away. "Dad's right."

Micki, too? Didn't they realize he had to go? Now.

He had to save his mom and Tessa. He had to get her out of this before...

His mind squeezed to the point of physical pain as it all gelled. Tessa's attack had been defining his relationship with her because he didn't trust the world not to hurt her, and he didn't trust her to rescue herself when she was in trouble. He'd taken it upon himself to right the wrongs done to her. Without her permission.

The only person he'd been protecting was himself.

Tessa was smart. Strong. Resilient.

She needed a partner, not some kind of avenging guardian angel.

"What you're saying is that if I want both Tessa and Mom to come out of this thing okay, I have to stop thinking of Tessa as a helpless girl. I have to stop thinking that I let her down and start believing she has as much control as any of us do."

Micki's smile was tight and sad, but it was a smile. "Remember that. She's not *anyone's* victim."

28

Although Tessa's heart was pounding so hard she thought she could hear it herself, she was relieved that Keith was keeping his gun pointed at her. As they made their way farther into the woods, he remained between Tessa and Jonah's mother.

Miss Joan lagged a step and shot a look at Tessa behind Keith's back, but Tessa had no idea what she was trying to communicate.

He herded them toward a massive red spruce with branches draping the ground. "Get under there," he ordered. Once they were all hunched underneath the low prickly branches, he told Tessa, "Get the duct tape out of the bag and strap her to the tree."

Oh, she didn't like the sound of that. It would mean Miss Joan had no chance of escape. "But how will she play that way?"

"I decided she won't. She'd drag down the pace," he said. "That's not her purpose." No explanation for what her purpose *was* though.

Miss Joan awkwardly put her back against the tree

between two branches, and Tessa began weaving the tape over the wood, behind her back but over her wrists. If she could just...

"Not that way," he barked. "Strap her down at the waist, hips, and shoulders. I don't want her interrupting the game."

Tessa tried to convey how sorry she was through her facial expression alone, and Miss Joan gave her a small smile. When Tessa made a lap around her waist, Jonah's mom whispered, "I'll be fine. You just take care of yourself. You can do this."

Her words shook Tessa. Obviously, Miss Joan believed wholeheartedly that Tessa could hold her own, that she didn't have to rely on Jonah to get them out of this situation. Something Tessa had spent the past ten years trying to prove to everyone, including herself. Only to find out she wasn't exactly the self-made woman she'd believed.

How could Jonah have taken that from her? He'd manipulated things behind the scenes while she was completely unaware. No, it wasn't physical victimization, but he'd still taken away her choice.

"Tessa," Miss Joan said. "Whatever my son did, he did because he wanted to protect you, because he cares for you."

"People who care for one another treat each other as equals."

"Equality isn't the same thing as equity, sweetheart. He wanted justice for you."

That should've been her choice, not his.

When she had Jonah's mom secured, Tessa turned to Keith. "What now?" Because it was time to get on with whatever he had planned. That was the only way to stop him.

"Turn around." He lifted the back of her shirt and checked the battery pack on her vest. Good thing she hadn't been able to disengage the wires on this one. He tinkered with the goggles perched on her head and yanked them down over her eyes.

That's when something dawned on her. She and Miss Joan were suited up, but Keith hadn't put on gear. Tessa had no understanding of the rules, and she suddenly felt as if she'd been plopped down in the middle of the *Hunger Games.*

HIS STOMACH A MESS, ROLLING AND CRAMPING, JONAH PULLED to the side of the road in front of the house he'd grown up in. His worry wasn't about defeating Keith Benery in a game of Steele Survivor. Screw the mods. He knew this game backward and forward.

But what if winning couldn't save his mother and Tessa? Benery had already proven he couldn't be trusted to play by the rules he himself had set.

In his rearview, Jonah caught sight of an unmarked car casually pulling to the curb a football field length behind him. Another turned into a driveway on the other side of the street.

Jonah got out of the car and under the pretense of adjusting his VR goggles, he inserted a second earpiece and mic. "Everything on target?"

In his ear, Maggie said, "Ready in less than five."

That meant his brothers were doing as he'd asked, so he tucked the earpiece and mic into his shirt because he didn't want Benery to realize he was wired. He ignored Maggie's tinny voice coming from the vicinity of his collarbone.

Jonah pulled down his VR goggles, pressed the attached headset into place and swung the mic up to his mouth. "I'm here, Benery. Let's play."

"In the backyard." For a fucking madman, Benery sounded remarkably sane. And based on the setting for the game, he knew about the significance of this location.

It wasn't a secret that Jonah had first played a sort of real-life version of Steele Survivor with his brothers in the woods behind this house. Once the game had begun to gain real traction, he'd become more careful about telling that story. A few overzealous players had found the address and come by to leave tributes of marbles and trading cards—game treasure—behind the house.

Once he'd walked in at Thanksgiving to find his mom had invited a trio of dudes from Minnesota to dinner because they'd been running around whacking at each other with wooden swords on her property.

Now, with the VR goggles on, Jonah was plunged back into the surreal zombie landscape Benery had created. The windows on the house had no panes, their emptiness like gaping dead eyes. Shingles that looked like strips of dried skin lay on the ground.

Keeping his back to the brick that he knew in reality did not look as if blood had been spattered on it, Jonah edged his way down the side of the house. At the corner, he peeked into the backyard, trying to spot Benery.

Nothing.

Yeah, playing out in the open would've been too easy. Which was the reason Jonah and his brothers had rarely done it. They'd preferred to wage their battles in the thick trees and underbrush between this house and the one a half mile behind it.

"Benery, you gutless fuck, come out and fight," he said into his mic.

"You know where this has to happen," Benery taunted. "So come get me."

The lack of leaves on some trees made visibility slightly better, but these woods were filled with pines, hemlocks, and cedars. Benery still had plenty of cover.

His brothers were supposed to be setting up on the west side of the property, so Jonah went east, his pulse thumping.

Yes, Tessa was strong and smart. She might even be out in the woods right now getting herself and his mom out of this mess. But he had to confront Benery because he couldn't bear to take chances with two of the women he loved.

29

TESSA PICKED HER WAY THROUGH THE DEAD UNDERBRUSH AND the trees with their grasping skeletal branches. Keith hadn't outfitted her with a headset or mic before he told her to move out and play the game, so she was down two huge advantages. Of course, he hadn't wanted her to be able to communicate with Jonah.

But talking was only one of many ways to communicate. What if she could make Jonah understand what was happening here? She looked around for something sharp, but the best she could find was a stick.

She was trying to maneuver it to scratch a T in the trunk of a tree when it felt as if her back had been flayed open. She was hit. Was it real or just the game?

Her knees succumbed to the pain and she fell face first against the tree.

Don't let him send you to the ground.

That was the worst possible position for personal defense.

Her back was throbbing, sending searing pulses through her. She touched her lower back, and her fingers came away dry. These sensors did more than burn. They simulated the painful damage of the opponent's weapon. How had Jonah survived them?

Tessa forced herself to move, with an awkward shuffle around the tree trunk, and stumbled behind some stubby evergreen shrubbery.

When she got a good look at her attacker, her heart felt as if it had been run through with an icepick. Her mind knew everything she was seeing had been distorted by Keith's tech changes to Jonah's game, but that knowledge did nothing to thaw her frozen muscles.

The person in front of her didn't look like Keith, nor did he resemble Jonah.

He looked like the teenaged version of Harrison Shaw, except zombified. Ragged khakis and a dark green repp polo with one arm dangling around his elbow. His light red hair partially ripped out, but the smirk... That was the exact leer Harrison had given her that night, not long before he'd slipped her a roofie.

That isn't really Harrison. You know that. He's in prison. This is Keith Benery.

She swallowed, trying to separate nightmare from reality.

The other player—it had to be Keith—turned as if looking for her, giving Tessa a chance to come at him from behind as he'd done to her. But self-preservation kept her from getting too close. Instead, she used her gauntlet as a gun, hoping she remembered the right sequence of movements.

Her virtual shot went high and caught him in the shoulder. The force of the bullet made him stagger forward and drop to his knees. Virtual blood bloomed in a dark circle on his back.

If she finished him here, would that mean the game was over?

She didn't get the chance to find out. Her attacker rose to his feet and whirled around, holding his hands as if he was brandishing a heavy sword. He came at her and swung his invisible weapon. It caught her across her abdomen, and Tessa looked down. The VR goggles made it look as though she'd been gutted side to side, her insides sagging out. Unable to help herself, she tried to push them back in.

Intellectually, she knew she was still whole, but the pain was excruciating. The mental toll from distinguishing reality from augmented reality was forcing her body into a state of shock.

Although she was mortally wounded, her attacker kept coming. A jab in her right arm set off the sensors high on her shoulder, rendering her entire arm useless. It hung loose as if the muscle and ligaments had been severed.

It went against every speck of her sense of self-preservation, but Tessa released her hold on her stomach and tried not to look at the visual trickery of her intestines looping down her abdomen.

She had to fight back, because with all this gear on, she'd never outrun him.

In all the years she'd studied self-defense, she'd always pictured herself fighting off a rapist. No other threat. But she'd been trying to protect herself from a past that she couldn't change. Trying to insulate herself from needing anyone else's help. Trying to remain removed from other people's traumas.

But this was a threat to her future in a way she'd never imagined. Even in the darkest days of her sexual assault recovery, she'd known she was alive. Known tomorrow—however painful—would come.

She'd understood her personal safety wasn't guaranteed. But she'd never actually looked death straight in the face before.

Today, she was seeing it in technicolor.

She advanced on her attacker. She could do this, take this risk. After all, she'd already risked her heart by giving it to Jonah, and there were no guarantees he wouldn't hurt her.

Although the fingers on her left hand still felt numb, she was able to fumble with the clasp on her right gauntlet and let it drop to the ground. Then she unfastened the other and allowed it to do the same.

She shifted her weight onto her back foot, but held her arms away from her sides in surrender.

C'mon, Keith. Get close enough so I can take you down for real.

He didn't seem to have his real gun, so the worst he could do to her now was some kind of fake kill. She, however, would inflict some very real damage.

He raised that wicked sword again, exposing his torso and giving Tessa an opportunity. Putting everything she had into it, she chopped him in the throat with her forearm. That opened him up for an elbow to the solar plexus.

Oomph.

Score one for Tessa. The contact jarred her, sending waves of pain up her arm. She ignored it and was going in for a knee to the nuts when he gathered himself and brought his sword around. Time seemed to slip into another dimension as it arced through the air a centimeter at a time.

But she clearly heard Jonah say, "Game over, Benery" just before the sword sliced her head from her neck.

. . .

THE PAINED CRY THAT CAME FROM BENERY AS HE CRUMPLED TO the ground was high-pitched. Too high-pitched. Jonah reached up to remove his goggles but was interrupted by the feel of a gun barrel against his temple.

"No, Steele, the game isn't over. In fact, I'm just starting. By the end, I'll have you begging me to kill you."

Jonah turned his head toward the voice, which positioned the gun against his goggles. Benery, who appeared to be a light-haired zombie with part of his scalp torn from his head, was upright and apparently unharmed. Jonah glanced down at the person sprawled on a mattress of dead leaves and pine straw. "Then who..."

Matter of factly, Benery said, "I don't think she's dead yet, but her sensors are set on the highest level. You may not have actually taken off her head, but the electrical impulses will eventually fry her heart. How does it feel to kill someone you love?"

As much as he wanted to yank off his goggles to discover if he'd just hacked through his mom or Tessa, he knew Benery would put a bullet through his eyeball if he did. He wasn't scared to die, but he'd be damned if he would leave Benery standing. "You said yourself that she's not dead."

He reached to remove his gauntlets, and Benery shifted the trajectory of the gun to aim it at the woman. Jonah froze.

Benery squatted down and punched the prone figure in the kidney. "You're not done playing."

She groaned and rolled onto her back, but in Jonah's virtual world, her head remained unattached. Fear that what he was seeing was somehow real rose up his throat.

Benery looked up at him with a smile. "Or maybe she'll get lucky and stop *your* heart."

Did the sensors really have enough juice to do that?

He'd easily endured the blisters on his skin, but if the power were cranked up...

"Why don't you put on the gear?" he taunted, so he wouldn't give away how fucking scared he was right now. "Hell, I'll even trade you my pansy-ass gear for that set." He gestured carelessly toward the ground. Anything to remove one of the loves of his life from this sick game.

"Nah. Because I want you to live the rest of your life knowing you were the one who killed her, just like I killed my brother." Benery's head was tilted at an angle as he shook it in a mocking motion. "And to think you invested so much time and money into her. But she didn't know about all that, did she?"

"Jonah?"

His name was a hoarse whisper, but that single word confirmed which woman Benery wanted him to kill.

Tessa.

Somehow Benery knew about Jonah's machinations. All his internal organs felt as if they were making a break for the exits. She would never forgive him for what he'd done. That was if he could get them out of this game alive.

"Let's see," Benery said. "There were five of them, right? Shaw, Johnson, Bledsoe, Levine, and Cartwright."

How the hell did he know anything about Tessa's attackers?

"I already let it slip how you screwed over Shaw and paid for Tessa's education. By the look on her face, she wasn't all that happy about it."

"God, Tessa, I'm sorry—"

"But I didn't have time to go into all the details. Charlie Cartwright's LSAT scores were questioned. Oops, there went law school and his political career. Some pictures of Johnson's johnson *accidentally* ended up on MySpace back in the day. Levine—who was a 4.0 student—somehow flunked out of Davidson. Last I heard, he was selling used cars in Raleigh. Such a shame. And Bledsoe...the one Steele here lured into a couple of porn sites... Well, he couldn't seem to shake his addiction to paying for pussy pics. That poor bastard blew his head off not too long ago." Keith's gruesome grin was sharp-edged. "Oh, I see neither of you knew about that one."

Jonah had wanted to make them pay, but he'd never intended for things to go this far. Shaw deserved prison and the others deserved to have their lives cut down to size. But death? No.

"Keith," Tessa said. "I don't think this is about me. It's about your brother, isn't it? Why don't you tell me about Steven?"

"I told you every fucking thing about him at Steele Trap."

"How did he die?"

For fuck's sake, this guy was trying his best to kill her and she was getting down to a therapy session with him?

"There's something you've been holding on to, unwilling to tell anyone. Why don't you share it now? If you don't want Jonah to hear, you can just tell me. What will it hurt, Keith? I'm going to die anyway, so I'll take the secret to my grave."

Her plea seemed to blow the guy's composure in a way nothing else had. His gun hand was no longer steady, and he swung his arms in agitation.

"You said something about killing your brother, but it was an accident," she prompted. "You know that."

Benery hitched his gun in Jonah's direction. "It was his fault."

"Okay," Tessa soothed, which only made Benery turn

the gun back in her direction. "Then tell me how Jonah was involved. I'm sure he wants to make it right."

"There is no making it right. Steven is dead. Dead, dead, dead."

When Tessa pushed her headless body to a sitting position, Jonah almost had a stroke. Benery didn't need any excuse to ramp up his recent twitch-fest. She placed a hand on the guy's knee. "Let it out, Keith. Maybe your gun went off accidentally while you were playing a silly game and—"

"Not just any game," he shouted, self-loathing dripping from every word. "We were playing Steele Survivor."

30

It all made such horrible sense to her now. Keith felt as if she'd somehow betrayed him by being unable to purge his guilt about killing his brother. Going after her clients was a way to discredit her, and he wanted to devastate Jonah as he'd been devastated. When a person was unwilling to accept blame—even if his transgression was an accident— the mind demanded that he hold someone accountable.

That's what she and Jonah were for Keith. Conscience cleansers.

Now all she had to do was figure out how to keep them both alive. This time, she wasn't in danger by herself. It was two against one, and those were odds she liked. Except Keith wasn't wearing sensors, and he had a gun.

"Benery, why don't you take Tessa's controllers and goggles?" Jonah taunted. "We can play this out where you have all the power, all the control."

At first, Keith shook his head, a vague movement. Then his focus shifted to where Tessa's gauntlets lay on the ground. "You're right. I have the real weapon."

His laugh was low and secretive, as if he were

sharing a joke with only himself. He yanked the goggles off Tessa's head, and she felt as if she could breathe again for the first time since he'd forced her to put them on. Besides, she could now clearly see the other player was Jonah, the man she'd believed she loved and trusted.

She still loved him, but could she trust him after what he'd done?

"Tell you what," Keith said to Jonah, "I'll even give you a head start. Let's see how long you can rabbit around these woods before I kill you."

"What proof do I have that you won't hurt Tessa once I'm out of sight?"

"None."

"Then no head start. You let Tessa walk away from here, and I'll stand still and let you put a bullet directly through my heart."

Tessa pressed a hand against her chest to keep her heart from pushing its way past her ribcage. What was Jonah thinking?

"What fun is that?" Keith's tone was sulky.

"You can't have it both ways, Benery."

"Fine. I won't hurt her until after I catch you."

"Tessa, do you know where my mom is? Is she okay?"

"Yes, but—"

"Go to her and stay there."

"Please don't do this," she pleaded.

He shoved his goggles to his forehead and stared at her, his face rigid with determination and desperation. "I don't think you're a helpless victim. But I need to handle this. Do you trust me?"

"I trust that you think you know what you're doing," she said carefully, but by the way his body stiffened it was clear he'd heard what she hadn't said. That she wasn't sure if she trusted *him*.

"That's more than I deserve." Before she could respond, he sprinted away and the trees swallowed him up.

THE LAST TIME HE'D LEFT TESSA TO GO FOR HELP, IT HAD risked both their lives. Jonah prayed to every god he could think of that he hadn't just made the same mistake again. Maybe he should've just risked it, grabbed Tessa and run like hell, hoping Benery's aim wasn't that good.

But all he could picture was Tessa being shot in the back and falling to the ground. Curling in a fetal position never to get up again.

That night ten years ago, when Harrison Shaw and his entourage of rich boys had lured Jonah to a white bedroom door in Shaw's house, it had opened to reveal Tessa drawn in on herself, lying broken on a bed.

"Game's on, Steele," Shaw said, a smug smile on his face. "But you gotta get your ass in here."

Jonah forced himself to take the steps. Once he made it through the doorway into the brightly lit room, the other guys parted so he could see the bed.

Oh fuck, oh fuck, oh fuck.

Arms limp over her head and legs dangling off the side of the mattress, the girl was sprawled out on the bed like a doll a kid had carelessly tossed aside. But that was where the resemblance ended.

Jonah tried to keep breathing, tried not to lose his shit.

But her skin. It was showing in places it shouldn't. Someone had ripped her pretty fluttery shirt down the middle and her bra was pushed up almost to her neck. Her jean skirt was bunched around her waist and a pair of pink panties dangled off her left ankle. She was still wearing a pair of high-heeled sandals.

If all that wasn't horrifying enough, there was blood on her golden-brown skin and in her dark curly hair.

The only thing that kept him from losing his ever-loving shit was the fact that her chest was moving up and down. She was in bad shape, but she was alive.

"Whatcha think? Want some of that?"

Jonah turned his head—it felt like slow motion—to find Shaw grinning. Perfect teeth gleaming white. So happy with himself.

What did he think? He thought he needed to get that girl the hell out of here. Jonah swallowed. Hard. "I think—"

"Rock, paper, scissors."

"What?"

"That's how we decide who goes next."

An overwhelming pressure built inside Jonah. They were playing a kid's game to determine who got the next chance to rape a girl. Jonah's hand curled into a fist and he leaned toward Shaw. He would kill this doucheface.

Shaw's eyes narrowed and he darted a look at his buddies, who moved in. "You must be into guys," he sneered at Jonah, "if you don't want that prime piece of pussy."

She wasn't a *piece*. She was a person. A pretty teenage girl. *Keep it together so you can get her out of here.* "She's not moving," he said, his voice scratchy and hoarse. "What's the fun in that?"

"You get between her legs and she's plenty of fun." Shaw fisted his hand in his other palm like a rock. "You in or not, man?"

Maybe he should run, just get himself and Micki out of here. Then they could call the police and...and it might be too late for this girl.

"Yeah."

Jonah's scissors cut Shaw's paper.

Then Shaw won rock over scissors.

By now, Jonah was sweating like a hog in August, but he was relieved to see his hand wasn't shaking as he faced off with Shaw the last time.

"One, two...three."

Jonah's glanced down and released a soundless breath of relief. He'd been right. Shaw wasn't smart enough to change his strategy. "Paper covers rock," Jonah sneered. "She's mine."

Shaw crossed his arms and stepped back. "So do it."

Oh, hell. They planned to stand there and watch. "You staying because you can't wait to get a good look at my dick?"

Shaw's mouth tightened and he hitched his chin at his friends. "Let's give the guy a few minutes."

"I don't blow as fast as your friends," Jonah said. "I'll need at least twenty, and I don't want anyone hanging out in the hall."

"Whatever." The guys filed out of the room.

Jonah watched them go and close the door behind them, but he couldn't bring himself to turn around and look at the unconscious girl. He waited a couple of minutes and then cracked the door. No one was in the hallway.

He wanted to turn off the lights so he wouldn't have to see how damaged, how broken, the girl was. But darkness might scare her.

He darted for the one window in the room, so fucking relieved to find it could be opened. Because there was no way he could drag this girl through that party.

Something rustled behind him and he swung around to find her stirring. She came to—just enough for terror to glaze her eyes. "D-don't…" She tried to hold out a hand to ward him off, but her arm barely made it an inch off the mattress before it dropped back. "P-please…"

"I'm not going to hurt you," he said in a low voice, walking forward slowly to kneel near the bed and keeping his gaze averted from anything but her feet. "Let me help you get dressed and then—"

"No!" She lurched forward clumsily, and hit him in the side of the head with her fist. It barely hurt, as weak as she was, but it momentarily stunned him. Enough so that she was able to get in another blow and rake her fingernails down his cheek.

He fell on his ass and crab-walked backward until he hit the wall. "I am not going to hurt you," he repeated. "I need help to get you out of here. I'm going to get my sister. Then we'll get you out of here. Can you stay here for five minutes? Can you do that?" He was babbling.

"I… Where am I?"

"You're safe. I'll lock you in when I leave."

Her eyes flared with fear again. "Lock me—"

"Just for a few minutes. Then we'll be back and get you to safety."

"Home. I wanna go home."

"Okay." Jonah pushed himself from the floor with a jerky shove and wrenched open the door before he thought better of it. Thank Jesus, no one was out there. He locked the door. Just a flimsy bedroom lock, but it was all he had. It would have to do for now.

Once he brought Micki back, it would take her all of ten seconds to pick the thing.

He stumbled his way downstairs and rushed into the crowd of gyrating bodies that smelled of booze, sweat, and something else—desperate lust—that turned his stomach.

"Micki," he called. It felt like one of those nightmares where you were running down the hallway, but it just kept getting longer and longer and...

There she was. Jonah shoved another guy aside and grabbed Micki's arm. "Micki, I need your help. Right now."

"What have you done? Did you find their computers and—"

Unable to control himself, he dragged her along behind him until they made it to the hallway. "She's back here."

"Who?"

"The girl Harrison Shaw and his friends have been gang-raping."

Jonah and Micki raced toward the wing of the house where he'd left the girl. The hallway was still empty and Jonah started to release the breath he'd been holding. But then the bedroom door opened.

A guy came out, still doing his fly. *Motherfucker.* He must've jimmied the flimsy lock. Jonah lunged at him, but Micki clung to his arm.

The guy looked up and Jonah recognized him as Andy Bledsoe. Son of a bitch had the balls to grin. "Guess you were supposed to be next, huh? Sorry 'bout that." He scanned Micki up and down. "But since you brought another date, maybe we could both—"

Jonah wrenched away from Micki's hold and punched him in the nose. Blood gushed, and the guy tried to protect his face with his hands, but Jonah caught him again high on the cheekbone, knocking him into the hall wall. "I'm going to kill you."

Micki pulled Jonah off and nodded toward the open door. "We need to take care of her."

The guy scurried away.

Inside the bedroom, the girl's clothes were still rucked

up around her body, but now she was curled in a fetal position. When she looked up to find him standing there with Micki, her eyes were dead. Flat as water in a stagnant pond.

She whispered, "You promised."

Yeah. All those years ago, he'd made Tessa a promise he hadn't kept.

And now, it could happen all over again.

"Jonah, what the *hell* is going on out there?" Maggie's voice boomed through his second earpiece, jolting him from the sickening memory of Tessa at her weakest, her most broken. "You haven't checked in since you left your car."

He covered the mic attached to his goggles and spoke into the other mic. "Sorry," he huffed as he ran. "Things got a little surreal there for a while."

"Did you get eyes on your mom and Tessa?"

"Just Tessa."

"She's with you?"

That hesitant feeling about leaving her behind rocked through him again. "No, but Benery's on my tail, so she's safe." He said it with confidence even though he'd heard no footsteps behind him. "Did Reid and Britt get the traps set up and clear out?"

"They didn't want to leave, but—"

"If their asses aren't out of these woods, I will stop running right now and let that fucker catch me."

"We're with Maggie, you asswipe." Reid's gruff voice was loud and clear through the earpiece.

"Then I'm headed in." He yanked off his second mic because he needed all the focus he could muster.

He used a few precious seconds to stop and listen. Leaves rustled off to the east, probably fifty yards out. He needed to let Benery catch sight of him for this to work.

Jonah knew when he'd been spotted by the noise.

Benery wasn't even trying to be stealthy anymore. He was crashing through the underbrush like a drunken elephant.

But Jonah had miscalculated the direction Benery would come from. He'd expected him to arrow in, but he'd circled around to the north. For the trap to work, he needed to lure Benery along an east-to-west trajectory.

And if Jonah didn't get some cover, Benery would be on top of him in seconds. His best option was a tall pine with a trio of branches a good ten feet over Jonah's head. He jumped, getting a finger hold on the chunky bark. Using his knees and every ounce of his upper body strength, he clumsily shimmied up until he could grab two branches. His brothers would laugh their asses off if they could see his less than graceful ascent.

He swung a leg up and straddled a branch, landing hard and racking himself in the process. Hugging the tree trunk, he huffed though the pain and prayed Benery wouldn't look up.

Benery darted out of a cluster of mountain laurel and paused long enough to scan the landscape before him. Jonah's grip tightened on the pine, and the bark bit into his fingers, sticky with thick sap. It didn't take long for Benery to move on, but he was still headed south. If he went too far in that direction, he'd hit the house's backyard and likely spot Maggie and the others.

Jonah quickly swung himself off the branch, hung for an instant before letting go and dropping to the ground in a knee-jarring crouch. He had to lure Benery to the east. He cut southeast to where a small stream ran through the property. The water was low, but there was enough for Jonah to splash through it. Not too loud, but just enough for Benery to hear.

A couple minutes later, the sound of leaves cracking and

sticks breaking made it clear the plan had worked. Jonah lunged out of the water and made no effort to be quiet as he ran, jumping over dead logs and dodging branches. One branch caught his sensor vest and it took precious seconds to break it off and get moving again.

By that time, Benery had gained on him. His grin was fierce and gloating as he bulldozed his way through the woods. Damn it, Jonah had let him get too close.

Expecting to feel the burn of a bullet to the back any second, he stumbled when Benery jumped him. Benery used Tessa's gauntlets to jab and parry, getting in close, actually driving his fist into Jonah's stomach. But that wasn't where the pain came from. It was the feel of serrated hunting knives punching into his body and the ragged rips they cut from his flesh. The intensely real sensation of blood flowing out of his body momentarily distracted him.

Why hadn't Benery shot him and ended the whole thing?

Jonah struck out at Benery, landing a glancing blow to his face. But a good old fistfight couldn't compete with the pain of knife wounds, real or not. The slice of a virtual blade caught Jonah low in his abdomen.

Benery came at him again, hitting the sensor directly over Jonah's real-life knife scar. Finally, a benefit to dead nerve endings. That reprieve gave Jonah enough clarity to turn in the direction he needed to lure Benery and run like hell, expecting a bullet in the back at any second.

He cradled his imaginary wounds to control the pain and tried to measure his strides as he ran. If he screwed up, he'd be the one knocked out cold instead of Benery. When he made it to the pivotal location between two tall pine trees, his legs almost failed him. But he pushed on, barely hurdling the trip wire in his path. Every instinct shouted at him to turn and watch for Benery's approach. But his and Maggie's plan echoed through his head.

Keep running so he'll keep chasing you.

His legs feeling as if they weighed two hundred pounds apiece, Jonah stumbled and rolled. Oh, shit. The plan hadn't worked. Benery was past the point where he should've tripped the wire. And Jonah was lying here like a fish just waiting to be scooped up in a net.

He scrambled up and the impact of a bullet train hit him in the chest. Unable to help himself, he looked down to find a hole gushing blood—down his torso, over his grasping fingers. Was it real?

If so, he was a dead man.

His mind shorted out except for one thought. *Tessa.*

Benery kept coming at him, arm extended. But with Jonah's wavering vision, he couldn't spot a damn gun.

Then the crack of real gunfire reverberated through the trees, and Benery's advance on Jonah stalled. The guy took one step, two steps before his left leg folded. His right didn't fare any better, somehow bending the wrong direction and sending Benery pitching to the ground.

Weapons drawn, Maggie and her deputies swarmed into the trees and cautiously approached the man lying on his side. Maggie hunkered down and touched Benery's neck. "He's out, but he's not dead."

The deputies quickly cuffed him and called for medical assistance.

Jonah tried to shove the goggles off his face, but hands weren't working correctly. "Wha...what the hell just happened here?"

Maggie looked over her shoulder and lifted her chin toward someone behind her. "Your girlfriend just saved your ass."

31

SHE SHOT HIM. TESSA STARED AT KEITH'S BODY ON THE TRAIL, then at his gun dangling from her fingers. She stopped him. She did it.

Jonah crashed toward her through the trees and skidded to a stop. His cousin pushed him aside and took the gun from her.

"I shot him," she said.

"But you didn't kill him," Maggie reassured her. "How did you get the gun?"

"He had to set it aside to put on the gear. I just reacted, grabbed it and ran, hoping he was so focused on Jonah that he wouldn't come after me. When I heard him moving in the other direction, I followed."

"Tessa, why the hell did you risk yourself like that?" Jonah tried to gather her in his arms, but Tessa wiggled out of his hold. Right now, she couldn't afford to lean against him. Soften toward him.

"Because it was time for me to do the protecting. The saving," she said softly. "Now you know what it feels like to have the choice taken out of your hands. Now you know how I feel about what you did."

The look on Jonah's face broadcasted his anguish, his apology. "I didn't want you to find out about the shit I pulled with Shaw and the others because I knew you'd look at me exactly this way."

When the EMTs tried to load Jonah and her into the same ambulance, she balked, telling them she wanted to ride alone. Soon she was lying in a St. Elizabeth's hospital bed with five leads snaking from her chest to a telemetry monitor. Apparently, Jonah had given the doctor the background on Benery's technique for trying to kill her, so that meant a full cardiac workup for her. And although she'd been given instructions to rest, that was impossible with a blood pressure cuff inflating every fifteen minutes.

The damn thing was just starting to pump again when the door opened and Jonah walked into her room wearing a hospital gown. The vee neck revealed burn marks on his upper chest. His face was as scratched as hers, and a bruise was forming on his left elbow. They were a pair all right.

Her heart seesawed in her chest, with love and resentment each trying to slam the other into the dirt.

"We need to talk." His voice was low and slightly slurred, probably from painkillers.

Talking was the last thing she was interested in doing. What she wanted was to go to sleep and wake up in the morning to discover none of this had ever happened.

That she'd never gone to Tucci's and opened herself up to being hurt by this man.

"Are you okay?" he asked.

Tessa could feel tears forming, but she'd be damned before she cried right now. "No. If I could wrap this blood pressure cuff around your neck, I'd happily do it. You tampered with people's lives."

His hazel eyes took on the sharpness of brass tacks. "I did, and I would do it again in a heartbeat. Tessa, Shaw and the others didn't just *tamper* with your life. They damn near destroyed it."

"So you felt like you had to step in and do something about it?"

"They needed to pay."

"That's what the legal system is for."

"A system you and your parents didn't use."

"So you took things into your own hands. Did you even think about how I would feel about you getting revenge for me? For manipulating *my* life?" She sat up and the leads pulled at her skin. Minor pain compared to what she was feeling inside. "Why? Why would you undermine me that way?"

"You'd been awarded some scholarships, but not enough to cover everything. I just topped off what the school had already provided."

"So you stole money to send me to college. Jonah, my parents would've helped me with the rest."

"But you wanted to do it on your own, didn't you?"

At the time, she *had* been proud. So gratified at the thought of having somehow paid her own way. Now, the memory of her full ride to U of W made her insides ache. She'd believed she'd earned that scholarship money, but it had been bullshit all along. "God, you were behind my graduate school fellowships, too, weren't you?"

"I didn't have anything to do with those. You earned them." Jonah lunged forward and reached for her hand, but she slipped it under the sheet. His jaw hardened, and he retreated to lean against the wall.

"Yay me," she said, not bothering to cover the cold bitterness of her tone. "Tell me, did you hack the dealership's system and give me that zero percentage loan when I bought my first car? Maybe you called these companies in North Carolina and blackmailed them into meeting with me."

"Now you're just being ridiculous. You've done all that on your own. But after the rapes, you were struggling. I just did what you and your parents couldn't at the time. Believe me, none of those guys got a fraction of what they deserved."

"What about Alex Bledsoe? Did he get what he deserved when he took his own life?"

"About that... Maggie called her contacts over in Mecklenburg County. They're already reopening that case, and it looks like it could've been homicide instead."

"What do you mean?"

"It's possible Benery was behind that, too. Regardless, he won't see the other side of prison bars for a long time, if ever." As if unable to help himself, he approached her bedside again. Touched the edge of the bandage on her forehead and studied the scratches on her cheek. "I was scared shitless to leave you alone with him."

She was tempted to lean in to his touch, just let all this go and move on. But she would eventually hate herself and Jonah if she caved. "You only did it because you knew he would follow you."

"No, I did it because this time I trusted you could handle yourself if it all went sideways. I won't lie and say I don't want to protect you. That's in my DNA when it comes to you. But just because I want to protect you doesn't mean I think you need my protection."

Tonight, she wasn't sure what she needed from him or if she could accept anything from him ever again. She'd loved him for years. Loved the man she thought was a hero, only to find his feet were made of clay just like everyone else's.

"I don't want to rescue you." His expression was so serious, so sincere. "What I've needed all along is for you to rescue me. I know you have feelings for me, Tessa. Otherwise, you wouldn't still be here."

"The doctors are making me stay for observation." She plucked at one of the leads. "It's not like I have a choice right now."

"For as long as I live," he said, "no one will ever take away your choice again. Not even me. I choose you and I hope you'll choose me back. I thought about coming in here with flowers or candy or hell, even diamonds. But I knew that wouldn't convince you of anything. All I can offer you is the truth. And the truth is that I've done things behind your back when what I should've done is told you how I felt straight to your beautiful face." Before she could pull away, he lifted her hand from under the covers and kissed the center of her palm.

Like a vow.

Like a promise.

"The truth is I love you. And I will for the rest of my life even if you can't love me back."

With the pain burrowing into her heart, Tessa knew the problem wasn't her love for him. It was whether or not she could be with a man who saw her as a perpetual victim. "I don't—"

"Don't say anything now," he told her. "Mom is having a holiday get-together at Tupelo Hill tomorrow night. Say you'll come. And if you never want to see me again after that, I'll get out of your life." With a gentle kiss to her knuckles, he squeezed her fingers. Then he headed for the door.

That's when she knew he was serious, that he cared for

her enough to do anything—even if that was nothing—for her. Because he'd apparently walked through the hospital with nothing on under his johnny gown.

Laughter bubbled up inside Tessa, but before she could release the sound, it turned to sobs.

This time, Jonah Steele *had* bared it all for her.

32

WITH A STEAMING MUG OF HOT CHOCOLATE CRADLED IN HIS hands, Jonah stood with his hip propped against the front porch railing, watching his family decorate a massive red spruce in his mom's front yard. Only a family the size of his could disturb the peace of a mountain evening. But he wouldn't have it any other way. This, this nuttiness, was a big part of the reason he'd maneuvered everyone into coming back home and staying here for good.

Tessa was right when she said he wasn't made to be alone. But without her, his life would be completely empty.

"Don't worry. She'll be here." Jonah looked over to find Grif holding up a bottle of Irish whisky. "Want some? Makes the cocoa go down even easier."

Jonah held out his cup for a generous splash. "This just for the guy who fucked everything up or did everyone get some?"

"Everyone over twenty-one and not packing a baby in utero."

"You're gonna be a dad, dude."

"Again."

"You'll be putting your tricked-out minivan to good use."

"I never imagined we'd all live here again." Grif settled against the rail as if he was planning to dig in and stay here to keep Jonah's miserable ass company. Looked like Grif had pulled the short straw tonight. "Hell, I sure never imagined you'd save this town. Steele Ridge, North Carolina."

"It's a good place, a solid one."

"You helped make it that way."

"I'm no fucking hero." And although hot chocolate, pricy booze, and family were an excellent combo on a December night, a chill had taken up residence in his chest when Jonah had walked out of Tessa's hospital room. It was a place inside him that might never thaw if she decided she couldn't live with what he'd done. "I've done shit."

"Good thing, too."

"I've lied and I've...what?"

"The women we love may not *need* us in order to make a life for themselves. Hell, Carlie Beth did it on her own just fine for a lot of years. But that means they *choose* us. And when they do, that's when you know it's gonna all work out." Grif nodded toward the driveway where a pair of headlights were cutting through the December darkness. "Told you so."

That freezer-burned part of Jonah's chest thawed a single degree. Tessa was here.

She got out of the car and freed Badger from the back. He hurtled across the yard like some kind of low-flying stunt plane, those ears almost taking him airborne. Jonah's heart expanded at the sight of Micki scooping him off the ground and hugging the crazy canine to her chest.

Gage was in the shithouse if he hadn't rounded up a Christmas puppy for her.

Every female in his family clustered around Tessa,

hugging and talking a mile a minute. She smiled at them, but her gaze sought out his.

Gut punch. He would never get used to how beautiful she was. But he'd come to grips with her strength.

He couldn't take a damn bit of credit for the amazing woman she was, but he was glad he'd had a small part in it. She, on the other hand, was the reason he was anything. If not for her, he might've been satisfied to be a back-room code monkey his whole life.

His family finally released her and she walked toward the porch. And now that she was here, his vocal cords seemed to have left the building. "You came," he croaked out.

With the white lights twinkling around them, she looked gorgeous wearing the sweater Brynne had given her. Even the bandage in the center of her forehead couldn't diminish her beauty. "Badger wanted to see Micki."

"He tell you that?"

Badger was racing around the huge tree. When Jonah's mom had insisted that it needed to be gussied up from the top to the low-hanging branches, Britt had borrowed a cherry picker from a friend.

Tessa frowned, not exactly the reaction he'd been hoping for. "Is that... Wasn't that tree in the woods where—"

"My mom has a soft spot for it now. She wanted you to have it, but I wasn't sure your condo would hold it. You're the one who really kept my mom safe, but I figured if I tried to put you in her yard, you might protest." He was teasing, but a part of him wanted to do just that, plant her where she could never leave Steele Ridge. Never leave him.

But it had to be her decision. She had to choose him and accept everything he'd done.

"Why aren't you out there helping?"

"Because I was waiting for you." He was trying to control his breathing, but his exhale came out in a long stream of white in the cold air. "Hoping you would come."

She nodded. "I've been thinking..."

He wouldn't have expected anything less. *Please say you've been thinking about forgiving me.*

"...about why Keith came after both of us."

Jonah's momentary hope deflated. "Britt found some evidence that someone had been camping here on Steele land. We're assuming it was Benery. That's how he was watching us."

"I was able to talk with his mom earlier today. Apparently, he'd been obsessed with working for Steele Trap since his brother died. Of course, she didn't understand the connection, but I'm guessing he blamed you all along. He may have been planning this for years."

"But why involve you? You had nothing to do with Steele Survivor."

"I realized that Keith never came back to see me after that night you and I were together in your office."

"He heard the recording of us?"

"When he hacked into the files, yes. I was so angry at you for keeping things from me, but I never told you the recorder was running while—"

"—we had sex."

"Yes. But I think Keith actually saw us together that night, which he felt was my defection from his side to yours."

"So he had no problem hurting you through your clients and using you to hurt me the way his brother's death devastated him."

"People are irrationally wired for revenge."

"And you think what I did to Shaw and the others was irrational."

"Did...Did you know that when we both had the VR goggles on yesterday, that Keith had programmed it so you would look like...Harrison Shaw?"

"Jesus. How could Keith have even known...? The recordings again."

"He was trying to bring us both down with things that scare us."

"Did he accomplish what he set out to, Tessa? Because I'm scared as hell that everything I've done has ruined any chance we had. I treated you like you were helpless. Like you needed me to fix things for you, without thinking about how my actions might also hurt you."

"Then be honest with me about something. Anything."

"Remember that app I mentioned?"

"The one you wanted to put a team together for."

"I didn't tell you about it. About why I came up with the idea." Unable to keep his hands to himself any longer, he reached for one of hers. He wanted to get downs on his knees, kiss her hand, and beg. But only the truth would win her over this time. "I don't want anyone else to have to go through what you did. If you'd had some easy way to get in contact with your friends at the party that night... The app will make it possible for a person to communicate with a small trusted circle of contacts if she—or he—ever feels threatened."

"Oh, Jonah." Her gaze softened and she squeezed his fingers, making his heart react in kind. "This... This is the man I've been reminding myself that you are. You're capable of incredible compassion for other people and even if you screw up, it's because you care so much. Me, on the other hand? I stifled my compassion because I was so scared of screwing up."

"I don't understand."

"I believed I was helping people all these years. Companies definitely need the kind of services I provided, but I've realized that I was protecting myself from people's real problems. Their real pain. I've been too afraid it would remind me of my own. But after seeing what you did for the shelter, after talking with Doris, I realized that's where I want to be. I want to help people recover from trauma. I know what it's like to be a victim, so I can connect with women and kids who've suffered abuse and sexual assault. Plain and simple —I've walked their walk."

"Won't that open up your past every day?" He didn't want her to have to relive that constantly, but he had to trust that she knew her own emotional limits.

"I'm sure it will from time to time, but it's also what will make me good at it. I've talked with the director at Sarah's Smile and she agreed to let me start there."

"Have I told you that I think you're the bravest woman I've ever met?" He released her hand and gestured toward the yard. "And I don't know if you've noticed, but I've got some pretty kickass women in my life. I'm sorry I treated you like anything less than that."

"Why did you?"

He stared down into his mug, into the swirling chocolate that reminded him of Tessa's eyes. "Initially? Because I felt like a fucking failure for not being able to protect you. I owed you something, Tessa. When Micki and I came back to that room and I realized you'd been raped again...I...I knew it was my fault."

She placed her hand on his cheek, forcing him to look at

her. "You were doing what you thought was right. What you thought would protect me."

"I made the wrong choice, so later, I wanted to make it up to you in any way I could. I wanted every one of those bastards to have something taken from them the way you did."

"You felt sorry for me. That's why you brought me on board at Steele Trap."

He wanted to pull her in, wrap her tight in his arms, and reassure her that he would never undermine her trust again. "I wanted you to have the best life possible. I could give you a little boost, but I had nothing to do with all the hard work it took you to get to where you are. The day you walked into the offices in Seattle, you were so put together, I couldn't believe you'd ever been a victim. I think I fell in love with you then, when I realized you had healed."

"But you didn't know how to stop thinking I hadn't. Which meant you wouldn't allow yourself to acknowledge your feelings for me."

"It felt wrong. Like I was just as bad as one of them. Because when I looked at you, I wanted you with a power that felt out of control. I fantasized about taking you... against the wall, in the stairwell, on my desk."

"I wish you'd told me all this years ago. You've been torturing yourself, convincing yourself we couldn't be together because you like to call the shots in the bedroom."

"Is it too late for us now?"

"I think that depends on if you've truly changed the way you see me. I'll always be a rape victim, but that doesn't make me fragile. I don't want or need to be taken care of like a child. I want to be treated like a woman, like an equal."

"Which means sometimes you protect me." It was really

that simple and that damn complex. A real relationship was fluid and no one got to play the same role all the time.

"Does that bother you?"

"I'd be lying if I said it felt comfortable, but I will do *anything* to make this work. I didn't fall in love with you out of pity, because you were a victim. I fell in love with you because I admire you, because you're a survivor. I love you and I want you, as a partner, in my life every day from now until the end. I can't promise I won't screw up sometimes and try to protect you. But I won't hide things from you anymore."

With a small smile, she glanced out at his family, where Reid had just thrown Brynne over his shoulder and Britt was trying to keep their mom from climbing into the bucket of the cherry picker. "It's obvious that you have a little caveman in your DNA."

"That's an understatement." But that didn't mean she could live with it. She still hadn't answered his question. Had he ruined everything?

"I love you, Jonah. I love you and wouldn't know how to stop if I tried. We'll both screw things up from time to time. But I trust you. I trust that you'll tell me the truth and listen when I tell you what I need, not what you think I need." Then she wrapped her arms around his waist, and the feeling of contentment that streamed through Jonah was bone deep.

"I promise." Jonah kissed her—a deep commitment to their future full of love, laughter, and unexpected visits from his family.

The whoops, hollers, and catcalls from the yard didn't deter him one bit. Tessa was his. And he was hers.

When they finally parted, lips clinging, Tessa's eyes were bright—with trust, happiness, and love.

"How would you feel about spending more time with the Steele family?" he asked her. "Maybe with a little less crime and a few more clothes? I'll even throw in Clementine if you're willing to go for it."

She laughed, and it lit him up inside, brighter than the trillion lights his mom had wrapped around that tree. "I feel like it would be the adventure of a lifetime, one I want to share with the man I love. Jonah Steele, you've got yourself a deal."

So with Tessa's hand safely in his, he stepped off the porch and into the beautiful adventure of their life together.

———

Now that you've had your fun with the Steeles, get ready for the Kingston cousins.

CRAVING HEAT

ADRIENNE GIORDANO

Enjoy an excerpt from Adrienne Giordano's *Craving HEAT*,
Book One in Steele Ridge: The Kingstons series:

"Hey," he said, "can we talk?"

When she didn't respond, he took that as a green light.
Of course he did. One thing about Marlene Tucker, she'd
taught him how to capitalize on situations. Besides, by now
Maggie could have hopped into the cruiser and taken off.
Which she didn't.

"I'm sorry," he said. "My crazy life put you in danger. You
have no idea how much I hate that. And, let's be honest, I
like you. You're funny and smart and, well, you carry a big
gun. I'd rather you not be mad at me."

She shook her head, but the smile tugging at her lips
couldn't be denied. Score one for the jock. He pointed to the
corner of her mouth. "I think you're smiling."

Pushing his luck—what the hell?—he inched his hand
closer. Close enough that the tip of his finger brushed the
insanely soft skin at the corner of her mouth and he
wanted...Jesus, he wanted his lips there. Right at that spot.

She wrapped her hand around his finger and—wow—if she'd wanted to get his mind out of the gutter that wasn't the way to do it.

"That woman," she said, still holding his finger, "is stone-cold nuts. None of this is your fault."

"Then why are you mad at me?"

Finally, she let go of him. "I'm not."

"Yeah, you are."

"You don't even know me. How would you know if I'm mad or not?"

He'd spent half his life surrounded by amped-up football players. More than anything, he recognized when people were pissed. "I've spent a career working in a team environment. Learning people's signals and moods. You're right, I don't know you, but I know when someone is angry. At least talk to me. Not that you owe it to me after today, but —" Damn. He shook his head. How to say this without sounding like a douche?

"But what?"

"Nothing."

Which, of course, was total bullshit. It was definitely something. Something that began with him looking at Maggie and liking it more and more. He met her gaze and inched close enough to hook his finger into her belt loop, pull her forward and ...

He dipped his head, studied the slope of her top lip and the air stopped moving. Everything froze. Including his lungs.

"I..." She peered down at her feet, dug the toe of her boot into the ground, then rocked back.

He took a hard inhale, held it until his chest slammed, and blew it out. Lord, he felt like a middle-schooler trying to steal his first kiss. "You what?"

She lifted her chin and the street lamp shined in her lush brown eyes and he was gone. Totally smitten with this beautiful, strong woman so unlike the soft-spoken females he went for. The ones who let him call the shots.

Maggie, Maggie, Maggie, what are you doing to me?

"I got distracted," she said. "During the press conference."

"There was a lot going on."

"That doesn't matter. I had a job to do."

"Maggie—"

She squeezed her eyes closed, jabbed her open palms at him. "Shut up."

Whoa. Shut up? "I'm trying to—"

"My lack of attention could have gotten you hurt." She pressed the fingers of both hands into her forehead. "I've been shredding myself over this, thinking about all the things I did wrong, every second I could have done something differently and yet," she dropped her hands "I stand here, looking at you and thinking, 'Gee, I'd bet he looks mighty tasty fresh out of a shower.' How stupid can I be? That's what I'm pissed about. It has to stop."

Not one to let a grade A opportunity pass him by, Jay tipped his head closer. "If you're thinking those thoughts, I don't want it to stop. In fact, I'd throw myself off the top of this building to make it not stop."

She gawked at him. Literally stood there, mouth agape, and instinct kicked in. "Honey," he whispered, "if you want me, I'm all yours."

Find out what happens next and order Craving HEAT

DISCOVER MORE STEELE RIDGE

Steele Ridge: The Steeles

The BEGINNING, A Novella

Going HARD, Book 1

Living FAST, Book 2

Loving DEEP, Book 3

Breaking FREE, Book 4

Roaming WILD, Book 5

Stripping BARE, Book 6

Enduring LOVE, A Novella, Book 7

Vowing LOVE, A Novella, Book 8

Steele Ridge: The Kingstons

Craving HEAT, Book 1

Tasting FIRE, Book 2

Searing NEED, Book 3

Striking EDGE, Book 4

Burning ACHE, Book 5

Want to help Kelsey, Tracey, and Adrienne get the word out about their Steele Ridge series? Write a review and/or recommend to a friend!

ALSO BY KELSEY BROWNING

PROPHECY OF LOVE SERIES

Sexy contemporary romance

Stay With Me

Hard to Love

TEXAS NIGHTS SERIES

Sexy contemporary romance

Personal Assets

Running the Red Light

Problems in Paradise

Designed for Love

BY INVITATION ONLY SERIES

Sexy contemporary romance

Amazed by You

G TEAM SERIES w/NANCY NAIGLE

Southern cozy mysteries

In For a Penny

Fit to Be Tied

In High Cotton

Under the Gun

Gimme Some Sugar

JENNY & TEAGUE NOVELLAS

Contemporary romance

Always on My Mind

Come a Little Closer

STEELE RIDGE SERIES

Romantic suspense collaboration with Tracey Devlyn & Adrienne Giordano

The BEGINNING

Going HARD

Living FAST

Loving DEEP

Breaking FREE

Roaming WILD

Stripping BARE

ACKNOWLEDGMENTS

This book and the entire Steele Ridge Series would've never come about if Tracey Devlyn hadn't said, "I have a crazy idea" to Adrienne Giordano and me one day over three years ago. I'm so thankful to these talented authors—for this amazing project, their love and support over the past nine years, and their friendship. Gals, we're pretty damn good together, but if Adrienne and I ever decide again that our characters should be twins, someone needs to stop that shit. LOL

A sassy unicorn thank-you to Heather Machel. I would have absolutely lost my mind over the past few months without your amazing help and calm demeanor. I keep promising that you've seen me at my worst, but it's possible I lied. ;-)

Donna Duffee, I'm not sure I can tell you how appreciative I am. You chase the numbers so that I can chase the words. I have but one word for you: priceless.

To my beta readers—Reva Benefiel, Amy Remus, and Kristen Humphry Johnson, thank you so much for raising your hand to help me troubleshoot this book. It's been a tough one, so your feedback meant the world to me.

Big editing hugs to Deb Nemeth and Martha Trachtenberg. You ladies push for my best work even when I'm not sure I have it in me. For that, I'm so grateful.

The Steele Ridge series wouldn't be what it is without our wonderful readers. Thank you to everyone who's told us how much they love the Steele family and couldn't wait for the next book. It's been a pleasure to bring the Steeles to life for you!

This book would've never made it to the page if not for my two technical advisors, Smarty Boy and Tech Guy. SB, thanks for helping me plot the non-sexy bits. TG, I'll try to stay away from tech topics for a book or two. That should save us a couple of...ahem...disagreements. I love you both more than you know!

TEAM STEELE RIDGE

Edited by Deborah Nemeth

Copyedited by Martha Trachtenberg

Cover Design by Killion Group, Inc.

Author Photo by Anne Yarbrough Photography

Print Edition, September 2017, ISBN: 978-1-944898-17-5

For more information contact: kelsey@kelseybrowning.com

ABOUT THE AUTHOR

 **Kelsey Browning** is a *USA Today* best-selling author of sass kickin' love stories and co-authors Southern cozy mysteries. She's also a co-founder of Romance University blog, one of Writer's Digest 101 Best Websites for Writers. Originally from a Texas town smaller than the ones she writes about, Kelsey has also lived in the Middle East and Los Angeles, proving she's either adventurous or down-right nuts. These days, she hangs out in northeast Georgia with Tech Guy, Smarty Boy, Bad Dog and Pharaoh, a (fingers crossed) future therapy dog.

Don't miss a new release! Join Kelsey's New Release Newsletter list!

For more information on Kelsey, including her Internet haunts, contest updates, and details on her upcoming novels, please visit her at:
www.KelseyBrowning.com
kelsey@kelseybrowning.com